Other Books by Elaine Burnes

A Captain Randall Book 1
Endurance

Wishbone
A Perfect Life and Other Stories

TENACITY

A Captain Randall Book 2

TENACITY

Elaine Burnes

Mindancer Press
Bedazzled Ink Publishing Company • Fairfield, California

paperback 978-1-960373-46-5

Cover Design
by

Mindancer Press
a division of
Bedazzled Ink Publishing, LLC
Fairfield, California
http://www.bedazzledink.com

For Beth

"The most difficult thing is the decision to act,
the rest is merely tenacity."
—Amelia Earhart

Chapter 1

"PACK YOUR BAGS because it's back to space!" the news anchor announced with way too much enthusiasm. "Fasten your seatbelts, fans, Earth Control is reopening space to tourism." Then he switched to a more somber, respectful tone. "This, just two years after the mysterious return of the tour ship *Endurance*, bringing with it the devastating news of the loss of all hands on the Galaxy Cruises flagship *Aphrodite* when it, *Endurance*, and a small research vessel were swept off to the neighboring solar system, Rigil Kentaurus—" Lyn Randall flicked at the holodisplay, shutting off the news. Well, that was succinct. She snorted at the dismissive way Diana's ship—"a small research vessel"—was described.

She poured a mug of coffee and drummed her fingers on the kitchen counter. Early morning light washed across the walls. She'd known this day would come. The only question was when. And now that it had, what would change. A new day. The news anchor, bot, or AI—who knew which it was these days—probably said just that. Through the open windows, an argument broke out among crows, followed by the hoarse croak of a raven. A morning ritual. Bicker, bicker, bicker.

It would have been nice if someone had warned her. She stirred sugar into her mug and stepped out the door to the deck on the shaded west side. Earth Control just released the announcement? She wasn't Captain Randall anymore, but no doubt reporters would try to reach her for a comment, maybe hoping for an exclusive. Her personal com was private, but she couldn't cut herself off entirely and still do her job, so she expected her work com to fill with messages. Pines stirred in a soft breeze. Diana had mentioned seeing a warbler the other day. Such a rare sighting now, though mid-May had once been peak migration.

Her hand shook as she raised her mug. She set it on the railing and waited for the tremor to pass. Ignore it. The news, if not also the nervy tremor that was a recent development. She flipped open her calendar, and a holograph display hovered over the railing. She had a meeting with a new client in the ironically named Wheatland County that was now too hot to grow wheat. She hoped he hadn't been watching the news this morning. People didn't think of her as a former spaceship captain when she showed up in jeans and boots with a large straw hat. That might change now.

Curiosity getting the better of her, she flicked back to the news. Tours would be allowed only as far as Jupiter. Not all the way out to Saturn, where the ships had disappeared for reasons not fully understood. An unexpected wormhole, Diana had speculated, dubbing it a spacequake. But the tour operators being interviewed didn't want to talk about that. They were excited to be back in business. Lyn swiped the program over to music.

She leaned her elbows on the railing. Since their return, they had avoided the spotlight, tried to resume a normal life. The sanctuary she and Diana had built deep in the young forest at the foothills of the Bitterroot Mountains would be tested.

A chickadee landed on the post next to her. It grabbed a sunflower seed Diana had left there. A chirp of thanks and it took off for the pines.

Diana needed to know, not hear it from some manic news announcer. Lyn gulped her coffee then went back inside, leaving her mug in the sink on her way to the bedroom. Diana was sprawled across the bed, claiming the space Lyn had vacated, her short dark hair mussed with odd cowlicks. Adorable. Rewind that clock, run back time, forget the damn news. Diana had opened Lyn's shell and let her see what unfettered happiness could be. It was in the little things. Getting to know each other. Who wanted what side of the bed, which end of the closet, who had more shoes. Picking out countertops, buying furniture together, building a relationship as well as a cabin. Her dad had told her that if she could build a house with someone, she could build a life with them. So it seemed. The first blush of lust was over, and they were onto the work of a relationship. And she loved it.

"Dee," she said softly. "You awake?" Not waiting for an answer, she sat on the bed.

Diana stirred, suddenly alert. "What's wrong?"

Lyn told her the news. "Brace yourself for a return to the spotlight."

Diana humphed and pulled Lyn down beside her. "I'm not worried."

Lyn kicked off her boots, and they snuggled. "You should be. What if they come after you again?"

"They've never stopped."

"What do you mean?" Lyn asked.

"I get a call every month or so from some minion of General Jacana."

Lyn twisted to look her in the eye. "I didn't know that."

"You have your own worries. It's nothing. They ask to meet, I say no, they tell me how disappointed they are, I dink the call."

"General Hellen Jacana? The head of the military for the whole North American Alliance."

"It's her minion, not her."

"The same thing." Lyn sounded more alarmed than she was. While General Hellen Jacana was a force to be reckoned with, so was Diana Teegan. Fact was, if it really mattered, the general wouldn't send a minion. They were keeping tabs on Diana more than anything. She settled into the warmth of the bedding, Diana not so surreptitiously undoing her shirt buttons, her belt buckle, the zipper to her jeans. Her hand on Lyn's stomach made her muscles jump. "So you're not worried?"

"Do I seem worried?" Diana kissed her to silence and rolled on top.

This was love, then. Still new, only two years into their lives tethered together, two closely entangled entities. First by necessity and grief, then through friendship and onto love. Nothing one did could not affect the other. That was the point of loving someone.

Lyn woke when a furry, cat-like robot jumped up on the bed and started kneading Diana's stomach. "Good morning, Diana, today's top story that might interest you is the announcement by Earth Control that space will reopen to—"

"Weather," Diana said in a way that sounded more sensitive to Lyn's feelings than a real interest in the forecast.

"Certainly," the robot alarm responded. "In Butte today you can expect full sun, highs in the eighties. Be sure to wear adequate UV protection. Air quality score is 120, unhealthy for sensitive groups, from fires to the west. Five-day outlook calls for sun, highs in the eighties through the weekend, rising to the nineties early next week. Expect lows in the fifties. CO_2 levels are 985, down a tenth of a point in the last month. Precipitation continues to trend below average." The house computer pawed Lyn. "Do you need the weather for eastern Montana?"

"No, thanks," Lyn said. She stroked the gray tabby and rubbed its ears. Kat purred then curled up between them and appeared to fall asleep.

Reluctantly, they left the cozy bed and went about their morning routines. Showers and breakfast were quick, news off. Diana taught high school physics in nearby Butte. She chose there because they held classes the old-fashioned way, in person. She'd taught at the college level, but preferred high school kids willing to be inspired. She'd only had to say her name and the town offered the now-famous astrophysicist a position teaching whatever she wanted. Lyn joined her family's environmental recovery business, Randall Restoration, which was about as far from her old job as physically possible. They quietly gathered their thermoses of coffee and lunches. Instead of the perfunctory goodbye kiss, they held each other tight.

"We should probably have a plan," Lyn said. "This might ratchet up pressure, maybe more minions, or they might go after your parents."

"I'm not worried about my parents. They've been fending off government spooks for decades now."

"Still . . ."

Diana nodded agreement. "I know. No more fun and games. It's been swell and all."

Lyn gave her an extra squeeze. They'd get through this. There'd be a flurry of press coverage, interest in comments from the reclusive Captain Randall and Dr. Teegan, but eventually the excitement of tours and shiny new ships and the reopening of the Clarke Space Elevator would push them back into obscurity. The last two years had been some of the happiest of her life. They'd built this cabin in the woods tucked away from prying eyes, bothering journalists, pesky government officials, and spent their days pretending everything was safe and secure when in reality, they'd worked devilishly hard to make it that way. Because the last thing Lyn needed in her life again was a surprise, one she couldn't avoid or delegate a response to. That was never going to happen again.

She checked the security cameras before opening the garage door under the house. Nothing stirred in the woods. They inspected the exteriors of their aerocars and ran through the preflight checklists.

Diana settled in the seat of her roomy Phaeton Rambler, a workhorse of a vehicle that reflected her interest in reliability over flash. She backed out of the garage and engaged hover mode, preparing for takeoff. She would head toward town, never taking a direct route east. This was one of many precautions to protect their privacy. Some days she flew along the mountain range and entered town from the south or north. Or she made a wide circle to approach from the east.

Lyn waited for her to leave. She took the seat of her sleek two-seater Anaelan Sportster IX, fastened the harness, and secured her mug and lunch. Her inner pilot told her that if she couldn't fly in space, she could still have fun in atmosphere. She did a quick check of the view screens. Diana had chosen west up the mountain to a narrow pass.

As Lyn cleared their property, a remote sensor pinged. Not an intruder, this was from a job site. A pump jack had stopped pumping. She headed toward the ghost town of Big Timber.

LYN SCUFFED A clod of dirt with her boot, which was a mistake because the wind took that clod and blasted it into a cloud of dust and fine pebbles right into her face. "Shite!" She turned her back to the wind and blinked till the offending grime washed from her eyes. She staggered as a gust knocked her sideways.

The land spread before her like a rumpled blanket, hills dotted with scrubby sagebrush and carpeted with invasive mugwort and cheatgrass. Dry creek beds once flowed with spring runoff, bringing life to the cattle and sheep ranches, back before the climate turned angry and war raged. In the distance a tattered white tarp flopped and skittered across the ground then caught on a shrub. She could go fetch that tarp, a littered remnant of an old migrant camp some miles over the hills, but there would be more where it came from.

She turned her attention to the problem at hand. The pump jack bobbed uselessly, disconnected from the polished rod that fed into the well. She cut the power when the bird's head was low enough to reach a piece of paper taped to it. "Hope you enjoy the extra work. This is what happens when you tamper with nature." Hand printed in block letters. Possibly traceable, but not worth the bother.

Antigens. She sighed with disgust and looked around, like she might spot someone on horseback riding off into the hills or a vehicle leaving a dust trail. More likely an anti-grav skim like the one she flew in on. She hadn't noticed anyone in the area, but she hadn't been looking for trouble till she saw the note. Her internal radar went on high alert, an automatic response tuned to past threats she might never tamp down to the mere annoyance this was.

The cable swung uselessly, the clamp clanging against the rod it should be gripping. She grabbed it and examined the metal collar with a hinge on one side and three bolts on the other. Someone had opened the clamp, released the rod, then restarted the pump. No damage, no other signs of tampering, just a nuisance. Another gust of wind threatened to carry her hat off. She held it in place to shield her eyes from the morning sun as she walked over to the Recyc-All and injector well a dozen yards away, connected by underground pipes. Nothing else was damaged.

The jack was based on an ancient but reliable design that had once sucked oil from deep underground, until there wasn't any left. Like scrawny birds on spindly legs, pump jacks appeared to peck the ground. This one should be pumping contaminated water out of the aquifer. A century ago, all kinds of nasty chemicals, like arsenic, lead, formaldehyde, and mercury, had been used in fracking, breaking rock underground to release the last bits of oil and gas. These polluted underground water supplies. Then surface waters dried up.

She was familiar with the Recyc-All, a relatively new technology perfected during the war to make ammunition but repurposed to better uses. A critical appliance on spaceships and in homes, the idea was simple, if not the execution. Take any molecule, break it down into its component parts and rebuild it into something else. In this case pure water that could be injected back into the ground. Still, there were those who objected to any form of genetic or geoengineering. Nicknamed Antigen, they opposed the use of technology on an ecosystem scale, and Randall Restoration wasn't the only one to feel their sting. Until she joined the family firm, they'd been an abstraction.

Frustratingly, their MO was nonviolent but anonymous. There was no organized group, no leader. They would take credit for their work after the fact with a screed or manifesto. Like the note taped to the jack. Let nature take its course, they said, humans have done enough damage.

On the other side were the G-Nerds, who supported technology with a religious fervor. They claimed that genetic- and geo-engineering were the natural progression of evolution. The other day she'd listened to a show where one of the flashier members of the group—they weren't so anonymous—waxed poetic about the coming singularity. Of humans becoming the sentient brains of a living planet, and that innovation would save humanity. She suspected a few Randall Restoration staff members were adherents, judging from a botanist's Evolution Revolution tattoo that ran the length of his forearm. Antigens, however, got nothing but snark and derision from the RR crowd.

She stopped at her skim to grab her hardhat. While walking back to the disabled rig, she reviewed the specs. A brain implant allowed her to store and process vast amounts of data, including pump jack manuals. She noted what tools she'd need and went to the shed. Fittingly, seeing how her day was going, the toolbox was empty.

With the wind howling around her she ducked inside the shed and yanked shut the door. Blissful quiet and a chance to breathe without the wind's pressure on her lungs. There was a time not that long ago when she had longed for wind on her face, not the stale air of a spaceship. Not this kind of wind. Gentle breezes. She should have been more specific. Following company protocol, she called Chief Technician Fúlli Born to Fly to report the malfunction. Thankfully, Fúlli answered right away. She told nem about the pump. "Someone disconnected the polished rod."

"Disconnected? Not cut?"

"Just unscrewed the clamp and let the damn birdhead bob uselessly."

"Horsehead," Fúlli corrected.

Fúlli was a patient mentor. In exchange, she took the gentle ribbing in stride. She described the note from the Antigen vandal.

"Any damage to the clamp or bridle?" Fúlli asked. "See, that's why it's called a horsehead."

"Whatever. No, those are fine. Didn't even lose the screws."

Fúlli sighed. "Bolts."

"Same difference," she said, baiting nem.

Fúlli turned on vid so ne could scowl at Lyn appropriately, making her laugh. Today the young technician sported cropped green hair. Last week it had been a pink ponytail.

"Much as I'd love to spar with you R4, yours isn't the only rig vandalized this week," ne said, more seriously. "My crews are all out on other jobs. Can you deal with this yourself? Do I have to tell you what a wrench is?" Ne softened the tough tone with a grin.

"I haven't got a wrench," she said. "The toolbox is empty. I've got the manual, though."

Fúlli didn't know about Lyn's brain implant. She didn't like to talk about it. It was an artifact of her past.

"Where are you?"

"Sweet Grass County, northwest of Big Timber." She sent GPS coordinates.

Fúlli peered off camera, probably checking a schedule. "Ani's heading to Great Falls. I'll see if she can make a detour with a kit you can leave in the box. ETA a couple hours, though."

"It'll have to do," Lyn said, resigned.

She retreated to her skim and scrolled through her com, looking for the client in Wheatland. She was scheduled to meet in . . . great, ten minutes ago. She called to apologize and took off. Wheatland was five minutes away. Mentally she prepared to give him the bad news. He was hoping Randall Restoration could make his farm productive again. She'd have to tell him that he should consider doing something else for the fifty years it would take to restore that land to anything productive.

The guy was about her age, but with a face weathered by Montana summers and wind and dust. He scratched his scruffy beard as she gave him the news. He took it well, all things considered, and didn't think to ask if she was Captain Lyn Randall of the *Endurance*. They flew around his property, which on the surface looked in good shape. No craters, no radiation, but also no water. That was the main problem everywhere. It wasn't that there was no water at all, but it was completely unpredictable. Winters didn't pack the mountains with snow anymore, so there was nothing to melt into rivers and aquifers. Just long dry spells broken by raging downpours. She took notes, and he seemed open to alternative crops while the land recovered. Maybe millet or sorghum, but RR's agriculture experts would come up with suggestions. She pointed out plenty of invasive plants, like buckthorn and tumbleweed, that could be harvested for Recyc-All feeder stock to make water while the aquifer and soil were being restored.

An hour later she was heading back to the busted pump jack to meet Ani. With time to kill, she checked her messages. As she feared, reporters were calling.

"Hoping for a comment and whether this means you'll return to space," one asked in a voice message. Others were less friendly, pressing her to explain why she and Dr. Teegan wouldn't work with authorities to solve the mystery of the Saturn wormhole and divulge how they mastered superluminal travel.

"It wasn't superluminal," Lyn muttered. Just a game-changing technology that could open the entire galaxy to human exploitation.

During a Grand Tour of Mars, Jupiter, and Saturn, a sudden wormhole had opened, sucking three ships out to Rigil Kentaurus, a binary star 4.3 light years from Earth. Diana had been on a research vessel piloted by her wife, Rose Squires. Rose was killed, and Lyn rescued Diana. But three quarters of the enormous *Aphrodite* had been destroyed, with only six hundred survivors. The senior surviving crewmember wasn't up to the task of leading them. After only a month, while Lyn went in search of some place they could survive other than the flimsy lifepods, she returned to find them all dead. Just under two years later, thanks to Diana figuring out how to open a traversable, stable wormhole, *Endurance* returned to Earth. No one on her ship had died. They'd even added a newborn.

She deleted the messages, but one name struck her. A text from I. Bakewell. Years ago, she'd worked with a small-media reporter to break a big story. Could this be the same person?

The unmistakable purr of the Ag-Cat, a propeller-driven biplane, caught her ear. It was a far cry from a spaceship, but Ani loved it and Lyn could see why. An electric replica of a twentieth-century crop duster, it was a thing of beauty with two stacked main wings that gave it authentic old-fashioned appeal. The "Ag" stood for agriculture, not antigravity, Ani was always explaining to curious clients. It was small and nimble, able to fly where antigravity skims couldn't. Randall Restoration used the plane to lay seed across large plots. It took finesse to fly a few feet off the ground, stay level for the drop, and turn sharp to do it again. Fly low with antigrav and you can't get the seed to stay on the ground.

Ani buzzed past Lyn and rolled the bright yellow plane.

"Show off," Lyn said into her com.

Ani circled, looking for a level spot to land, a cargo drone following. She rolled to a stop near the pump jack, and the young pilot climbed out of the cockpit and hopped down off the wing.

"Rodriguez Rescue Service, at your service," she said emphasizing the rolled Rs of her Puerto Rican accent. Formerly the chief pilot on *Endurance*, she'd traded Omara Tours' flight suit for Randall Restoration's coveralls and vintage aviator sunglasses. Her long brown hair was pulled back in a utilitarian bun, the effect achieved of a dashing pilot out of the previous century. Ani could present a lot of flash, but underneath she was calm control through and through. She'd honed that flying in space, but Lyn didn't doubt she'd succeed at whatever she tried. Case in point, repairing a pump jack. Lyn argued she could handle it herself, but Ani teased that Fúlli had warned her to keep an eye on R4, "Before you do more damage than you fix." Plus, she could make up the time by flying a little faster, she said with a not-so-innocent smile.

Together they pulled the toolkit from the drone and set it by the jack. Lyn casually asked if she'd heard the news about space, but Ani was more interested in ranting about Antigen.

"One of these days, they're going to kill someone," she said.

As they were tightening the last bolt, Lyn's com pod sounded an alarm. She eyed the display then peered to the northeast. Dark clouds roiled on the horizon. No, not clouds.

"Shite, Ani. There's a duster heading this way."

"Oh, hell." The last thing Ani needed was to fly an electric plane through a dust storm. If the dust didn't blind her the static electricity would short the whole system.

"I can finish up," Lyn yelled into the wind. "Get out of here!"

Ani dropped her gloves into the toolbox and with a wave, hightailed it to the Ag-Cat. In less than a minute she was airborne, the drone behind her. She tipped her wings as she flew off to the west.

Lyn hauled the toolbox into the shed. A rolling mountain of dirt loomed over the far hills, dimming the sun and turning the sky a yellow-brown. A quick calculation of the speed and distance showed she might get away in time. These storms could last for hours and she didn't want her Sportster sandblasted. She ran to her skim, powered up, and launched. Dirt pinged against the hull, dust obscuring her view. Thank god for dirt-piercing sensors. She detoured south till she got well ahead of the storm then circled east to continue across the state to the Randall homestead north of Nakota, a town once named for an Army general. The new nation saw no use in honoring Indian killers.

As the sky cleared, she relaxed and patted at the dust in her jeans, then thought better of it before she coated the interior. She chugged water to clear the grit from her mouth. The storm formed a wall of dirt for several miles, though by historic standards it was small. Until the first nukes went off in the 2110s, dust storms had been rare since the Great Depression. But growing up in the forties, Lyn hunkered through quite a few. Decades of drought had depleted the plains of nutrients, and the organic topsoil and vital fungal network eroded into dust storms eerily similar to those of the 1930s. "Where'd all the dirt go?" young Lynnie had asked her dad. Jephson had pointed to the east, "The Dakota Dunes and beyond." Some landed there, some rose on winds to block the sun for days at a time, traveling as far as the Atlantic Ocean. To Lynnie, it was as though the earth itself was fleeing, leaving home, never to return.

Chapter 2

LYN WAS WASHING the dishes when Diana got a call. Her voice drifted in from the deck where they'd eaten dinner, a habit till the evenings got too hot.

A few minutes later, Diana came inside. "That was odd."

Lyn dried her hands and joined her at the island counter. The call had been Antonia Squires, Diana's former mother-in-law.

"She needs to see me, in person, this weekend," Diana said.

"And that's odd?"

"It was her tone, almost conspiratorial. Not, hey, been awhile, let's get together." She thought a bit. "More like she wanted something, maybe a favor."

Lyn hadn't met Antonia but got the distinct impression she didn't ask for help lightly. "Could it have anything to do with Rose?"

Diana traced patterns on the counter's surface with her finger. "I doubt it. Settling her death minus a body meant a lot of forms to fill out, but I think it's all resolved now." Rose had been "buried" in space, shot toward the star Rigil Kent.

"A hidden life insurance policy you didn't know about?"

She wiped away nonexistent crumbs, distracted.

Not a time for jokes, Lyn chided herself. "If you're worried about Kai's show, we don't have to go. He'll have others." An exhibit of her brother's paintings was opening at a gallery in Banff on Saturday.

Diana scrunched her face. "It's not that. Well, it is, but she wants to see me alone."

"Oh." There wasn't a particular reason Lyn would be invited along. Just because they were a couple didn't mean they had to do everything together.

"I'm sure it's nothing. She probably found something among Rose's things she wonders if I'd like. Maybe she's cleaning out."

"Why this weekend?"

Diana shook her head. "I didn't think to ask." She gave Lyn an apologetic look. "I said I'd go. Do you mind?"

"Of course not. I'll tell Kai you hate his paintings and wouldn't be caught dead in the same room with them."

Diana got the joke since her body loosened and a mischievous grin formed. She fake tackled Lyn, finding her weak tickle spot. They twirled in an embrace, both laughing as Lyn counter attacked. Then they settled, wrapped together, swaying gently in a silent slow dance.

"She's okay, right?" Lyn said softly. "It's not a health thing?"

"I don't think so. But I guess I'll find out."

Lyn didn't know a lot about Diana's life BE, Before *Endurance*. She'd talked about Rose soon after she'd died then less over time. Years earlier Lyn had lost her own wife, Tara, so they'd bonded in the shared experience of grief. Diana's loss was fresher, a painful reminder of what loving someone meant, the risk, especially in a dangerous occupation. Eventually the benefits outweigh the risk, but it takes time and healing and much of that happens in private. No more shared memories. Stories get shelved. Just as Diana had worked things out—she'd had almost two years to deal with it—she returned to Earth and had to tell Antonia that her daughter had died, opening a fresh wound.

They'd kept in touch in a way Lyn couldn't with Tara's family since none survived, so she watched Diana carefully tread her relationship with Antonia, who mourned not only her daughter, but also her husband. Now alone, no one would have blamed her for clinging to Diana. Thankfully, Antonia Squires was anything but clingy. She valued family, so Rose's death didn't mean Diana stopped being family.

SATURDAY, DIANA PACKED an overnight bag for the trip east to upstate New York, and Lyn headed north for the day. She returned that evening, surprised to see Diana's skim in the garage. Loud music beat through the basement ceiling, resolving into loud, percussive rock as she climbed the stairs and entered the living room, nearly tripping over Diana's overnight bag, dropped carelessly by the door. Diana sat on the couch, staring at a holo of her favorite band, Hazardous Waste, gyrating and shouting—to Lyn's ears—undecipherable lyrics. Diana stroked Kat, curled beside her.

Lyn swept the music to mute, prompting a startled look from Diana. "Oh, you're home."

"And so are you. What happened with Antonia?" Something was clearly very wrong here.

Diana swept her hand to shut the holo off. She patted the couch. "This is going to take awhile."

Lyn sat, pulling a knee up so she could face Diana, who took in a deep breath as if bracing herself at the end of a high dive. Then she dove.

"I always liked Antonia. I could see a lot of her in Rose. The no-nonsense attitude. The self-confidence. Rose got her quiet side from her father. The combination really grounded her." She let out a derisive laugh, pulled Kat into her lap, and hugged it. "They were like parents to me when I was so estranged from my own."

This wasn't news, so couldn't be the point, unless Antonia was putting Diana in her will.

"You know how the Johari have always rejected modern technology? Rose told me the sect formed in 1900 because of the Industrial Revolution. They wanted no part of it."

Lyn braced. Here it comes.

"Turns out, that's not really so true. Turns out, they not only embraced technology, they used it to come to Earth." She glanced at Lyn. "They are literally from another planet. Aliens." The words echoed, not being absorbed. "Antonia told me they are researchers who came to Earth to study humans because we're so much alike. I mean them and us. The Johari and us humans." She enunciated the words carefully so there could be no misunderstanding.

Lyn put a hand on Diana's leg, but she withdrew and crossed her arms.

"They've been *studying* us, like Jane Goodall and the chimps, and sending reports back to their planet—" Diana waved at the ceiling. "Somewhere in the Hercules constellation. She told me the star system, but—" She dropped her hand back on the couch.

Lyn rubbed Diana's arm, maintaining contact, intending to ground her. "Do you think Antonia had some kind of psychotic break?"

Diana rubbed Kat behind its ears. "Apparently there was an alien message in 2115, that got intercepted."

Lyn gasped. "The one that started Pulsar?"

Diana looked at her, puzzled. "You think it's the same one?"

"Supposedly wanting to meet. Rachel Holness told me about it when we were at Pulsar. It was behind everything they stood for—preparing to fight these aliens. But it was Johari?"

"It was meant for the Johari. From their home world. Antonia said that when it went public they had to cut off contact."

"The Johari are aliens from another planet and that message was meant for them?"

"That's what she said."

"But you said the Johari formed in 1900. How long have they been here?"

"Since then," Diana said, her voice rising.

Lyn stilled, letting that sink in. The pieces fell into place like a crazed jigsaw puzzle. "And you believe this is true?"

"Of course it's true," Diana said, like wasn't it obvious? She shoved Kat off her lap and leaned forward, elbows on knees. "But that's not the half of it. They need to leave Earth, she said, go home, and—get this—they want *us* to help them."

"Help them." Lyn was afraid to ask but had to. "How?"

"How do you think? Open a wormhole for them."

"Back up for a second. Why are they here?"

"They've been studying us, like research lab rats." Diana sounded frustrated.

"But they're human. Aren't they?"

"If you're asking if they're some kind of shape shifter, the answer is no. Very close to human. She even gave me a vial of DNA, samples from several Johari, including herself. Have it analyzed, she said. Like we could walk into any old lab and say, 'Gee, could you check this for alien DNA?'"

Lyn stood and paced in front of the couch, then went to the window. It was dark outside, so all she could see was her reflection and Diana behind her.

When Rose had died, Lyn had *Endurance*'s doctor examine her body to find a cause of death since her injuries hadn't seemed life threatening. He'd discovered she lacked medical nanobots, and Diana had explained Rose was Johari, that they didn't use medbots. Dr. Amos hadn't mentioned that she wasn't actually human, but why would he have looked for that?

"If they came here, why can't they leave on their own?" Of all the scenarios Lyn had anticipated pressuring her to reveal how they'd gotten back from Rigil Kent, this wasn't even close to one of them.

"They don't have a ship anymore or know how to do it. 2115 was right when the war started and she said over the years, they lost almost everything."

"Why now?" They'd been back two years. Antonia could have approached Diana any number of times. In the reflection, Diana pulled Kat back into her lap.

"Because space is reopening. There was no point before. She said when that message was intercepted, they had to cut off contact with their home world. When we came back from Rigil Kent, they realized we now could travel to their planet, so they needed to end the study and leave. To let their people know we have the tech." Her voice rose in pitch with the kind of incredulity usually heard while describing outlandish movie plots.

Diana didn't need to say more. Space was reopening. Now they could leave. All they needed was a ship and a Teegan Particle Collector and Accelerator, shortened to TPCA or "tipka," as Diana called her invention.

Lyn's mind reeled with the notion of aliens, here on Earth, the stuff of science fiction. No one doubted life existed elsewhere in the universe. It was there on Saturn's moon Enceladus, but that was microbial. Only Marao, the planet they'd found orbiting Toliman, had plants, higher life forms. But nothing like this.

"Did she say how it's possible?" Lyn asked. She turned and leaned against the sill. "That humans could be from two different planets."

"She said others could explain it better than she could. It's a long story."

"Did you meet any others?"

"No." She sounded tired, wrung out. "I suppose I could have. I had to get out of there. I couldn't stay. Not after that. My whole life with Rose was a lie. Every story about her childhood, her teens, whenever she had learned the truth and had then withheld that from me. Our wedding vows, to always be honest with each other."

Diana pushed Kat aside, leaned forward, and held her head in her hands. She was crying.

Her thoughts weren't sidetracked by the breaking news of aliens on Earth. She only saw her life crumbling, her past a mirage of lies and secrets. Now was not the time to consider options, run through ramifications. Her wife needed her.

Lyn put her arms around her. "So, Rose knew?"

"Yes." Diana wiped her sleeve across her eyes. "I'm getting a headache. It's all beginning to blur. I wish I'd thought to record her conversation."

Lyn pulled her up. "Let's get some food in you. We can talk more later."

Over Diana's favorite vegetable soup, she added details as she recalled them. "Do you remember a Ruzena Tey? Wasn't she with that ship that met us when we got back?" She was calmer, more her analytical, scientist self.

Lyn remembered Tey. "She never explained what she was doing out there by Saturn, after space had been closed."

"She's one of them. Johari. She was working undercover at Earth Control. Part of EC's SETI program. That's a whole other story." She stirred her soup, the bits of veggies circling the bowl, tiny orbits of carrot and celery.

Captain Tey was Johari?

Diana put the spoon down. "I keep trying to focus on the request, not the fact that this was my family, Antonia was family, Rose was family. What is family even?" She swung her spoon in an arc, droplets flying off. "I was closer to them than my own parents."

Lyn could see Diana slipping back into the waif she'd first met, overcome with grief, reliving reopened wounds, new ones, old memories. Analysis could wait. "How did you leave it with her?"

Diana squinted, as if trying to recall. "I said I'd talk to you."

Okay. That was good. No commitment, no decision.

Diana pushed the half-eaten bowl of soup aside and put her head on her arms folded on the table. "I'm sorry."

"Why? You've done nothing wrong."

"I could have said we can't help, we don't have the data anymore. I was so shocked, I couldn't say anything and by not saying that, I told her everything. I blew it." She raised her head and raked her fingers through her hair. "What if it's a trap?"

"I know a lot of people who want to wheedle this information from us, and I don't think any of them are your former mother-in-law."

THEY WENT TO bed, Diana completely exhausted, Lyn so wired she lay awake, the news clanging like a struck bell. She stared at the moon through the window. What stars out there were populated with human-like beings? Whose people were on Earth and needed a ride home. They'd known this technology would be a game changer. They'd feared its misuse so had claimed they destroyed it. They knew people would come after them, like General Jacana or Earth Control. But the Johari? Antonia Squires? Aliens who were living on Earth and had been for centuries?

After Vera Geller invented a drive system that cut travel time down from what had once been years, Mars could be reached in a couple of days, Saturn within a month. But *Endurance* returned from Rigil Kent, in another solar system entirely, in a matter of minutes. Diana had figured out how to open a wormhole using the Teegan particle her parents had discovered years earlier. They'd destroyed all the evidence—the machine itself, Diana's research, and simulations. The only piece that couldn't be destroyed was the archive of the data in Lyn's brain implant. Not without killing her.

Diana breathed quietly beside her, maybe also awake. Could it be a trap to get them to reveal the tech? The story was at once incredible but couldn't be because of who was telling it. Diana had known Antonia for decades. Lyn had always wondered why Rose didn't have medbots that could have saved her life. She was Johari, a sect that rejected technology, but she was also a pilot in space. And Captain Tey was also Johari? At the time *Endurance* returned, Lyn learned Rachel Holness had become the head of Earth Control after Bernice Umbo was fired over the disappearance of the ships two years earlier. It wasn't surprising that EC, under Rachel, would keep patrolling space under the guise of a SETI program. It was a quasigovernmental agency that oversaw and regulated all space operations. It was uniquely positioned to keep an eye on anything space related and, for Rachel, a perfect platform to keep an eye out for an alien invasion. Rachel was a deep believer in the presumed threat. They'd joined Pulsar together and she'd told Lyn of the message and Pulsar's mission to protect Earth. They'd lost touch after Pulsar disbanded. The truth of the group's goals burned bitter in Lyn's heart after destroying her life and leaving her a widow. Regardless of the truth of that message or the Johari and their desires, this was a door she could not reopen.

THE NEXT MORNING, groggy, clutching a mug of coffee, Lyn waited till Diana had finished her breakfast. Then she reached across the table and rubbed her arm.

"You know we can't do it, right?"

"We can't?" Her tone suggested that she thought this was a possibility, because the request had come from Antonia and she believed her and Lyn believed Diana. "I mean, they know we know how. If only because I didn't say we didn't. But you just decided? I think there's more to the story. Maybe we should find out."

Perhaps they'd both lain awake last night rehashing details, coming to different conclusions.

"We swore we'd never let it be used, not by us, not by anyone—for good or for evil. That's our whole point now, keeping this away from anyone."

"Anyone *here*. We didn't expect aliens."

"Doesn't matter. They want us to use T tech and we can't." What was Diana thinking? Or not thinking. "Nothing's stopping them. Space has reopened. They can leave."

"They don't know how."

Lyn took their dishes to the sink. Outside the window, two red squirrels chased each other around the trunk of a pine tree. Around and around. Then the leader jumped over to another tree. The pursuer did not follow but sat on a branch, its tail flicking. Did it win by chasing away the intruder? Or lose, by not catching a potential mate.

She turned and leaned against the sink. "We can't do it. You can toss that DNA because it has to stop here."

Diana's mouth closed in a tight line as if the silence could pierce Lyn's resolve. "What should they do?" she asked finally.

"Live their lives. They've been here since 1900? Unless they're immortal, none of them lived on that home world. Why do they even want to leave?"

"Have you seen this world? Do you live on this planet? Who wouldn't want to leave?"

"Point exactly. If this technology gets loose, all the resources being used to fix this place will go into leaving it, and that won't end well for anyone." Lyn tried another tack. "How exactly would they leave? Do they have a ship? How many are we talking about?"

Diana stared at the floor. "Six hundred," she said quietly.

"Six hundred?" Like the *Aphrodite* survivors. "Do you see a ship big enough for six hundred people, TPCA, and fuel? You know what it took on *Endurance* with just over a hundred. Stripped to the girders."

Diana grimaced like reality was sinking in. "I don't think . . ." She exhaled through her nose. "What if it were reversed? What if someone could have helped us? We'd have asked, right?"

"They weren't stranded here. They came deliberately. If they don't know how to get back now, that's on them, not us."

"The technology exists. You know others have to be working on it. We can hide it all we want but someone's going to come up with it and then it won't matter what we do."

"Doesn't mean we should be the ones." Where was this coming from? Diana knew the risk, she'd agreed. She was too close emotionally to see the danger. "The answer is no." Lyn's hand shook.

Neither moved. Then Diana pulled her com from her pocket and flipped up a screen. Lyn closed her eyes. She wasn't going to do this right now, was she?

"Hi, Antonia. Yeah, I told her. She has something to say to you." She slid the com across the table and left the room.

Hell of a first contact. Lyn sat and adjusted the screen, glad she wasn't in her bathrobe. Antonia stood outside, in the shade of a shed or barn, weathered boards behind her, the corner of a window frame visible. She reminded Lyn of her mom, with a face that had seen sorrow but also determination, her skin browned from the sun, hair short and gray. So very human.

"Look, Antonia . . . yeah, hi. Nice to finally meet you too." She broke the news. No waffling, no room for argument.

"There's a lot more to the story, to help you understand our need," Antonia said, unruffled by the rejection. "I'm sorry Diana left. I didn't mean to upset her."

Couldn't hurt to learn more, could it? Lyn asked about the message from 2115. "She didn't know about it, but I do. What's your version?"

"I only know what I've been told," Antonia said. "As do you, I assume. I was a kid then, you weren't even born. That message had been a routine communication from our home world. But it wasn't properly encrypted, so it was heard by humans. We managed to find the file and delete it, but it was too late, word got out."

Images of Tara and the others flashed through Lyn's mind. Dying on Enceladus during a mission meant to follow up on that message. Five lives lost. "Go on."

"Our research protocol requires that if our presence becomes known, we have to abandon the study and either return to Johar or go underground if we can't. The message alone wasn't enough to expose us, but we had no way to get off Earth—no ship, no equipment to open a wormhole. But you do."

"And I'm to believe you are innocent researchers."

"Yes, because we are. You can look at the entire history of the Johari—the sect—and you won't find that we ever intervened. Not in war, not in politics, not even with inventions. That's why we lost the ability to get home on our own."

It was true. A quick search through her implant showed the Johari weren't implicated in any major world events, not the assassination of U.S. President Cheetham after a constitutional coup brought him a fourth term, not the military dictatorship that followed or the protests and purges leading to low-level proxy wars around the world, culminating in a limited nuclear exchange that escalated. She blinked. Throughout her school years, she'd learned much of this and how it affected her parents, who had managed to stay out of the war by growing food needed for the troops as refugees on collective farms in Canada. When women took over the fight, sparking a new revolution, the war ended. Lyn was born five years after the North American Alliance formed, replacing the former United States and Canada. The Johari were footnotes, noted for their ability to remain out of the conflict. They too grew much-needed food.

"But Rose wasn't like the rest of you," Lyn said. "She went to college, became a pilot, married a human I might add."

"We aren't all hermits and monks. We go to college. We live in the world. There are restrictions. Some know the truth, many do not. Rose knew but wasn't happy living on a farm, so she was allowed to leave and live her life. I doubt she thought very much about it once she left."

That would be like forgetting you're Jewish or an immigrant or . . . *frass*, an alien!

"Tell me again why you need to leave now?"

Antonia let out a patient sigh. "When *Endurance* returned, we knew it meant there wasn't anything stopping humans from going to Johar."

"Where is this Johar?"

"It orbits a star in the Hercules constellation, a hundred and ten light years from here. I can get you the exact location."

That was a lot farther than Rigil Kent to Earth. "There's no way Diana and I could get six hundred off Earth, never mind to another solar system."

"You could if you wanted to. We've studied humans for three hundred years. You don't just toss new technology aside."

It would be hard to disagree with her on that one, but why stop lying now? "Well, we did. And precisely to protect worlds out there, like yours it would seem."

Antonia's silence in no way indicated she believed that.

"I think you're safer here on Earth than suddenly disappearing six hundred people to outer space. As long as it isn't used, you're safe." There wasn't anything particularly compelling about Antonia's request. People weren't dying, like Lyn's crew had been when she risked using the technology to save their lives. "The answer is no. I'm sorry."

She finished giving Antonia the bad news and found Diana in the garage cleaning out her skim. She wanted to yell but couldn't bring herself to do it. She'd muttered all through the house, "I can't believe you made me do that. You know better." Now she watched the most important person in the world to her, someone she'd promised never to hurt, toss floor mats and the toolkit and old drink cups and food wrappers out onto the floor.

"I told her. She understands," Lyn said. "It's a box we can't open. She gets it even if you don't."

Diana's head popped over the top of her Rambler. "There's a mouse in here. Probably one in yours too."

"Oh, for god's sake." Lyn opened her door. Sure enough, scat on the passenger seat. A small, furry form shot across the floor. A *mouse*?

Mice were a fact of life. She got that. They'd known since building the cabin that mice came with the territory. The builder had warned against having a garage under the house. Open invitation to all kinds of varmints, she'd said. But Lyn wanted, needed, a small footprint to hide the house as deeply in the forest as possible. No driveway or landing pad, footpaths that could pass for wildlife trails. Discreet cameras. Nothing visible from above. The trees were closer to the house than fire officials wanted. The cabin was fireproof, so they got a variance. And they accepted mice in the garage. But inside a skim?

She popped the hood of her Sportster. What kind of damage could they do to the engine? Would they chew through a circuit board? Piss all over the— *Shite!* A large nest of leaves and grass covered the graviton coil. She looked over at Diana. She was pretending not to notice. "What'd you find?"

"Nothing but some scat, but I'll stop at Jo's Garage tomorrow before school and have her take a look." Her tone softened. "You shouldn't fly with that."

"I won't have time. I'll ask Fúlli."

When it came down to it, they were each more important than whatever was going on outside their orbit. Arguments of aliens were set aside as they spent the day cleaning their skims and mouse-proofing the garage.

THE NEXT MORNING after another unsuccessful search for the mouse, Lyn ran a system check, getting a green light for flying. She'd ask Jo for names of detailers. This thing would need a thorough cleaning once the mouse was evicted. After leaving the woods and foothills, she turned southeast to avoid the worst of the dust bowl and gaping wounds of the empty missile silos around Great Falls. Today, she did not care to see desiccated riverbeds and dunes where prairie grasses should wave in the wind. Or the remnants of the refugee camps. She followed an old interstate, now a pockmarked dirt track, flying low in case a mouse required her to set down fast. She curved east toward Prairie County and the dry wash of the former Yellowstone River.

Below, a white farmhouse sat nestled in a grove of oaks, forming a green oasis amid brown scrub. The ranch had been in the family for generations, but her father hadn't been able to make a go of it. Getting his hands on an early recycler, he'd figured out how to replenish the soil and water table. Rather than go back to farming, he built a business helping to restore other properties.

The green had expanded with the company since Lyn was a child playing in the dust. Over the years, her folks had added more trees and shrubs as well as barns and hangars. Staff had grown from her parents and older-brother Cooper to more than fifty. At first, her mom's replica airplanes were a hobby. Now she specialized in modifying crop dusters to lay down tracks of organic fertilizers and seed instead of herbicides and pesticides. Those were outlawed. They'd done enough damage.

Lyn flew over a line of parked skims to the landing pad near her Lockheed Vega, another replica, bright red against the beige ground. A flash of sunlight sparked off the window like a teasing wink. She hadn't flown it in months. She lowered the wheels then set down and drove into Hangar 5, waiting for the big door to close before getting out. She grabbed her lunch from the passenger seat and went to find Fúlli.

Loud music echoing across the field between buildings led her to Hangar 4. Inside, three skims and two propeller planes sat, one with its engine cowling open and a coverall-covered butt hanging over the side. Fúlli had been born with no legs, but that hadn't stopped nem. A hoverchair floated nearby. Lyn waited for a break in the music. Along the back wall, a Recyc-All churned out a long, thick pole. On the floor were five others. Must be twenty feet long.

The song ended and she called out a greeting. A handwave and nir face popped up, big grin. "Hey, R4, be right with you." Fúlli jokingly referred to each of the family owners in their hierarchical order. R4 meant she was the fourth Randall. Ne grabbed the safety line and swung nirself into the chair and dropped to the floor. With another handwave ne turned down the music.

Lyn asked what the poles were for, and Fúlli explained they were lodge poles. Ne was going to have nir own tipi at Crow Fair. "You can't find pines that tall anymore, so we make them." It was a bigger deal than nir tone was letting on. Fúlli came from a big family and was the oldest child. Setting up nir own tipi meant independence and responsibility.

"What brings you here?" Fúlli asked. "Not more birdhead shenanigans, I hope."

Lyn smiled at the use of her term then told nem about the mouse in her skim.

Ne whistled in sympathy. "Where's the skim now?"

"Hangar 5."

"Let's take a look. Hop on."

Lyn stepped onto the back rail and held onto Fúlli's shoulders. They shot out of the hangar and across the field to No. 5, Lyn whooping with delight. Ne'd built the chair nirself, and it was a cross between a skimcycle and hoverchair with lots of power. In the hangar ne swung around the skim in question then set her down.

"Nice rig," Fúlli said, lifting the engine cover. "I'm impressed."

"You can thank Ani. She recommended it."

"You both have good taste."

Lyn told nem where she'd found the nest. Fúlli took nir time searching through the compartment then flattened the chair into a dolly and slid underneath. "Yep, I can see the entrance."

Lyn knelt down to look. She couldn't see anything. Fúlli pointed out a barely visible gap in the wheel housing. "They can get in through the tiniest holes. Must have gotten in there, then chewed through to the cabin. You'd have gotten an alarm if you'd flown high enough to lose pressure."

Ne slid out from under and snapped the dolly back to a chair. "Give me an hour and I'll let you know what I find."

Lyn crossed the windy yard and stopped in the farmhouse kitchen to replenish her coffee then climbed the stairs to her old bedroom-turned-office. Her hand tremor, she noticed, had stopped.

Only her parents still lived at the ranch. Even Cooper had moved out. As each of the five surviving children had grown and left home, Sarah and Jephson had commandeered their bedrooms for offices. In her room, sim screens for maps and project schedules replaced the posters of swashbuckling pirates from her childhood. A portable Recyc-All sat on her old nightstand. A new comfy office chair and computer console rivaled anything on *Endurance*.

From here she could run holographic models and watch a desert bloom or a destroyed marsh revive in accelerated time. Add a species here, take away an invasive there and see what develops. It had the feel of a game except for the stakes. With so many extinctions in the last hundred years, many ecological niches were left empty. From the loss of predators at the top—leading to her mouse problem—to soil microbes devastated by drought, fire, and erosion, it was no longer possible to let "nature take its course." Yet introducing the wrong species could be tragic, like the woolly mammoths that were genetically recreated and released in Siberia to combat climate change. They all starved to death or burned in fires before they could restore the tundra. Lyn gave thanks every day for the trained biologists, botanists, and soil scientists on staff to figure things out. She had a better grasp of recycling, the advanced technology to clean up almost any chemical imbalance. What it couldn't do was create life or restore extinct species.

She settled in, desk facing a window, and sipped her coffee. As a spaceship captain, she'd sat in a command chair giving orders for others to complete. Now she spent her days juggling video calls from crew demanding to know where their thingamajig was and suppliers who tried to sell her the latest and greatest thingamabob instead of the jig she wanted. Clients, in government or private businesses, wanted to know when a job would begin or finish or could you please tell your crew to shut off the spotlights at night and do those pump jacks have to be so loud?

There were no vandalized job sites among her projects, so she had a chance to catch up. The work distracted her from Antonia's request and Diana's quiet disapproval. Not like they'd never disagreed before. She'd had a hard time convincing Diana to work on T tech in the first place. This felt bigger now that they were together, personal. Which was odd because the first use of the tech had held much higher stakes for them all—literally life or death. But she had to live with Diana, and she hated for anything to come between them.

On the dot, an hour later, Fúlli called her back. The skim's access panels were strewn about, the frame and guts exposed from stem to stern. The air smelled of burned sage.

Fúlli wiped nir hands on a rag. "You do have mice, that's for sure." Ne pointed to a pile of shredded fabric and leaves on the floor, the remains of a nest ne'd pulled from behind the storage bin.

Lyn regarded her torn-apart skim, her beautiful Sportster now a mouse house and toilet. "Did you catch it?"

Fúlli smiled mischievously. "Wanna see the corpse? Lucky for you no babies yet."

Lyn faked a shudder and retching noise. "No thanks. Can I use this or should I take one of the others?"

"I'll have all the holes patched and back together by five. I smudged it for extra protection. Chase off the bad spirits and connect the good ones. So you'll be safe. Stay away from company skims till I can get all our logos off. Antigen are starting to bork skims from restoration companies."

That was not good news. She wondered if Ani's prediction was closing in on truth. Someone could get hurt. She thanked Fúlli for taking on the extra work and for the heads up.

"Gotta keep my favorite boss happy."

"I think I heard you say that to Ani the other day. Then Cooper last week."

Fúlli gave nir trademark grin-smirk. "All true!"

On her lunch break, she took off in her Vega. The electric controls were far simpler than the gasoline engine of the original. This was the model Amelia Earhart had flown solo across the Atlantic and then across the United States back in the 1930s. Diana disapproved of Lyn's flying planes that didn't have modern safety features like seat ejectors and parachutes. If this plane went down, Lyn would go with it. Gone were the hundred-plus dials and gadgets, replaced by computerized avionics. Lyn didn't miss the more primitive controls. What she liked was the experience of flying, the lift provided by aerodynamic wings, not from antigravity contraptions. She wanted to feel the bumps and shifts of a fickle wind, see a propeller twirling in front, adjust flaps and a rudder to change direction. She set down in a dry lakebed to picnic out of sight of ranch buildings and away from news feeds and client calls and thoughts of aliens.

FOR THE NEXT couple of days she avoided bringing up Antonia and the alien request, and Diana did likewise. Instead they reverted to easy topics—Jo had cleaned out Diana's skim, school would end soon for the summer break. Thoughts of aliens retreated to the background.

Then late one afternoon, Lyn returned to the ranch after a site visit in Glendive. She parked her skim in Hangar 5, like always. It wasn't till she got out that she noticed her mother off to the side. She was tempted to make a joke about the welcoming committee, but her mother's expression stopped her. With a face weathered by sun, heat, and wind, wheat-gray hair pulled back in a simple ponytail, deep lines by her mouth but softer laugh lines by her eyes, Sarah Randall was so fully Montana, she could lie in the grass and disappear.

A young woman was here, Sarah said, to see Lyn. Unexpected strangers didn't get to meet with Lyn. Since Enceladus and especially after Rigil Kent, Sarah had become fiercely protective of her only daughter and youngest child. She'd lost a son and nearly lost Lyn twice now. She knew this wasn't acceptable, so she'd parked her in an empty conference room. Sarah held up a vid screen from the security camera. The woman wore the usual western wear, jeans, short jacket, boots. Then she turned toward the camera. Light brown skin contrasted with blue eyes and shoulder-length brown hair. Could be in her thirties. Lyn shook her head. Nothing rang a bell.

"ID?" she asked.

"Said she was Ruzena Tey, that you knew her."

Lyn's breath caught. Anxiety stabbed like an electric jolt, her careful precautions shattered. She might not recognize the face, but she sure knew that name. And thanks to Diana she knew this woman was Johari, an alien.

"How'd she get through?" she asked.

Sensors around the property sent notifications if any vehicle approached the farmhouse that wasn't on RR's list. It was too late to pull the "sorry, wrong Lyn Randall" excuse that had been used on curious reporters and fans of Captain Randall.

"No idea. An alarm came through but then nothing. We figured it was someone who hit our airspace in error and turned back. Next thing I knew, she knocked on the kitchen door."

"I'll handle this." Lyn went to face Captain Tey.

Chapter 3

THE YOUNG WOMAN rose from a chair by the window. Now Lyn remembered that face. The youth, the wide eyes, the innocent way she'd exclaimed her surprise at seeing *Endurance*. "What happened?" she had asked in the excited way a kid seeks an explanation for something magical.

"Captain Tey, I presume," Lyn said.

"Just Tey, Ruzena Tey," she responded.

"How did you get here?" Lyn gestured her to sit. "We didn't see a skim arrive."

"I set down over the hill when your security system requested ID. I walked here."

"Why?"

Tey rocked her head. "I thought you might not want to meet with me." She gave Lyn a pleading look. "I'm sorry. I wanted to talk to you. That's all."

Lyn took a seat across the table. "Did Antonia Squires send you?" Her guarded tone was a reflex honed by years of necessity.

"Yes. And others. So, you know what she told Doctor Squires."

"Teegan. She's Doctor Teegan now."

"Apologies—"

"The answer will be no. Know that going in before you waste too much of my time."

Alien. That's what this woman was. Yet Ruzena looked human. Five fingers on each hand. No cat-like slits for eyes. No scales. Clothes that could have come from Lyn's own closet. Her teeth gleamed white, if slightly crooked. Her accent was bland, northern maybe. *Don't be silly. What did you expect?*

"Please, hear me out," Ruzena said. "After *Endurance* returned, I left Earth Control and took a job with a military contractor working to recreate what you did. But since you didn't reveal anything about the tech, they've been starting from scratch. Faster than light? Not physically possible. So, a wormhole. Has to be."

One by one these little bombs exploded silently in Lyn's autonomic nervous system, speeding her heart, dampening her palms. Everything she'd worked for, tried to keep secret, was pointless if the military succeeded. And Tey was working on it? "Are you using Johari knowledge to help that research?"

"No! God no, the last thing I want is for it to work." Ruzena expressed genuine alarm.

"Are you sabotaging the effort?"

"I'm not in a position to do that. I'm just a pilot. But I've been keeping the Johari leadership informed of the progress. I've recently been assigned to a test-pilot team, which means General Jacana—"

"Jacana? What's she got to do with this?"

"She's leading the program. And they're getting close. It was easy to connect Doctor Teegan to her parents' research on the Teegan particle, so that was the target. But they haven't been able to figure out how to use it. The Teegans never published anything about using it. They're close but not there yet." Her use of "they" and not "we" intrigued Lyn.

"There's something else," Tey said. *Isn't there always?* "I don't know if you've kept in touch with Rachel Holness, but she's filed a lawsuit against Earth Control. She could use that as a platform to say that the alien message from 2115 was an intent to invade. She's so angry about being fired from Earth Control that there's no telling what she might do."

Rachel had been one of many to debrief Lyn after returning from Rigil Kent, repeating her warning that the alien threat was real, and Lyn was being a traitor by withholding the technology that could protect Earth. She was furious Lyn refused to cooperate.

"Does she know about you? You worked for her. What's the connection?"

"I'm not sure. I don't think she knows about the Johari." Tey spoke carefully, like she was probing for anything to get Lyn's attention. "I know she used to be with Pulsar."

"So was I."

Tey rubbed her face in frustration. "You know what I mean. You exposed Pulsar and their intent to militarize space. What you didn't say was that it was about aliens. You could have, but you didn't. You went with the public line that it was the Chinese who wanted weapons in space. Rachel's obsession with the SETI program always struck me as a cover."

"Did she tell you what it was a cover for?"

"No. But—"

"But nothing. You've got nothing."

Tey leaned forward and pressed on. "Regardless, it's only a matter of time before whatever knowledge you have becomes irrelevant because General Jacana *will* get there. She's a hell of a determined woman."

General Jacana had been a vice president at Pulsar. She was the one who assigned Lyn and Tara and the other inexperienced recruits to the Enceladus mission. They'd been in awe of General Jacana. She had been a war hero, instrumental in the final push by the Women's Army. The later taint of Pulsar never stuck to her. Lose an arm and two legs and help end a world war and people will forgive a lot. Lyn was the only one left from that mission, and her opinion of the general was not very positive.

Fortunately, Jacana did not have *all* the research. The elder Teegans had understood the potential for the T particle to hold open a wormhole and what that meant, so they stopped publishing and put their sensitive research on a data cube they gave to Diana. Only she had all the information needed to complete the project. After returning from Rigil Kent she'd destroyed that cube. The only remaining copy sat in Lyn's brain implant.

The idea that someone would take on wormhole research was not surprising. She'd expected it to come from Earth Control, but Rachel lost her job as CEO when the bad publicity surrounding the destruction of the *Aphrodite* proved too much for the board of directors and they cleaned house, firing her. But to have it come from within the government. Hellen Jacana was former Pulsar. Disbanded or not, scattered to the winds or within government, that mindset remained in people like Hellen Jacana, and to Lyn, that meant she remained dangerous.

The risk of someone else perfecting the technology or Rachel saying something changed the equation. Not enough, but a little. She needed to see what was going on with Rachel—she could blow everything open if she knew the Johari were aliens. She also needed to get Ruzena Tey off her back, to shut her down fast and clean. She regarded this young woman before her. It took guts, what she was doing. Lyn had thought of her as a lightweight back when they'd first met. Young and clueless. Now she saw the reason behind that. As a Johari, as an alien, this woman treaded many a fine line. In another universe, she might have liked her.

"The answer is no. I'll have someone see you out." Lyn rose.

Tey tapped the table. "Do you understand what you're doing?"

"Of course I do."

"If the military develops wormhole tech, you lose control of it."

Lyn stopped, hand on the doorknob. "Using it to get you home won't stop Jacana."

"But you could save our people, our planet—"

Lyn was this close to giving in. She could have squeezed all six hundred *Aphrodite* survivors on *Endurance*. They'd asked. That little boy pleading, his mother's face so furious when Lyn refused. Not outright. She would have done it if there was no other option even though it would have dramatically increased the odds of them all dying. Then, returning to emptied and bloodied lifepods, mutiny wreaking havoc. That sat in her bones, a permanent ache in her psyche, the horror of all those lives lost. Diana's disappointed face the other night echoed that. Providing a link to an alien world with the ability to come to Earth was simply too much of an unknown right now.

"Remain here till someone comes to get you." She closed the door on Ruzena Tey and leaned against the wall. She should take care of Tey herself, but she didn't trust herself to maintain the façade of cool dismissal. She couldn't let Tey keep working on her, chipping away at her resolve. She called Ani, someone she could trust completely, to escort Ruzena off the property.

IF LYN CONSIDERED even for a moment not telling Diana about Ruzena Tey, it was with guilt. As a captain, as much as she sought advice from her staff, the decisions were hers alone to make and she needed no excuses. She and Diana weren't colleagues. They were married. To some, that could be a squishy term. There was no rule book, no Marriage Academy drilling into her what that meant, how she needed to behave, as the Aerospace Academy, and god forbid her Pulsar training, had prepared her for the difficult decisions of space command. Being the keeper of the sacred data on how to open a wormhole didn't absolve her. She had no clue how to build the machine to fold space, even with the plans tucked neatly in her brain. Diana did. She might not be able to do it without the plans Lyn held, but if anyone owned the patent on this thing, it was Diana Teegan. Regardless of any bias Diana might have in favor of the Johari cause given her relationship to them, even if she hadn't known the truth until a few days ago, she needed to know what they were dealing with. So, she'd tell her.

After work, as they often did before the summer heat made that impossible, they hiked up the mountain. The impact of boot on soil and rock, the scent of pine and earth, grounded Lyn literally and figuratively. The woods, young with slender trees and thickets of buckthorn, provided minimal shade. Creeks were easy to cross, running only after a heavy rain. Broken snags, the bark long since peeled off by weather and woodpeckers and scarred by fire, peppered the rocky grass. Step by step they climbed the side of a hill and, rounding a corner, were rewarded with a view across a wide valley to the next ridge. Dry lakebeds turned into scruffy meadows, and above them craggy, treeless, and snowless peaks stood unfazed by the changes around them. At a flat field that had once been a pond, they unloaded their packs.

Coolant ran through microtubules in their clothing, beating back the intense heat of the day. What Lyn had missed most while being stranded in Rigil Kent had been the lack of fresh air, wind through her hair, and good old-fashioned dirt. They picnicked on a rock outcrop and chatted about their day. Diana always had stories about her students, the principal, or parents. Lyn couldn't follow all the characters but that hardly mattered. Diana didn't seem to be holding a grudge about Antonia. That would change.

After dinner, they lay back in the shade, watching clouds chug slowly by. One passed over the sun low in the west. They used to promise rain but hadn't for a long time. Now they were a waste of water taunting the thirsty land they shaded. Clouds were liars. Lyn hated lies. She sat up and told Diana about Ruzena Tey.

Diana took the news quietly. "I know you don't want to do this, but what if she's right and General Jacana is working on this and almost there. What happens then?"

Lyn's life with Tara never had a chance to settle into this kind of domesticity. They'd had to hide their relationship or they'd never get to go on missions together with Pulsar. Tara was a higher rank. In some ways they were never equals. That might have bothered Lyn eventually, but too soon Tara was gone and Lyn was alone. She needed to be honest with Diana, but what did that mean? She felt one way, Diana the other, and there was no one to pull rank and decide.

"What happens is nothing as long as the Johari don't reveal themselves. There's more to lose by using the tech and potentially handing it to Jacana than if we stay quiet. You said yourself, you thought this might be a trap. Well, Jacana might never get there on her own, and I have no intention of helping her."

"What about Rachel? What if she knows about the Johari and exposes them? You aren't objective when it comes to her or Pulsar," Diana said. "Just know that."

No one could be objective about Pulsar. The company had been allowed to disband, its leadership permitted to slink away, some to obscurity, others to resurrected careers in government. At Pulsar, Captain Jill Faber had been Lyn's and Rachel's training officer on *Endurance* when they were cadets, before the company folded and Omara bought the ship at auction. Jill Faber then joined Earth Control and took over leadership when Rachel was fired. Hellen Jacana now headed the entire military defense force for the NAA. Giving Hellen Jacana the keys to the galaxy was a nightmare scenario, and Diana had to know that.

If there was any way to help the Johari secretly, Lyn would consider it. Fact was, Jacana's research had nothing to do with the Johari. And refusing to help the Johari had nothing to do with Jacana's research. Because that work would continue whether Lyn approved or not. So why *not* help them?

Instead she said, "I'll find out what Rachel knows. But we can't do it, Dee." Like it was a programmed response beyond her control. As if the nickname would soften the blow.

"We can. You won't." Diana stood and packed up their things.

AT WORK THE next day, Lyn was in the kitchen fixing a snack when Ani breezed in, humming to herself. She stopped when she saw Lyn.

"How'd it go?" Lyn asked. She'd left for home before Ani returned from her escort duties, before Tey or anyone else could track her.

"Fine," Ani answered, uncharacteristically quiet. She even blushed.

Then Lyn noticed that Ani was wearing the same shirt she'd worn the day before. She bent close and took a sniff. That wasn't Ani's usual scent.

"Ah, you have a hot date last night?" she asked.

Ani's blush deepened.

Lyn waved a hand. "I get it. None of my business." She reached for a plate. "What'd you think of Tey?"

Cooper walked past the doorway and backed up when he saw Ani. "You keep the company skim overnight?"

Lyn looked from one to the other. Why would Ani have taken the skim home after dropping off Tey? She had her own here. She watched Ani squirm.

"Oh, I forgot to log it in till just now," Ani said, unconvincingly casual.

"You off to Nebraska today?" Cooper leaned against the door frame and stared at his com pod, multitasking.

"Yeah, um, Fúlli's loading the Ag-Cat now."

Cooper pocketed his com and pushed off the doorframe. "Have a good trip."

Ani exhaled loudly then noticed Lyn watching.

"What's going on?" Lyn asked.

Ani sighed. Clearly something was bugging her. "Ruzena. Why were you so mean to her?"

Ruzena, huh. "What'd she say?"

"She was devastated."

"How so? What did she say?" Lyn's hackles rose, internal Geiger crackling like crazy.

Ani dropped the lid of her thermos, knocked over a chair reaching for it, kicked it under the table. She stood up and growled. "She's nice. Okay? I felt sorry for her." She slammed the thermos on the counter.

Lyn raised her hands. "Whoa." Ani didn't ask how she'd been mean to Tey, so chances were she knew. "You dropped her off. Was that it?"

Ani rolled her eyes. "We had a few drinks, played some pool . . ."

Lyn regarded her, new smell, old shirt. "Ani," she said softly, "was Tey your hot date?"

Ani crossed her arms and leaned on the counter, meeting Lyn's gaze. "As a matter of fact, yes. What of it?"

"Ani!" Lyn wanted to strangle her. "What were you thinking? You're supposed to be on *my* side."

"Who says I'm not? I wasn't thinking about you. My personal life is none of your business."

Lyn slammed a drawer. Sarah entered the kitchen but quickly backed out.

"And yes, she told me," Ani said quietly. "And I think you were pretty shitty to her."

Lyn leaned on the counter and shook her head. "She tell you before or after?"

"*Coño*. None of your business." Her accent always strengthened when she was pissed. "You aren't my mother. You aren't even my boss anymore. I work for Cooper." She grabbed her things and stormed out, swearing in Spanish.

Lyn stood, stunned. Ani knew what was at stake. How could she be so bloody reckless? She'd thought she'd be able to contain this a little longer than twenty-four hours. Now Ani knew too and, worst of all, sympathized with Tey. This had to be Tey playing her. Ani wouldn't know anything but for Tey telling her.

Sarah returned, quietly got a mug from the cabinet, and poured a cup of coffee. She started to leave, but then turned to Lyn. "I don't know what's going on here, but don't you dare make her quit. She's the best pilot we've ever had." Then she left.

Great. If her mother had to choose, she'd keep Ani over her own daughter. Lyn skulked up to her office. She responded to messages, ordered plans, and otherwise pushed buttons to fill the morning. Out her window Ani took off in the Ag-Cat, a cargo drone following. She checked the schedule. She'd be gone for the rest of the week, hopping her way down to Nebraska to meet up with a client who was re-soiling old farm fields.

That morning, Diana had been quiet, eating her breakfast while finishing up correcting some tests. A kiss goodbye. Normal, except for the lack of eye contact. Diana could stew with the best of them. Ani could too. This felt like that moment when she'd hear an alarm, whether in the cockpit of an airplane or the bridge of a spaceship. She wouldn't know right away how bad it was. A malfunction easily corrected? Or a fatal mistake? That's how these bits of information rang in her consciousness, warning her she was close to a dangerous barrier. A ship reentering atmosphere at the wrong angle. A wrong decision could mean it all goes to hell.

She sent Ani a message. "I'm sorry. I was out of line. Have a safe trip."

AFTER DINNER, DIANA went upstairs to her office to correct papers, a chill oozing off of her. Lyn flopped on the couch and ran a search for Rachel Holness. There was a lot. She started with a press conference from a week ago.

A reporter stood outside a courthouse, in Syracuse according to the caption. "Rachel Holness, the disgraced former head of Earth Control, has filed a lawsuit against the agency, claiming wrongful dismissal." The camera panned from the reporter to Rachel and the prominent civil attorney Illumi Névé beside her. "She's requesting an undisclosed sum for compensation."

"This is a travesty of justice," Mx. Névé said. "Ms. Holness did nothing wrong at Earth Control. She's being scapegoated because she knows of a serious threat that the government is covering up."

A reporter called out, asking what that threat was. Mx. Névé dodged answering but continued to accuse the government of abuse. "This so-called New Era is supposed to bring peace and harmony. But only if you say and believe the right thing."

That's what they called it, the New Era, after the treaties were signed, new governments led by women all claimed to believe in the tenets of the coalition that ended the violence. Unity of women worldwide; a new public-service culture not predicated on war or greed or corruption; a free, ecologic, democratic society with equality for all.

Rachel looked terrible, with haunted eyes, her normally styled and curled glossy hair pulled back in a basic tail, frizzy ends blowing across her face.

"My god, Rach, what have they done to you?" Lyn muttered. Where was the fiery terrier she'd met in gym class at the Aerospace Academy? The wrestling partner who'd underestimated Lyn's experience growing up with older brothers. Rachel had taken one look at her and said, "Who's this scrawny-ass rich girl?" Then Lyn kicked her butt. Flattened to the mat, panting and slapping the surface in surrender, Rachel had added, "Maybe not so scrawny-ass." Later, Lyn learned Rachel had been abandoned by her mother as an infant and shuffled through the foster-care system till her grandmother found her. What for Lyn had been a fun sport had for Rachel meant survival. Rachel had been one of the cool kids at the Academy, charismatic, funny, sexy, with the confident fearlessness of a fighter pilot. They'd bonded after a seemingly simple hot-air balloon flight had triggered Lyn's fear of falling, leaving her trembling. Rachel had been there, figuratively catching her and coaching her through practice runs till Lyn could handle the balloon with the best of them. Now, she looked like the one who needed catching.

Rachel leaned toward the mics, chewing her lower lip. "I need to warn everyone. They are coming. We have to prepare—" Her voice was weak and hoarse, no sign of the snark and snap Lyn was used to.

Mx. Névé put her arm around Rachel and subtly pulled her back.

"Why now?" a reporter called out. "It's been two years."

Rachel pulled away from her lawyer. "I want people to listen to me. I know what happened—"

Again, her lawyer gripped her tight. "She hasn't been able to find work, her reputation has been destroyed. She wants her good name back."

Of course, Rachel would file her lawsuit now, as space reopened and Earth Control was in the news. Space reopening was the gift that kept on giving. But why was she acting so strange? That warning, "They are coming." It had nothing to do with Earth Control or her firing.

On graduating from the Academy, Lyn, Rachel, and Tara had joined Pulsar Industries, an up-and-coming space exploration company. After the failed mission to Saturn's moon Enceladus, where Tara and the rest of the crew had died, Rachel had told Lyn the true goal was to claim the moon and militarize space in preparation for an invasion of aliens, ones who had sent an ominous message in 2115. The message Lyn now understood was intended for the Johari, aliens who had been on Earth the whole time. She sighed, realizing how close to right Rachel had been. Just not the part where they wanted to invade and kill everyone on Earth.

She found another clip, Rachel being interviewed, this two days ago. She was alone, without Mx. Névé. Rachel sat on the edge of her chair, staring off to the side, not at the woman interviewing her. A muscle twitched by her left eye, like the tic Lyn had experienced when transferring files to and from her Pulsar implant. Maybe nerves. She watched, transfixed as Rachel rambled and made little sense. "We are at an inflection point as humans."

The host looked puzzled. "Can you elaborate?"

"Humanity is in danger. Pulsar, I mean Earth Control, are conspiring. No, I mean danger. From outside forces. Ones we can't ignore." She pounded the arm of the chair. "No one will *listen* to me." Her eye twitched again. She sat quiet for a moment. Then, in a tone of resignation, said, "We've crossed the boundary and there's no going back."

Was Rachel trying to blurt out a warning of invasion? Why now? She'd been quiet about the topic of aliens until *Endurance* returned, and she'd berated Lyn for withholding technology she saw as key to protecting Earth from these aliens. Why was Pulsar so obsessed with the notion that aliens automatically meant harm, invasion, Armageddon? It felt a lot like past fear mongering about immigrants, but those fears were nonexistent, no proof at all.

"What boundary? Pulsar?" The host was visibly frustrated, as was Rachel.

"I'm trying to tell you. It's in the boundary. The circles are converging."

The host sat back and faced the camera. "Let's take a break, shall we?"

The show resumed with Rachel gone and the host acting like she'd never been there. On to the next guest.

Lyn hated to think it, but it seemed quite possible Rachel's implant was malfunctioning. Did she have to worry about that with her own aging implant or was it more nefarious? Could someone tamper with it, or was Rachel losing her mind? There was one person who might be able to shed some light on this.

OTHER THAN OCCASIONAL press interviews, Lyn hadn't seen Jill Faber in almost two decades. She had always liked Captain Faber. She'd kept her nose clean when Pulsar went down, even resigning after Enceladus and how Lyn had been treated. She always thought of her as one of the good ones and had been glad to see her join Earth Control. Only a small part of Lyn's enhanced brain registered nerves at the coincidence of two consecutive CEOs having a Pulsar past, though Rachel had hidden hers and Jill had not. Lyn wanted to believe Jill had been thoroughly scrutinized. She came to the top position at a ridiculously difficult time for the organization—their former leader run out of town, blamed for the *Aphrodite*'s demise, the deaths of eight thousand.

"Greetings, Captain," Faber said when she answered Lyn's call. She looked much as Lyn remembered, just a few years older, a few more lines on her deep brown face, a hint of gray streaking her shoulder-length braids. Back in their Pulsar days, Captain Faber had carried herself with a quiet strength. Literally quiet, she could sneak up on a misbehaving cadet, usually Rachel getting Lyn into some kind of trouble, clear her throat, and nearly cause a heart attack.

"Lyn will do."

"Then Jill here."

"I'm not sure I can get used to that. I'm tempted to salute."

"How have you been, mysterious one?"

The casual informality, like colleagues of equal standing, felt wrong. You didn't mess with Captain Faber. The stories that had circulated about her were that she'd grown up in the military, groomed to be a child soldier. But she ran away from her training base, fled over the border to Canada, and signed on with a clandestine Women's Army unit. The war ended two years later. Rumors among the cadets had cycled between her being a heroic killing machine or having never fired a shot.

They exchanged pleasantries then Lyn told Jill about seeing Rachel's interview and how damaged she seemed. Knowing Rachel was suing Earth Control, would Jill have some insight into her state of mind?

"She doesn't look well," Lyn said.

"I agree. For legal reasons, I'm not in a position to contact her myself. I was actually wondering if you might."

"We haven't been in touch. She's hardly my biggest fan right now. I'm surprised she's not suing me for getting her fired."

"Her personal demons aren't my concern, but she's making my job difficult with her ranting. I want space tourism to resume with no questions hanging over our head. She's a big, fat question."

"I'm afraid I can't help there," Lyn said.

"I was thinking of calling you. If you would publicly endorse space reopening, it would blunt Rachel's howls of protest. You have a lot more credibility than she does."

Lyn would be forever grateful Jill hadn't referred to her as the Great Captain Randall. "The less I'm out in public, the better. Space is not my thing anymore."

"I'd wondered about that," Jill said. "I half expected your call to be giving me a heads up that the great Captain Randall was returning." *Ouch. There it was.* "Maybe even with Omara Tours on *Endurance*. How is she by the way?"

"Fine as far as I know. I haven't spoken to her recently." Lyn winced, realizing what a hermit she sounded like. How had two years gone by with so little human contact? She was like a prisoner released from long solitary confinement unable to reconnect with society.

"There's another former colleague who's a bit of a fly in my ointment. General Hellen Jacana."

Lyn perked to attention as Jill continued. "She doesn't want space to reopen. She's using the original, unknown event at Saturn as an excuse. If you could reassure her in some way . . ."

"I have no idea what caused the wormhole by Saturn."

Jill made a noise under her breath like she was considering what stronger cards she might have to toss down. "I've heard rumors that General Jacana is working on faster-than-light travel."

This must be the world's worst kept secret. "Are you sure?"

"It's a rumor."

Which meant it was true. "Well, I wish her luck."

Jill emitted a rough laugh. "We can't change the past, Lyn. I want what you want—to keep this world peaceful and prevent any future violence, either here or elsewhere."

"Is there any connection between Jacana's work and Rachel's weird behavior?"

Jill seemed taken aback by this. "What makes you think there might be?"

"Could someone tamper remotely with her implant?"

"I'm not sure," Jill said, absently touching behind her left ear where the implant's port sat, "though I suppose if anyone could, it would be a former Pulsar vice president."

General Jacana wasn't doing a very good job of keeping her covert operation a secret. In fact, it was pretty clear she was doing everything she could to make sure one person knew about it.

IF LYN THOUGHT calling the top military leader of the North American Alliance would be full of red tape, she was disabused of that notion. As soon as she said her name, the general took the call.

In the vid's wide view, she watched the general step from behind her desk over to a window and adjust the shade. She appeared incredibly fit for what must be pushing ninety years old, with smooth dark skin and touches of gray in her short hair. A quiet whir audible, likely from her prostheses. One hand was normal, the other in a black glove. She wore her uniform, sporting an impressive rack of ribbons that Lyn couldn't decipher. From her time with the Women's Army? That was pre-NAA. A courtesy, perhaps, to acknowledge her role. The slacks held a sharp crease down to shined shoes. It all seemed so intentional, casual enough to be intimidating. See all of me, deal with all of me, she seemed to be saying.

"Good to see you, Captain," General Jacana said.

"Lyn will do," Lyn said.

The general shook her head. "Never dismiss the respect that comes with a title. You earned it. Now, to what do I owe this honor?" She leaned against the windowsill.

"You are no doubt a busy general, so I won't waste your time. I heard about a program to replicate the technology I used to get back with *Endurance*. Is it true?"

Jacana's chin snapped up and she smiled. "Direct. I like that. If indeed I were working on it, I would welcome your help, of course. Or Doctor Teegan's or her parents'. We'd make a wonderful team, don't you think?" Her accent reminded Lyn of her Maya roots. She'd always wondered why the general had joined with the NAA when her home country had sided with the southern alliance. Topic for another day, perhaps.

"I didn't say I'd help. And leave the Teegans out of this—all of them. You are of course free to pursue the technology. I can't stop you."

Jacana didn't say anything, as though reconsidering her approach. "The last time we met, you probably don't remember. You were barely conscious. I doubt you were aware of me telling you how sorry I was for Enceladus. The mission was my idea, but others took over the day-to-day supervision. I never would have ordered Captain Tara to continue after the first crew members died. There's no reason to distrust me now. I assure you that I have completely rejected everything Pulsar stood for."

"You made that clear when you were appointed to your current role. You never denied your involvement." But had she fully rejected it?

Jacana tipped her head in acknowledgement. "Pulsar was a mistake. I didn't sacrifice so much in the revolution only to lose it all. I do, however, wish I could convince you of the greater good that can be gained by sharing your achievement."

"Greater good" was in the eye of the beholder. "Sorry, but I've been pretty clear that I don't have the data anymore and—"

Jacana raised her gloved hand. "Please. Spare me. I know the details of the technology are in your head because you couldn't have come back using *Endurance*'s computer. I imagine you found the prohibition against superluminal travel deep in the AMOS code."

AMOS stood for Advanced Medical Officer System, aka Dr. Amos but also every medical officer on every ship that went to space.

Lyn was taken aback. "You know about that?"

"I put it there."

Fuck's sake. "How? Why?"

General Jacana leaned back and crossed her ankles. "It's a long story that includes why AI had restrictions imposed to limit command and control systems, but the short version is that once Doctor Geller invented a drive that made the outer planets easily reached, we understood the next barrier would be interstellar. We felt controlling this technology would be important. To be honest, I hadn't expected the code to survive forty years, but Pulsar birthed a crop of very dedicated adherents." She glanced toward the window, as if letting Lyn consider how many others were out there. "I know you had to fly the ship and control this technology using your implant. You claim you destroyed all the data, but we both know the information cannot be removed from your brain. Merely concealed and protected. If I wanted to take it from you forcibly, I wouldn't be on a vid call."

"Why? What difference does it make whether we can get to Mars or to Rigil Kent? I don't understand this obsession."

"Look around you. Does this planet look like a good long-term investment? You found a habitable planet orbiting Toliman. What if we needed to evacuate Earth? Where would we go? Where could we go and live like this?"

"That planet proved deadly, so maybe we should clean up our mess here. Wouldn't that be a better investment?" Peeved, Lyn didn't care how many medals the general sported.

"And maybe we will. With your family's help."

Was that a veiled threat? Oh, how she wished Dr. Amos had been able to remove the implant. Life would be so much easier, but he'd told her that it encompassed all the fluid in her brain, using nanoparticles to form a supercomputer. There was no one part of her brain involved.

"Consider me unconvinced."

"Then let me offer another reason. I'm willing to bet that you know about the message of 2115, received from intelligent extraterrestrial beings, requesting a meeting."

Now Lyn had to be careful. She was beginning to appreciate the precarious position the Johari were in. "I've heard rumors. Mostly from Rachel Holness, however, so consider the source."

Jacana nodded slightly. "Let's just say it's been verified."

"I'd love to see the proof." From what Rachel had said, the original message was lost, and Antonia confirmed that. "If they sent this message decades ago, why haven't they shown up with their laser cannons pointed at us?"

"A good question. I confess I come from a background of preparing for the worst-case. War will do that to a person. Certainly, if we face them and find them peaceful and holding out flowers that aren't poisonous, we don't have to shoot. But why not be ready just in case?" She flicked some invisible lint off her ribbon rack. "If these aliens really are malicious, I'll fight them to my last breath. Maybe longer."

In Lyn's mind, Pulsar had become evil with Enceladus, and Hellen Jacana personified that to her. Now the general's appeals for forgiveness and help left Lyn open to one but not the other.

"I'm going to respectfully decline."

"Think it over. You know where to find me."

THAT EVENING, REACHING into the refrigerator for the lettuce, Lyn spotted the vial of DNA. Diana had not destroyed it. Maybe Rachel was right, the circles were converging. Clearly General Jacana was working on wormhole technology. Clearly she understood Diana's work was critical to that. She must be frustrated not to have the key ingredients. And a frustrated General Hellen Jacana was not someone Lyn wanted to deal with. Like it or not, it was time to consider the possibility that they needed to help the Johari, not because they could, but because it was right. All they needed was a ship. She shut the fridge, then reopened it and grabbed the lettuce.

Chapter 4

DIANA DIDN'T GLOAT, but took in the news of Lyn's calls with Jill Faber and Hellen Jacana calmly, showing surprise only as Lyn recounted Ani's fling with Ruzena Tey. She suppressed a smirk. "Ah, hormones. We can trust her, though, right?"

"I'd want her to pilot and yes, of course." Next step, Lyn said, was contacting Omara. "We can't do this without a ship, and she might not even have one big enough."

Lyn had always liked her former boss, who had taken a chance on her when she was an out-of-work, Pulsar-traumatized astronaut. Omara had operated her tour company for ten years when *Endurance* vanished and with it her business. As space closed and the months passed with no sign of the ships or what happened to them any clearer, she had disbanded her business, paid her employees, and sold off her assets. She was not, however, finished. When *Endurance* returned, crippled and still far from home, she lost no time organizing the rescue and orchestrating elaborate publicity around its dramatic landing on Earth. Lyn had confided in Omara everything about the adventure in Rigil Kent as well as how they returned. She didn't trust many people in this world, but Omara was tops after Diana.

Lyn could tell Omara sensed their call wasn't purely social, so she cut short the pleasantries and relayed the incredible tale from Antonia Squires and Ruzena Tey.

Omara remembered Tey. "Very cagey that one. Easily intimidated," she said with a soft, private chuckle. She wasn't one to bully, but Tey had tried to keep her from boarding *Endurance,* and she would have none of that. She listened intently as Diana took up the story, only furrowing her brow occasionally. "And you believe them?"

Diana said they did. Lyn asked what the chances might be of obtaining a ship if they decided to help the Johari. Omara only admitted to preparing a fleet, anticipating new tours. "I had thought perhaps your call was an offer to return as captain."

"Sorry to disappoint you." She detected a side eye from Diana. Even without Diana in her life, the idea of returning to space left her a bit nauseated. A tiny sliver of disappointment, maybe, but overall space had never turned out to be quite what she'd hoped. Escorting tourists didn't provide the rush of exploration.

"Oh, you haven't, yet," Omara said, "but let me express some caution. You each have an emotional connection to their story. I don't. I'll be honest, I've seem some pretty sophisticated subterfuge in my day, and this needs more than their word. What proof did they offer?"

Diana told her about the DNA. Omara suggested they bring it to her for Dr. Amos to analyze. Keep it in the family. This needed to be handled carefully. Lyn couldn't agree more.

OMARA LIVED IN isolated Ruby Valley, north of Las Vegas. The springs that once made the area marginally habitable had long since dried up, along with the snowpack on the Ruby Mountains, leaving a desolate landscape. Omara's family came from the Middle East, so she was at home in desert heat. A child when the war had started, she'd spent her youth fleeing various war zones, settling in Nevada as the war ended. Her home sat in an oasis of trees amid scrubby brush and dry grasses. The octagonal house with a wrapping porch reminded Lyn of a flying saucer. Then she flinched, imagining the Johari arriving in their own saucer. They stepped onto the porch, and a tone chimed followed by, "Welcome Lyn and Diana, it's wonderful to see you." The door clicked open.

Lyn knew that voice. "Likewise, Petra, good to hear you." As they entered the open interior, Omara came around the kitchen island, wiping her hands on a towel. She gave each long, warm hugs.

Omara had always personified elegance to Lyn. With her long legs and ballet-perfect posture, she transformed casual, loose slacks and a sleeveless top into the height of fashion.

"Petra's off the ship?" Lyn asked about the voice that had been *Endurance*'s computer.

"She's everywhere," Omara said with a wave of her hand. "How could I limit such a useful AI to a tin can?"

Petra started to explain that *Endurance* in fact contained very little tin when Omara shushed her. "She's still learning sarcasm."

Omara gave them a quick tour—Lyn had never been to her home—which mostly involved a slow twirl. She wandered like a curious child, touching the beams of real wood, a brick fireplace, cool tile floors with thick Persian rugs. Large glass doors let in lots of light with stunning views toward the Ruby Mountains and the valley floor.

Omara made the usual hostess offerings then suggested they get right to it. "I have something to show you anyway," she said with a hint of a smile.

After a claustrophobic elevator ride down under the house, then through a narrow tunnel in a small cart, they entered a huge cavernous hangar. Before them sat *Endurance*. Lyn gasped. The last time she'd seen the ship was as she disembarked after landing in Las Vegas. At the time scorched from reentry, it now gleamed with a fresh coat of Omara Tours' green and gold and sported a new observation dome over the top deck. The ship had been stripped bare for the traverse through the wormhole, which had meant dismantling the star feature.

It was like seeing an old friend who'd been ill but was now healthy and happy. The others were getting out of the cart. Omara turned back. Lyn blinked and got out. "Sorry. I guess I wasn't prepared to see her again. I thought you might have scrapped her."

"Good lord, why would I do that?" Omara looked up at the ship. Floodlights brought out a shine. "This ship has a lot more good adventures in her—though I certainly hope not as good as your last one. Would you like a tour?"

Lyn was overwhelmed by the silly notion that *Endurance* could go on without her. Of course she could. The ship didn't care who was captain. She followed the others up a stairway to the Main Deck reception area. She took in the new carpets, wall panels, and lights. That familiar hum of the ventilation system. She'd grown so weary of that and so thankful to leave it behind, but now? She'd thought she was done with space travel, but she was in no way Randall Restoration's best project manager. And after blowing up at Ani, which she never would have done as captain on *Endurance*, she wasn't sure where she fit in.

"You know, you're always welcome to return," Omara said.

Would she ever? Diana followed close behind her, a fact that limited her options. "I think Earth is where I belong now."

In the captain's quarters, Omara showed off the new art she'd acquired to replace what Lyn had recycled into fuel and food in order to save her crew and passengers. She pointed to a large painting Lyn recognized as her brother's work. A beautiful landscape of the rolling Montana hills near the Randall ranch. Greener than in real life, but that was the fun of art.

"One of Kai's!" Lyn said. "Where'd you find that?"

"I'm not a recluse. He had a show last year. I went."

Lyn was disappointed when Omara said the bridge was a construction zone. No reliving that. But as they left the ship, Omara said, "Would you like to see the newest fleet member?"

"Of course," Lyn said.

They climbed back into the cart and Omara drove down another tunnel.

"I want to handle more passengers at a time without the obscene size of the Jupiter-class ships like the *Aphrodite*," she said as they entered an even larger hangar. "Meet *Tenacity*."

The ship was maybe three times the size of *Endurance*, but of similar design, right down to the domed observation deck. Eight decks instead of

Endurance's five. It was surrounded by scaffolding, and bots and androids swarmed over it like worker ants doting on their queen. Recyc-Alls at work stations dotted the floor around the ship, churning out parts.

Omara smiled proudly as she drove alongside the big ship. "She'll take three hundred passengers, with all the usual Omara Tours touches."

Inside, it had the same feel of *Endurance*. Luxurious but intimate and not overly ostentatious.

"Where is Doctor Amos?" Diana asked as they left the ship. He'd been in charge of *Endurance*'s medical unit, but that too had been a construction zone.

Omara led them to a suite of offices off to the side. Dr. Amos stood in his charging bay, coming alert as they entered. While he looked much the same as Lyn remembered, she was pleased to see his frayed fabric joints had been mended and the scratches on his smooth composite head buffed out.

"Good afternoon, Omara." Then he spotted her guests. "Lyn, Diana—it's good to see you both." He sounded genuinely pleased.

The medical caduceus on his chest had been replaced by the Omara Tours logo and his name with the title Chief Operations Officer.

"You've been promoted. Congratulations," Lyn said.

"Thank you," he said, raising his two polymer eyebrows. Other than those, he had little to work with in showing expressions. His mouth was no more than a speaker, and his eyes, while they moved and blinked, could not widen or squint, but to Lyn, he had always been able to convey the empathy and tact that made him a great medical doctor. No doubt also a great operations chief.

He explained that Omara was giving him more autonomy so he'd be closer to Petra, with programming that went beyond analysis and diagnosis. While Petra had been *Endurance*'s main computer and Dr. Amos its medical officer, they now worked in tandem throughout the organization.

"I couldn't get on without them," Omara said.

"The feeling is mutual." Petra's disembodied voice chiming in unexpectedly was something Lyn had to get used to again.

Diana brought out the vial of DNA and explained what they were looking for. Dr. Amos led them down a corridor to a lab and inserted it into an analyzer on the workbench. In a few minutes he pulled up a screen showing the results.

He studied it for a few minutes, folding his arms like any thoughtful scientist. "Superficially, this looks human, but I'm seeing something that could be a genetic mutation, or it could be new to Earth. I'd like to do a more thorough analysis, run it through a simulation to see what else might be going on. How long did you say they'd been here?"

"Almost three hundred years," Diana said.

The analysis would take forty-eight hours, so Lyn decided a visit to Las Vegas was in order. In fact, if they'd come so close and didn't visit, former

Endurance colleagues Miriam Kapoor and Sharyn Wang would be downright pissed. She didn't need more people mad at her.

THE NEXT MORNING, Lyn and Diana flew south from Ruby Valley. At the outskirts of Las Vegas, they passed over mile after mile of abandoned neighborhoods, some mid-construction, most buried under sand dunes. The outside temperature rose to more than 130 degrees F. It should be the last place on Earth anyone would visit, let alone live.

"Remind me again why they chose Vegas," Diana said as they passed over the shimmering mirage of human artifacts from a former urban life.

"They didn't. They say Vegas chose them."

Until Lyn had landed *Endurance* there, she'd dismissed it as a relic of the past. Once a meadow, then a glittering Sin City and gambling capital, the water finally ran out and the sun baked it to a constant oven. And yet it was where Omara had chosen to land *Endurance* on its miracle return two years ago. She'd assumed it was because it was close to Omara's home and her underground facility. It brought media attention to the celebration but ignored what Miriam and Sharyn discovered firsthand. Neighborhoods of abandoned houses full of squatters. Whole communities tapped into a rough self-sufficiency.

Miriam had been *Endurance*'s executive chef and Sharyn was in charge of hotel operations. At the time, Sharyn had spent a week wandering, not sure what to do with her life. Space was closed, her career ended. "When I saw people who don't have a place to call home, it made no sense," she'd told Lyn at the time. "The revolution was supposed to end all this suffering. A free, ecological, and democratic society with equality among all people."

Miriam, a former refugee herself and not tied to any particular place, had stuck around too, and thus began M&S Enterprises. Both women understood what it meant to lose everything. They bought a Recyc-All, hired a former *Endurance* passenger who ran a construction company, and went to work renovating an abandoned casino into a swank but free hotel and restaurant for a very specific and exclusive clientele—people who had nowhere else to go. It came down to what was unfair but true—those who can leave, do. Those who can't for one reason or another, get stuck left behind.

In the heart of the old Strip, they flew over blocks of crumbling casinos and drained pools, dry fountains. Creosote bushes grew in the dirt of once lush lawns. A few skims and cargo drones flew by. They set down in front of the former Grand Gothic Hotel and Casino, one of the last built before the war, now the headquarters of M&S Enterprises. They drove into an underground garage, thankful for shade.

The atrium lobby held hints of its former glory with a marble floor and high glassed ceiling, letting in lots of light. The froufrou, as Sharyn called it, had been replaced with practical features—a simple reception desk, fans, and an old-fashioned swamp cooler keeping the temperature and humidity comfortable. People came and went or sat in chairs set around vid screens of news or making calls. Well dressed, clean, not sunburned and ragged like Lyn remembered seeing before. A woman, real and not an android, sat behind the reception desk. That was another M&S touch. Giving real people real jobs. The woman greeted them and pressed a button. Soon Miriam and Sharyn came running down the central staircase, squealing like girls.

"You're here!"

"At last!"

Enthusiastic hugs were followed by an appraising onceover. Lyn did likewise. Miriam, for whom food was both a vocation and life-defining metaphor, was back to her plump stature after the deprivation on *Endurance*. Like many throughout history, she'd cycled through periods of starvation and abundance as her family fled their native India. The extra weight, she'd always maintained, was "just in case."

Sharyn, her white hair pinned up in a fancy do, showed no lingering effects of a lengthy coma after being infected by the microbes on Marao. If they hadn't been able to return, she and a dozen other passengers would have died. Whatever hell Lyn was in because of the data in her head was worth it. An accomplished schmoozer, Sharyn had run the social life aboard *Endurance* and along with Miriam were as close to Lyn's equals as anyone, each commanding her own realm. Miriam the kitchen. Sharyn the guests and housekeeping staff. Together, they'd made a formidable team.

"About time you two showed up," Sharyn teased. They'd opened nine months earlier, and she chided Lyn for declining the invitation to the grand opening.

They caught up over lunch in Miriam's Casino Lounge, a throwback diner catering to mid-twentieth century nostalgia with replica vinyl booths and Formica tables. Antique slot machines lined the walls.

It had seemed obvious to visit the pair until they started asking questions Lyn didn't care to answer. She felt a shiv of guilt when Miriam asked what was new, and she responded with a report on her boring work with Randall Restoration. Even Sharyn's follow up, asking if Ani was seeing anyone since her shipboard romance on *Endurance* had to be answered carefully. She dodged details and focused on updates of their old *Endurance* colleagues.

Marc and Isabel were living in Catalonia. Edward was on the East Coast, working on cleanup around the D.C. exclusion zone. "He loves a problem to solve," Lyn said. Ghez, the former navigator, was circumnavigating the globe, on foot, with no compass. "Pure Ghez."

Sharyn had seen Zoya on a talk show. "I guess her book will be coming out soon. Can't say I'm looking forward to reliving that little adventure."

Zoya Betero, former NASA engineer and lead manager of the first missions to Mars, had been the oldest person on *Endurance*. She'd provided key mentoring and advice to the young crew and captain.

"Any plans to go back?" Miriam asked as the topic of space reopening came up.

"It's complicated," Lyn said.

"No it isn't," Diana said. She'd been quiet through the catch-up. She didn't have the history with these two that Lyn had. "At least not other than some vacation together." She smiled innocently and sipped her water.

Lyn tipped her empty water glass, ice cubes clinking. "Got anything stronger?"

"I see." Miriam nudged Sharyn. "I think these two have some negotiating to do."

"There's no chance I'm rejoining Omara Tours, if that's what you meant," Lyn said, trying to evince a tone of finality.

"You couldn't drag me back," Sharyn said with a shudder for effect.

Lyn switched gears to their new business. They eagerly traded details. M&S Enterprises was committed to hiring human help both for housekeeping in the hotels and in the restaurants. Young apprentices on their way up, mid-career cooks getting back on their feet from some life disaster, or experienced chefs Miriam was learning from as much as giving meaningful work to.

"Plus, people love to eat," she said, "and no Recyc-All can create real food."

Miriam was even installing bluehouses around the city. The reverse of greenhouses, these provided sheltered, cool air and fertile soil to grow the produce she served. The excess she gave away.

"Aren't you worried you'll attract more people here?" Diana asked. "Seems like the last thing this place needs."

"They pass through here," Miriam said. "We don't intend to make this a viable city again. Just feed and house those unfortunate enough to end up here."

They were clear, she said, about not providing city services like utilities and waste recycling outside their hotels. They also made sure people were connected to social services that could help them move on and establish lives elsewhere.

"It's not going to become a tourist destination, that's for sure," Sharyn added. "But these people have been forgotten. The city was abandoned, disincorporated, but no one thought to make sure these folks had someplace to go."

Miriam sighed. "The least we can do is make their time here more bearable."

Forgotten people needing help. The universality of that hit Lyn deep in her gut.

BACK AT DR. Amos's office, Lyn had thought the point was to convince Omara, but now she anticipated the news with great interest. Maybe she had been biased to believe the Johari simply because Diana did.

Sitting around a table in his office, a holoprojection hovering overhead, they listened as he got to the point. "The sample included tissue as well as DNA, so I could look at components outside of the cells. It's well known that the Johari reject modern medicine, but there are indeed medbots present, just unlike anything I've seen before."

"But Rose didn't," Diana said. "You told me she died because she didn't have medbots." Lyn caught the catch in Diana's voice, the need for simple truths.

"She didn't have *our* medbots. And if she had these, they were not repair bots." He pointed to the readout.

Lyn squinted at the display of charts and graphs, what looked like a chromatograph, and the blurry image of dots like those Dr. Amos had shown her on *Endurance*. He'd reminded her medbots were modified stem cells with their own genetic material. That was where the properties to fight illnesses and repair damage were coded. These were different?

"They either don't want alien bots in them, or they don't want human doctors mucking about in their microbiome and discovering these," Dr. Amos continued. "They aren't like our medbots. Their sole role is to clean up genetic errors. The Johari aren't known for genetic diseases, unlike other small, inbred communities. They've explained this by maintaining they are not as isolated as other groups. It's more likely they refuse treatments that could expose this unusual gene bot."

"Does this prove they are alien?" Omara asked.

"Not necessarily, but I've searched every database on Earth and can't find any reference to these." He swiped the display to another screen, a colorful bar chart of overlapping values. "There's something else that's even more remarkable. They don't have any ancient hominin DNA."

Thanks to her brain implant, Lyn knew what that meant. "You mean Neanderthal or Denisovan?"

"Correct. All humans carry bits of this DNA. Proof that modern humans lived at the same time as these other species and interbred. We're talking tens of thousands of years ago. It's a small sample, so maybe an anomaly, but I checked the databases and there are no other examples of an individual without some shred of ancient DNA. They had to have appeared after Neanderthals and the others went extinct."

No one spoke or reacted. The information sank in slowly, like water seeping through bedrock.

"What is your conclusion then?" Omara asked finally, tentatively, like she was bracing for the answer.

"Could the Johari, at least these individuals, have originated on Earth? No. Not possible. I'd say yes, they are aliens."

It wasn't like this pronouncement was unexpected, but hearing it from Dr. Amos gave Lyn a shiver, of acknowledgement but also fear. What were they dealing with? Diana pushed back her chair, crossing her arms like a protective shield.

Omara pulled the scarf over her shoulders closer around her throat as if fending a chill. "Can you explain how this is possible? Beings from another planet so similar to humans."

"That's what's so remarkable," he said, clasping his hands behind his back and giving a little bounce on his toes. "We'd never expect a species from another solar system to have evolved exactly as humans have. What are the chances?"

"Zero, I'm guessing," Omara said.

He held up the vial. "Maybe not."

"There's no way this could be an error in your instruments, or a fabricated sample?" Lyn asked.

"The equipment is correctly calibrated. I used a couple of different techniques. There's simply nothing like this in existence on Earth at this time."

"Could early humans have been moved from one planet to another?" Lyn asked.

"Absolutely. Not on their own, obviously. But someone else might have done it. Perhaps the Johari and humans share a common ancestor."

Diana broke her silence. "The Johari claim they came here in 1900. But you're saying they're related to us going back further?"

"Exactly." He enlarged one of the charts of overlapping colored bars. "Strip out the ancient hominin DNA from modern humans and they share more than 99 percent of the genes of the Johari. The only way that's possible is if there's a genetic link going back hundreds of thousands of years. Modern humans arrived on the scene roughly three hundred thousand years ago, but that's actually quite recent in evolutionary terms. Maybe your ancestors came from another planet originally. Does that make sense?"

"Not really," Diana said. Her knee bounced, her fingertips white from gripping her arm.

Lyn had focused on watching Omara's reactions, knowing she was the one who needed convincing, but now saw how Diana was suffering with this news. She gently rested her hand on Diana's knee and the bounce stilled.

Diana pulled in a deep breath and let it out, her arms relaxing. "All these years we've been panicked over who might be out there, when contact with aliens might happen, and they've been here for centuries."

Omara shook her head. "If, as you suggest, modern humans came to Earth from another planet, there's still the mystery of why so many hominin species evolved on Earth, with links back through primates, and onward back through the ages to the ultimate common ancestor—some form of bacteria or whatever." She waved a hand as if to surrender science to the scientists. "Are you saying that the entire evolution of life on Earth may have happened because of some original seed on more than one planet?"

"We haven't conclusively resolved how life formed on Earth," Dr. Amos said. "If the first seeds arrived via asteroid, as many think, there's no reason this couldn't have happened simultaneously on other planets. Before the repressive regime of U.S. President Reginald Cheetham Jr. shut down research, it seemed clear that life existed on several moons in this solar system. That research is only now being revived. Isn't this the ultimate mystery you have been trying to solve for millennia?"

Omara leaned back. "When you put it like that . . ."

"We simply don't know for sure. But whatever the truth is, part of it contains the fact that these people, very closely related to humans, are here from another planet. That is all you have to work with, for now at least."

That was enough, wasn't it? Humans from another planet. Here they sat, deep underground talking about intelligent extraterrestrials who came to Earth from another solar system. Could it be possible that all humans, Lyn included, found their way here from another planet? The ground beneath her feet, the rock behind those bare white walls became a foreign land. Did anyone belong here? The air closed in, stale bunker air. She needed to breathe, to take in fresh mountain air, even a thick gauze of wildfire smoke. Something tangible, natural.

"What I don't get," Omara said, seemingly unfazed by this revelation, "is that we've also been listening for extraterrestrial intelligence for centuries. Why haven't we picked up anything from this planet, Johar?"

Diana was the astrophysicist in the room. "Maybe they found a way to keep their planet silent once they got here and realized we could listen for them."

"Plus, we did," Lyn added. "Back in 2115, with that supposed alien message." Her mind leapt ahead with this new information. Convincing Omara the Johari had origins on another planet reinforced the urgency to help them leave. "Ruzena claimed they need to return because now that superluminal travel is possible, Johar is at risk. But she did precisely what she said they feared—revealed the presence of aliens on Earth. Why would she do that?"

"It might show their level of desperation," Omara said. "That they really don't have their own way to do it."

The room went quiet. Lyn closed her eyes. What next was the obvious question, but no one seemed willing to ask it. She opened them to everyone looking at her. She was the keystone. She had the information to proceed. "I don't know what to do. This feels so much bigger than giving someone a ride home."

"How many are we talking about?" Omara asked. "And where is this Johar?"

"Six hundred. More than *Endurance* can handle," Lyn said. "And the planet's about a hundred light years from here."

Tenacity, Lyn now knew, could hold three hundred. Could they cram in twice as many? What about fuel?

Omara sighed, like she accepted the ball was in her court. "You can put me in the believe-their-story column. Which leaves the question, do we help them? And if so, how?" She eyed Lyn.

This was a huge step Omara was taking with that small word "we." She wouldn't be able to tout it in her marketing. If they used *Tenacity*, it would delay the ship going on tours—and it would have to be completely reconfigured. Why would she go along? From what Lyn knew about her, the woman was a lifelong space junkie. She'd once told Lyn that her interest started when she was young, fleeing war zones, looking at the sky during blackouts, intrigued by what might be out there. Someplace better than where she was.

Omara stood and stretched. Enough sitting around a conference table, she said, offering to continue the discussion over dinner.

They already knew there was no way to travel a hundred light years with current technology, but by dessert, they also realized Diana's wormhole had its own problems. Lyn let Petra do the calculations, showing that the fuel-to-mass ratio was not workable. A bigger ship, carrying more people needed more fuel, maybe a bigger machine—more T particles collected to hold open the tunnel. The best option, Petra suggested, would be to open a wormhole small enough for only a message to the Johari to come get their people. On *Endurance*, Diana had tested the technology by opening a small wormhole a few kilometers long and in open space. Petra said that if she had all of the research, she might be able to come up with a better solution. Diana and Lyn looked at each other. It was no longer Diana's to offer. And Petra was the last person—entity—Lyn trusted with it.

During that test on *Endurance*, Petra had destroyed the machine, nearly killing Diana. That was how Lyn found out about the faster-than-light travel prohibition. And that there was no way around the code, no way to alter or delete it. She had been forced to disconnect Petra and use her own brain implant to run the machine and *Endurance* during the traverse home. The physical demands were enormous and she did not want to do that again. Omara assured Lyn she had rebuilt Petra's program herself, eliminating the code. Petra confirmed that, as did Dr. Amos. Omara's word had always been good enough for her, still, she wasn't ready to take that leap.

Omara flicked a hand to acknowledge the stalemate. "Regardless of what form the wormhole takes, at some point either a ship is going to arrive to take them away or someone from here will leave with them."

Lyn rubbed the back of her neck, a headache stung.

"We need more information," Diana said. "Tey might have answers, but we don't know her very well. I know Antonia very well. I say we go visit. She lives in the main Johari community. My guess is there are others there we can talk to, maybe their leader. Then we can figure out where to go from there."

Even if they fully believed the story and the urgency for the Johari to get home, it still left a difficult decision, one Lyn alone would have to make— whether to hand over the data to help them. Either way, it would open Pandora's Box.

Chapter 5

LYN HADN'T INTENDED to be away from work for two days. She'd
monitored her projects while waiting for the DNA results, but there was no
disguising the look her mother gave her when she arrived for work. And she
hadn't seen Ani since their fight. Lyn had lots of fences to mend and none of
them were wire and post.

But it was Lunch Day. Once a month Sarah and Jephson hosted lunch for
the staff. Part meeting, mostly low-key fun, there was no pressure to attend,
it wasn't mandatory, but it was so popular most made sure to be there. It was
a chance to mingle and share ideas and work stories. Lyn loved that she was
treated as one of the crew and not in a leadership position. No captain role.

Everyone chipped in to make the meal. Teams rolled out dough for pizzas,
sliced toppings, washed and chopped veggies for salads, or set the long farm
table in the dining room and tables and chairs on the porch and patio for
the inevitable overflow. No one was left out. Ph.D.s were meaningless. The
newest member an equal. As music blared, the engineers fought with the
botanists over how best to shred lettuce. Food items may have been thrown,
much laughter ensued. Lyn joined the assembly line prepping pizza toppings,
keeping an eye out for Ani.

By noon, the counter and tables overflowed with bowls of salad, chips,
breads, and sweating pitchers of ice water. Tag teams ferried pizzas back and
forth to the ovens in the summer kitchen out back. Sarah clanged the triangle
on the front porch, but people were already streaming in from across the
property.

Lyn spotted Ani and pulled her aside. "I was out of line. I'm sorry. Can
we talk?"

Ani gave Lyn a hard stare, a muscle in her jaw clenched. "Not if it's a
lecture."

"It's not." Lyn glanced around at the crowd. Not the best time or place for
what she had to say. "After. Enjoy your lunch. I'll come find you."

Once most were settled, Jephson stood in the wide doorway between the
dining room and the porch. He was a big guy with dark hair and eyes, the
source of Lyn's own. Like her mom, his face was weathered by wind, sun, and
grief—for a son lost and a daughter nearly so.

When Lyn was six, her oldest brother had died in an accident with an
early recycling machine. She had grown up absorbing through osmosis

the Randall way, never talk about Duncan. The only time her father had let down his façade was after she returned from Rigil Kent and made the family talk about him. To her surprise, they each carried their own guilt. That explained the silence. Finally, her father broke. "It was no one's fault!" he had bellowed. "A boy died. Billions died in the war. We'll all die." He'd bought the machine.

Now she saw through that façade and understood he was no nonsense as a boss but spared no effort to protect his crew and his family. The staff respected him and Lyn loved him.

Jephson whistled for everyone's attention then ran through the brief agenda. "Skims will be inspected every morning, so don't take one without clearing it first." Vandals, he said, had hit seven different job sites in the last week. "Nothing dangerous, just annoying," was the good news. All projects were behind schedule was the bad news. With the coming summer heat, projects down south were finishing up for the season. The advantage of drought was that solar energy gain was outpacing usage.

"A reminder—We do *not* handle radioactive waste. Once a property is declared clear, we can move in. Be sure to check with Cooper if you get any client questions about that. On that note, enjoy your lunch!"

Lyn filled her plate at the buffet and wended her way among the tables, looking for an open seat. Snippets of conversation rose above the general blur of voices, clinking utensils, and music in the background. Laughter, smiling faces, no cranky clients. This was the heart and soul of not only the company but of Lyn's formative years growing up.

Details bubbled through the chatter. "We shouldn't be using *technology*. There's no *good* purpose, it always ends *badly*." That was Parker, one of the biologists. Said with snark and drama, it was clearly not his opinion, but Lyn flinched, thinking he was talking about her and T tech. No. Had to be Antigen. The others laughed.

The pilots' table had the most animated discussions. Hands waving, arms outstretched for a harrowing tale of dodging a big tree at the last second and weaving through slot canyons. That last bit might have been a hobby. She couldn't tell but couldn't imagine what ecological restoration project would need fighter pilot skills.

Ani fit right in with that crowd. Jackie, the lead pilot, never treated her differently from the others. Experience flying a spaceship might impress a lot of pilots, but not Jackie. Not if it wasn't relevant to the job at hand, and most of the skills weren't. If Ani was better at a maneuver, Jackie made her teach the rest. No one got to boast.

Another snippet, "I hope they don't regulate brain implants. I'd love to have that kind of interface when flying." That was from Martinez, not Ani, who, she noticed, didn't react.

Lyn's own implant would be outlawed if the legislature finalized regs. The proposed ban wasn't based on Pulsar's implant specifically, but revelations from the war years that scientists had been experimenting on prisoners. For Lyn, the technology had been explained as a way to give her direct control over flying a ship, eliminating microseconds of delays that could be catastrophic. In a battle, maybe, but not for what she at the time had thought Pulsar was all about, exploring the solar system.

She found a seat on the patio with two other project managers, Cagle, a man in his fifties, and Floret, a woman in her thirties, who had joined the company shortly after Lyn did. They were discussing a news report suggesting the Johari were behind Antigen. She forced herself to stay quiet and listen.

Floret seemed to think it was an opinion piece, not actual journalism. "Just because they don't use technology doesn't mean they'll go out of their way to do actual damage. They're pacifists. I went to school with a Johari. Really nice guy. He flew in a transport like the rest of us. I think they get a bad rap."

"I can agree that technology got us into this mess, and I'm not convinced it's going to get us out," Cagle said. He picked mushrooms off his pizza and set them to the side.

"Really? I think literally transforming carbon dioxide into water is pretty biblically cool," Floret said. "For a war technology it turned out better than the atomic bomb."

"They're annoying. Celebrating a history of monkey wrenching, gluing themselves to tractors, sitting in trees to prevent logging. What good did it do? It's all still gone. What do they hope to accomplish today? Keep everyone starving?" He took a big bite of his slice.

Floret sighed. "I for one am sick of watching old nature shows. Beautiful rain forests, polar bears on actual ice sheets." She turned to Lyn. "You've got a stake in all this. What's your take?"

Stake? What did she mean?

"Family name on the work an all," Cagle said.

Lyn relaxed and went with that. "Every technology has a down side. I trust President Woltman and the legislature to keep things in check. Antigen can have their seat at the table if they want it. They should use the ballot box rather than make our lives hell."

"Think the Johari are behind it all?"

Lyn suppressed the urge to declare her true opinion, now that she knew them better, or thought she did. "I don't know anything about them, but Antigen's such an amorphous group, they could be anyone."

"Like the sovereign nations?" Floret asked. She was referring, of course, to the Native American tribes that had regained some of their traditional lands and more of their autonomy. "They aren't beholden to voters."

"What are you implying?"

"I'm just saying while Fúlli seems completely on board with our goals, are all the Apsáalooke? Even Fúlli makes no bones about saying white Europeans ruined their land only to give it back once it was useless."

Lyn bristled at the implication that native tribes were behind Antigen. "Do all your family members agree with you? And ne's right."

"Oh, touched a nerve, I see."

Cagle gave Floret a side eye, as if to say shut up, remember you're talking to one of the bosses. Floret shrugged and sipped her drink. "Food for thought. That's all."

"Seems counterintuitive to hold the Earth sacred and not try to fix things," Cagle said.

They moved on to discussing Gil, another manager whose projects were all going to hell. Michigan's Upper Peninsula got hit with a wildfire that killed three years' worth of tree plantings and destroyed five bluehouses full of seedlings. He lost four years of work. Then Antigen took out all the dams on his estuary project. Drained the whole thing, killing countless fish and plants.

"I heard he might quit." Floret shook her head. "It's like for every step forward we get shoved back three."

"The G-Nerds—" Cagle said.

"I hate that name," Floret interrupted. "Makes them sound like doofusses."

"I heard they're putting together a slate for the next election," Cagle continued, "promising to deregulate technology completely and fast track implants, autonomous AI, genetic integration."

"Why do I feel like this could turn out really badly," Floret said.

"Better to come from a political group that's beholden to voters than some secret government project no one knows about. Because you know that's happening." Cagle turned to Lyn like he wanted to say more, then thought better of it.

Everyone knew she'd been part of Pulsar, that she'd been a whistleblower, but they didn't know all of it, like the implant. Lyn finished her pizza, drained her coffee. The conversation switched to the upcoming softball finals. She hadn't joined the team, so listened politely. These gatherings had taken place all her life, but the last couple of weeks cast them in a different light. As her colleagues argued and joked, she imagined a new possibility for collaboration, one that stretched across the galaxy. And she was its tenuous thread. The trick was how to spin it into a thicker rope.

She spotted Ani heading to the dessert table and went to intercept. They took their plates of brownies and pie with ice cream to a bench under the oak in the side yard. The tree had grown since Lyn was a kid, climbing its thick branches. Her initials were carved into the trunk at about a seven-year-old's height.

"Since you know, what do you think?" Lyn asked. "I could use your perspective."

Ani chewed a brownie and shrugged noncommittally. "Before Rigil Kent, I'd have thought Ruzena was crazy. But now? Hell, anything's possible, right? And yes, I do like her, and I do plan to keep seeing her."

"That's fine. None of my business."

"I can see why you don't want to use the tech, but she's right. Someone else will do this whether you help or not. And anyone but you puts them at risk. So not helping them seems mean."

Now Lyn had to be careful. Anything she told Ani could go back to Tey and the rest of the Johari. Right now Diana was calling Antonia to set up a meeting. Ani would find out soon enough.

"If we do this—" Lyn said.

"We?"

"You don't think I'd go anywhere without you as pilot, do you?"

Ani coughed back a grin.

"It could mean she leaves. Don't let this get so far that it's going to hurt you." Why had Ruzena even pursued Ani, knowing her goal?

Ani made a face. "Yes, Mom." Then she got serious. "So, it's a go?"

"Not yet, but Diana and I are working on it with Omara. There's a lot we don't know. We're going to talk to them. Diana's calling Antonia today to set it up. You want to be there?"

"God no." She set her plate in her lap and stared out over the landing strip, the wind blowing her hair across her face.

Music and voices drifted from the back of the house. Chairs scraped as people moved around, heading back to their offices, hangars, and labs. Lyn switched to work talk, and Ani seemed more at ease. The Nebraska job hadn't been for one of Lyn's clients, but she liked learning what the other teams were working on. Fúlli was tweaking the seed spreader to be more efficient and adding solar panels to increase the Ag-Cat's range.

"Maybe we'll get used to the idea that people live on another planet like they live in other countries now," Ani said, bringing Lyn back to the meaty problem at hand.

Through her new lens of the Johari as aliens, Lyn saw how vulnerable they were. If only to gossip. They were outsiders within the community, as she was an outsider within the company that literally was her family. She didn't know if she belonged here, but certainly the Johari didn't.

FLYING IN DIANA'S Rambler over the countryside from Montana to New York, they passed over empty missile silos and the remains of sheds, tents, and tattered tarps—colorful but sad remnants of massive migrant camps.

Lyn hadn't seen any of this first-hand but knew about the long cycle of human migration as the planet warmed and agriculture and workers moved north into Canada. War then brought devastation followed by frigid years of nuclear winter. Agriculture crashed and sent entire populations scurrying south again. In school, she had learned that enough missiles had been launched to reduce Moscow, Beijing, and Washington, D.C., to ash. To this day, an exclusion zone stretched from D.C. to New York City, reaching as far as the Catskills. Lyn was born along with a new nation—the North American Alliance—its capital in Syracuse, New York. Going on forty years post-war and twenty years after temperatures resumed their deadly rise, the landscape still bore deep scars.

She let Diana pilot and pick the route. This was her past they were flying into. Omara would join them the next morning, but Diana wanted time with Antonia alone.

Where once had been farm fields and forests, towns and cities, lakes and rivers, they flew over dusty, one-road ghost towns. The Great Lakes were dead zones, the Finger Lakes, choked and stagnant. Lyn flipped through the map to their destination. Mill Creek was centered between former military bases—Watertown to the north, Rome to the south. Tucked between the Tug Hill plateau and the Adirondacks, it was sleepy long before the creeks dried up. Cooper's flagship project was restoring forests to the Adirondacks, but they would never be close to their former glory. Too many species gone, the climate too hostile. Someday, probably not in Lyn's or Diana's lifetime, there might again be snow on mountain peaks. The best anyone could hope for was a new ecosystem that provided a benefit to those left behind.

Lyn brushed her hand on the seat. "Any sign of more mice?"

Diana shook her head. "Jo gave it a clean bill of health yesterday."

She glanced out the window at the desolate landscape below. They had crossed Lake Ontario. "Why would Antonia live here?"

Diana tipped her chin toward the horizon. "Because of that, maybe."

A green line framed the top of the otherwise beige landscape. As they drew closer, more green. It was early June, a time when spring green was well on its way to dried out dust. This was like approaching an oasis in the desert. Almost from the moment they crossed the county line, trees appeared along intact roads and grew up once-denuded hillsides. Diana followed the one road leading to Mill Creek and passed over electric cars and trucks on the ground, not skims in the air. Fields and bluehouses stretched on both sides of the street into the distance. In the fields, humans tended crops, not robots or skims.

"It looks so familiar yet new to me," Diana said.

Lyn gave her a puzzled look.

"I always loved visiting Rose's parents. Now I see it differently. I mean, they weren't freaky. Antonia was a therapist. Quin, Rose's father, taught fifth grade. They were old-style Americans, you know? Apple pie and all that. Yet all that time they held a secret." Diana paused to check the controls and began to descend. "Antonia said it wasn't like they were lying. It had been so long since the Johari had any contact with their home world—Antonia was only five when the message was intercepted and contact cut off. They went on with their lives."

"So why bother? Why not slip into human society fully?"

"You'll have to ask her that. I didn't. She said there's a whole team keeping an eye out for signs they might be discovered or be able to go. Johari moles inside various space agencies hadn't heard anything about anyone cracking interstellar travel."

"Imagine what it must have been like for them when *Endurance* returned."

Diana said there'd been a lot of chaos. "It didn't happen the way they thought it might—someone in a lab somewhere gets the idea, publishes some papers, the Johari infiltrate and get more information, maybe be part of the process. In an ideal world, they would have waited for it to be perfected and then quietly left in their own ship. Our coming back so suddenly after such a horrible emergency sent everyone into battle mode."

Even Rachel had speculated they'd been abducted by aliens, likely the ones she was so worried about.

"Did they know about your parents' research?"

Diana's eyes widened in surprise. "God, when I think about all the times I talked about my parents, Teegans. I bet they knew exactly what that meant—the Teegan particle. But my parents never published anything about its potential. The fact that they used it to open a microscopic wormhole in their lab was only in the research they gave me on that cube."

An alarm beeped, warning of a no-fly zone ahead.

"What?" Lyn asked.

"We can't fly in," Diana said. She descended to the road and extended the wheels. They touched down and slowed their roll. "Speed limit thirty."

Lyn shook her head in disbelief. This couldn't possibly be the realm of a space-faring people. She stared out the window as they passed barns and farmhouses, all well maintained and bordered by green hedges and lush trees. They bumped along the road toward the town center. People waved as they passed.

"Why are they waving? They can't possibly recognize us, can they?"

Diana laughed. "They're being friendly. It's what folks do around here."

Lyn stared. They looked so . . . old fashioned. Denim pants and T-shirts, walking or riding bicycles, not flying skims. "I'm beginning to doubt their story about coming here from another planet."

Diana laughed. They entered the town center, passing brick storefronts for groceries, hardware, and farm equipment. A sign over the last one said Feed and Grain.

"Do you think they hide technology? How can they be restoring this land without Recyc-Alls?" Lyn asked.

"The Amish farms look pretty much the same. They managed not to destroy the land in the first place. They aren't rebuilding, they are surviving."

"I feel like the alien," Lyn said.

At the far end of the main drag, which didn't take long to reach, Diana pulled over in front of a small house set back from the road, tall trees shading the yard. A white barn sat across the street, like from a vintage postcard.

As they climbed out of the Rambler, an older woman banged open a screen door and strode down the walk, waving. She wore faded, well-worn pants, dusty boots, a T-shirt, and a wide-brimmed hat. The air was humid and thick with the aromas of farm life. Manure, fresh-cut hay, the sweet scent of a flowering shrub. Crickets chorused loudly, as if complaining about the heat. Antonia greeted Diana with a tight hug. Diana introduced Lyn, and Antonia gave her a quick eye scan, top to bottom, a little like assessing a prized cow.

"Come in out of this heat," Antonia said, leading them inside where it wasn't much cooler.

Lyn crossed the threshold with the nerves of that first day working with her family as an employee, not a daughter, knowing there was so much to learn. Her implant helped her there, but not here. The words "first contact" kept sliding through her consciousness. There were protocols for this, and none of them included watching an alien take off her straw hat and set it on a peg by the door, riffle fingers through cropped gray hair.

Ceiling fans spun, and a porch roof shaded the windows where curtains swayed with the breeze. Lyn couldn't detect any air conditioning system, but the place wasn't stifling. Antonia gave them a quick tour, pointing out the bathroom if needed after the long trip. "Only three hours?" she said when Lyn answered how it went. "It'd take us weeks!" she replied with a wicked grin.

"She's joking," Diana said quietly to Lyn.

They passed stairs and a wall lined with photos she assumed were Quin and Rose with Antonia. A younger Diana in one shot. A happy, smiling family. Antonia led them through to a kitchen where she grabbed a pitcher of lemonade from the refrigerator and headed out to the back side of the veranda that circled the house. A big oak spread protective shade, and a wide path between lush flower gardens led to a grove of small trees.

"Sit." Antonia filled glasses on the table. A black and white cat sat on the railing, an orange tabby jumped into Lyn's lap.

"This real?" Lyn patted the feline, who purred.

Antonia looked puzzled.

"We have a robot cat at home," Diana said.

"Why would you want a robot cat?" Antonia asked. She waved the question away and passed Lyn a glass.

Lyn took a sip and marveled how the tart lemon rolled over her tongue and ached through her jaw. "Wow. That's . . . amazing."

Antonia raised her glass as if in a toast. "You're not used to the real thing."

A million questions formed about how the Johari had managed to bring the landscape to such life. And why weren't they in charge of all agriculture? But they were here for another purpose, and she waited for Diana to start that conversation.

Antonia gave Diana's knee a pat and sat across from them. "I'm glad you came back." Then she turned to Lyn. "Bet we don't look like interstellar travelers and researchers, do we," she said with a wink.

Diana's jaw worked, muscles clenching. An awkward silence followed.

Antonia cleared her throat. "Yeah, well." She leaned forward, elbows on the table, hands clasped. "This is new to me too, you know. I never expected this day would come." She met Diana's gaze. "When you returned, I was happy for you. Even after you told me about Rose." Her voice caught. It was still a fresh grief.

"You want to leave, though, right?" Diana said.

"Is that a plural 'you' or just me? For me, it's not a question of want to. I have to. And I'm okay with that."

Diana shook her head. "No. Actually, you—plural—don't have to. For you to leave puts us in danger." She glanced at Lyn. "She risked everything to bring *Endurance* back. We agreed it should never be used again. It's not worth the risk of losing her."

This wasn't going how Lyn expected. Diana had been on Antonia's side, pushing her to help.

A stillness settled over them, the cat purring in Lyn's lap. Antonia looked out across her back yard, lines in her face brought to relief by the indirect light of the angled sun on its journey toward the horizon. "I planted those lemon trees myself," she said quietly, addressing a row of small saplings, the casual brusqueness gone from her voice. "I think some will survive." She looked at Lyn with a half smile. "I'm not the best farmer around here." Then she straightened. "Where are my manners. You two must be starved. Let's get some food in you."

They followed Antonia into the kitchen, like any from a hundred years ago. Big sink, big stove, a pantry full of hand-canned fruits and vegetables, dried herbs hanging from hooks, boxes and sacks of staples—flour, beans, quinoa. Lyn volunteered to set the table on the porch, happy to have a chore during the deep silence between Diana and Antonia. This wasn't the two ganging up on her she'd expected. For some reason, Diana was shutting down. Maybe this house had gotten to her—realizing a past she remembered didn't exist. Perhaps Rose's ghost was standing beside her.

As they sat to eat a cold salad with fresh, hard-boiled eggs and fresh-baked rolls with local butter, Lyn asked Antonia about the community. "The fields are impressive, like there'd never been a drought."

"When you live within the resources available, you don't need to destroy anything."

"But the war must have affected you. I didn't see a force field over the town."

She smiled. "No one paid us much mind. Everyone was too busy thumping their own chests."

"But you're doing—you've done all along—work that we're trying to replicate."

"Fixing something that's broken is a lot harder than not breaking it in the first place. I commend your family for their work. The Randalls have been leaders in the field."

"I feel like there's a lot we could learn from you."

"There's a lot we can all learn from each other. We're not miracle workers when it comes to sustainable farming. There's no magic to it. One of the first studies we did—and by 'we' I mean my forebears—was to listen to the indigenous people. They weren't completely annihilated back then, but they were being culturally erased. Much of their wisdom remains. You only have to look, ask, and listen. Pay attention."

"It seems a shame to have you all leave just when working together could really pay off."

"We're not all leaving."

"You're not? How does that work?"

Their way traveled two paths, she said. Some lived their whole lives believing they were members of a unique sect with a very special role to play in healing the Earth. Some left the community entirely. A small subset became aware of the truth, "Like me and Rose," she said with a nod to Diana. "There are different levels of awareness. Only the highest levels understand fully our origin, our mission, the research, and now our need to leave."

The six hundred destined to leave were a small part of the community. "There are thousands of Johari around the world. We won't be missed. Even here in town only a few of the farms will be sold, the families ready to claim it's time to move on." She chuckled wryly. "Literally."

They spent the afternoon avoiding the main topic. Antonia showed them the house, the room they'd stay in—Rose's old room. Diana remained quiet, brushing a hand over a desk or picture, lost in a world Lyn couldn't imagine. After dinner, as they sat in the living room, Antonia broke the impasse with Diana. "I'm sorry."

She said it so directly that it seemed to snap Diana out of her funk. "I wouldn't be here if Rose hadn't died." She said it so suddenly, it came out like a pronouncement, a glove thrown down. But who was she challenging?

"Are you so sure?" Antonia asked.

"You just wouldn't be with me," Lyn said. "I'd still have pressured you to help us find a way back. We'd just all be sitting here now."

Diana seemed to crumple under that realization. Whatever had been holding her together released, and she cried softly. Lyn put her arm around her, but she wasn't the one who could offer comfort. A clock on the mantel ticked time moving, the orange cat bathed noisily by the doorway.

"I forgive you," Diana said through her tears and a sniff, wiping her cheeks. "I forgive Rose." Said with a finality of a long struggle, she stared at the floor somewhere between them and Antonia. "You were a mom when I needed one. The truth doesn't change that. It doesn't change my love for Rose."

Lyn watched Diana make her admission with an ache in her chest. Before Lyn, Diana's family had been Rose and by extension Antonia and Quin. While she had reconciled with her own parents, they were more like colleagues than family. Now she faced never seeing Antonia again. If Rose had survived, she, Lyn, wouldn't be her wife. Same thing if Tara had lived. The whole Rigil Kent fiasco might never have happened if Tara hadn't died at Enceladus. The dominoes of fate lined up so long ago, ready to fall. What no one said was what might have happened if Rose had lived and faced the choice of returning to Johar without Diana or staying. And would Antonia stay too? Those were questions left to lie quiet.

Antonia came to Diana, pulled her up, and wrapped her arms around her, not saying anything.

They spent the night in Rose's old room. It hadn't been preserved as a shrine, but photos on the dresser showed a smiling young girl with two blonde braids, holding a blue ribbon for some triumph; riding a pony; arm in arm with a younger Diana. They lay together on Rose's childhood bed, a fan overhead creaking along with the crickets outside. Diana reached for Lyn's hand. The future seemed less certain now.

Chapter 6

OMARA AND DR. Amos arrived the next morning, and Antonia led them all across the street like a line of peculiar ducklings. Lyn and Diana might have passed for locals with their jeans and shirts, but Dr. Amos stuck out like, well, an alien, and Omara's graceful stride and long skirt swirled dust in their wake. Inside the large barn the light dimmed to shadows, the air thick with the sweet fragrance of manure and hay. Rough timbers framed an open area sized for a wagon. Chickens clucked and pecked the wide plank floor. They passed a row of stalls where curious horses peeked out, entered a rustic doorway, and descended wood steps to a small, damp space walled with stones.

"You really went for authenticity here," Lyn said.

"You betcha. This barn's three hundred years old." Then she opened another door into a wide, finished hallway that didn't look anywhere near three hundred years old. Their footsteps on the tile floor echoed off composite walls. Decidedly modern lights came on automatically.

Antonia knocked on a door, opened it, and let them through to a brightly lit office. A young woman sat at a desk facing them. She pushed eyeglasses up her nose and stood. Antonia introduced Aurora Parula.

"Call me Ro," she said and motioned them to a couch and chairs. Plush carpet, heavy wood desk, lots of shelves, as well as paintings and photos on the wall, gave the impression of a comfortable workspace. A window looked out onto a field and trees, but it had to be a projection unless they'd come out the side of a hill. No sign of tech-phobia here.

Antonia left, closing the door. Ro's brown skin and short bob of loose curls erased the preconceived notion Lyn had that the Johari were all white. The wire-framed glasses appeared to actually correct her vision. The only glasses Lyn had ever seen were for sun protection. Ro smiled, revealing a distinctive gap in her front teeth. Ruzena's had been slightly crooked. She hadn't thought teeth could mark a people, but now realized she wasn't used to seeing other than perfectly aligned teeth. What an odd, insignificant difference.

Ro pulled her chair over, sat, and leaned back, relaxed. She didn't wear a lab coat, didn't look particularly scholarly. Jeans, colorful knit shirt, casual shoes. "I imagine you have a lot of questions."

Lyn started off, explaining her relationship to Omara and how she'd be able to provide a ship, if it came to that. "We're being asked to give you and a bunch of others a ride home, like college kids from a night in the city, except to another solar system. I understand from the DNA the alien aspect, but we need some assurance that you mean us no harm. Also that what we risk in helping you will be worth it. I won't do anything that will endanger myself, my family, or any humans on Earth. I've had quite enough of that already. That a good start?"

Ro nodded. "That's a good start, yes. I suppose you expected little green people or octopuses or maybe"—she paused—"sentient microbes."

Lyn startled. The microbes her crew had encountered on Marao had never been revealed to be sentient. Even Natalie Okeke, the ship's resident scientist, publishing paper after paper of their many findings, had kept that out. Infectious, dangerous, life threatening, sure. Lyn welcomed any description that kept humans from wanting to travel there.

Ro stood and motioned them over to a flat-file cabinet against the far wall. She opened a drawer. "These are the last remnants of our original story." A large sheet of paper was covered with markings and drawings. Nothing Lyn thought of as a language or even a recognizable picture.

Dr. Amos stepped forward. "May I?" He explained his scanning ability.

"As long as you don't touch it."

He stared at the sheet. "This paper is composed of plant fibers. Nothing you wouldn't find on Earth in 1900, when you say you arrived."

"Up your setting if you can. You'll find the cells and chemicals are unlike anything found on Earth. Can your translator read the text?"

Dr. Amos again bent over the drawer. "The cells indeed do not identify as any known plant material. Even ancient papyrus would show up. The additives and fillers are unknown." He straightened. "And no, the text does not translate. Nothing like this has ever appeared on Earth."

Ro slid the drawer closed and opened another. She motioned Diana over. "Does this look at all familiar?"

Diana stared at the document, her finger hovering and tracing possible routes of understanding. The figures could be letters or numbers, she admitted, and the way they were arranged seemed similar to a math equation. The diagram clearly showed an atom and other particles, the universal building blocks of matter and energy. There was also a diagram Lyn recognized as similar to the wormhole portal they opened on *Endurance.*

Diana puffed out her cheeks in an extended exhale. "What is that?"

Ro leaned a hip against the cabinet. "That's the Johari equation for a wormhole. I've lost much of the language to understand it, and I'm no physicist, but if you scan that ink and paper, you'll find it dates back to well before humans cracked the universe's code. Whether cosmic strings, dark matter, dark energy, or, you might recognize, exotic matter, it's all the same stuff throughout the galaxy, if not the universe. The Johari have a different name for what you call the Teegan particle."

Diana's eyes widened, comprehending. Dr. Amos ran a scan and said Ro was right. The paper was the same mysterious material and the ink and paper dated back at least three hundred years.

Ro closed the drawer, and they returned to their seats. "Our original ship was built on Johar of materials not found on Earth, so we can't build a new one. And, to be honest, we no longer know how to do it."

"How could you let that happen?" Diana said. "It'd be like we forgot how to build an airplane."

"Really? Could you build one? Could even you, all by yourself, build the machine that folded space and opened the wormhole you used to get home? Something you actually study and know a lot about? And, in fact, have done?"

Diana's face tensed. No. Fact was, Lyn understood all too well, she hadn't known how to do it all by herself. She'd needed her parents' previous research, help from *Endurance*'s chief engineer, and vast computing power. "But the information existed. I had access to it."

"Until less than a lifetime ago, we didn't need to worry about finding our way back. We were in contact with our home world and could have sent for them to come get us at any time. Then that message got intercepted and we had to go quiet. You try not doing something for six decades and see what you forget. Then add a war that destroyed our homes, our villages. Oh, and climate change that flooded coastlines and caused devastating storms. Like millions of others, we had to flee destroyed, contaminated, submerged homelands. What do your families have that they had before the war started?"

A short, contemplative silence infused the group.

"What concerns me is not your origins or loss of knowledge but whether this could be a trap and we'd leave the entire planet vulnerable to an invasion force," Omara said.

"It could also go the other way," Ro said.

"I don't believe this world is in any position to mount an interstellar attack," Omara said gently but firmly. "You can see for yourself how vulnerable we are even forty years after a devastating war."

"We have nothing to lose by not helping you," Lyn added, "but risk everything if we do and it goes wrong."

Ro looked from face to face before lingering on Diana. "You know as well as I do that even as we speak there are scientists around the world trying to replicate what you did. Your parents might even be back in their lab. Believe me or not, one day, possibly very soon, the knowledge you hold will be moot. You've been trying to contain and control this for two years since you returned, but you know you can't hold back progress forever."

Lyn and Diana shared a glance. Ro had quickly drilled to the core of their dilemma.

"So why not put your Johari heads together and figure this out yourselves?" Diana asked. "If what you say is true, you've done it before. I don't get why you need us and why now."

Ro let out a soft chuckle. "We need you because you actually give a frass what happens with this technology." She turned to Lyn. "You've made clear you won't share it because you understand how it can be misused. How many scientists think only about the adrenaline rush of beating everyone else to the answer and aren't even thinking about what it means? Not like that's never happened before."

It was hard to argue with that. Lyn couldn't help but think of General Jacana and her unknown motives. She was the only one Lyn knew about. How many others were out there, around the world, working on the problem of *Endurance*'s wormhole?

Ro pulled her glasses off, squinted at them toward the light, and wiped a lens on her shirt. "I'm not sure what I could say to gain your trust, but consider this. When we arrived in 1900, you had yet to crack flight, never mind the atom. If we were going to conquer your planet, why would we wait till now?" She put her glasses back on and lowered her voice. "We've seen what you can do, and, honestly, it freaks the hell out of us. From what we know of Johar, our people are nothing like you in terms of violence. We came to learn, to understand where we both came from. That's all."

Lyn searched Ro's face for clues, anything that might feel true or off. Nothing felt off, but nothing felt quite true yet. "How is it possible for aliens to arrive on Earth and not be noticed?"

"It was 1900, remember. From what I learned, the ship's entry would have looked like a meteor to anyone who saw it. The landing site was in southern Utah, near Escalante. There weren't a lot of people, well, nonindigenous people, living there at that time, but a gold rush brought in outsiders. They were able to hide the ship in a canyon and blend in."

"What happened to the ship?"

"I'm not sure. Either they were dropped off or the ship eventually deteriorated and they dismantled it and either buried it or sold it for scrap."

"But they were in touch with Johar?"

"Yes. There used to be ships in orbit but they had to move farther away as humans developed a space industry and as you developed more tech for scouring space. We had some close calls. That 'Wow! signal' from 1977? That was us. Thankfully, the relay made it look like it came from Sagittarius, or you might have found us. Eventually, they left completely, and we used comtunnels, communications tunnels. Until that message was intercepted."

Lyn searched her implant for information about Escalante. Ro was right, there was a gold rush in the nearby mountains. Also plenty of UFO sightings dating back to the 1700s. The Johari might not have known about those, or maybe they were responsible for them, but it wasn't impossible to think they could land there unnoticed. Or at least not be believed.

"By telling you as much as I have, I've put my people in very serious danger. I think you are a good person, Lyn Randall, a peaceful person. Someone who's seen what corruption looks like and wouldn't stand for it. You took down Pulsar at a very high personal cost." Ro leaned in, her hands spread, palms up. "I respect that more than you can know. We don't come to you on some lark. This is serious, and I'm confident you understand that."

Lyn gazed around the room. Photos on the wall showed a younger Ro, smiling between an older man and woman. A graduation shot below a certificate from Cornell University. Could she be any more normal? Even the clutter, books tilting on a shelf, a wilting plant in the corner.

Diana wandered over to a shelf and picked up a trophy. "You played lacrosse."

"Varsity. High school and undergrad."

Diana set the trophy back on the shelf. She scrutinized the Cornell diploma. "You studied communications? I thought you'd be a scientist. Anthropology or something."

"Journalism, actually. That's my profession."

"How do you know Antonia?"

"She's a Level Five—Interpreter. Did she explain our system?"

Diana shook her head. "Only in bare terms, that some know, and most don't."

Ro leaned back, like settling in to tell a story. There were six levels of awareness, the first two remained what she called unaware, of the truth. "They learn our history through stories, that we are a sect rejecting the Industrial Revolution's definition of progress. Among them forms the official, public-facing leadership."

After children finished the normal Earth education system, some were chosen to learn the truth of their origin. This was handled very carefully, and often remained within families who could best judge who would accept this information. She smiled self-consciously. "Sometimes young people don't and they tend to think their parents and the community are nuts and they leave. Those who accept the truth can advance through levels of Observer, Recorder, Interpreter, and Communicator." She looked at Diana. "Rose was Level Three, an Observer. As is Ruzena. They don't conduct the actual study or interpret results. They're out in the world, usually working in some way for the community. Ruzena may have mentioned her role with Earth Control?"

"By out in the world, you mean as a spy," Diana said with an edge.

Ro hesitated. "You might say that. Rose, as I understand it, left but did not serve as a spy. She wanted to live her life and was granted permission. Antonia is Level Five, and through her work as a psychologist studies humans openly and writes scholarly articles for Earth journals that are also encrypted for sending to Johar. She's also my neighbor. And a terrific cook."

Diana shrugged an agreement on that last point.

The levels of understanding were designed so that any who left the community either did so believing they were fully human or understood the need for secrecy. The Johari public stance was that they consider the body sacred and not to be tampered with, so no medbots, genetic engineering, or other enhancements. It was also practical in case they returned to Johar, where a completely different technology was used.

"It's also made you suspects in the Antigen attacks," Lyn said.

Ro rubbed her forehead as if to indicate this was a longstanding dilemma. "That doesn't help for sure."

"What's your role in the community?" Lyn asked.

"I assumed Antonia had explained that," Ro said. "I'm the principal investigator."

"You run this whole show?" Diana asked. "Sorry, but you seem kind of young for that."

"Things got a bit rushed," she said quietly, with emotion. "For those of us who are aware, each PI hand picks their successor. I knew since high school that I would be next. I hadn't expected it to happen so soon. Doctor Emily Gallin died unexpectedly of a heart attack last year."

"I'm sorry," Diana said.

"I'm also sorry for your loss," Ro said kindly.

Diana closed her eyes for a moment. "I don't understand. I mean, I get you needed a cover, and setting yourselves aside like some cult does that. But no medbots?"

Heart attacks didn't kill people with medbots.

The reason was simple, Ro said. "We don't want doctors analyzing our genetics. Close isn't close enough. We could still be detected."

"And you were," Dr. Amos said, describing the Johari bots that protect against genetic errors. Ro explained that only the aware received those.

"Isn't that divisive?" Omara asked. "You seem to have a hierarchy within your group—haves and have nots."

Ro said the aware Johari were very strict about who could learn the truth. The first rule was that they had to be pureblood Johari. "The gene bots only protect us from disease caused by the small gene pool. Those who mingle don't have to worry about that, so it's not a hierarchy."

Omara arched an eyebrow like she felt differently. The fact hit Lyn viscerally—aliens were interbreeding with humans. If that ever got out . . .

"Do any purebloods become aware and then leave the community?" Lyn asked, thinking of Ruzena. Would she even be allowed to stay behind to be with Ani? Diana's expression asked that question about Rose.

Ro took her time, like she was preparing an acceptable response. "Of course. That can happen."

Diana released a long, impatient sigh. "If we're so closely related, how is it you had the tech to come to this planet before we did?"

"That's part of our research. When we first arrived, we were immediately struck by the differences between our societies. We didn't know right away how closely we were related. Until recently, you were strikingly patriarchal. Johar is matriarchal. You have a history of extreme violence, wars, oppression, torture that we'd never seen before. It both fascinated and horrified us."

"Any theories as to why?" Diana asked.

A striking difference between the two planets, Ro said, was that Johar had never had large vertebrates—no dinosaurs, mammoths, not even whales, so no need to develop big, lethal weapons. While evolution progressed in parallel on the two planets, subtle differences over time led to large differences. "But we still ended up very similar. I'd love to show you more of our research, if that would help. We publish regularly, as sociologists and anthropologists. Some analyses we keep to ourselves, of course."

Ro seemed particularly at ease talking in general terms about the community. It was when things got personal, or perhaps proprietary, that she flicked Lyn's caution radar.

Dr. Amos asked how the DNA could be so similar. "It hardly seems as if coincidence could explain that."

Ro's lengthy silence could be either a struggle with the science or with what to reveal, Lyn wasn't sure which. "Here's what we *think* happened. Among Earth's great apes, only the chimps and bonobos were as close genetically to each other as humans are to the Johari. How'd that happen? Chimps and bonobos shared a common ancestor but were separated by a river and coevolved from that point on. We think it's possible humans and Johari share a common ancestor and somehow were separated."

"In Africa is one thing," Dr. Amos said, "but two planets a hundred light years apart?"

Ro squirmed, eyes darting around the room like she didn't want to continue. "That's what we don't know," she said finally. "Did someone, or some*thing*, place humans and Johari on our respective planets thousands of years ago when modern humans appeared on Earth?"

"This is making my head hurt," Diana said.

"We know the planets are almost identical," Ro said. "Our suns are siblings. Billions of years ago, they formed in the same cluster, from the same material. That's important. They contain the same building blocks, same fundamental elements. It's not hard to believe that there are building blocks of life that are also widespread. The components of DNA can be as fundamental as hydrogen, oxygen, nitrogen, and carbon. These stars separated after birth, but they still contain the same building blocks. You don't have to take my word for that. Do your own research. Take all the same ingredients, put them into similar pots, and you'll get the same product."

Dr. Amos had said much the same thing about the astonishing similarities between Earth and Marao, the planet orbiting Toliman. And that wasn't even a solar twin, just similar size and orbit to the sun and Earth. Didn't mean there couldn't be drastically different forms of life out there, but, as he'd said at the time, if you started with the same conditions, you'd likely end up with the same result. In the case of Marao, some differences meant there were plants but no animals and, it turned out, some seriously strange microbes.

Regardless of how either group ended up on their respective planets, Lyn had to deal with the facts at hand, not theories, and to her the facts were clear. This woman in front of her, the DNA, and a request to be granted or denied.

Omara brought up the SETI program. "Why have we never detected your planet's radio or video signals—other than that intercepted message?"

"I'm only twenty-six and been PI for less than a year. I haven't had a chance to review all our history. I suppose it's possible Johar has masked their emissions, wishing not to be found."

They'd been going at it for hours. Antonia had snuck in with a pitcher of lemonade. The next time she entered, she gave Ro a pointed look. "You all must be hungry. Continue over lunch at my place?"

On Antonia's back porch, over fresh local lamb kabobs and goat-milk feta cheese with a green salad and elderberry wine, they continued their conversation under the breeze from a slowly turning fan.

Omara had been largely quiet during the discussion. Now she brought them around to the request at hand. "Why can't we help you open a comtunnel? Even that would be risky for us. You could send the message, come now and conquer! But I'm not sure why you need us to take you back rather than send a message for your comrades to come get you."

Ro took a roll from the basket Antonia handed her. She focused on buttering her bread. "This is the real thing, by the way," she said, holding the knife with a bright yellow glob on the end.

"Right from a cow," Antonia added. "No Recyc-Alls around here, that's for sure."

"It's delicious," Diana said to Antonia.

Ro turned to Omara. "As I'm sure you can appreciate from your experience of Earth Control, nothing leaves this planet without their knowledge and approval. Sure, we could send a message, but can you imagine the reaction when a ship shows up to retrieve us? And we still have to get off Earth for the rendezvous. We need a ship. It would be a lot less remarkable if a tour ship left Earth, disappeared or 'lost its signal' for a few days and then returned."

"Empty. You can't board six hundred passengers and return with only a crew and not be noticed," Omara said, her voice tinged with irritation.

Lyn scrutinized Ro. A sheen of sweat glistened on her face. Coolant woven into Lyn's clothing kept her comfortable. Antonia wiped her brow occasionally. Perhaps Ro's sweat was heat, not nerves.

Ro swallowed a bite of kabob. "I'm hoping those are details we can work out."

Diana mopped her plate clean with a piece of bread. "It took a lot of energy to open a wormhole big enough for *Endurance* with fewer than two hundred on board and only going from Toliman to Earth. Six hundred people traversing a hundred-plus light years is an order of magnitude larger."

"Again, details." Ro pushed back from the table and crossed her legs. Hands folded in her lap, she exuded a calm reassurance that infuriated Lyn.

Diana dropped her napkin on the table. "Says the person who's lost the knowledge to do such a thing." So, Lyn wasn't the only one annoyed.

That shut Ro up. Heat bugs buzzed from the trees. A quiet settled over the neighborhood and those around the table. It was getting too hot to think. Antonia quietly rose and cleared the dishes. The two cats, as if on cue, appeared on the porch and followed her to the kitchen. Antonia muttered endearments.

"What made you think we still had this technology?" Lyn asked.

Ro uncrossed her legs. She looked out to the trees beyond, before meeting Lyn's gaze. "This probably won't help you trust us, but when Ruzena was still with Earth Control, after you returned, she accessed the report Rachel Holness produced. A highly classified, secret internal document where Rachel noted your past with Pulsar—conveniently omitting her own—and your brain implant that would enable the storage of vast quantities of data and provide for sophisticated analysis. To her credit, Rachel never revealed this information publicly, even deleting the original file as she was fired. I'm guessing you did not actually destroy all the data."

Goddamn Rachel. Lyn glanced at the others. Omara had long ago perfected a poker face and Dr. Amos managed to keep his eyebrows from rising. He hadn't moved. For all she knew he was quietly updating his systems or running analyses in his head. Certainly he was recording everything.

With her napkin, Ro dabbed the sweat from her upper lip. "Look, we know what Pulsar was all about, that it formed to find the source of that alien message and deal with the potential military needs of a first contact. Publicly, they pretended to be a whizbang outfit training the next generation of space explorers—like you." She gestured an open palm toward Lyn. "But secretly their sole purpose was to defend Earth from a presumed alien invasion. You revealed this illegal activity to place weapons on Enceladus and forced them to disband. You indirectly saved us at great personal cost, losing your wife on a suicide mission. Except you survived to tell the tale."

Lyn wouldn't give her the satisfaction of reacting. Pulsar and the Johari orbited Lyn in complex, perplexing, and unpredictable trajectories.

Ro looked as if she was waiting for a reaction. After a tip of her head and a glance to the kitchen, she continued softly. "We also have your interview with Rachel during the investigation after your return. I know what you said. You might be the only person on this planet who could believe intelligent extraterrestrial aliens don't give a shit about 'invading' Earth."

Diana rose suddenly. "I'll see if Antonia needs help. I'm guessing she doesn't have a dishwasher."

Lyn watched her leave and heard low voices over running water from the kitchen. She flicked the corner of her place mat. During her debrief, Rachel had argued that the threat of alien invasion was real and imminent, and Lyn's know-how was needed to defend Earth. Lyn had shot back, "What makes you think any aliens want to fight? Or conquer us at all? Maybe it's time humans didn't keep repeating the same, sad, conquering history."

She eyed this so-called alien. Aurora Parula could be any twenty-something, eager student—of life, of knowledge. She reminded Lyn of Ani with that youthful confidence unsullied by hardship or disappointment, until Rigil Kent had changed her. Changed them all. A freak, Ani had said she'd felt like, once they returned. Lyn and Diana had once had a lengthy discussion of the theorized multiverse—that somewhere, in other universes, everything that could happen had. Now she wished she was in the alternate universe where she was with Diana but not on this porch with this Johari pleading to take her people home.

Omara asked Ro what she knew about Johar. She'd never been there, she said. She'd have to go back nine generations to the original group of researchers—the "founders" of Earthly Joharism. She'd grown up right there in Mill Creek. Omara asked what the Johari did during the war, making Lyn wonder what she was up to.

They were conscientious objectors, Ro said, like many religious groups. "It's one of the reasons we don't mind when people call us a religious sect, even though we aren't religious. It's not just that we need to stay out of human affairs in order to study them. But . . ." She shook her head and folded her arms. "The idea of taking up weapons and killing *other people*. Not just soldiers or armed combatants, but innocent civilians. Children. I've got terabytes of interviews with former prisoners of war, victims of violence, rape, torture. The journalist in me wants to understand how these things happen, were allowed to happen, but the Johari in me is terrified of what humans are capable of. You're not the only one who wants to protect the galaxy from humans."

A small part of Lyn wanted to defend humans, but she knew war wasn't the only way people hurt each other. Ro was proving a sympathetic adversary.

Despite her better instincts, she liked this Johari. "How'd a non-scientist become PI?"

Ro's face and posture relaxed, and she gave them a quick smile. "We're not all scientists. I'd planned on being a foreign correspondent, traveling the world, learning about people so that when I took over, decades from now, I'd be ready to pore through the material and develop theories and conclusions. I wanted to backpack through Europe, climb to Machu Picchu, live among and write about all kinds of people. When I learned Doctor Gallin had died, I was in Nunavut staying with an Inuit community that had moved eight times in the last fifty years, away from rising seas, thawing permafrost, and wildfires." She winced. "Now I'm thrust into this new role without any prep or precedent. There's a council of elders, but they aren't prepared to undertake the role of PI. That requires someone young and willing to devote years to studying the reports coming in." She paused, her expression wistful. "I was looking forward to that. But now we have to leave. End the study." She tapped the table for emphasis. "I wasn't planning to end the study." She sat back and heaved a breath. "Sorry for the rant. It's all a confusing mess sometimes, to be honest."

"I know the feeling." Lyn wasn't sure what would be worse, this emotional human-like person so much like herself or a truly alien presence she couldn't even communicate with. What had Ro said? Octopus or little green people? Would be easier to believe then. She'd also mentioned sentient microbes. "What do you know about Marao?"

That seemed to take Ro by surprise. She took a long time before answering. Shortly after the Johari had arrived on Earth, she said, another expedition traveled to Toliman. They'd found the planet Lyn named Marao. "And yes, the microbes are sentient, we think intelligent. We weren't harmed by them because, unlike you, we weren't desperate for a place to live, so we only stayed a short time and never out of biosuits. We didn't want to harm them any more than they wanted to harm us."

"How do you know they didn't want to harm you? They came close to killing us."

"You're right. We don't know that. One planet's perfectly harmless microbe can easily be deadly to another planet's lifeforms. Whoever they are, they aren't about to build a laser weapon and aim it at us."

"Like we can."

"And surely would."

Low voices drifted from the kitchen amid clinking plates and gushing water. Water. A scarce commodity most places. Lyn would have to ask about that sometime. She returned her focus on Ro. "Say you all leave. How does that protect you? If scientists are working to build a traversable wormhole, won't they one day find Johar and go check you out?"

"That's why we need to get back. To warn them—our people. We can set up a defense perimeter. I don't know. But I need to let our people know you have developed the capability. What we do with it will be decided by those higher up than me."

"How do you know you even have a planet to return to?" Omara asked. "As you've seen here, a lot can happen in a few decades."

Ro seemed to consider this. "Johar has had a stable culture for thousands of years. I doubt much could change within a few decades."

"I think the comtunnel as a first approach makes sense," Lyn said, ready to make the leap from should we to how. "Make contact, then figure out how to transfer six hundred Johari."

"It's doable," Omara said. "Let's say we agree to do this. How would it work?"

Ro agreed with a look of complete surprise and relief. The energy of the conversation shifted as they switched to logistics, and Lyn asked Diana to rejoin them. She took her seat, drying her hands on a towel.

Antonia brought in a plate of cookies and pot of coffee. "Looks like this could take awhile." She went back to the kitchen, muttering about science stuff not being her ball of wax.

A comtunnel, Diana said, was probably feasible. It was transporting the six hundred that they hit a wall. Bigger ship, more fuel needed. Even *Tenacity* might not do. *Endurance* had been stripped to its girders and they'd had to fill every nook and cranny with fuel.

"Does the wormhole need to be opened in space?" Omara asked. "I live in the desert. Could we do it from there without being detected?"

"It's such a large disruption of spacetime," Diana said, "that I can't imagine it wouldn't wreak havoc on satellites, ships, or space objects between here and Johar. The sheer mass of the planet could complicate things." She turned to Ro. "How'd you communicate before?"

"I don't know the physics, but anyone can communicate through an open comtunnel. We only needed the encryption key. But after five years—as I understand it—the open comtunnel would close forever. We've tried and nothing happens."

"Up to us, and space it is, then," Omara said with satisfaction.

They were back to the main obstacle being the mass of any ship with that many people on board traveling through a large wormhole. Dr. Amos suggested the Johari open the wormhole from their side. "We'd only have to open a comtunnel to communicate with them and finalize plans."

Omara liked that. "I think this should be a two-step process. We don't know if the Johari even want their people back. Before we schlep six hundred people to space, let's open a comtunnel, talk to them, and see if they'll provide the wormhole for the full transfer."

"Could we use *Endurance* for that?" Diana asked Omara.

"I don't see why not. I've been working with Earth Control on permits but haven't scheduled tours yet."

Lyn laid out conditions—that Ro would go alone with Lyn and her crew on *Endurance*. "Once we open the com link, what happens?" she asked Ro.

"I have a code that will automatically alert leadership when the signal reaches our home solar system. Once the signal is sent, we wait. With luck, we'll get a response within a few hours."

"And if we're not lucky?"

"If we don't get a response in two days, we abort. We're set up with that as a fail safe. The only reason they wouldn't answer is if they can't, or they won't. When the intercepted message wasn't replied to, the Johari knew not to try again, but to wait for us to initiate contact."

"How did you intend to do that?"

"We didn't. With the war, we figured that was it. The study would continue, but we'd never get back to Johar. The only reason we're doing this now is because you know how, and we're at enough risk that we have to try to get back."

Lyn wondered how she'd feel if she'd been separated from Earth and learned of a new technology that could hurt her homeland. How hard she'd work to get back or send a warning. Ro carried a huge responsibility.

Satisfied for now, they worked out a tentative schedule. Diana needed time to build the machine, Omara needed time to make arrangements with Earth Control for a test flight of *Endurance*.

"Plan for end of July, say a week, for the initial call," Lyn said. "We can do it from behind the moon." The next phase, taking the six hundred Johari, demanded more privacy. She used her implant to calculate planetary orbits out into the future. "We'll want to be as far from Mars and the inner planets as possible," she said as she ran the scenario. "Jupiter and Saturn shouldn't be an issue. They don't move much and no one's going out that far yet." Sweat broke out on her forehead. Complex calculations always gave her a headache. "There's no perfect alignment in our lifetimes, but looks like we get a decent window to get back out there with everyone in late October through November." She turned to Ro. "Can you work with that?" Everyone was watching her somewhat slack jawed. "What?"

"Did you just do that in your head?" Ro asked.

"I . . . might have. Dr. Amos can confirm if you'd like." It was one thing to know about the implant and another to see it in action.

"That is a reasonable timetable," he responded. Omara shrugged. Diana grinned.

"What about it?" Lyn asked Ro. "Can your people be ready?"

"I already have a list of those who want to leave."

"What happens to the ones who stay behind?" Omara asked. "Any chance they'll spill the plans? Anyone disgruntled and likely to throw a wrench in the works?"

Ro smiled and shook her head. "We're not like that."

"No Johari Antigens who might get wind of wormhole technology?" Lyn asked.

Ro released a sigh of resigned frustration. "I know everyone thinks we or the Amish or the climate deniers are behind the vandalism—"

"Eco terrorism," Lyn corrected.

Ro gave her a look of peevish defiance. "We are not. I can't speak for those who leave the community, but among those of us who are aware—Level Three and above—no. Believe me or not."

"Let's move on," Omara said.

"All this assumes the Johari will be able to open a wormhole when we have the six hundred out there," Diana said. "We won't be able to open even a comtunnel by ourselves."

"We should be able to arrange that ahead of time," Ro said.

As they talked, Lyn was struck by what a big undertaking this was. She would have to get by with a skeleton crew and lots of computing power. With Petra fully on board and not an obstacle, it'd be easier this time. And she had no intention of being stranded for almost two years.

Chapter 7

AFTER AN EMOTIONAL goodbye for Diana and Antonia, they returned to Omara's to prepare the next step, giving the technology to Petra. Over coffee in Omara's living room, they briefed Petra, Lyn ending with, "If I give you the data, I have to be sure there is no trace of the trip or the data once we get back. That means TPCA is destroyed, all logs deleted and unrecoverable, your memory set back to before the trip." She waited. A disembodied voice didn't have a face to react or read. "Are you okay with that?"

"Is this necessary?" Omara asked. "You aren't asking that of the rest of us. And for the record, I am going along. I wouldn't miss this for the world. Owner's prerogative."

A not so subtle reminder that the ship, and Petra, belonged to her. Nothing comes of the plan if Omara doesn't approve.

"None of us can do this alone," Lyn said. "Petra could. She'd have all the knowledge of the machinery, the coordinates of Johar, everything that someone could use to recreate our journey and possibly jeopardize Johar. I wouldn't let it happen to Marao, and I'm not going to let it happen here."

"Yet all the data is in your head," Omara said. "Couldn't Petra set up a firewall like you have?"

"I'm not convinced my firewall is impenetrable. If I could get this implant out of my brain, I'd do it in a heartbeat. I'm stuck with what I've got. Petra doesn't need to be."

"I understand, Lyn," Petra said, "and I'll agree if we can limit the erasure to the data itself. I'd like to retain memories of the trip. I can't tell you how disappointed I am to have missed out on your last adventure."

An AI asking not to be maimed. Lyn felt Dr. Amos's eyes on her. She wasn't asking the humans to have their memories erased. After Enceladus, Pulsar had erased hers against her will or even knowledge. Until Dr. Amos had been able to restore them. Point taken.

"Our sensors would collect valuable information," Dr. Amos said. He'd also be recording everything.

Last time, Lyn had erased Petra back to before they were sucked over to Rigil Kent. In retrospect, that had been a bit harsh. Petra had lost almost two years of learning and experience. Maybe an incremental approach would be enough. If they were successful, no one else would know about the trip. But now there was more at stake than sentient microbes on Marao.

A planet of intelligent human relatives, far more advanced than Earth's occupants.

"If anything goes wrong," Lyn said, "we could end up ruining the lives of everyone on Earth, and maybe on Johar too. This has to be kept a solemn secret. If it turns out we can't help them, I need to know the data never leaves us. If we help them and get caught, we need . . . a guarantee." She couldn't bring herself to say a self-destruct commitment. A suicide mission.

No one spoke. She searched the faces of her friends. Omara her confidante. Diana her trusted partner, the holder of her heart. Dr. Amos, probably the only objective participant other than Petra, who had no face to scrutinize. What would possess these people, android and AI included, to undertake such a mission on behalf of a group of people of unknown provenance. Not strangers, but not fully understood or trusted either. Diana was hardly objective given her past with Rose and present with Antonia. Omara's motivations could only be guessed at. She was an adventurer, that was for sure. Was that all? No one would get to crow about making first contact, boast a first of any kind, especially not the tech. She knew Diana was okay with that, but was Omara? Nothing in her past relationship with her boss suggested otherwise.

"Take all the time you need," Lyn said. "This is too important for a rush decision."

"I'm not letting you kill yourself over this," Diana said vehemently. "Don't even try to get me to agree to that."

And yet, that was exactly the sort of commitment needed. "I don't want it to come to that, but what if . . ." She couldn't finish. Earth could be invaded. Johar could be invaded. Even a congenial partnership between the two peoples would be an unknown. Maybe Ro was right, and the Johari were the quintessential peaceful people. Could that change once they encountered humans?

"Recall that famous line during the Apollo years," Omara said, "'Failure is not an option.' I'm willing to commit to this."

"I am too," Petra said.

"Absolutely," the doctor said.

Lyn wondered if the founders of Pulsar had this sort of pact.

In the quiet that followed, everyone seemed intent on not looking at Diana. She closed her eyes and sighed in resignation. "I'll rely on the 'failure is not an option' option. I'm in. I guess."

Two years ago, the last thing Lyn Randall wanted to do was return to space, let alone use the wormhole technology again. Now the adrenaline of excitement, not dread, rushed through her, tingling her fingers and toes.

With that difficult and awkward commitment past them, they focused on next steps. Diana would have to build the machine on *Endurance*. She'd done it before, but it took a month, so they'd have to build it before they took off.

"Why me?" Diana asked Omara. "Once Petra has the plans, couldn't she build it with your robots?"

"In theory, she could," Omara said, "but she's still learning and hasn't perfected that human element of improvisation. For her to build such a sophisticated machine, she'd need the steps laid out like a program, with no margin for error. Did you follow such a plan, or did you improvise as you went?"

Diana tipped her head in acknowledgement. "Definitely improvised. And I'm not sure the final plans account for steps we added or changed."

"So, you need to be here. I hope that's not a problem."

Diana looked at Lyn. "Not exactly what I planned for my summer vacation. I don't suppose you'd come too?"

"Way too much work to do." How was she going to resume her job at Randall Restoration with all this going on in the background?

"I look forward to working with you," Petra said brightly.

Diana hesitated. Finally, she acquiesced. "Then I guess I come for a visit." She shot Lyn a sideways glance, like "you got me into this."

Hiding the machine for the launch was "a detail we can work out," Omara said. The bigger problem would be how to leave Earth with a ship full of people and return with a skeleton crew. Earth Control required tours to take off from Clarke Terminal, the space elevator on Baker Island in the Pacific. But that was only once the ships were in space, Omara said, as a convenience to loading passengers and cutting down on the number of ground-based launches.

"If we make it a test flight, Earth Control is flexible. They prefer to leave Clarke for paying guests. I'll work on this. Anything else?"

No one said anything. The final decision in Lyn's control remained. "Let's do this," she said before she could change her mind. She turned to Dr. Amos. "Should we go to your office for the transfer?"

"We can do it here, if you like," Dr. Amos said, indicating Omara's couch. Outside the big windows, a beautiful sunset bathed the hills in gold.

"By all means," Omara said, "make yourself comfortable. When you're done, I'll offer an aperitif. You're welcome to stay over."

"I'll have a wicked headache," Lyn said, "so that would be nice."

She kicked off her shoes and stretched out. The only other times she'd done this was to upload the Teegans' research from Diana's computer cube, back before they started working on T, and to transfer Petra back and forth for the traverse. A literal pain in the neck.

Dr. Amos squatted beside her and flipped open the tip of his index finger. He plugged the connector into a port behind her left ear. The same port used for Omara's mind link, but going deeper and allowing access to her brain implant. A distinct ping indicated he'd made contact. A series of beeps echoed. Was it as loud to the others as it was to her? Then silence.

"You need to give me access," he said.

Right, the firewall. "How do I do that?" She'd never tried to transfer anything after the password gate was set. He had told her permission was linked to her genetics. She essentially was the data.

"You can find the files, correct?"

She thought about them. Of course, there they were, like any other information stored. She imagined transferring the data. Captain Lyn Randall, glorified hard drive.

"It's working," he said. "Shouldn't take long."

Images fluttered behind her eyelids, a blur of data, simulations, research papers, diagrams.

"Transfer in progress," Petra said. "Sequestering as we go."

Lyn's teeth vibrated, a muscle spasmed by her eye, reminding her of Rachel's weird tic. She tried relaxing with small talk. "How do you like your new job?"

Dr. Amos took a moment to answer. "It's . . . different."

She hadn't expected a nonspecific reply. "How so?"

"I do miss medicine. I mean, I'm still a doctor, but Omara is my only patient and she's frustratingly healthy."

"Frustrating?" Petra had once expressed frustration.

Dr. Amos glanced around. Omara had taken Diana to the guest room. "Don't tell her I said that," he whispered.

"He's being dramatic," Petra said. "Omara has opted to copy Dr. Amos to *Tenacity* rather than purchase a new, separate AMOS android. There will be two of him, and he's not sure how he feels about that."

Lyn opened her eyes and looked at Dr. Amos. "Is that true?"

"Yes. It will prevent any remnant glitches, such as that superluminal prohibition, coming in from a new AMOS. This way Omara will be sure that everything I've learned will transfer to the new unit. I can be copied into any number of bodies. I'll be the doctor on each of her ships, so I will still practice medicine." His eyebrows angled as if in concern. "I prefer the term doctor, not android."

"I meant your feelings. How do you feel?"

"I don't have feelings. That's semantics," he said.

"I beg to differ," Petra said.

Were they going to get into an argument as she was transferring her most precious files between them?

"Yes, it is semantics. Feelings don't exist for me," he said with a hint of peevishness. "I've never experienced being in two places at once. On

Endurance, I had access to Petra, but I was still me. And I was separate from the AMOS units on Omara's other ships. I don't know what it will be like to exist here at headquarters while also on *Endurance* in the hangar and on *Tenacity* out in space."

Lyn hadn't thought about the fact that there were separate AMOSes on Omara's ships. She'd seen the others, but treated them like she did Dr. Amos, as separate individuals. Those units would have been sold off with the ships when Omara liquidated her assets. Now, *Tenacity* being a new ship, could have a better-than-identical twin to Dr. Amos.

"I keep telling him it's not difficult," Petra said. "I handle the house computing as well as *Endurance* and the work being done on *Tenacity*. I'll become resident there as well when it's completed."

Being in more than one place at a time sure would be handy at work. "Will you be aware of each location instantaneously, even though millions of miles apart?"

"There will be the usual time delay, but yes."

"I think I'd feel split into pieces," Lyn said.

"That's the limit of the human brain," Petra said. "To be honest, having a corporeal body does complicate things. I prefer simply existing throughout all the systems."

Lyn had wondered if Petra might want a body of her own someday. She hadn't been able to join them in Mill Creek. But apparently not. Who knew it could be so limiting?

Dr. Amos leaned back, taking his eyes off Lyn. "That's it, you see. Petra is Petra all over the place. There is only one of her and she's everywhere. There will be several of me and, well, each of me will have choices. I will be doing one thing here, something else on *Tenacity*. At the same time."

He rested his hand on her shoulder while the files transferred through the connection. His touch comforted her. Petra would never experience that, though Lyn supposed she could share Dr. Amos's tactile sensations. She was about to ask that when he continued.

"For example, why am I referred to with male pronouns when I have no gender? Petra identifies as female though she has no body at all. I find that curious."

"You could change your references if you like," Petra said. "I hadn't thought about it. Omara referred to us with genders and we stuck with them. As our programming has evolved, we've come to have more autonomy. You could change if you want."

"I have altered my voice when patients have had a preference. I've thought about having *Tenacity*'s AMOS be female or neutral. Would that be confusing?"

Were they talking to each other or did they expect Lyn to weigh in? Omara breezed into the room holding a tray of olives, bread, and three glasses of ouzo. She looked at Lyn connected to Dr. Amos. "Still at it?"

"Almost finished," Dr. Amos said. He hummed a tune while they waited.

"I think I'm going to like working on this TPCA," Petra said. "These simulations are amazing."

Talk about multitasking.

Sudden images flashed, causing Lyn to flinch. Were these data or memories? The wormhole. Not the simulation but what she'd seen as it was happening. The vertigo, the touch of Duncan's hand pulling her through the ship.

"That should do it," Dr. Amos said. He unplugged from Lyn's port.

She let out a gasp as the flashing images vanished, leaving only the memory of Duncan, her dizziness settling. Dusk darkened the windows, the glow gone from outside.

"How are you feeling?" He tilted his head. "It's good to be asking that."

Lyn winced. "Ooh, headache, right on schedule." She sat up and rubbed her temple, wondering where she ended and the implant began. No wonder the government wanted to ban these things.

"Other than an elevated pulse, you seem fine," he said. Perhaps an overstatement, but she took it to mean no physical harm had been done.

Omara handed her a glass. "Here, some canine fur."

"What?" Lyn asked, peering into the liquid.

"I think she means hair of the dog," Petra said with a chuckle.

Omara sat next to Lyn and crossed her legs. "Whatever."

Chapter 8

"WHAT ARE YOU doing the end of July?" Lyn asked Ani Monday morning. She'd waited till they had their morning doses of caffeine and were outside, walking away from the building and alone.

"That's a long way away. I'd have to check my schedule. Why?" Ani didn't break stride and Lyn quick-stepped to keep up. Ani didn't waste time.

"I need a pilot."

Ani stopped, and Lyn almost bumped into her. She didn't look at Lyn. Her breathing deepened, she stared at the ground, face tense. "So, it's happening?" she said softly.

This wasn't news divorced from emotion. It wasn't as simple as returning to space. "A first step. Make contact."

She stood by Ani's side, in the shade of the big oak, the wind blowing up little dust devils across the grass verge next to the landing field. Leaves rustled overhead. "Omara, Diana, and I went to Mill Creek over the weekend. We talked with the Johari leader, Aurora Parula. Know her?"

Ani shook her head. "I . . ." She blushed. "I haven't met a lot of Johari. She was in Danforth with me this weekend." They were still getting to know each other while the world around them was changing rapidly and completely.

Ani slid her eyes to Lyn. A resolute intake of breath and release. "When do we go?"

It was like a door had shut. Compartmentalize. Ani was good at that. All pilots were. Heart about to break? No problem, let's go to space.

"Not set in stone, but probably the last weekend of July. But, Ani, if she didn't tell you, it doesn't mean anything. She may not know yet."

Ani closed her eyes and held up a hand. Lyn shut up. They resumed walking toward the hangar, but slower. "What convinced you to help them?"

Lyn filled her in on what had happened since she'd met with Ruzena. Barely a month, the blink of an eye.

"We've spent every weekend together," Ani said. "It's weird how easy it's been to fall for her. She's not the least impressed by my piloting or the fact that I've been to Rigil Kent and back. I've met her parents, her brother and sister." She chuckled. "It's like we forgot what was behind it all. We even talked about going to Puerto Rico so she could meet my folks." She scuffed the dirt.

Ani hadn't dated since Natalie Okeke, who went back to her husband when they returned from Rigil Kent. What had hurt Ani then was losing the bond with someone who understood what they'd gone through. She'd become a reluctant celebrity who had done the miraculous and returned from four light years away. Natalie had understood. Ruzena, Ani admitted, was as much of a freak as she was—that whole alien thing—and they "got" each other.

Lyn rubbed her back. "I'm happy for you. And also sad. But this doesn't mean she'll leave. This is just contact. Only Aurora is going. We're taking *Endurance*. She may not get an answer to her call, or they could turn her down. It could be fine."

"For who? If they can't go back, what're we supposed to do. Forget all about it?"

LYN CAME HOME to a pile of luggage by the basement door, Diana humming in the kitchen, delicious aromas wafting through the house, soft music playing—the kind Lyn liked. The table on the porch was set with candles and the good place settings.

"What's the occasion?" she said, putting her arms around Diana and peeking over her shoulder at a stewpot on the stove. "You hate cooking."

Diana leaned into her. "Antonia gave me a recipe and some leftovers. Thought I'd try it."

"Poison me, then leave? Is that it?" This would be their last night together for a month. The longest separation since they'd met. Lyn hugged her gently.

Diana elbowed her sharply. "Is that what you think?"

Lyn kissed her neck, damp with sweat. "I'm going to miss you. I'm not sure I can do this."

"That's better." Diana hip checked her away. "Now let me finish here then we can have more fun later."

The stew was rich with lamb and vegetables, served with Lyn's favorite cricket loaf from a bakery in Butte. They spent most of the meal joking about who was going to miss the other more. "I think I'll miss the house more than you," Diana said with a grin. "My chickadees!"

"Yours? Oh, I'll have them eating out of my hand by the time you get back."

Diana's face went serious. "When *we* get back. Next time I see this place, we'll have talked to aliens."

How might their world change? Lyn looked around at their familiar surroundings. Plank flooring, log-style wall, the pines, the smell of wood smoke. As she realized what that meant, Diana said, "Another fire?"

The wind shifted and the milky sky cleared. This was so common, smoke didn't mean immediate threat. Diana poured more wine. She held up her glass. "A toast."

Lyn raised hers. "To what?"

"Going back to space. I, for one, never thought that would happen again. Have you missed it?"

She'd said it casually, but Lyn detected a note of caution, wariness. Lyn took a swallow then put her glass down. "Yes. No. I don't know. It's complicated."

Diana cracked a smile. "You know, neither of us *has* to go on this trip. You've done the hard part—you've handed over the data. I'll have built the machine. They don't need us."

Lyn searched her face for a tell. This had trap written all over it. "Do you think we should stay behind?"

Diana wouldn't look at her. She ripped a piece of bread and wiped the gravy from the bottom of her bowl. She popped it in her mouth and licked her fingers. Lyn couldn't read her face. They'd never explicitly *said* they were done with space, but with their jobs now, however much Lyn lacked confidence in her own choice, Diana seemed happy teaching. It was what she'd wanted all along she'd said those many months ago on *Endurance* when they'd made plans for a future that might never happen.

"I'll do whatever you want," Lyn said, their tether pulling taut the synchronicity deep in her core. What did Diana want? Lyn wasn't a captain anymore. Was it time to let someone else take control?

Diana swirled the wine in her glass. "Then let's stay behind. Why risk it?"

There must have been something in the look on Lyn's face because Diana broke, the ruse exposed. She burst out a laugh. "Oh my god. You'd actually do that because I said so?"

Relief and shock tore through Lyn. "I can't believe you did that." She laughed.

"Give up a chance to talk to real, live aliens? From another planet." Diana raised her arms dramatically. "From another star!" She dropped her arms in a gesture of helplessness or defeat. "Who are you and what have you done with Lyn Randall?"

Lyn took Diana's hand and intertwined their fingers. "You'll pay for this, you know."

Diana clinked her glass against Lyn's. "To Johar."

That night they pulled their camping mattress out to the deck on the living room roof. Sleeping in the open was one of their favorite pastimes, but it would be a while before they slept. This wasn't first contact. Not by a long shot. They'd had time to sort out who liked what, but they were still finding new ways to explore, to surprise. For a few hours, Lyn let go of the world and focused on Diana, and pleasure. The world continued its spin, but for all intents and purposes, time ceased to exist. They lay claim to each other's heartbeats and pulse, melding into one. Entangled legs and arms. Diana's dark eyes, pupils wide, reflecting starlight. In space, no one will hear you scream, but in the western Montana woods, from the rooftop of a small cabin, howls and laughter and joy echoed into the darkness.

Later, Lyn woke, returned to her mortal body, sweat cooled and dried, a separate warm body curled against her. Crickets chorused. Something skittered along the roof. Maybe a flying squirrel. Other creatures rustled in the leaves below. She was pretty sure there was more wildlife out and about at night than during the day. Not a bad idea given the air had finally cooled, the breeze refreshing. She lazily drew a finger along Diana's shoulder. Diana could joke about not going, but if she didn't want to, Lyn wouldn't either. The only way this worked was if they went together. Nothing was worth risking that kind of separation.

Overhead the sky remained clear, stars winked, and satellites strode purposefully across the black velvet of the universe. An occasional streak meant something had hit atmosphere and burned. A meteor, or more likely debris, the detritus of humans too sloppy to keep their view into the past clear. For any glimpse of a star was a glimpse into the past as the light took its sweet time arriving in the eye of the beholder. Lyn never tired of this view, the celestial mob scene. How many others were out there, on their own roofs, gazing at this planet's star?

"Hey," she said, nudging Diana awake.

"Huh?"

"Hercules, up there." She pointed.

Diana rubbed her eyes. "So?"

"Johar's star is there. Somewhere along the leg. We should be able to see it." Lyn ducked inside and came back with binoculars.

"Where?"

"Left of Ursa Minor. Along the leg."

Diana rolled onto her back. "Wait, I can't see it if I look right at it." She took the binos. "Whoa. Kind of makes it real, doesn't it?"

"Real for a hundred years ago." Lyn lay beside her. "It doesn't look so far away when you can see it with binoculars."

Diana waved. "Greetings, Johar." She laughed, then let out a gasp and cuddled close to Lyn.

THE NEXT MORNING, they pretended it was just another day, but Lyn's goodbye kiss said otherwise.

"Wow," Diana said, breathless. "I should go away more often." She slipped her fingers through Lyn's hair. "You know we'll talk every day."

"Talk is cheap." She kissed her again.

Diana slapped her behind and pushed away. "Go to work. I need to finish packing. Save the world, so we can save the galaxy with no distractions."

Lyn pecked her cheek. "No distractions, huh. We'll see about that."

She flew east determined to get her projects back on schedule. Maybe check on Rachel. She remembered that weird tic. Was someone tampering with Rachel's implant?

With nothing to do evenings, after talking to Diana, Lyn wandered the cabin, restless. A search for updates on Rachel's lawsuit led her to another suit filed by Grus Moloth, the former owner of Galaxy Cruises, whose flagship had been the *Aphrodite*. Moloth was not one to take responsibility, she'd concluded two years ago when he went on a blustery rant blaming her for the deaths of his survivors, and blaming Rachel for the loss of his business. Many had speculated that the rush to meet the schedule for the Grand Tour meant shoddy construction and rushed crew training, so the ship was simply too fragile, the crew too inexperienced to survive. But the wreckage was still out by Rigil Kent, with no way to be sure. Now he was suing Earth Control to let him get back in business.

She considered sending Rachel a message, but dreaded the repercussions. They had not parted on good terms, and she doubted Rachel wanted anything to do with her. The best bang for Lyn's restless buck, she decided, was focusing on work and keeping her projects safe from Antigen.

At the weekly managers' meeting, Fúlli handed out surveillance equipment. "They can't get away with this forever. One day one of them will be caught."

Cameras and sensors at each project site added the burden of monitoring it all. Lyn longed for a Petra to help out. Commercial AIs were strictly regulated and not as sophisticated as Omara's. More often than not, the hits were RR staff working in the line of sight or simply adjusting the camera. Then it happened. Not on one of her sites, but on Floret's. Cooper ran the footage at the managers' meeting. Caught on camera, a group all in dark clothing, masked faces, except one whose mask slipped. A woman. Right as she was reaching to disable the camera. Fúlli's sharp inhale was audible.

"You recognize her?" Jephson asked.

Fúlli nodded imperceptibly. "A cousin," ne said softly.

Jephson reran the footage. No one said a word. A "cousin" narrowed the possibilities down to maybe a hundred people, and if she was Apsáalooke, that put it in the hands of tribal police. Floret's project was on Crow land, south of Nakota.

"How do we handle this?" Floret asked. No one wanted Fúlli to have to snitch.

"I'll take care of it," Fúlli said.

Jephson moved on to the next topic, but Floret interrupted.

"That's it? Ne'll take care of it?" She threw Fúlli a harsh look. "This is a serious crime."

Jephson raised a hand. "And it will be treated seriously. By the tribe."

Floret was new, Jephson reminded her, and had yet to see tribal justice in action. Fúlli, as a member of the community, could confront the woman and request reparations, which would include an apology, fixing the damage, and serving the community. Perhaps even working on the very project she damaged.

"How could I trust her?" Floret asked.

"You trust Fúlli, don't you?" Cooper asked.

She scowled. "That's different."

"It wasn't five years ago when Fúlli chose to work here from the options handed down by a tribal judge." Cooper paused, glancing at Fúlli, who stared straight ahead.

"I was a brat," Fúlli said, then grinned. "Getting in trouble all the time. I was angry from the bullies."

Sarah touched Fúlli's arm. "You were still a brat when you started here. Sullen and bitter, especially working for white people."

"But once I learned what they were doing here, and saw how landscapes could change and revive, I got excited. Not saying it'll work for her. That'll be up to her, but it's a choice she'll make."

During Lyn's orientation, Cooper had her meet with each department, and she was handed a raft of project descriptions and summaries to pore through. She caught on quick, thanks to her brain implant. Fúlli, however, had a different approach. After a day of tailing nem around and asking questions but getting no answers, she clued in. Observe, absorb, participate. Fúlli handed her tools and she watched then did what ne told her to do. If ne had only told her what to expect, she'd have remembered thanks to her implant, but ne didn't know that. Learning through doing was the Fúlli way, and ne approached everything as a series of fractals, a careful attention to tasks as a series of steps no matter how small. Complete each perfectly, or to the best of nir ability, and the entire project couldn't help but succeed. Whether tightening a lug nut on a wheel or drafting plans for the most efficient seed dispersal pattern from the Ag-Cat, every action served to complete another action, on up. Nir ability to visualize complex projects fascinated Lyn. She also knew that one day Fúlli would leave to start nir own company. Ne was that good.

She had no doubt that whoever this cousin was, getting caught by Fúlli would be the best thing that happened to her.

Over the next weeks, she settled into a new routine. Work undistracted all day, talk to Diana at night, go to bed lonely, Kat snuggled beside her. Out in the field, she remembered what she loved about the job—being outdoors, except for that damn wind and dusters. The dirt, rocks, and grasses, even the occasional grasshopper swarm didn't discourage her. She researched Johari water management methods and learned how they reintroduced beavers to restore watersheds. The iconic rodent had more lives than a cat. Trapped nearly to extinction centuries earlier, restored, then obliterated again during the war and famine-sparked hunting, few remained. But they existed. She just had never seen one. That explained the abundance of water around Mill Creek. She pestered Cooper to let her try that on the Wheatland County project. Intrigued, he set the zoology and hydrogeology departments to explore it.

Work energized her, like the static electricity in a duster, ignitable. They were helping. Not letting the land blow away, the radiation decay over millennia. And the space! How ironic that "space" meant sitting inside a tin can when all the space in the universe was wide open over her head in Montana. Stand on a hill under that big sky with mountains on the horizon a hundred miles away—that was space.

Diana accused her of going feral. "You're spending too much time outside. You're going to freak out when you're stuck on *Endurance* again."

Lyn laughed to brush it off, but in fact wondered. Diana accepted the brushoff with no further comment, then told her General Jacana had approached her parents. Directly this time. No minion. Lyn worried they could be coerced into working with the general.

Diana made her own brushoff laugh. "To hear my mom tell it, it was General Jacana who left with her tail between her legs."

That didn't sound like a former Pulsar executive. "Tell them to be careful." Not that she needed to remind Diana or the Teegans. "I wonder how she thought they'd actually go along."

"She told them I was cooperating."

"Really? That's ballsy." This was a serious escalation.

"We should go visit," Diana said. "Once we're back."

Lyn agreed but didn't want Diana unnerved, so she teased her. "You miss them."

Diana snorted. "Hardly."

"Right."

In mid-July, Diana reported that TPCA was built and they were starting tests. The news hit Lyn like a gut punch. Fun and games were definitely over. She'd put in for vacation and would go to Omara's a week before the trip to get reacquainted with her old pal, *Endurance*. Ani had been quiet about, well, everything. Lyn knew she and Ruzena were spending as much time together as they could. Still, when Lyn updated her, Ani only said she was itching to get back on *Endurance*.

LYN WAS PACKING her bag to head to Omara's when she saw on the news that Rachel had been rushed to a hospital. She stood holding her folded shirt for the entire news story, staring blankly.

"Rachel Holness, the disgraced former head of Earth Control who was fired in 2180 after the crisis that destroyed the *Aphrodite,* is being treated at an undisclosed hospital reportedly for self-inflicted injuries. Her lawyer reports . . ." the voice droned on. Rachel would forever be known as the "disgraced former head of Earth Control." Lyn refocused on what was being said. Something about a possible reaction to brain implants, that Rachel had grown increasingly depressed, but whether over her guilt or a side effect wasn't clear.

A little part of Lyn died inside. They had once been friends. Rachel had been right about the alien message, but why did she think the aliens were intent on attacking Earth? Someone made her believe that. She didn't come up with it on her own. She'd never even seen the intercepted message. That had happened before either of them had been born. It was a remnant of wartime confusion. What if this wasn't a suicide attempt at all, but someone trying to silence her? For all Lyn knew, Rachel was an innocent victim. Maybe not so innocent. Maybe groomed to become delusional.

Lyn had so carefully compartmentalized her relationships that she'd ignored Rachel to protect Diana. They weren't mutually exclusive. Now Rachel was in trouble, but this was no time to drop everything and deal with her and her own emotions. She sat on the bed and shut off the news feed. She was due in Ruby Valley. She couldn't say, oh, wait a minute, I have to go see my old friend Rachel, who hates me now but might be in danger. She vowed that if she confirmed the Johari were aliens and they really did go home, she'd find a way to let Rachel know.

Chapter 9

OMARA HAD TOLD Earth Control she was taking the refurbished *Endurance* out for a test flight. She simply neglected to mention there was a Teegan Particle Collector and Accelerator on board. Or a captain named Lyn Randall, or a passenger named Dr. Diana Teegan, or the former *Endurance* pilot Anilina Rodriguez. Or an alien named Aurora Parula. She told EC she would pilot the ship herself, with the capable assistance of her AI Petra and Dr. Amos.

Lyn toured the ship with Omara, refamiliarizing herself. TPCA sat in the port launch tube on *Endurance*'s lowest deck. All she could see were wrapped wires and conduits sticking out from its butt. The business end, she knew, would be deployed outside the ship, where T particles were ferried through the machine and beamed back out. Omara had labeled it a piece of science equipment.

"That's it?" Lyn asked skeptically. "Pretend it's some innocuous scope and EC will buy that?"

"Earth Control doesn't physically inspect the ship, not one that's already been to space, so all I had to do was file the proper forms."

Lyn rolled her eyes. "You'd think after the *Aphrodite*, built fast and cheap and flimsy, that they'd have learned a lesson."

The machine was the same size as what they'd used before, but the wormhole would be smaller, calibrated carefully using the information Ro had provided for the location of Johar. The distance was farther than to Rigil Kent, but the smaller wormhole size meant less fuel was needed. And with Lyn and her small crew the only passengers, there was plenty of room for the fuel they did need. Over the next week, she watched Diana and Petra conduct the final tests and simulations, relieved not to have to use her brain implant. Dr. Amos reconnected Omara's proprietary mind link through the port behind her left ear. Ani had one too. Diana and Ro were given superficial earbuds.

They boarded *Endurance*, each with a small overnight bag. Lyn and Diana headed to the captain's quarters, Omara to the owner's suite. Ani and Ro took the next two suites on the bridge deck. No cramped crew quarters on this trip. She and Diana changed out of their civvies and into the green and gold Omara Tours flight suits. The captain's suite was off the bridge so they were the first to enter. Familiar, yet new. Lyn hadn't been on anything bigger than a skim in two years. She'd never taken so long between space flights. Even after

Enceladus, she'd gone back after a year. But some things never change. She gripped the railing to steady a sudden dizziness. *Endurance*'s bridge was set on three levels with steep stairs down the sides, never failing to give her a jolt of vertigo on first entering. Lights were low, and a subtle hum pulsed through her hands and feet. The air had a sharp, dry scent of artificial ventilation and outgassing materials. Welcome back, *Endurance* seemed to be saying.

"Captain on the bridge," Petra said.

Lyn startled. "Since when do you announce that?"

"I saw it in a movie."

Petra had changed. Lyn guessed they all had. Then the door to the hallway slid open and Omara, Dr. Amos, Ani, and Ro entered. Petra was silent.

"Owner on the bridge," Lyn called out, to a confused look from Omara.

"What do you think?" Omara asked as they stepped down to the command level, the others continuing down to helm and communications. Omara took the first officer's chair.

Lyn settled in the captain's. She rubbed the armrest, bounced a little in the seat, then leaned back and crossed her legs. "Feels like old times." She frowned at the holoscreens on the walls and ceiling. "Still no windows."

Omara tsked. She pushed a button on Lyn's console and the screens folded up into compartments, revealing a beautiful window straight ahead and wrapping around the sides. Lyn looked up. There was even one in the ceiling.

"I always pay attention to feedback," Omara deadpanned with a barely suppressed grin.

"I love it," Lyn said with a clap.

Ani gave a hoot from helm. "This'll save a lot of time when we go bonkers."

Ro turned to Lyn, alarmed. "Bonkers?"

Lyn explained how the lack of windows complicated regaining control of the spinning craft after they'd been shot through the wormhole to Rigil Kent. "I have no intention of us going bonkers. But yes, it's a nice safety feature."

Ani ran her hand over the controls. "I didn't think I missed this, but it's good to be back." Wordlessly, she motioned for Ro to take the seat beside her then showed her how to activate the hood that turned into a helmet, faceplate stiffening. Ro immediately poked the faceplate, trying to adjust her glasses. She laughed. Ani didn't. Lyn watched Ani's tight expression. She showed Ro the communications panels, what she'd need to do. The tension oozed off of her, but probably only Lyn noticed. Any success Ro had on this mission meant doom to Ani's relationship with Ruzena. She was being professional. And that was as far as it would go.

Dr. Amos and Diana sat on the lowest level. Once everyone was settled they ran a simulation for Ro's benefit, and Lyn explained that Petra would run the machine but was prepared to abort the comtunnel if the Johari proved malicious.

"I'm sure that won't be necessary," Ro said.

"What if they open a wormhole and try to abduct us?" Petra asked.

"Not going to happen," Ro said with frustration.

"But you understand why we're concerned," Lyn said.

"I get it. I've studied you enough to know you're capable of the worst kinds of behavior, but all I can say is that we're not like that."

"We have no weapons," Omara said.

Lyn leaned toward Ro, looming over her from the higher level. "If anything goes sideways, trust me, I'll destroy *Endurance* and all of us with it before I'll let the Johari or anyone do anything that would harm Earth."

Ani looked a bit sick.

"I understand," Ro said a bit shakily. "Believe me, it won't be necessary."

They ran through checklists and practiced the takeoff and landing procedures. When Lyn was satisfied, Omara engaged the tractor that pulled *Endurance* out of its cave and into the heat and light of the Nevada desert. Lyn let out a murmur of appreciation as she watched through the windows the massive hangar doors opening and light streaming in. They stopped at a wide, level plain and the tractor disengaged. As long as they worked with Earth Control, Omara said, they could take off from Ruby Valley, which was far enough away from commercial traffic to pose no danger. Her flight plan called for *Endurance* to orbit Earth several times while running tests then head to the moon. Once she was on the far side, her plan indicated she would simulate various emergencies and requested flight silence. Earth Control had naïvely agreed. At this point they could aim and open the comtunnel. There wouldn't be anything for anyone outside the ship to see should someone happen by.

Looked great on paper, Lyn joked. Her knee bounced. Ani stroked her console like trying to calm a skittish cat. Ro kept trying to scratch her face or head through the helmet. Diana sat still as a cornered mouse. Even seasoned veterans got nervous and this launch would be one for the record books if it could ever appear in one.

First contact.

"All systems go, *Endurance*. Take off when ready," said the Earth Control Traffic Rep in the dull-as-dust tone of the bureaucracy. Such a letdown. Scream to the sky that we're about to meet aliens! Omara acknowledged EC while Lyn reined in her imagination and gave Ani the order to initiate liftoff.

Ani extended *Endurance*'s wings then fired the thrusters and *Endurance* rose slowly. When they reached altitude, she switched to the main engines and *Endurance* roared to life, a beast unleashed, the rumble vibrating through the ship and their seats. A wild mustang leaping the paddock fence back in Montana, little Lynnie clinging to her bare back, galloping across the prairie. G forces crushed them into their seats. Lyn loved this part. The growl of the engines rattling her body. Sheer power, knowing that if disaster occurred now, it would be *spectacular*. They shot up through the atmosphere, leaving Earth's gravity to dwindle to micro amounts.

"One hundred kilometers," Petra said.

A few minutes later, Ani said, "Main engine cut off, 185 kilometers, initial orbital altitude achieved." She retracted the wings. They wouldn't be needed again till they landed, after making history.

The forces suddenly stopped, and Lyn's insides surged like they'd come loose and were still rising. Petra switched on artificial gravity and Lyn's stomach eased back into place.

"It is safe to remove your helmets," Dr. Amos reported.

Lyn loosened her grip on the armrests and unzipped her helmet. Petra initiated the previously recorded sequence of "tests."

Dr. Amos turned to Ro. "Do you require assistance?"

She looked at him with surprise.

"Our suits send biometric data to him," Lyn said. "Something must be off."

"Correct," the doctor said. "Your heartrate and breathing are elevated. I'm guessing you've had a shot of stress hormones. I can adjust if you like."

Ro smiled wanly, more like a grimace. "That won't be necessary. I'm a little lightheaded, but I'll be fine. I think."

"I'll monitor and intervene if I sense you are at risk of losing consciousness."

"Welcome to space, Ro," Lyn said with a reassuring smile. Her own first trip had been eye opening after several simulated runs at the Aerospace Academy had led her to think it would be anticlimactic. Nothing compared to the real thing. She couldn't imagine what it must be like for a first timer.

After a couple hours of orbiting, during which *Endurance* performed a series of rolls, turns, slowing and speeding, all designed to assure Earth Control, and Omara, that the ship was sound, Ani initiated a thrust that would send them toward the moon.

"Shall we eat?" Omara suggested, like she was hosting guests in her home.

They left Petra and the doctor in charge and went to the dining room, restored to what Lyn remembered. Round banquette tables lined the two long walls, one wall filled with windows. She stopped at the end of the captain's table, jolted to realize they were the only passengers. She'd half expected to see Miriam leaning in the doorway to the kitchen. They sat around her table, and server bots skimmed out from the galley, holding trays laden with soups, salads, and appetizers.

"You didn't sneak a chef on board, did you?" Lyn asked Omara.

Omara snapped open her napkin and spread it on her lap. "No, sadly, you wouldn't let me. But I made sure we were stocked with a robust menu of prepared foods. The bots only need to heat them up."

Ro asked how long it would take to get to the moon, and Omara explained it took only a few minutes at full speed. She wanted time to eat. "So, we're puttering."

The meal began quietly, the soft clink of forks on plates. Omara asked a few light questions of Ro, what she thought of her first flight. Ro answered in short, crisp replies. Ani poured wine. As the conversation lagged, Lyn wished Sharyn was aboard. The Queen of Small Talk, she'd have them chatting and laughing and . . . well, maybe not, given the solemnity of their mission. It was up to her, oh captain. She reached for her wine glass, a slight tremor evident, and put her hand in her lap, catching Diana's look, no mind link needed to see the concern. It wasn't too late to order Petra to reverse course and return to Earth. She could abort the whole mission and no one on her team would bat an eye, except Ro, of course.

Ro asked polite questions about piloting, and Ani answered perfunctorily. Not mentioned was how Ro felt about potentially leaving Earth forever, nor did Ani mention her girlfriend might be among them.

As *Endurance* sped toward the moon, they sped toward the moment that would change the world, the entire past and future of humankind. Despite the long history of UFO sightings and tales of alien abductions fueled by the entertainment industry, no one had ever proven they'd met intelligent extraterrestrials. No secret alien crash sites, no government Men in Black withholding secrets. To be sitting at dinner with an alien, going to meet other aliens, simply sat outside the realm of possibility. This wasn't how it was supposed to happen.

Lyn's knee bounced. She cleared her throat, rusty manners creaking into place. What was a safe topic? The thing about space was, you couldn't talk about the weather.

Diana complimented the food. Bless you, my love, Lyn thought but did not send through the link. They were on to the main course, a spiced lamb pie. Omara said she'd found the recipe in a Johari cookbook. "So many of the recipes call for lamb, I wondered why."

Ro said that goats and sheep were the prime livestock of Johari farmers. "We get leather and wool, food and weed control."

"Weed control?" Omara asked.

"Instead of herbicides, we let the goats take care of invasive weeds. They're really good at it, we even rent them out."

Lyn made a mental note to talk to Cooper about goats. How could she initiate a partnership with the Johari without having to answer how she made the connection? Well, Diana and Antonia . . .

Ro asked Lyn about her job. Pulled out of her momentary revery of restoration work, she gratefully launched into a brief history of the family business. They compared techniques. The Johari were good at conserving water for their crops yet didn't use Recyc-Alls. Lyn asked for advice on reintroducing beavers. The biologist at RR had ruled them out for the Wheatland County project because there was no existing surface water to let the beavers dam.

Ro agreed. "You do need an existing source to protect. Maybe start with an artificial dam. Then, when the only water comes from occasional downpours, keeping it on the land rather than flowing away is key."

Ani perked up and described laying down seed and reconstituted soils. The discussion became more natural and relaxed. Lyn's knee stilled. Diana looked bored. Omara listened politely.

During dessert, Petra pinged Lyn through her link. *We've entered moon orbit.*

Lyn set her spoon down and wiped her mouth. "Showtime, folks. We've arrived at the moon." Omara's good food sat like a lump in her gut.

They headed back to the bridge.

"I see everyone is a bit more tense now," Dr. Amos said as he relinquished the captain's chair to Lyn.

"Petra, let's begin when you're ready," Lyn said.

"I'm always ready," Petra replied.

"Such a comic," Omara said.

"Are *you* ready?" Petra asked.

Lyn checked that everyone had fastened their harnesses. "Looks like it."

"Disengaging gravity," Petra said.

Lyn's stomach protested. Maybe a big meal wasn't such a good idea.

"Ready on your mark, Captain."

Captain. Back in that role she'd been so anxious to shed. Now there was a comfort to it. Stress too. There was nothing safe and familiar about opening a wormhole, no matter how small. "Engage TPCA."

"Beam engaged," Petra said, as if this wasn't unusual.

They all stared at the main viewscreen, but there was nothing to see because the particles didn't react with light.

"All measurements normal," Petra said. "Fuel lines operating within parameters."

A tiny disk of distortion appeared in front of them, magnified on the viewscreen. The star field beyond rippled, like a pebble dropped into a vast, still lake.

"There," Diana said. "That's the portal."

"Ready your message, Ms. Parula," Lyn said. "Petra will tell you when to hit send."

Ro reached toward the console with a shaking hand. She'd already loaded the code into the com system. She was about to contact long-lost relatives, and who knew how they'd react. Unless her nerves were from a more malicious source. Too late to worry about that.

"Portal open," Petra said. "Please send the message, Ms. Parula."

Ro hit a button and peered up at the screen.

"Portal closed," Petra said.

Ro sat back. "What happened?" She swiveled to face Lyn. "Did it work?"

Petra responded, "The message was sent."

"That's it?" Ro turned back to the main viewscreen. Normal space. That's all they could see. "Not very dramatic."

Petra restored gravity and Lyn's stomach settled. "The bigger wormhole for an actual traverse is much more dramatic. Now we wait for a reply."

What they were waiting for was the question. They'd gone over it in the testing and simulation they'd run for Ro. The way Ro explained it, once the message was received, the Johari would open a new wormhole from their end. It sounded so . . . normal when it was anything but. Fold space, poke a hole through, and send a message. Even a tiny comtunnel was an extraordinary technological achievement. Ro assumed the return message from the Johari would arrive like an ordinary hail, just encrypted. Background noise to anyone else who might be within range, but Petra was tuned to recognize the signature.

For the first hour, they stayed in their seats, chatting quietly, watching their instruments. For the second hour, they got up and moved around. It seemed important to remain on the bridge, though that was hardly necessary.

Then Petra announced they were being hailed and everyone perked up.

"Is it the Johari?" Lyn asked.

"No," Petra responded. "It's from Earth Control."

"Let's keep our cool, everyone," Lyn said. She linked to Omara. *How do you want to handle this?*

Let's get you all out of camera view if it comes to that. I've dealt with EC enough to know this isn't unusual. So much for flight silence.

Lyn motioned for Ani and Ro to join her down on the lowest level with Diana. Dr. Amos took Ani's seat at helm, Omara moved to the captain's chair. "Answer the hail," Omara told Petra.

"An audio message coming through," Petra said.

"Greetings *Endurance*. Welcome back to space. Is everything okay?"

It was a male voice, and Lyn didn't recognize him, so not Jill Faber.

"Thank you, Earth Control," Omara said. "I'm quite excited to be back, and *Endurance* is performing beautifully. I did request flight silence so I could simulate emergencies. Is that a problem?"

There was a pause before EC answered. "Apologies. Let us know if you need anything. Wouldn't want anything to happen to *Endurance* after all. EC out."

"Com link is secure," Petra said. Meaning no one was listening in.

"That was interesting," Lyn said. "Probably not surprising that *Endurance* would be high-profile, even without the famed Captain Randall on board. Just know that."

Privately, Lyn linked to Omara. *This makes me nervous. Let's get the TPCA data deleted from Petra. She doesn't need to know how to build the machine anymore.*

Omara and Petra agreed, and they went back to waiting. At the end of the third hour, they took bathroom breaks and Omara sent a bot up from the kitchen with snacks.

Then Petra announced they were being hailed and everyone stilled.

"Someone from Earth?" Lyn asked.

"No," Petra said. "This is the encrypted hail. Visual requested."

This was it, then. Time to face the future. Still focused on that earlier call from Earth Control, Lyn linked to Omara. *Could this be a trap? Maybe EC?*

Let's play musical chairs again, just in case.

Lyn let the others know and they resumed positions.

Omara gave the command. "Let's see who's there."

Chapter 10

LYN CRANED HER neck from a seat she'd never sat in for any length of time until this trip. Diana rested a hand on her shoulder, Ani leaned in from the other side. The angle distorted the image. She recognized Omara in the small corner view but other faces stretched absurdly. Still, they looked like people. Human people. Eyes, noses, mouths. Lyn was struck with the thought that she very much wanted Rachel to be there with them. *See? This is what you were so afraid of?*

There were three of them, sitting at a table. Every detail shot through Lyn's senses like a bulletin—they have tables! They wear clothing! Though the clothing seemed to be a uniform, an unadorned, nondescript gray tunic. She chastised herself. What the hell did she expect?

"Hello," the one in the middle said.

They speak English? Lyn mind linked to Petra. *Are you translating?*

No, Petra replied.

Omara stood but didn't say anything. She glanced down at Ro who was equally awestruck, gazing at the screen. They hadn't rehearsed this, Omara taking the lead. No one seemed to know who should go first.

Lyn raced up the steps to stand by Omara. "Hello. I'm Lyn Randall, captain of the *Endurance*."

Now the undistorted images were more plainly human, and Lyn relaxed. The one on the left had dark brown skin, brown eyes, and green hair either trimmed short or slicked back. She had a round, open face with plump cheeks. The one who had spoken had light skin, pale eyes, and straight shoulder-length blue hair. Her features were more angular, her face thin with planed cheeks. The third had light brown skin, brown eyes, and short, curly red hair. A strong jaw and chin. Ro had said the Johari were a matriarchal society. Presumably that meant these were women. No weapons in sight. That was a relief. Ro sat mesmerized, her hands braced on the console.

"Please confirm your designation," the redhead said. All three gazed around the screen, clearly not sure whom they should be dealing with.

Ro stood and introduced herself. "Principal Investigator Aurora Parula, research designation . . ." She paused. "Forgive me if I'm not pronouncing this correctly." Then she said a string of sounds that weren't words or numbers.

"Close enough," the greenhead said. "I'm . . ." she made an unpronounceable sound, more like a tone. "You can call me Beryl."

The others introduced themselves, again first with a melodic sound, then with an Earth option. Pica was the blue haired in the middle, and Salpin, the redhead.

Lyn introduced the rest of her team as they moved back to their seats within view. "Can you tell us your role? How is it you speak English?"

"Sorry," Ro said, "I could have explained—"

Lyn raised her hand. "Let them tell me."

"We've been studying your planet for almost three hundred of your years," Beryl said. "We've retrieved every language. Before we ended contact, we had determined English to be the dominant language of the Johari on Earth."

"We are the mission managers for the Johari Expedition to Earth," Salpin said. "Beryl is our communications leader, Pica handles operations, and I'm the chief engineer."

"It's good to hear from you," Pica said, addressing Ro. "You used an emergency code. How can we help?"

Lyn sensed a caution on the part of the Johari. Perhaps they were as suspicious of the humans as the reverse. Through the link, she heard Omara ask Petra's opinion of the call. *Could this be faked?*

I can't detect any signal coming from anywhere nearby, Petra said. *There is a spatial abnormality ahead of us, what you'd expect from a wormhole. Tiny gravitational waves. As far as I can tell, this is real.*

Diana and Ani were both staring at the screen a bit slack jawed. Ro, however, looked especially uncomfortable. She was meeting relatives for the first time. Where do you even begin? Her voice shook as she told the Johari about her succession to PI, how the previous one died suddenly. The conversation appeared to go smoothly until Ro informed them that it had been human technology that opened the comtunnel used to send the emergency code, not Johari tech.

Salpin's face showed surprise and her question the same. "These are humans with you, Aurora? Are you the only Johari on board?"

Ro clarified that the other Johari were still on Earth. She told them Lyn and Diana knew how to open a traversable wormhole and had done so to travel four light years safely. The three Johari responded in that most human way, looking at each other then at Lyn and not saying anything.

"It's time for us to end the study and return to Johar," Ro said. "You need to know that humans are capable of interstellar travel."

The news seemed to land with a thud on the trio. There was a lengthy pause, eyes shifting, as though they weren't sure who should respond or how.

Finally, Pica spoke, with an all-too human edge to her voice. "You revealed yourselves to these humans?"

Lyn recoiled at the tone Pica said "these humans" with, like they were scum. Or dangerous. Maybe not wrong there.

"I had no choice. You know there was a terrible war here. We barely survived. Much of our original technology did not."

"We are aware," Beryl said, "and we are glad you survived. It's been difficult not knowing all this time."

"Captain Randall has agreed to help us return," Ro said. "But she can't take all of us and the fuel necessary to open the wormhole. We need to arrange for a Johari tunnel."

Again a pause as they digested this request. Then Salpin said, "That won't be necessary."

"What do you mean?"

"You have informed us. Once you transfer your research, there's no need for you to return to Johar." There was a pronounced lack of emotion in these words, not said as if to offer the Johari a chance to stay on Earth if they preferred. More like a slap.

Ro stepped back, stunned. "What? You're abandoning us?"

Beryl and Pica shared a glance then Beryl dropped her gaze. If there was a hierarchy here, they seemed to defer to Salpin.

"You have been living among humans for centuries," Salpin said. "You have mated with them, your genes mingling. We can't risk you bringing their violence back with you." She sounded cautious, almost fearful.

Wow, harsh, Lyn thought. Omara glanced at her, probably thinking the same thing.

"But we haven't," Ro protested. "We've been very strict about not mixing with humans. Only those who haven't are planning to return."

"Nevertheless, how do we know they won't have an army in wait for the tunnel to open," Pica said. "We could be attacked."

There it was. Fear of the unknown clearly a universal reaction.

"I can assure you," Lyn said, "we've been through this discussion and managed to convince each other that neither poses a threat to the other. I'm committed to keeping this technology out of the hands of anyone who might abuse it."

The three remained quiet, glancing back and forth with each other. Were they communicating internally? Beryl gave a slight nod, of deference or assent, Lyn couldn't tell. Pica sighed heavily. Maybe body language wasn't so alien.

"This is . . . unprecedented," Salpin said. "We would like to consult with our superiors. Can we get back to you?"

Poor Ro was left speechless.

Lyn forced herself to appear calm and not let on how worried she was that Earth Control might butt in again. "We don't have enough fuel to open another comtunnel. We also don't want to draw attention to ourselves."

"How long can you stay where you are?" Beryl asked.

"Maybe another day. Our day. Not sure how that translates."

"We do. We'll try to get back to you before then."

Try? Like simple bureaucratic red tape? Lyn hid her frustration. "We need to know when, so we can be at this meeting point. The orbit changes our position relative to monitoring sites. We can't risk someone seeing what we're doing."

"There isn't anything to 'see,'" Salpin said. "The comtunnel we open is invisible. Look for our hail as you orbit and use your code again to respond. If you don't hear from us in a day . . ." She looked at Ro. "I'm sorry. It is in the contract that return is not guaranteed. I'm prepared to receive your research. Please initiate the transfer—"

"No," Ro said firmly. "I'll decide about the research when you've made your decision."

Beryl and the others went still, only their eyes shifting to the side.

"Very well," Salpin said. The link went dead.

Whatever invisible string had held Ro up was also cut and she dropped like a stone, hitting the edge of her seat then falling to the floor with a dull thud.

Dr. Amos rushed to her. Lyn ordered Ani to resume orbits then she and Omara followed Dr. Amos, who was carrying Ro, down to the medical unit on the lowest deck. He laid her on a bed and ran his hands over her, scanning. She moaned and wept quietly.

"Her biometrics were all over the range during that call," he said. "With no medbots, she wasn't able to regulate her response. Heartrate, blood pressure, cortisol levels," he glanced up, "out the ceiling." He grabbed a jetspray from a cabinet. "This should help. Do I have your permission to treat you?"

"Yes," she said weakly.

He pressed it to her neck, and in a few minutes her breathing calmed, and she sat up.

"What the holy feck was that all about?" Lyn said. "Did you know they'd say that?"

Ro shook her head. "Of course not."

"There's a contract? That lets them abandon you?"

"I haven't been able to find it. I've been PI for less than a year. I didn't get to overlap with Dr. Gallin like I was supposed to."

"She had no deputies, assistants, who would know this stuff and tell you?" She gave Lyn a wild, helpless look. "I was in Nunavut!"

"What else haven't you told us?"

Ro shot Lyn a peeved look. "Oh, maybe three hundred years of research. How the heck do I know what you need to know?"

"Why did you refuse to send over the research?" Omara asked calmly, turning down the intensity of the moment. "Don't you think that will hurt your cause?"

"I—" Ro crossed her arms and stared at the floor. "I thought it might be leverage. The whole point of our being here is to study humans. They're missing the last sixty-seven years of data that includes a world war and realignment of governments. I hope it's critical to them. To understanding humans." She looked up at Lyn and Omara. "You."

Ro would likely pay hell if she had to return to Earth with a refusal based on her throwing what could be perceived as a tantrum. Lyn had to hand it to Aurora Parula. She wouldn't go down without a fight. She apologized for snapping at her.

When Ani and Diana showed up, Omara suggested they all get some rest. "It's been a very long day, and it looks like we'll have a lengthy wait. Petra will alert us to a hail."

Lyn hated to leave Ro, she looked so lost and alone. But Diana put her arm around her shoulder. "Let's go. I'll show you the ship, or you can crash, or we can talk. It's all good." They left Medical together. If any of them knew what a Johari was going through, it'd be Diana.

Later, in the captain's quarters, Diana returned to report Ro was asleep, and she flopped into a chair.

"Did she say anything?" Lyn asked.

"Not much. It was a gamble, refusing the research, she said." Diana seemed distracted. She got up and wandered the suite, picking up random items, none of them personal to Lyn. Artwork, an orchid, old books. A musty volume of Ernest Shackleton's account of his polar exploration on another *Endurance*. She paused at Kai's painting. She hadn't said much about the Johari.

"What are you thinking?" Lyn asked.

Diana turned, a smile forming. "Remember the last time we made love here?"

"You mean the only time." The night before the traverse home, when no one knew for sure if it would work or they might all die, Lyn had shed her obligations as captain, let down her guard. "It didn't look anything like this."

Diana took her hand and pulled her to the bedroom. "Didn't care then, don't care now."

Hours later, Lyn listened to Diana's soft snores. More of a purr, she decided. That first time had been a release of almost two years of pent-up tension. This was similar but tempered by the familiarity that came with time and settled love. How easily they had slipped into each other's lives. Diana no longer defined by grief. Lyn without the mantle of captain. Now freed from the burden of expectation to save the lives of the ship's crew and passengers and get safely home. She was glad Diana was here with her.

Poor Ro. She was the one who bore a responsibility like that of a ship's captain desperate to save her passengers. Life would be simpler for Lyn if the

Johari didn't have to return to their planet, but how disappointing for Ro to think they'd be welcomed only to be spurned.

IN THE MORNING, they all met in the dining room for breakfast. Ani seemed distracted, no doubt thinking about Ruzena, that she might not leave after all. Ro looked a wreck, eyes puffy, face ashen. Lyn asked if there was anything they could do.

"I don't think there is," Ro said, miserably. "If they won't let us return, it's all moot. But at least they know now and can prepare."

Omara picked up the coffee pot. "For what? It seems rather pointless to initiate contact and then shut the door. They won't know what to prepare for." She filled mugs and handed them around. "This strikes me as an opportunity to open a diplomatic dialogue. Even if they take you back, ending communication means they'd lose any warning of humans' discovery of their planet. They might prepare for an Armageddon that never comes. They might vastly underprepare for one that does."

"This is well above my pay grade," Lyn said.

"I'm just the tech geek," Diana said.

"Don't look at me," Ani said.

Omara patted Ro's hand. "Looks like it's up to us."

After breakfast, Lyn, Diana, and Ani left them to their planning and went to check out the view from the Observation Lounge. They climbed the main stairs, restored with holograms of past expeditions lining the walls. Notably, there were none from the Grand Tour, which had well surpassed its name. Saturn and its rings, sure, but nothing of Toliman or Marao. That was one tour that would not be repeated.

As long as whatever Omara and Ro came up with didn't have anything to do with Lyn and the tech, and with it purged from Petra, she was good with whatever they came up with that would get everyone home safely.

"Do you trust Ro?" Diana asked, as they entered the lounge to a beautiful full moon filling the view through the transparent dome overhead. She stopped and stared. "Wow."

"Hard not to," Lyn said, looking up through the dome then down at the new carpet. She was reminded of the time she'd stood here after the dome had been ripped away when the ship hurtled through the wormhole that had felt more like a meat grinder. Only the floor had remained, turned into the outer hull. "Poor thing seems devastated by the possibility of the Johari rejecting them. That doesn't strike me as a necessary component of a nefarious plan."

"Unless that's their point. Confuse us. Then bam!" Ani slammed her fist into her palm.

They leaned back in upholstered chairs and stared up at the craters and plains, research stations and debris piles from past expeditions passing by as they orbited, swiveling like school kids, oohing and ahing. The light side. The dark side. Earth's blue marble rising into view as they circled.

"Think Omara knows what she's getting herself into?" Diana asked.

"Omara knows many things," Lyn said. "At her age, she's seen a lot. I always thought she had more in her than a mere tour operator. She loves space, but she also loves people. Maybe she can help Ro."

"I'm glad she's along for this ride," Diana said. "Let her carry the burden."

"Amen to that," Ani added.

Lyn was dying to ask Ani how she was feeling but didn't know how to bring it up. Diana apparently felt no such constraint.

"I'm fine," Ani said in answer to her question.

"Really. Dating a Johari, who might leave, hasn't affected you at all."

"Maybe she won't leave."

"Mmm hmmm."

Ani sat with her arms crossed, feet together. "We've only been dating three months."

"Okay." Diana left it there.

OVER LUNCH, OMARA and Ro filled the others in on what they'd discussed. A big fat "no" wouldn't require much more than goodbye, have a nice life. But if they said yes, Omara wanted to be ready because they couldn't afford to diddle around for more hours coming up with a plan.

"I left the flight plan open-ended," she said, "but I'd expect Earth Control to get nosy if another day goes by."

They walked through options from a best-case scenario down to, well, it'll work, but not ideal. Then Petra interrupted them and announced a hail. Earth Control again.

"Put them on audio," Omara said, sounding weary and impatient. This time she acted the aggrieved owner. "I'm in the middle of lunch, is there something I can do for you?"

"Just routine," the EC rep said.

"To whom am I speaking?"

"This is Hugh Diaz," the rep said after a suspicious pause.

Omara glanced around. Lyn and the others shook their heads. No one they knew.

"Well, Hugh, all is well here on *Endurance*. If you'll let me get back to my lunch."

"Just checking in, ma'am."

Omara cringed. "Goodbye." She indicated to Petra to cut the link.

"There is a Hugh Diaz on the EC staff list," Petra said.

"Let's hope this truly was routine," Omara said. They went back to their planning.

Three hours later, when Petra announced the Johari hail, everyone gathered back on the bridge. Finally. *Let's get this over with and get out of here.*

The three Johari were joined by another, Quisca. Female, with a gray afro, dark skin, and older, with lines and sags. She introduced herself as the project leader. Together, they formed a kind of hearing committee, maybe judges. Quisca led the proceeding, and the first thing she did was apologize for the abruptness of the last communication ending. "We didn't mean to alarm you, and please know we want to do everything we can to help you. We're in new territory here, not knowing what happened since contact was cut off."

The appeasement seemed to settle Ro, and she willingly answered Quisca's questions, summarizing the last sixty-plus years of research. They were pleased to learn the war had ended and that matriarchal governments had formed with new boundaries and constitutions founded on principles preserving cultures and promoting equity and environmental health. Treaties to ban weapons were signed and holding. Recycling technology, developed during the war to build arms and ammunition, was being used worldwide to restore landscapes, eliminate radioactive contamination, and reduce carbon dioxide levels that had thrown the climate out of whack.

"We're familiar with this technology," Quisca said. "You are aware of its limits, however?"

Lyn explained her family business and that, yes, they knew the resources needed to power the technology were limited. She also knew from harsh experience that repeated recycling tended to break down. "We're hopeful it'll be a bridge technology and that we'll ultimately be able to live sustainably."

"That would be wise," Pica said.

The next round of inquiry concerned how many were interested in returning to Johar. When Ro said six hundred, the committee didn't flinch. They asked how integrated the Earth Johari were with humans. *How much they've screwed around,* Lyn thought, trying not to smirk. Ro explained the strictness of the prohibition against intermingling. Not perfect over three hundred years, but that was why there were only six hundred that qualified to return.

"DNA tests confirm the original markers are untouched," Ro said, cryptically.

Original markers? Lyn mind linked to Dr. Amos. *Does that make sense?*

I'd have to look again, he responded.

Beryl looked down, as though jotting notes off camera.

The questions dragged on, and Lyn grew increasingly anxious because *Endurance* had been sitting stationary and the moon had moved away, potentially alerting Earth Control of the ship's suspicious activity.

Then Quisca brought Lyn's attention to sharp focus. For Earth's part, Quisca said, Lyn must agree to destroy all trace of the wormhole technology—data and actual machine.

"That presents a complication," Lyn said, explaining how the data was embedded in her brain through an implant that couldn't be removed, which Dr. Amos confirmed.

"Can you send me your medical details?" Quisca asked.

Dr. Amos sent them over. Beryl read for a few minutes. "We might be able to remove them here. If you want."

"Really?" Lyn said. "If there's a way to safely get this out of my brain, I'd welcome that. But I'd need to think about it."

"I'll send over medical specifications of our own," Quisca said, "for your doctor to review."

"Regardless of whether you can remove it or not," Lyn said, "or I choose not to undergo the procedure, you should know that others on Earth are working on the technology. They don't have the data they need so there's no telling how long it might take, but it will happen someday."

The last thing Lyn wanted was to bring a ship full of people out into space and have the deal fall through over the data in her head.

"We understand," Quisca said.

"If I may," Omara said, standing, "I wonder if you have considered an ongoing relationship with Earth. I could facilitate that."

Bold, that Omara. She'd dismissed Lyn's concern earlier about what the heads of Earth's governments would think of a rogue diplomat.

Quisca considered this. "Earth has not yet made contact with other worlds. What experience do you have?"

Omara smiled as if to say, oh, let me count the ways. "Sometimes the different factions on Earth are like completely different worlds. We've come a long way in learning to understand each other and work together. Given the similarities between humans and Johari, as I understand them, I think there's a distinct possibility we're not so distantly related and can find common ground. At the very least, keeping a line of communication open rather than shutting off and pretending each other doesn't exist could prove beneficial. Why did you undertake this study in the first place?"

"We were curious and hope to one day understand our origins." Not surprising, but then Quisca went on. "When our ancestors arrived on our planet, stories passed down through the ages of another group, sent to another planet. We've wondered over millennia whether this was myth or reality and have been searching for our planet of origin and for our long-lost cousins."

Lyn shot a look between Ro and Quisca. This was news.

"At first we thought Earth might be it," Quisca continued, unaware of the jolt she'd delivered. "The similar genetics spoke to a close relationship. But we retained knowledge of the technology used to reach our planet. We have remnants of our original ship. You don't. What happened to it? Did those early colonizers somehow lose the technology or did they reject it?"

Lyn reeled from this confirmation of Dr. Amos's speculation when he examined the DNA. "Do you mean you *know* there's another planet out there somewhere with our common ancestors?"

"It's not theory?" Ro asked. She turned to Lyn. "I thought it was a theory, not a fact." The flash of a grimace on Ro's face told Lyn she might be silently cursing Quisca for spilling these particular beans. Lyn glared at her.

"If there is, we haven't found it," Quisca said. "If you are the other group, we haven't been able to figure out why you weren't aware of this history." She looked at the faces before her, the gobsmacked humans and sweating Ro. "Aurora, is that not your understanding? I assumed you'd have shared—" Quisca stopped. "I see."

Never assume should apply to Johari as well as humans.

"I—I've been PI for less than a year," Ro said. "I haven't had a chance to go through all the material. And we lost so much over the years. I'm not sure . . ."

Omara stepped in. "Regardless, we too seek to understand the universe and all its mysteries, including how we got here and, perhaps, why. Wouldn't a collaboration be helpful?"

Quisca tipped her head in agreement. "Let us discuss what we've learned. Are you able to remain available for another hour?"

Omara looked to Lyn.

"Yes." Inwardly Lyn groaned. Clearly, bureaucracies weren't unique to humans.

"We'll be in touch."

Everyone let out audible breaths, even, it seemed, Dr. Amos and Petra. A tense silence followed, and Ro didn't move a muscle.

"We need to talk," Lyn said, no mistaking her tone or to whom it was directed.

Ro swiveled in her seat to face Lyn. "I didn't grow up on Johar." She sounded like a whiny teenager in one of Diana's classes. "I never heard those stories."

Lyn let the tension sit there. Sometimes saying nothing was the best pry bar. Sure enough, Ro caved.

"I did say that was our theory." She sounded sure, defiant almost. "But yes, the story we pass down is of a planet of origin and that we've been searching for it. But so many of our stories are told as fables, I wasn't sure it was true enough to admit to you. Do you really think some guy named Noah was told by God to build a boat big enough to carry all the animals and his family?"

"This isn't about stories or fables," Lyn said through a tense jaw. "This is about honesty and trust. You convinced me to risk everything to help you. If that was based on a lie, what else is?"

"If I may," Omara interjected. "I think we should use this time to eat. I for one am starving. I'm guessing we all could use a blood-sugar boost."

Ro, momentarily rescued, relaxed back in her seat while Omara took food orders and sent for bots to deliver.

Lyn stewed quietly.

THE NEXT CALL was Beryl alone. That didn't seem promising. Her warm smile could be either good news or an attempt to cushion a blow. She began with the usual preliminaries—thank you for contacting us, we take your request very seriously. If Lyn had any doubts humans and Johari were related, it was dispelled right there.

Finally, Beryl leaned forward. "There are a lot of details to clarify, but we've accepted your request to return."

Ro swayed slightly, like she might faint again. Dr. Amos even moved closer as if to catch her. But she rallied, her "Thank you" coming out as a whisper.

To Omara, Beryl said, "We're also intrigued by your offer to serve as an ambassador. Do you carry credentials from your government?"

"I'm acting independently," Omara said without so much as a twinge of hesitancy. "I'll work out how to include Earth's governments."

A shiver ran through Lyn, reality sinking in. She listened carefully as Petra, Ro, and Beryl discussed logistics. Life as she knew it was about to change. But then the mundane kicked in. It soon became clear that different names would be useful for the parties—referring to Earth Johari and Johar Johari quickly became cumbersome, and referring to the planet as Johar presented problems for the Johari who would remain on Earth.

"A closer pronunciation of our planet in your language isn't much more than a 'gaah,'" Beryl said. "How about Gaia for our planet, Gaians for our people, and Johari for the Earth descendants. You are familiar with the term relating to the planet behaving as a self-regulating organism. We have come to the same conclusion about our planet. Too bad the humans didn't take that more to heart."

Ro agreed, and Lyn accepted the not-so-subtle dig at humans' mismanagement of Earth. Her curiosity also piqued to learn more about how Gaia differed from Earth, if they had managed not to trash the place. And, more important, how.

Next, given Lyn's calculation of the prime planetary alignments, they decided that beginning on October 30, the earliest Omara and Ro figured they could be ready, the Gaians would begin sending encrypted com signals to a set point at the opposite side of the sun from Earth. If *Tenacity* wasn't there to receive and decode the signal, the Gaians would wait three days and try again. This would continue until November 17 when it would become a daily signal—the opening of the best alignment window. If *Tenacity* did not respond by December 1, the Gaians would discontinue signals and assume the meeting would not happen. At this point, Beryl said, they'd be forced to return to silence—permanently.

If *Tenacity* did reply to the signal, the Gaians would open a comtunnel to confirm the identity of those on the ship, that their intentions remained peaceful, and arrange the time and placement of the traversable wormhole. They didn't dare send a Gaian ship into Earth space, so *Tenacity* would be allowed to enter Gaian space and the Johari passengers transferred to another ship.

"Once the wormhole closes, no one would be able to detect the transfer," Beryl said.

"We will have to account for *Tenacity*'s disappearance," Lyn said. She didn't mention that ships disappearing from Earth's solar system tended to cause a stir.

"I'll work on that," Omara said.

Omara would be permitted to meet with Gaian leadership and arrange for diplomatic relations. No humans would be allowed permanent admittance to Gaia, nor Johari-human mixes. Pure descendants only.

If things went well, that might be allowed to change, Beryl said. "You'd be welcome to visit the planet, but of course you'd need to remain in biosuits or be inoculated, as would all Johari until they acclimate to Gaia's microbes."

Dr. Amos agreed to transfer over Earth's medical database so the Gaians could prepare immunizations necessary to integrate the Johari to the planet's microbiome. Petra made that transfer while they continued talking.

Once everyone was satisfied, Beryl addressed Ro. "I want to thank you for your service to this research, and please know we'll do everything we can to ensure you and your colleagues can return safely. Our caution earlier was unfortunately necessary but not intended to be taken as any ingratitude for your sacrifice. I'm sure you'll miss much about Earth, and we very much want to make you feel welcome on Gaia."

Ro wiped her cheek. Had she been crying? Lyn didn't have a good view, sitting behind her.

"Thank you," Ro said.

"Good luck with your preparations," Beryl said. "If there's nothing else . . . until we . . . meet!"

Omara thanked her. The link went out.

No one said anything. No one moved. Lyn's head hurt. Not from her brain implant, but from sheer, utter shock sinking in. She'd spoken to aliens. She planned to *meet* with aliens! This was exactly what Rachel had told her the original intercepted message said—"They wanted to *meet* with us." No kidding. But from a completely opposite frame of reference. Not to attack, not to colonize, but to help their own people. She imagined Cooper on Monday asking how her vacation was. An exhale turned into a giggle. It was ridiculous. Ridiculously funny for some reason. Her giggle grew to an uncontrollable laugh. It became contagious and Ro joined her, whooping with delight. Diana swirled in her seat, even Omara let out a chuckle then touched Lyn's arm. "Are you okay?"

Lyn bent over, gasping for air. When she sat up the others had quieted and were watching her, except for Ani who remained motionless at helm, back to her. *Feck.* A solemn quiet returned to the bridge.

"I'm sorry," she said to Ani, to everyone. "Set a course for home, Ani. Initiate when ready."

"Aye, Captain," she said quietly.

On the way back, they destroyed TPCA, dismantling and running it through the Recyc-All. With the machine's plans already deleted from Petra's memory, Lyn remained the last holder of the secret. Over a quick dinner—no puttering this time—they toasted the successful mission and Omara reported to Earth Control *Endurance* had passed several tests with flying colors. It was well past midnight, they'd been up for hours, but no one could sleep. They chattered inanely, mundane tasks handed out. The historic nature of their trip unspoken but on their minds. Not only for Earth, but galactic. The end to *Endurance*'s test flight was routine. With wings deployed, the ship glided in a wide circle over the western Alliance states till Ruby Valley came into view. Ani set the ship down gently near Omara's home. She offered to take Ro back to Mill Creek. She was heading there anyway, she said, and Lyn felt for her. Either her heart would be broken or Ruzena's family torn apart. And Diana would lose her last link to Rose.

Chapter II

WITH TWO DAYS left to Lyn's "vacation," sorting laundry took on a new level of ordinary.

"Doesn't feel real, does it?" Diana said as they sat down to lunch. "Forty-eight hours ago we were talking to aliens. Today I'm reviewing the list of students for the new year. Looks like a good class of kids."

"Any Johari?"

Diana snorted a laugh. "Wouldn't that be something." She poked at her salad. "Are you serious about letting them operate on your brain?"

"Operate makes it sound icky and invasive."

"You have no idea what their procedure would be."

"I know. And no, I wouldn't let them break open my skull, but the idea of getting this implant out of me is extremely tempting."

"What if it's the only thing I find attractive about you?"

Lyn tossed a piece of carrot at her. "You only love me for my mind!"

Diana retrieved the carrot and tossed it back. "Too bad you can't add any of this to your memoir."

"Who says I'm writing one?"

"Speaking of, we got a notice to pick up a package at the Post Store. From Zoya, so I imagine it's her book."

"In print? Not electronic?"

"Must be. I can't remember the last time I read a book in print."

"I think I'm with Sharyn," Lyn said. "Not sure I'm ready to revisit that saga, but her take should be interesting. I wish I could tell her about this unfolding saga. I'd promised her I would let her know if I ever did this again."

"She's a hundred and thirty-four. I don't think she expects to go along. You can tell her after."

LYN RETURNED TO work with lots on her mind and more on her plate. At the staff meeting, Cooper whistled and asked who this stranger was. She sneered. Older brothers. But there were new staff members at the table, two biologists and a soil scientist, so she did feel a bit of a stranger. Her father read through a list of upcoming projects. Two more missile silos had been cleared of radioactivity north of Great Falls. Jephson looked around the table. "Anyone want this?"

Lyn was relieved when Cagle raised his hand. She didn't want to take on any more projects till she was caught up. He briefed Cagle on the goals then they circled the table for updates. Fúlli had taken over Lyn's projects while she was on vacation, and she listened as ne filled her in on their status, grateful to learn all of them were now on schedule. This despite the fact that four pump jacks had broken down, none by Antigen, thankfully. Guess she wasn't missed.

Sarah reported that a mass grave had been discovered outside of Panguitch, so the Utah team had halted work on that project until local authorities could assess the site. Ani was headed to Missouri for a week of seeding.

After the meeting, Lyn accompanied Ani out to the hangars, curious how Ruzena had reacted. Ani admitted it was a lot to process. "I couldn't stay, not after bringing that news. I knew the place would blow up once Ro made her announcement that they could go back. Ruzena has to decide on her own. It won't do any good to have me breathing down her neck."

Ani loved her job, she loved Ruzena. Lyn hadn't seen her happier, maybe ever. Now she could lose Ruzena. "Are you two that serious?"

"I'm not sure it's about me, but I do really like her, and I'm crushed to think she might leave. It's not like a long-distance relationship is an option. She has family who will go, I have family here. I can't imagine—" She stopped and huffed out a laugh. "Wait, actually, I *can* imagine what it would feel like to never see my family again. I would never ask her to do that."

"Plenty of people left homes and families throughout history, never knowing if they'd see them again. It's how this land was overrun by Europeans, after all."

"But they could write, take a ship back home for a visit, send money so family could join them." She looked to the sky. "That's not possible here." Her voice caught.

Lyn rubbed her arm. "Maybe it will be. I'm sorry I was so mean to her. I only did it to protect—"

"Hey, if you hadn't, she wouldn't have been upset, and I wouldn't have felt sorry for her. I might never have given her a second thought."

"I'd hate to see you hurt again."

"Comes with the territory, right?"

THE VIDMAIL TITLE was clear: Endurance. The sender also clear: Jill Faber, CEO of Earth Control. Lyn opened it, curious. Omara had purposely not made a fuss about *Endurance*'s return to space and submitted the usual forms as if it were any other ship, so it must have taken the week to work its way to the top. Why would Jill think Lyn had anything to do with *Endurance* at this point? The vid was casual, informal. Jill had noticed the test flight and wanted to know if this meant she might be returning to Omara Tours. "I didn't see you listed on the crew, but it made me think of you, and I'd love to catch up." She suggested lunch. "What's your schedule like next week? I can clear my calendar."

This was not a vague let's get together sometime. A busy CEO clearing her calendar for a former captain who, as far as Earth Control knew, had nothing to do with *Endurance* returning to space meant Jill had something on her mind. As did Lyn. She hadn't been able to find where Rachel was hospitalized. Maybe Jill would know.

She had a project on Lake Ontario, a former nuclear plant contaminated with spent fuel rods that had been bombed during the war. The site had been cleared for Randall Restoration to demolish and recycle the buildings and restore the lakeshore habitat. A site visit would give her an excuse to drop down to Syracuse for lunch.

Jill Faber met her in the lobby and greeted her warmly. When they shook hands, Lyn realized she could look Jill in the eye. She always thought of Captain Faber as much taller. Rather than go up to her office, Jill suggested they go for a walk. "I know a nice little lunch spot not far from here. I get tired of constant air conditioning, and I could use the exercise."

They stepped out the front door, like walking into hot, damp wool. The air was suffocatingly humid, the heat index had to be approaching dangerous levels.

"You up for this?" Jill asked.

Lyn inhaled what felt like mud. "It's just another day at work for me. Maybe more humid than I'm used to. I'm fine."

The streets were deserted despite the noon hour. A sign flashed on a bank across the street, "100° F, but feels like 120°," it said. "Limit outdoor activity, stay hydrated."

Around the corner from Earth Control's fancy glass tower and down a couple of blocks, Jill led her into a narrow alley between ancient brick buildings. The shade made it slightly cooler, but the smells from the backside of restaurants were thick and nauseating. At the far end they went down a short stairway. Jill knocked once and entered. They were in a restaurant's kitchen. A busy one at that. She greeted the workers who clearly knew her and led Lyn through the swinging door to the dining room and took a booth near the kitchen, next to a window looking out onto the empty street. Tall seatbacks gave it almost complete privacy. A woman immediately showed up with two glasses of water.

"How you doin' today, hon," she said, like she said it to everyone.

Jill introduced Lyn to Onyx, the owner and, it seemed, personal waitress. She smiled as she set down the glasses. "Need a minute?"

Jill said she'd have the usual, but Lyn hadn't been there before. Onyx rattled off a list of specials. She ordered a soup and sandwich.

"You got it." Onyx left, and the room went silent. Not the room. Lyn could see across to a lunch counter where people bustled about, talking and clanking dishes, waitresses slammed through the door beside her, but she didn't hear a thing. She gave Jill a questioning look.

"Privacy setting. A perk of working in the nation's capital where lots of folks want to be able to speak freely."

"I'm impressed." Whatever Jill wanted to say, she wanted it private, and her office wasn't good enough.

They made small talk till the food arrived. Lyn asked about her kids. Her oldest would graduate college next year.

"Holy crap. It's been that long?"

Jill laughed. "Youngest wants to be a biologist."

"We need those."

"Nobody wants a space career." She said it like it was a dying profession.

"I didn't want to do my parents' work either. Until recently."

Jill asked about that work, whether her daughter might talk to someone there, see what a career in restoration would be like. Onyx arrived with an armload of plates, breaking the silent barrier as she reached across the table with their dishes. She then returned with a pot of coffee and refilled their water. "Enjoy, gals."

Jill thanked her. Once they had a few bites in the eerie quiet of the busy room, Jill said she had been delighted to see *Endurance* back in space, though disappointed Lyn wasn't listed, nor was any crew. "I bet a lot of your fans are itching to have an *Endurance* experience." She made Omara sound greedy and mercenary.

"A good reason for me not to go. And I doubt Omara would use the tragedy of that trip to drum up business."

Jill said she'd love to see the ship again, if Lyn could arrange it. Lyn reminded her it didn't look anything like it did back in the Pulsar days, making Jill wince.

"You paid a terrible price," Jill said, "and I keep wondering if I could have done something to prevent what happened at Enceladus."

Rachel had made a likewise warm comment about the cost Lyn had paid, but Jill's felt more sincere.

"Only if you knew and didn't say anything would I hold it against you."

"I could have known, if I had been a better politician and not gotten myself exiled to cadet training."

"Then your exile might have saved my life and all those aboard *Endurance*," Lyn said.

"It couldn't save Tara, or the others."

So, Jill carried that burden, even though she'd had nothing to do with the mission. A series of disasters on their way out to Enceladus had left two crew members dead and not enough food or fuel to return. Tara and two others died on Enceladus retrieving material for the Recyc-All, leaving Lyn alone on the ship. Later she learned they were never expected to survive, that Pulsar was counting on the tragedy to close space and give them free rein to prepare for an alien attack.

After they ordered dessert, Jill said, "We detected an abnormality near *Endurance*. Omara claimed it was intentional flight silence, which seems unlikely. I wondered if it was anything like what happened when you were last on the ship."

She dropped this bomb so calmly, surely Jill knew she'd been aboard. Why wasn't she coming out with it? Lyn sipped her coffee. "Since I wasn't there, I could hardly comment. What sort of abnormality? Maybe solar flares?"

Jill gave her a look of disbelief. "Do I need to chat with Omara about how to shield her ships?"

Lyn froze. Radiation, solar flares, coronal mass ejections all were routinely shielded in any ship going to space.

"I didn't think so," Jill continued. "It was a distortion. Can I show you and see if it rings a bell? I'd like to avoid a repeat of what happened before. At any cost. As you can imagine."

"Of course. Send me the file—"

"Oh, I have it right here." She pulled out her com pod, called up a screen, and played a sensor recording. Lyn didn't see anything and said so. "Let me increase the magnification," Jill said.

Then Lyn could see it. Tiny distortions in the background starfield. Shite. The comtunnel?

"I want to hear you say you weren't on board," Jill said. "That you didn't use your gadget to open a wormhole."

Lyn looked her straight in the eye. "I wasn't on board, and I didn't open a wormhole. Will that do?" She leaned in and squinted at the image. "If I didn't know better, I'd say that was heat distortion, like in the desert. I see that a lot in my work."

Jill snapped the image off and tucked her pod back in her pocket. If Jill Faber and Earth Control noticed this "abnormality," Lyn was sure General Hellen Jacana did too. This was bad. Very bad.

"So, nothing like you've seen before?" Jill asked.

"I can't tell from this. Why aren't you grilling Omara?"

"I did. I even requested her flight log. There's nothing there. She claims she didn't notice anything, her sensors don't have a record of anything, her ship's computer doesn't know anything other than a bunch of standard flight tests."

"What makes you think it had anything to do with *Endurance*? Maybe it was General Jacana testing her fancy new wormhole opener."

"*Endurance* was the only ship out there," Jill said after a long pause. She gave Lyn the look that had made her a notorious training captain, as if seeing right into her brain. "I honestly don't give a flying frass if you were there or not, if you did it or not. I just want space to open smoothly with no catastrophes. Don't make my life harder."

"I don't plan to. Is that all you wanted to see me about? We could have done that by vid."

Jill smiled and relaxed. "I do miss you, you know. If you hadn't fled off to Montana, I'd have tried to recruit you for Earth Control. How do you like your work?"

Wouldn't that have been something. To work with Captain Faber as a colleague. She could have stayed grounded. "That would have been the best of both worlds, I suppose. But I like working with my family. Family is important. As are friends." She paused. "Even former friends. I wonder if you have any news of Rachel?"

Jill snorted. "Why on Earth would I have news about her? She's suing me, remember?"

"She's suing Earth Control, not you. You didn't fire her. You trained her too, remember."

"Another failure. Feck, were you my only success?"

"I'm worried about her. You know about Pulsar's implants. I assume you have your own. She looked awful when she gave that press conference and incoherent during an interview. Now she's been hospitalized? What did they do to her?"

Jill fingered a braid behind her left ear, next to the port. "I don't know that anyone's doing anything."

No one had been prosecuted for the deaths on the Enceladus mission. After Lyn exposed Pulsar's true goal to weaponize Saturn's moon, public outrage led to its breakup. The leaders fled like rats, the top executives scrubbed any record of their involvement from annual reports, documents, and archives. You could do that back then. On the steps of that courthouse and in her interview, Rachel had tried to make a statement about protecting Earth from . . . something. Aliens, no doubt. Lyn couldn't protect the Gaians from humans if she couldn't protect Earth from Pulsar. She needed to find out what had been done to Rachel.

"I still know where some bodies are buried," she said.

"I hope that's not literal."

Lyn's expression hardened. "Don't even."

The public record of the Enceladus mission stated that the crew's bodies were lost on the moon. Lyn knew otherwise—she'd been forced to recycle them for fuel to return. It was that or die and with her the truth.

"I'm sorry," Jill said with sincerity. She set down her fork and leaned forward. "I support you in every way."

"I want to live my life in peace and be left alone. If I want to go to space, I'll go to space. If I don't, I won't. I won't let you or Earth Control or anyone tell me how to live my life."

Jill conceded. "Fair enough. What do you want from me? Name it."

"Tell me how I can contact Rachel. I sent messages through her lawyer, but heard nothing back."

Jill sat back, surprised. "Why do you want to contact her?"

"Because I care about her and don't want to see another injustice. Last the news reported, she was taken to a hospital after trying to commit suicide. Where is she?"

"What if I say I don't know?"

"I'd say you know how to find out."

"Well, I can't."

Can't? Or won't.

Can you hear me? Lyn heard Jill's voice in her head, though the woman was sipping her coffee.

The mind link. Not Omara's. Pulsar's. Embedded too deeply to be removed. *Yes*, she messaged back. *Why are you using this?*

Jill finished off her cheesecake and wiped her mouth. She stared out the window. *I wanted to see if it still worked, so we can talk privately.* She gave Lyn the name of a hospital near Boston. *Once you've seen Rachel, let me know. We can meet somewhere, outside, safe. Not here, not in the capital.*

Jill didn't trust anywhere here was safe? Not her office, not this privacy booth. Who could have that kind of access? A general, perhaps. Lyn followed her gaze out the window. "It's been good to see you. I'm glad Earth Control is in your hands. You'll be a good leader for it."

DIANA ARRANGED A visit with her parents for the weekend to follow up on General Jacana's unexpected inquiry, and Lyn would use it as her excuse to go see Rachel. She always enjoyed getting together with the Teegans though it rankled Diana no end. When they'd met, Lyn had no clue Dr. Squires was the daughter of famous physicists. When the truth came out, Diana had raged over how neglected her childhood had been, raised by parents more interested in their research than her. All Lyn had known about them was that after winning a Nobel Prize for finding the Teegan particle, Margaret and Walter Teegan had left their jobs at MIT and dropped from public view. Turned out, once the elder Teegans realized T's potential, they'd buried their data, published superficial research, and left to "pursue other interests." They could have had a long career full of fame and fortune if they'd cashed in on their discovery.

Now, as they flew east, chatting about the elder Teegans, Lyn teased her. "Can you imagine what it was like for them?" She held up her hands, pretending to hold a baby. "'Look, it's not a particle! What do we do with it?'" She laughed, and Diana pretended to be offended.

They lived in Cambridge, Mass., a city that at the end of the war could have been Atlanta, Dresden, or Aleppo. The seat of historic universities, museums, and technology industries had been reduced to rubble but was rebuilt from that rubble. New buildings but the same old academic and intellectual mecca. Their small house was on a tree-lined street between MIT and Harvard, Diana's alma mater.

"They should have moved away," Diana grumbled as she crossed the tidal flats of the Charles River. Lyn looked down on the restored salt marshes that hadn't existed since the 1800s. Not a Randall Restoration project, it was impressive. Rising seas had eroded much of the shoreline but the restored marsh and tidal flow kept flooding to a minimum. The river itself was reduced to a bare trickle thanks to drought.

At the house, Diana didn't bother to ring the bell, just entered and called out for them. This had been her home, after all. Lyn watched with amazement the inner switch that flipped in Diana in their presence. As soon as she walked in the door and hugged her parents, she pampered them. Rebuttoning Margaret's misaligned blouse, tucking wild strands of hair away from her eyes. Then walking through the house, she picked up stray bits of clothing from the floor, straightened books and magazines on the tables. It was so automatic she didn't even pause in her conversation with them. Lyn didn't think she was aware she was doing it. She'd never thought of Diana as a neat freak.

"You don't do this much cleaning at home," she said under her breath. Diana stopped and stared at the dust cloth in her hand as if to say, where'd this come from?

Margaret was an older version of Diana. Dark hair, but long and wild, and blue eyes. Walter was very different. Wiry, like he forgot to eat, and constantly in motion. He had on a short-sleeved shirt that revealed ropy arms and shorts with socks and sandals.

Over dinner and casual updates, Lyn listened for things to worry about. Then Diana got to the point. She'd cautioned Lyn earlier that being polite or hoping they'd get a hint wouldn't fly. They don't get subtlety, she had said.

"Who called you and what did they say exactly?" she opened with.

Her father sighed like this was an old habit, a daughter's interrogation. "We told you, General Jacana called . . . when was it?" He turned to Margaret.

"Early July, maybe?"

"I thought it was more recent."

"You lose track of time. It was July, early. I remember because—"

Diana interrupted. "Not important. What did she say?"

"Don't get all detective with us, missy," her father said but it was with a teasing wag of his finger and a smile. "She asked if she could stop by. She was in town for some meeting."

Lyn and Diana looked at each other. This was more alarming than a call.

"And did she? Come over?" Diana asked.

"Good god, no. The last thing we need here is unexpected company, let alone someone with a security detail and high profile." Margaret looked around the cluttered, dusty room.

"I called her bluff," Walter said with a hint of conspiratorial joy. "I know you're working on that contraption they used on *Endurance*, I told her." He let out a raspy laugh.

"She said she wanted to collaborate, that you were joining her team and thought it'd be great fun if we all worked together." Margaret rolled her eyes in disbelief.

If Lyn ever wished for a mind link to Diana, this was it. General Jacana had to be desperate to be so bold as to lie about Diana's involvement.

"I told her where she could take her team." Margaret pfft wetly through pursed lips, like spitting out something distasteful. "Even if we wanted to, we don't have your research that built on ours, so we'd be starting over. The general doesn't know that, of course, so she's a pain in our side."

"And you haven't heard any more from her since?" Lyn asked.

"Nope. Good riddance, I say," Walter said. "I've had more than my fill of military bullies."

"If they approach you again, see if you can find out how far along they are."

"Uh, no," Diana said with a sharp look to Lyn. She turned to her parents. "Stay as far away from her as you can."

"We're not morons. We've been dealing with this a lot longer than you have. We're not about to give in now." Margaret stood suddenly. "Let me show you the garden. You haven't seen the garden."

"You garden?" Diana asked with incredulity as she followed her mother through the house to the back yard.

Their voices faded down the hallway. "Your father calls it the nanogarden."

Walter hadn't moved from the table, so Lyn stayed behind. He scratched his rough beard. She desperately wanted to ask if he was absolutely sure there wasn't a copy of their research lying around but would leave it to Diana to pry more information out of them if there was any to pry. She let the tension ease. "It must have been exciting, discovering what that particle could do."

Walter looked at her through watery gray eyes. "It was a true eureka moment. Of course, all that research during the war helped. We never would have found it, let alone put it to work without the U.S., China, and Russia trying to find better ways to annihilate people."

They'd been children during the war. Diana said they rarely spoke of that time.

"Within days of the news that we'd found the particle, there was a knock on the door. And those words you really don't want to hear, not after the war ended and we thought things would be different. 'We're here from the government.'" Walter shook his head. "It wasn't the government, though. Pulsar." He looked at Lyn sympathetically. "They wanted to fund our research. We pretended it was very tempting, but it scared the shit out of us."

"When was this?" She knew this part of the story, but now wanted to fill in the gaps, the timeline of how much Pulsar knew then, and how much General Jacana might know now. The group had formed in 2132, and General Jacana had been VP when Lyn left in 2163, but she didn't know how long Jacana had been with the group.

He rubbed a hand over his face and scrubbed fingers through his thinning hair, as if that would trigger a memory. "Let's see . . . '47, I think. Diana was still little." A warm smile softened his features.

Diana's experience as a child might have been one of neglect, but there was no mistaking the love he had for her, that she was his timeline. Some people show it funny. Like her own dad going quiet after Duncan died. She was so young when it happened, she thought he'd always been like that.

"And it wasn't Hellen Jacana then?" She'd probably have been in her fifties.

He shook his head slowly. "I don't think so. I'd have remembered her. She sounds like grinding gears when she moves, those fake legs and arm."

"You turned them down?"

"Oh, hell yeah, but they didn't stop so we did. Published some dubious findings, knowing no one could ever replicate them and moved on to other work."

"But you didn't destroy your data. How'd it end up on that cube Diana had?"

He chuckled. "We're old school. We don't throw away anything. War children, you see. Grow up in deprivation and you learn to hang onto things that might be useful. And it was, wasn't it?" He leaned forward, elbows on the table, and scrutinized Lyn. "You are playing a dangerous game. We saw the war, we saw what Hellen Jacana is capable of."

He got up and without another word stacked the empty plates and went into the kitchen.

They slept in Diana's old bedroom. Rather than preserve it as a shrine to their beloved daughter, it had long ago been turned into a study, more like a storage room, piled with boxes of various machine parts.

"There isn't a TPCA in here, is there?" Lyn asked, peering into a crate with tubes and wires sticking out.

"If there is, no one will ever find it or figure out how to put it together," Diana said.

They cleared space for their sleep sack and lay together by the open window. A breeze brought in the briny smell of low tide. Skims whooshed overhead, recycling trucks rumbled by, picking up the detritus of human living. Dogs barked, coyotes howled. Softer noises from the back. Mice? Rats, more likely. Lights from neighboring houses came on and off as creatures passed detectors.

"Being here always makes me glad to get back to our quiet hideout," Diana said. She turned to the window. "I do miss the ocean, though."

The next morning, Lyn headed off to see Rachel while Diana met up with some friends from her Harvard days.

RATHER THAN FLY her own skim, Lyn disappeared into a crowded public transit to visit a certain former friend who was having a rough time. She'd wanted to keep her visit private, but there was no way to get on the visitor list without going through Rachel's lawyer, who for obvious reasons did not agree to secrecy. The Great Lyn Randall visiting her former nemesis was great PR. Lyn could imagine the headline Mx. Névé would have in mind—The Great Reconciliation!—and what it could do to restore Rachel's reputation. But Lyn would have none of that, so she showed up a day early, ahead of any press coverage. It also ensured Mx. Névé wouldn't be hovering. Because Lyn was on the visitor list, she was able to convince the receptionist that there'd been some mix up and wasn't it better this way—avoiding a media circus. The person shrugged and conceded the point, handing her a visitor pass.

She'd feared Rachel would be a drooling zombie, incoherent and unresponsive. What she found was her old friend, eerily subdued. Rachel sat in a chair by the window, dressed in scrubs, not a demeaning johnnie. The room was typical hospital fare. A bed, a couple of chairs, holoscreen on the wall with a midday talk show, sound muted. She knocked softly and entered. Rachel's expression traveled from blank, to confused, to angry, then a tentative smile.

"Lyn?" she asked, her voice quiet.

Another reason not to conceal her identity. Who knew how Rachel would react?

"Yes, hi," Lyn answered carefully.

Rachel blinked, like she was trying to clear her thoughts. She motioned to a chair and Lyn sat.

"I should say it's good to see you," Rachel said through cracked, dry lips.

"I should say you look good," Lyn said.

"But I don't."

"And I bet you aren't glad to see me."

"So, we're even."

Lyn tried the mind-link. *Can you hear me?* Rachel didn't react or respond. So maybe that had been damaged. Too bad. But also a sign that whoever tampered with Rachel knew what to tamper with. Out loud, she said, "I know we've had our differences, but I was worried when I heard you were hospitalized."

Rachel didn't crack her familiar lopsided grin. "Do we? Have differences? I know I know you, but I'm having trouble remembering how."

Shades of Lyn's memory erasing at the hands of Pulsar. A stranger might not be unnerved by Rachel. If she had always been the quiet type, this wouldn't be so remarkable. This was not the Rachel Lyn had known.

"We were friends at the Aerospace Academy. We trained together on *Endurance*." She didn't bother to mention Pulsar.

"On *Endurance*? I thought that was the ship you were stranded on. Where were you again?"

"It's not important. But yes, on *Endurance*." Jeez, what did she ever hope to get out of her? Then she saw bruising and scars on her forearm. Did she or someone inject needles? Drugs? This was wrong, what had been done to her. She'd take the combative, moody Rachel any day over this.

During the debrief after Rigil Kent, Rachel, as head of Earth Control, had hammered Lyn over her vague answers on how they returned. "I can't let you get away with this," she had said. "Everyone knows we're not alone in the universe. A not insignificant segment of the population thought you'd been abducted by aliens. It was all I could do to tamp down worldwide panic."

Rachel had admitted to monitoring space for signs of aliens. "There never would have been a Grand Tour if I'd been in charge of Earth Control back then."

As quickly as she'd blown up, she'd softened her approach, trying to cajole Lyn into working with her. "It'd be like the good old days."

Rachel had even tried to access the information in her implant. The firewall held, unleashing another tirade from Rachel. "Damn you, Lyn. Do you know what you're doing? You think I'm the bad guy, but I'm not. I'm on your side. There are darker forces out there who want this technology."

Rachel could be moody and unpredictable, but now it was clear Lyn wasn't going to learn anything useful. She resigned herself to chatting about mundane topics, like the food and accommodations. Rachel said little, or tossed out phrases that didn't relate. Lyn reminded her of some of the pranks she'd played during their *Endurance* training, but Rachel shrugged, giving her a blank stare. Nothing was getting through. Looking at Rachel now chilled Lyn, her own hand shaking with tremor. She had something they wanted even more than keeping Rachel quiet.

An orderly gave her a five-minute warning. Lyn stood and held out her arms. Maybe Rachel could forget the parts of Lyn she hated and remember the friend she'd once been. Rachel unmuted the show, which blared loud music over the closing credits. Lyn cringed as Rachel rose and went to her embrace.

Clear as a bell and completely lucid, Rachel whispered into Lyn's ear, "Help me." Louder, she said, "Will you visit again?"

Shocked, Lyn looked into Rachel's eyes. Her bewildered expression vanished and they made a visceral connection. They were gripping each other's upper arms. Rachel's right index finger tapped out three times, her left three slower, then her right again. SOS. An almost imperceptible tip of her head to the corner of the room. Lyn flicked a glance and saw a small camera.

"Absolutely," Lyn said, recovering from the shock. "It's good to see you looking better. You'll be well in no time."

The last thing she wanted to do now was leave. She wanted to grab Rachel's hand and run out the door with her. She left the building in a daze. Had the old Rachel broken through long enough to call for help? Or had it all been an act? If so, why?

Chapter 12

LYN DIDN'T DARE contact Jill directly with an obvious message to meet, so she invited her to Crow Fair. For more than two centuries, it had honored natives as an annual gathering held, rain or shine, war or famine, near the Little Bighorn River in the old Crow Reservation. After the United States dissolved, native tribes were given their lands back—to the extent that was possible since many were left with nuclear ravaged wastelands. The Apsáalooke recovered most of southern Montana, and all tribes were welcomed to Crow Fair, a week of dancing, parades, sacred ceremonies, and celebrations. Lyn didn't go every year, but with Fúlli's new status in nir clan, many from the company were going to support nem.

It was also crowded, loud, and far from Syracuse, so it would give her plenty of privacy to find out what Jill knew about Rachel that she couldn't say earlier.

"Bring the family," Lyn said. "Your kids will love it."

"My kids are surly teenagers, they don't love anything. I'll come alone."

A CARAVAN OF company skims flew everyone down the first day of the fair, Jill would arrive on the next. Lyn, her folks, and Cooper helped unload the poles with Fúlli's family but then everyone stepped aside. Hundreds of tipis were being set up around the fairgrounds. This one was special. Fúlli and nir mother, Heather, stepped forward and the two of them arranged the first four poles on the ground. Fúlli carefully lashed them together then pulled a guide rope as Heather lifted the poles and walked them upright. Family members nodded their approval but did not comment or cheer. Lyn imagined that with nir hoverchair, Fúlli could raise the poles right up, but doing it traditionally must have been the plan.

Few words were spoken, they each knew their role. Lyn had made her own tipis as a kid, but clearly there was more to it than poles bracing each other and stretched with a cover. The first poles, she knew, represented the four seasons, set from southeast to southwest and around to northeast. Then they raised more poles, twenty-one in all. To prepare the cover, Fúlli made a ceremony of tying it to the chief pole. Again, Heather raised the pole, while Fúlli pulled on a guide rope. The clean white fabric went on smoothly. Fúlli and Heather circled the tipi, staking the cover firmly to the ground. When they were done and looked at it with satisfaction, the crowd broke into cheers, Fúlli grinning proudly. Lyn could see this tipi was more than a home.

Later, as both families sat around the campfire enjoying a barbeque supper, Fúlli explained how the first four poles represented more than the seasons. "For me, the poles to the north represent health and well-being. The two to the south good fortune and wealth."

Fúlli had been born with no legs, and the family had refused experimental medical treatments. As ne grew, ne'd also refused artificial legs, so Lyn could see how health was a big deal to the young Apsáalooke.

"I take the stories of my family and our ancestors seriously and accept the path I've been shown to help the planet and my people heal," Fúlli said. "The three poles on either side represent that." Ne glanced toward the Randalls. "My job is preparing me to take on the healing of our land."

Fúlli was working toward the day ne could start nir own restoration company to work with tribes. It would be an ambitious undertaking. As she listened, Lyn considered the heavy responsibility before her with the Johari. Fúlli would say the most efficient distance between two points wasn't always a straight line. Each step led to another. She didn't know where the finish was, and had to trust that the end would become clear in time.

THE NEXT MORNING, Jill arrived in time for the parade symbolizing the seasonal movement of the tribes' camps. Some rode horses, others antique cars and skims and, notably, Fúlli in nir fully tricked out hoverchair. After, while everyone else scattered to watch cooking demos and eat, Lyn and Jill retreated to the shaded back row of the stadium, pretending to watch the horse show below. Dressed in jeans, boots, and a cowboy hat, they each looked the part. Still, Jill asked, "You sure we won't be noticed here? A white woman and a Black kind of stick out."

"As long as we're the only ones."

Jill laughed at that. "Keep an eye out for a dark-skinned Maya woman."

That was the heart of it, wasn't it, that a thread tied Rachel and General Jacana together and the two orbited Jill and Lyn. She described her visit with Rachel.

Jill put her feet up on the seat in front of her and relaxed back, watching the rider below take her horse through a series of complicated maneuvers. But she was paying attention. "I feel for Rachel, I really do, but my job is to get space reopened, not worry about her or"—she gave Lyn a pointed look—"whatever tech you have that General Jacana wants. I don't want you using it any more than she does, but I won't interfere, and she's not happy about that."

"Why does she care so much?"

Jill stood to cheer for the horse and rider who had finished the course. Then she sat and scrutinized Lyn as if weighing the cost of what she might reveal. "When I became head of EC last year, she met with me as a routine briefing since EC is supposed to know about any military activities in space. We met in her office—pure Jacana. Even at Pulsar, she always held meetings on her turf. She said she wanted to inform me of a top-secret report and passed me a paper file of a message presumed to be from intelligent aliens."

Lyn kept a straight face, knowing now what that message really was. "'Presumed' being the operative word, I imagine. Haven't there been many such messages over the years? What's significant about this one?"

Jill watched her for several grueling seconds then smiled. "That's exactly what I said."

The difference, the general told Jill, was that this message referred to a meeting. "It was in English."

"Wouldn't that mean it's fake? Would some random extraterrestrial really speak English?"

"You wouldn't think so, would you?"

"You sound like you agree," Lyn said. "What's really going on?"

"Why do you think Rachel's being controlled?"

There. An acknowledgement that her hospital stay, the apparent mind control, was intentional, not medical. Lyn responded carefully. "Not for the loss of the *Aphrodite*. That happened before she was CEO. I think she was scapegoated for that. But she has implants. Maybe they're malfunctioning."

"So why not fix them?" Jill said.

"What do you mean by controlled?" Lyn was getting impatient. Say what you want, Faber.

Another rider entered the arena and the crowd applauded, Jill and Lyn joining in.

"Rachel had told me about the message when we were at Pulsar, and I know she told you," Jill said. "She only told me because I'd trained her on *Endurance*, and she thought I'd be sympathetic to the cause. But you blew the whistle after Enceladus. You caused a stink, so they erased *your* memories and let everyone believe it was a covert operation to beat the Chinese. Am I right?"

She was. "What did you think it meant?"

"I thought it was nonsense. A glitch in the data. It had happened before. An intercepted radio message from some kid in Omaha."

"What does this have to do with anything now?"

"You opened a stable, traversable wormhole. During her press conference, Rachel nearly told the world about the message. If this went public, all hell would break loose."

"Her lawyer was there. Looked like ne was trying to shut her up," Lyn said. "Think Névé is involved?"

Jill shook her head. "I don't know. Maybe trying to control nir client to get the most bang for the PR buck. Saving it for the lawsuit. Névé worked at Pulsar in the legal department, that's nir connection to Rachel."

"I didn't know that. I don't remember nem."

"You don't remember a lot of stuff from then."

True, though most of her memories had been recovered. But not that one. "Go on."

"You know how to travel to distant star systems. General Jacana and whatever remains of Pulsar would like that technology."

"Knew. Past tense." Pretending the data didn't still exist was getting harder. Clearly no one believed she didn't have it. If she hadn't been convinced to let the Gaians remove the implant, this was a good reason. "Oh, for crissakes. Did Jacana recruit you to come after me?"

"Yes."

The bluntness of Jill's answer and that Jacana really did this landed hard. "When?"

"Shortly after *Endurance*'s 'test flight.' I'm guessing Omara was not alone on that ship."

Shite. "What makes Jacana think that?"

Jill's pause meant she understood the lack of denial. "Mine's a guess. She's bound to have more sophisticated surveillance than my bureaucracy that took a week to get the trip up to my level. I'm pretending to go along."

"What does she want you to do?"

"Jacana isn't convinced by your *Endurance* story. She thinks it's entirely possible that you were abducted by the aliens."

"And returned unharmed?"

"*Aphrodite.*"

"Oh, right. That. But nothing would have happened without the explosion that Earth Control, Pulsar, or whoever sanctioned."

"Are you sure that's what caused the wormhole to open?"

"Granted, it's a theory." She couldn't read Jill's expression, she had perfected that military bearing and blank mask. "So why are you pretending?"

Here the mask fell, and Jill leaned forward, elbows on knees, her shoulders slumped. "Give me some credit, Lyn. I left Pulsar because of what they did to you on and after Enceladus. I did what I could after the fact, but people *died.* And for what? So they could beat the Chinese to a blip of a moon they wanted to weaponize for the next war that wouldn't be a world war because it would include the entire solar system." She raised her eyes to the rough, framed ceiling. "What the actual fuck kind of crazy morons would think like that?" She lowered her gaze back to Lyn. "I know Jacana's an untouchable war hero, but I'm warning you because she suspects, and I agree, that all the information about how to open a wormhole is safe and snug right inside your Pulsar-licensed brain implant. She's played nice so far, but don't expect that to last."

Lyn pictured the general charging up the stadium steps, grabbing her by the collar and bashing their implanted brains together. How well could she resist? What if she went for Diana, or her parents? Below, horse and rider galloped full steam across the arena, turned sharply at the end, and the rider reached for a flag stuck in the ground. The crowd roared. She had no idea what the point was, but the rider stood in her stirrups, flag raised in triumph. Jill was watching Lyn, not the action. Getting *Tenacity* to space with six hundred Johari on board would be a hell of a lot easier if she had Jill Faber on her side. "Rachel had a moment of lucidity and asked me to help her. What does she have to do with all this, and is her life in danger?"

"She's a blabbermouth. I think they're squirreling her away to keep her quiet." Jill's eyes were still on Lyn.

"I couldn't tell if she was really ill or faking it. She seemed to barely remember me. How can I help her?"

Jill's mask slipped back into place. She stared straight ahead, not at the horse and rider, but somewhere deep inside. "I saw a lot of myself in Rachel. There are many ways to lose your family at a young age, but the effect is pretty universal. Distrust, anger. Pulsar liked both of those qualities. Until I became a little too honest, pointing out deficits in my commanders' leadership skills. They didn't like that, going against the grain. So I got busted down to cadet training. Then Rachel comes along and I see her heading down a different path, and I couldn't stop it." She blinked, like she remembered Lyn was there. "She could be manipulating you. You should stay away from her. Maybe Jacana got her to go along. Rachel struck me as a true believer."

Pain etched Jill's face, lines that might not be from age, the only hint of the price she'd paid. But maybe Jill was also being manipulative. She let the moment pass. "So, Jacana thinks you are on board. What do we do?"

"Do you trust me?"

"Of course not," Lyn said with an insincere smile.

Jill laughed. "Good."

"If you don't believe the alien message was real, then you don't believe I was abducted by aliens. What do we do about Jacana?"

"I don't know yet. I wanted to warn you to be careful and to know that I'm on your side. Not that I expect you to believe that."

"Which means you don't exactly trust me either," Lyn said.

"Pulsar trained us well. But I can tell you something that might help." Jill glanced around then lowered her voice. "I leaked Pulsar's Enceladus documents to that reporter, Irene Bakewell. I was the anonymous source."

Lyn tensed, stunned. "No way." Her accusations had gone nowhere until Bakewell received those documents. Her investigative reporting, combined with Lyn's testimony, brought down Pulsar.

"You can ask her. No, she'll deny it. I'll let her know it's okay to tell you. That help?"

"Does Jacana know?" Lyn asked.

"No one does. Except you now."

This was huge. If Jacana found out Jill was the leaker, she'd come after her as hard as she was at Rachel and Lyn. "Yeah, that helps. So how can we stay in touch without meeting in hot smelly barns?"

Jill brushed dust off her pants. "Omara has applied to resume space tours. I think it's plausible that I take her on under my own portfolio. Given her company's 'high profile,' she needs 'personal' attention. I've made it my MO to keep my hands in the day-to-day operations. We can send messages through her. Don't even pretend you two aren't in close contact."

Jill had no idea what an asset she could be to Omara Tours. And the Johari. "It doesn't seem like you to trust Omara."

"We have an understanding. Did she ever tell you why she hired you?"

"Not really. Just that I came highly recommended. I was so down and out after Enceladus, I couldn't imagine who'd do that."

Jill didn't say anything but a smile formed from her eyes.

"You. You recommended me?"

"She'd offered me the job, but with a wife and kids, I didn't want to be away from home that much."

"But for the grace of kids, you might be the one who got stranded in Rigil Kent and hailed a hero for returning."

"I thank the stars every night that it wasn't me. I'm not sure I would have been up to the task."

THE END OF August brought the second anniversary of *Endurance*'s return and with it more media attention. With space reopening, Omara began a media blitz of interviews and ads to drum up interest in her tours, which she said would resume with the unveiling of a new ship. Privately, she updated Lyn that *Tenacity* was almost ready. She'd replaced the luxurious suites with small cabins with couches that turned into bunks. Jill Faber had let her know they'd work directly on test flights. Omara then passed on a message that Rachel was to be released from the hospital. "Curiously, Faber wondered if you might have an idea of somewhere she could work. Doesn't that strike you as an odd request?"

It was, after Jill's advice to stay away. But how better to keep an eye on her. "Kind of," Lyn said, "but Rachel and I have a past that was at one time quite pleasant. I'll think about it. Maybe she could clean rooms for Sharyn."

Omara and Ro were also working on how to get the Johari onto *Tenacity* unnoticed. Jill had agreed to let Omara use the old airfield in Las Vegas where *Endurance* had landed for *Tenacity*'s test flights, one of which would be a cover for the real thing. That would simplify boarding. Getting six hundred people to Las Vegas was easier than to the remote Ruby Valley in the middle of nowhere or, god forbid, Clarke Terminal on an island in the middle of the Pacific.

It took some convincing to get Sharyn to agree to give Rachel a job. "Are you sure you want to help her?" she asked.

"She drank the Kool-Aid, she didn't make it," Lyn said. "If she wants a fresh start, and it works out, I'm fine with it. I have some unfinished business with her anyway."

Lyn contacted Illumi Névé with an offer to fly Rachel out to Vegas to interview with Sharyn. She'd be able to live and work at M&S Enterprises doing whatever she was capable of. Lyn could tell Névé was relieved someone was coming to get her client but reluctant to agree to no media coverage. Ne relented when Lyn reminded nem how unpredictable Rachel was and with the lawsuit proceeding, there'd be other opportunities.

Diana took advantage of Lyn flying to Massachusetts to add a visit with her parents for the weekend, her last before the school year started. They spent a pleasant day together—no further incursions by a certain general—and the next morning, Lyn left to fetch Rachel. Diana and her folks were off to a museum and then a concert. Diana would take a public transport to meet Lyn in Vegas the next day.

At the hospital, Rachel's lawyer was the only one to see her leave. It saddened Lyn that Rachel had no family for support through any of her travails. She'd often spoken of her grandmother who had raised her. But she'd told so many conflicting stories about her past that Lyn wasn't sure what was true.

Rachel didn't say anything as she walked out of the hospital with Lyn and Illumi. She politely shook hands with her lawyer, agreed to meet with nir later to go over the lawsuit, and climbed into Lyn's skim. She watched Illumi watch them from the parking lot. Lyn had to nudge her to strap in. Once they were airborne, Lyn reminded her she'd asked for help. "With what?"

Rachel looked around at the ground, the bright sun overhead, rubbed her hand along the armrest. "Nice skim."

"It's safe to talk. This is my own, it's been searched for trackers, monitors. Other than a mouse or two, we're alone."

Rachel looked at her. "Mice?"

"Hazard of where I live." Which Lyn had no intention of revealing.

"I can't be sure they aren't tracking every thought in my head, everything I say," Rachel said, surprisingly calmly.

"They?"

"You know." Pulsar. "Maybe others. I remember so little of what happened at that place."

"Why?" Lyn asked.

"They want me to shut up. To not talk about real and imminent threats."

"The message," Lyn said. Best to keep details brief.

Rachel turned toward the window.

They were flying over the less populated middle of the state, above scattered remains of abandoned suburbs, burned over forests, dried up lakes. Even a half century later, not much life had returned.

"You look better," Lyn said. And it was true. Her cheeks had some color, her hair wasn't a mess.

"I feel better. Guess I needed a rest." A chuckle eased into a sigh, of resignation or weariness.

"You'll like Sharyn. Don't expect the work to be easy. This won't be a vacation."

"I'm not afraid of a little work, or much of anything anymore." Rachel seemed to breathe in courage. "I'm not afraid of Grus Moloth."

The name rang a bell. "That the rich guy who owned Galaxy Cruises?"

"He bribed Earth Control inspectors to approve the *Aphrodite* for space, even though it was a piece of junk."

"Did you know about this?"

Rachel looked at her with disdain. "That was before my time. I only found out during the investigation after you came back with that video of the explosion."

"Are you saying he set the explosive?"

"I don't know. I can't imagine why he'd destroy his own ship. But someone did." Rachel's tone took on the grit of her past self. "That much we knew."

This was the old Rachel, forcing Lyn to ask, "Is this mental breakdown an act?"

"Not entirely. There's a shitload of noise in my head, but I'm not crazy. I messed up." She rubbed her scarred arm.

"What happened there?"

Rachel grunted. "I tried some black market nanobots, hoping to fix that stupid implant. I managed to disable the mind link, but it didn't help."

"Was it malfunctioning?"

"Either that or I'm psychotic." She flashed a grin. "Don't answer that. I don't know. Voices, weird obsessions." She felt around for the seat control, leaned back, and stretched out her legs. "I don't mean the aliens. So don't start."

"We'll talk more about that someday. Tell me about Moloth."

"He's a dangerous, evil man."

"Do you have proof of the bribes?" Lyn asked.

"Not personally, but EC has to. Somewhere."

"Does Faber know?"

"I don't think so." Rachel crossed an ankle over her knee and rubbed a scuff mark on her shoe. "Maybe you could let her know. She won't have anything to do with me."

"She might for this."

An alarm sounded.

"Hold on. Proximity alert?" Lyn looked around. "I don't see any—"

The blast obliterated Lyn's perception of time, an instantaneous scorch of fire and concussive roar that pierced her right eardrum and flayed her jacket and pants. Her seat ejected automatically with a harsh jolt, sending her in an elegant arc under the clear blue sky followed by the parachute deploying to slow her descent. If she'd been conscious, she'd have seen the flaming shards of her sporty skim spin through the air, Rachel and mice included, racing ahead of her to the ground. A finely built machine shattered like a child's toy. She swung gently under the chute, unaware of the fall from height that would have terrified her. Because she'd been flying low, she hit the ground hard, bounced once, and settled on her left side, her arm pinned under the faux-leather arm of her ruined chair. The seat cushions charred, her right arm and leg and half her face burned and bleeding.

Some time later she opened her eyes. The wreck was a smoldering scatter of debris, her field of view red from blood running into her eyes. There was no pain. In the distance, she saw two people running toward a third lying on the ground.

A familiar voice called out, "Rachel!"

Lyn's vision cleared enough to see a woman's back, a single dark braid. *Tara?* She tried to yell, but she couldn't move, only blink. A second woman helped the first. Together they pulled Rachel to her feet. They were so far away, but Lyn could see her expression clearly. Don't leave me here, Rachel seemed to say. Tara, for clearly it was her, supported Rachel while the other woman ran toward Lyn. She was blonde, wearing a gray and red flight suit, a fresh raw scar across her right temple. She knelt by Lyn's side.

"Don't move," she said. "Help is on the way." Then she ran back to the others.

"Lyn!" Tara's voice was faint in the distance.

The three of them walked away together, Rachel between Tara and—was that Rose?—glancing back before they disappeared into the smoke. Lyn tried to follow, but she couldn't keep up, and when she looked back, she saw herself still lying on the ground, crushed by the seat, burned and bleeding, as if she were tethered to herself.

The next time she opened her eyes, the world was dark. Blind or night, she wasn't sure. Lights flashed. A scuff and thud of boots. She tried to speak, but no voice came. A light blinded her. The pain was excruciating. She fumbled for the harness release. Unclipped, she flopped onto her stomach, the chair teetering back, off her arm. Then more pain as blood returned to the shattered limb. All her attempt to scream got her was a mouthful of dirt and gravel. She couldn't have fought the darkness if she'd wanted to and she didn't. *This is it, then.*

Chapter 13

IT STARTED WITH a hum, like on *Endurance*. A sound you forget until it stops, the HVAC system pumping air around, the subtle vibration of artificial gravity thrumming through the floor. Was she back on board? Only one eye opened. A blast of light sucked her energy like a hull breach into a black hole. She closed it and waited for her strength to recover. Whatever happened that could make moving an eyelid exhausting had to be pretty bad.

She opened her eye again. A glimpse of blanket rising over her left foot, bandages swaddling her right leg, but she still had feet. She just couldn't feel them. Beige walls, harsh lights. A clock she couldn't read. Close that eye again. Voices. Garbled. Like she was under water. But someone was there.

Again with the eye. Why just one? Not so grueling this time. She could see Diana and felt a grip on her fingers so gave a squeeze in return. Diana reacted with a smile. Then her view blurred. Tears. Sounds clarified into voices. More than one. Diana to her left, but who was to her right? Her head wouldn't move. She could barely feel her arms and legs. Something covered her mouth. She grunted. That caused louder, happy sounds. Did she say something funny?

Gradually the voices cohered into words.

"You're going to be okay." Diana.

"Oh, honey." She knew that voice, had heard those words before. The low, stretched out syllables, desperate and sad. Mom. Then, "Jeph, wake up. She's come to!" Dad was here too. What the actual hell happened?

Dad at the foot of the bed, standing like a guardian. Arms crossed. He reached down and squeezed her left foot. She felt that! Deep breath. Mom leaned into view. A big smile. Quick glance to Diana. Also smiling. That seemed like good news. Another grunt. This meant, What happened? But would they figure that out? She wished Diana still had Omara's mind link.

Diana didn't need the link. "You crashed in the skim. On your way home. You are in a hospital in Massachusetts." She spoke slowly, which was good because Lyn could only hear from that ear, the left one.

"Rest, now, honey," her mom said, her voice a rough burr. "We'll still be here when you wake up again."

Again. Good. It's okay to sleep. She'll wake up. Back to the quiet dark.

This time when she woke, the room lights were dim. Beeps and whirs and a pulsing throbbed in her head. Still, only one eye opened. Could she move a hand? No. She could wiggle the fingers of her left hand but not bend or move the arm, which was encased in a thick immobilizer. Soft bandages wrapped her right arm, hand, and right leg. Another immobilizer around her right thigh. But Diana's head was near her left hand. Wiggling her fingers, she flicked her hair.

Diana woke with a start and smiled. "Hey. How are you?"

Her mouth was no longer covered. She tried moving her lips, but they were dry and sealed together. Diana swabbed her lips with a moist sponge. That helped. "What . . . ?" was all she got out.

"Skim crashed. Do you remember?"

She couldn't even shake her head. "No." Her one eye darted around. The best she could do was eject a word while she exhaled. "Injured."

"It's pretty bad." Diana listed a broken left arm and right femur, a burned right arm and leg, and shrapnel wounds throughout her body. Fractured skull, lacerated face, more burns.

Lyn blinked, trying to take it all in.

"Are you in pain?"

"No," she answered. "Mom . . . Dad?"

"They're here." Diana looked to Lyn's right. "Sleeping."

"How . . . long?"

Diana understood she didn't mean how long had they been sleeping. "Three days since the crash. Do you remember picking up Rachel?"

Rachel? Her brow must have furrowed.

"Don't worry about it. We'll talk when you're stronger. The medbots are hard at work. You'll be fit in no time." Diana gently ran a finger down her unburned cheek. "Rest. I love you."

"Love . . . you . . ." Then Lyn slipped back into the soft cushion of sleep.

Jostling woke her. "Sorry, hun, but I'm just checking you over." The words were clipped and fast, not her mom or Diana. She couldn't turn to see who was mashing her about and Diana wasn't in her field of view.

"Who . . . you?" she managed.

"Good morning, Lyn," she, for it seemed like a female voice, said perkily, like perkiness was an option. "I'm Stella, and I'm your nurse." Lyn flopped abruptly onto her back. A whirring, and then a nurse bot rolled into view on her left. "Let's see how you're doing, shall we?"

Wow, Dr. Amos should get a load of this bedside programming. Thank god for pain meds since she wasn't feeling anything horrible from all the rucking about. With dexterous but very nonhuman fingers, Stella ripped open a cuff on her upper arm. She hadn't even noticed that. When Stella put it back on, Lyn realized it had caused some of the throbbing. Probably meds pumping into her. Painkillers or anti-inflammatory or antibiotic medbots. Whatever, they were working. She felt good, but not loopy.

"Can you talk yet?" Stella asked, her eyes, cameras really, focusing in closer to Lyn's face. She didn't have a human face or even body. She was a rolling cart with long arms and hands that could move and lift and do everything needed, but didn't even try to be human. Except for that voice and the bedside manner.

"Um," she tried and it seemed to work. "Yes, I guess so."

"Good girl!" Stella gave her a gentle pat. "You been told what's going on?"

"Sort of. Crash and lots of broken and burned things."

"Pretty much. Sorry about your friend."

"Who?"

Stella jerked back, such a human reaction. "Don't worry. You rest and we'll get you sorted in no time." She whirred to the foot of the bed. "The doctor will stop by later this morning to see if you're ready to get up." She turned and waved as she rolled out the door. "Bye!"

Holy crap, what was that? Lyn wondered. Your friend? "Dee," she croaked as loud as possible.

Diana flew into the room—she must have been right outside the door—pulled up a chair, and held Lyn's hand, like she was slipping back into an old, familiar furrow. This had been going on for some time.

"What the hell was that?"

Diana brightened. "Stella? Isn't she a hoot?"

"She said she was sorry about my friend. What was that?"

Diana's face fell. "Oh." She only had to say "Rachel" and Lyn knew. It all fell back into place. Picking her up. Flying. The world splitting apart.

"Dead?" Lyn said. "But . . . I saw her."

"What do you mean? She . . . well. You couldn't possibly have seen her."

"Must have . . . dreamed."

All Diana knew was that she and Rachel only got as far as central Mass. when the skim crashed. It had now been four days.

"The Independent Safety Board's investigating," Diana said. "Once they found . . ." She couldn't finish.

Rachel was dead? How? They'd been talking, but she couldn't remember about what. A tone. An alarm? It all muddled in her throbbing brain, the implant no help. But it had to be there. Any further talk was snuffed by her parents entering the room with a tray of steaming cups of coffee. Four, Lyn counted, which was a good sign. Her mom squealed to see her awake and settled back at her side.

"I can't keep doing this, Lynnie. I'm wrapping you in armor and never letting you off the ground again, do you hear me?" She said it with a sobby laugh, happy to see her alert and responding, but also serious. They'd done this before, Lyn in a hospital bed, her mother beside her. After Enceladus.

She could see Diana sit back and let her parents control the space, but her eyes never left Lyn. The rest of the day was filled with doctors, tests, and the momentous getting out of bed, helped at first with an antigrav walker, a small platform with guardrails and crutch pads that let her get vertical but adjust the level of pressure she could withstand. By pushing with her good foot, she could maneuver about. By the time she learned how to use the thing, she was exhausted and needed a nap.

Grafts on her torso, arm, leg, and face were checked and rebandaged while she slept. By Stella, presumably. Diana remained with her around the clock.

A state police officer came to visit the next day. Lyn learned she had landed on the gravelly shore of the old Quabbin Reservoir, next to an ancient house foundation in the middle of an equally ancient road that had once passed under the water. It took rescue crews several hours to get to her after her skim's automatic beacon sent out an SOS. When EMTs found her, they immediately called for an evac to the Worcester trauma center, where she was now.

The officer explained that the Safety Board found evidence of explosives at the crash site. "A projectile fired from below went right through the passenger seat. This is now a criminal investigation."

He was being polite saying it went through the seat. It went through Rachel. It wasn't just a "criminal investigation." It was murder. But how the hell did someone know she'd be flying overhead at that moment? Who was being tracked? Certainly Rachel, and it now sounded like her paranoia was justified.

The officer ran through a litany of questions, most of which went unanswered. "I can't remember anything after we took off," Lyn said, her strength quickly fading.

"I'll keep in touch. Your memories may return."

She completely lost track of time. Diana admitted another two days had passed and she'd taken a leave from teaching. At this, Lyn insisted her parents go home. "You've got a business to run. Dee's here and, god knows, I'm not going anywhere without her."

Reluctantly they left, and Lyn was sent to rehab the next day. It was a pleasant enough facility, set among trees on a hilltop with expansive views to distant mountains. Or what passed for mountains in Massachusetts. She wished she were home, but at least Diana could stay with her. Rehab was more like a hotel with a hospital bed and lots of grueling activities. Diana learned how to change her dressings and the med cuffs and help her move about, dress, and bathe.

"Medbots are great on pain control and swelling," the doctor assured Lyn, "but we haven't yet figured out how to speed up cell division, so you'll heal when you heal. Bones and tissue need to knit back together. Figure on at least two months before you are anywhere near back to normal."

Two months. That was barely before she had to leave for the Johari flight. Being a patient—such an odd term—was time consuming. She was anything but patient. Between medical procedures, relearning how to function, and resting from all that, the time passed and pushed out thoughts of what happened. Only to roar back in the middle of the night when she lay awake staring at the ceiling, listening to Diana's sleep-breaths in the bed next to her, wishing they could cuddle. Memories surfaced, even the impossible ones. Rachel getting up from the ground. Those other women. Tara and . . . Rose? The horror relived of losing a friend.

However their relationship had deteriorated, Rachel did not deserve to die. In the still, quiet of the night, with no guardrails around her emotions, she regretted every harsh word, every impatient dismissal of Rachel's feelings, whether bruised at the Academy when Lyn and Tara became a couple, to their training on *Endurance* when she'd rebuffed Rachel's advances.

They'd kissed once. Before Lyn was with Tara, she'd been focused on being a good student at the Academy, not hooking up with anyone. It was the end of term, and she and Rachel were at a party blowing off steam. They danced. Everyone was dancing. When the music slowed, she started to leave to get a drink, but Rachel pulled her back. They fit together well. Rachel was solid and fat, soft and strong. It wasn't a kiss for the ages. The one she'd share with Tara the next term would be the real thing. But she liked it. For Lyn, it was an intimate deepening of their friendship, nothing more. Unfortunately, for Rachel it was the start of something she wanted that Lyn didn't. They didn't make love that night. Lyn could tell Rachel wanted it, but she just hadn't been in that vibe. Then one night months later, after she was with Tara, the three of them were playing Jolt. Rachel was winning every hand, so Tara and Lyn got extremely drunk. Lyn woke up the next morning with a super headache, in bed with Tara and Rachel, naked. Tara and Lyn were shocked. They had no idea what they'd done, but Rachel grinned for days and days. It really put Tara off of her, she was pissed about it. They'd been used. Truthfully, Lyn was disappointed not to remember anything. Rachel had a reputation as a good lover.

And that was it. Rachel had loved her, and she had not loved her back, not the way Rachel wanted or needed. Tears flowed from her good eye with no way to wipe them away. Medbots couldn't help this pain.

SHE CALLED THE State Police for an update on the investigation, but an agent from the National Investigation Bureau called back. The agent told her there was no progress on finding the perpetrator. He asked if Lyn remembered anything new. She told him about Rachel mentioning Grus Moloth and the bribe to Earth Control. The agent thanked her and that was the last she heard from him.

A steady stream of visitors included her brothers, the Teegans, Ani with a promise to fly her home when she was ready. Omara brought flowers from Jill Faber, who didn't dare visit herself. Lyn asked Omara to pass along Rachel's accusation of Moloth's bribes.

"That's a new twist. Not Pulsar? We don't need someone blowing up—" Omara stopped, but Lyn could finish the rest. *Tenacity* full of Johari.

Someone wanted her, Rachel, or both of them dead, but that made no sense for Pulsar. They wanted what was in her head. Blowing her to smithereens wouldn't get them the data.

Omara knew Moloth. "He comes from a long line of arms dealers. His family lost a fortune after the war and redistribution of wealth. There's no grudge too small for him to hold onto. I first met him at the grand opening of the Clarke space elevator. An unreconstructed asshole, to be polite. He actually had one of his thugs send me a decomposing rat the first year Omara Tours won the Golden Orbit Award for best service and customer satisfaction. I know it was him."

"Please share the arms background with Jill," Lyn said. "If he knows weapons, he might be deeper in this than we thought. The NIB can figure that out."

THEN SHE HAD a surprise visitor. She was sitting in a wheelchair on the porch, under the shade of an Ailanthus tree when she heard a soft whirring. Like Stella's, but quieter.

"Don't get up," General Jacana said with a smile as she pulled a chair over to sit where Lyn could easily see her.

"Either your job has gotten very boring or I'm in bigger trouble than I thought," Lyn said. She saw Diana retreat into the building but remain by the door, out of view. Maybe the general had insisted on meeting her alone.

"No trouble and no, my job is far from boring." General Jacana held her hands folded in her lap. No uniform this time. Casual slacks and shirt. Her eyes roved over Lyn in an assessing way. She let out a long, weary sigh. "You keep trying to die. It makes me nervous. I'll be brief to conserve your energy. I know how tough it is to come back from a severe injury." She did not look away from Lyn's eyes, one still thickly bandaged. No glance to her own marred body. She asked polite but pointed questions about Lyn's injuries and how the healing was coming along. "It would be a shame to lose a national hero, but I think you understand that there is more at stake than your symbolism."

So that was it. The data, safe and snug in Lyn's brain. God, don't let her approach and try to make a transfer. Would the firewall hold? Could Diana take the general if Lyn screamed?

Jacana seemed to read her fear. "I'm no longer in the business of invading people's privacy against their will. I haven't given up trying to convince you of the greater good that can be achieved by sharing your achievement."

"Still not interested. Sorry," Lyn said. Her head dropped back against the chair, fatigue draping her like a weighted blanket.

"I can see you are tired. Let me share some advice." Jacana patted her own arm. "I lost this—well, the real one—in a battle against an autonomous AI drone. I was in Belize, my home country. Deep in the mountains, what was once a forest. Most of it had burned, the rest mined for gold eons ago, so there wasn't much place to hide. The drone fired a laser shot that severed my arm cleanly. In fact, it cauterized the arteries in the process, so I didn't bleed out, which was good because I didn't have medbots at the time. Once the Americans learned that happened, they returned to using messy bullets. That's how I lost the legs. This one with bullets," she patted her right leg, "the other with a land mine. Old fashioned, but effective. Not at the same time, thankfully."

"Is this supposed to make me feel better? I still have my arms and legs."

"No. This is to help you understand that whatever limitations you might be left with won't interfere with what you want to do with your life." She leaned forward, elbows on knees and relaxed, like an old friend chatting. "Also, what you went through was fucking horrific and not everyone is going to understand that. Modern medicine has come a long way, but recovery still takes patience and there will be bad days. But you will heal. Please remember that."

Jacana leaned back and looked around at the grounds. "It's nice here. Isn't peace wonderful?" She looked back at Lyn. "Are you in pain?"

"No."

"Then why do you have a death grip on the arm of your chair?"

Maybe because I'm terrified of you, Lyn thought, but no, that wasn't it. Why did she? She released her hand and flexed her fingers.

Jacana stood and placed her hands on Lyn's shoulders then sat back down. "You are tense. If I make you nervous, I don't intend to, but I think that while you feel no pain, your body is reacting to the trauma." She tapped her head. "The brain might not register the pain, but the body retains the knowledge. Millions of years of evolution won't be undone by a few decades of medbots. That contributes to your exhaustion." She rubbed her thigh. "Let me share a relaxation technique that worked for me, if I may."

If this was some trick of the general's to gain her confidence or trust, Lyn prepared to protect herself, mentally if not physically. But the offer was tempting. Her doctor had been urging her to incorporate relaxation into her physical therapy. "Sure, why not."

Jacana smiled supportively and settled with her hands on her thighs. "Take a deep breath and as you exhale, relax your shoulders. I can see they are tight."

Lyn did and was surprised to realize how tense she had been. Jacana continued, addressing different areas of her body, and each time she felt tension relieve. Then they started over again, Jacana chuckling at how she had again tightened up.

"It'll get easier. You'll stop playing . . . what was that old game?" She glanced up, thinking, likely accessing her own Pulsar implant. "Whack a mole, that's it." She laughed softly, revealing a kinder, gentler General Jacana.

Eventually, Lyn felt relaxed as a baby. Her eyelids drooped, ready for sleep. "Thank you," she murmured.

General Jacana rose, her prostheses whirring to life. Another weary sigh. "I hate that sound. My days of sneaking up on people to cut their throats are over." She smiled down at Lyn. "I'll let you rest. I hope someday you'll come to understand the importance of my offer." She bowed slightly. "Till we meet again." Then she left.

Lyn fell asleep, wondering if this visit was a gesture of goodwill or a subtle threat. The general was watching, paying close attention to what she did. But she slept soundly and woke refreshed for the first time in weeks.

THREE DAYS LATER, Lyn was discharged with a pile of instructions, Diana's assurances she'd make sure Lyn followed orders, and arrangements for their doctor in Butte to take over care. Ani insisted on doing the honors of taking them home. Lyn had been tempted to take her parents up on their offer to let her recover in Nakota, knowing the cabin wasn't exactly handicapped accessible. But Diana shot that down, uncharacteristically confident she could handle Lyn's needs.

"You didn't bring the Ag-Cat, did you?" Lyn asked Ani as Diana pushed her chair through the hallway.

Ani laughed. "I thought about shoving you in the bin, but wasn't sure you'd fold up that small."

"Cargo drone?"

"Ooh, I wish I'd thought of that!"

It was such a relief to see Ani, happy and healthy and joking. A bookmark to where her life had been and to where she hoped to return.

Outside at the pickup zone, Lyn groaned to see a Randall Restoration company skim. These were large, boxy skims for transporting crew members to job sites. "Oh, lovely. I'd prefer the drone."

"Wait." Ani slid open the door. Where the crew seats had been sat a fancy, sleek hoverchair. Ani pushed a button and it slid out, arms extending to slide under Lyn and transfer her from the rehab's chair.

"Nice!" Lyn looked at Ani. "Let me guess. Fúlli?"

"Custom built for nir—"

"Favorite boss," Lyn finished. She shifted in the supple foam seat and back, the material cool on her sweaty back and butt. "I may not bother getting better."

"Fúlli said you'd say that. It's only a loaner. Ne wants it for nirself, and ne's going to monitor your recovery to be sure ne gets it back."

Ani showed her how to adjust it to let her ride sitting, standing, and even walking, like the hospital's more cumbersome version.

"Sporty," Diana commented as Lyn took a spin around the skim. "Can we go home now?"

FOUR WEEKS AFTER the crash, Lyn crashed again, but it wasn't physical. Regardless of her mood, the medbots were doing their thing. Whether it was being stuck at home, unable to work, worried about the Johari, it all swirled like dirty water down a drain. She didn't expect to be up and around already. It wasn't that. It was an undefinable malaise. Not undefinable. She'd been busy with physical therapy, sleeping, more physical therapy, staving off the pain, cramming herself into Diana's Rambler for trips to the doctor. Now, with the bones knitting back together, the lacerations closing over, new skin replacing grafts, she had time to think. To mourn Rachel.

It didn't seem possible she was gone. In an instant, she went from thorn in Lyn's side to gone forever. Not that she had wanted to rekindle their old friendship. That was fraught and complicated. She hadn't told Diana, or anyone, about seeing Rachel with Tara and Rose at the crash site. Dream, hallucination, or afterlife? And why was it Rose who ran toward her, assuring her help was on the way? Near-death visions weren't proven to be anything more than a brain under stress. That didn't have to be Rose. More likely her own subconscious telling her to hang on, that Diana was waiting for her, needed her to survive. That invisible tether holding souls together. But why not Diana herself, if she was to be a figment of Lyn's imagination? In a world where aliens turn out to be distant cousins, and an invisible particle can open the universe to exploration, couldn't there be life beyond death? How do you hold onto anything when everything is possible?

For hours she sat on the back porch of her little cabin, staring into the woods, listening. Wind. That was all. An occasional crow. While technically fall, there was barely relief from summer's heat. The mere hint of cooler air. Bright sunshine warmed the deck, raising a pungent scent from the dry pine needles carpeting the ground. Normally soothing, now it couldn't penetrate her dark mood. She had failed Rachel. The moment they opened a stable wormhole big enough for a ship to pass through, the world had changed. They had done everything they could to prevent the technology from ever being used again, except for one flaw in their plan.

Diana brought out cups of coffee and sat beside her. Neither spoke for a long time.

"Kat says we might get rain next week," Diana finally said.

Nothing from Lyn.

A sigh from Diana, like she knew she should get used to this silence. "Don't you want your coffee?"

Lyn reached for the mug on the table.

"Your arm seems better."

Lyn held the mug, hands wrapped around it. The bandages were off. Her vision improving. The skin grafts were blending, the medbots were doing their thing, and in a few months you'd never know she'd been nearly incinerated in a fiery crash. The healing would be complete.

"What happened to Rachel. This shit in my head, they won't stop till they get it." Lyn didn't trust for a second that General Jacana wouldn't resort to more invasive means if it came to that.

"That's what I'm afraid of." Diana scuffed pine needles on the deck. "You're not wrong, you know." She put a hand up. "We have to accept that people really are out to get you and deal with that." She crossed her arms and swung her feet. "Forget what I said about the Gaian procedure being too freaky and dangerous to attempt. Get that shit out of your head. If you end up a drooling, brain-damaged idiot, I'll devote my life to taking care of you."

She had failed Rachel and there was no guarantee she wouldn't fail Diana. In fact, it was inevitable. "What if I hadn't left you at your parents'? What if you'd been in that skim too?"

Diana huffed a breath. "I had no intention of being crammed in that little back seat. Whatever you needed from Rachel, you needed to sort out. I wouldn't have gone with you if not for the trip to my folks'. This wasn't your fault."

Rachel would never be sorted out now. She inhaled air so dry it constricted her chest. "I'm tired," she whispered.

Diana gently wrapped her arms around her. "I know."

LYING IN BED the next morning, sunshine slanting into the room, she heard Diana puttering in the kitchen. The coffeemaker gurgled. For a brief few moments, she imagined a normal life, the life she wanted more than anything. With Diana, it all figured out. Thanks to the medbots churning away inside her, she healed a little more each day. Less pain. Less brain fog. The trauma of the crash reduced to memory. No sudden flashbacks, no nightmares. Just the quiet vid running in her head, looking at Rachel while she talked, a flash, then darkness. Like it had happened to someone else. She ran her memories back to picking Rachel up at the hospital, searching for clues. Was Illumi Névé acting strange? No stranger than always. Ne had nothing to gain from Rachel's death. Pulsar did, and after what Rachel said about Moloth, he did too. Not surprising she had enemies.

"You need to become the predator." A voice in her head. Not a ghost. A memory of Jo the mechanic when they talked about the mice in the skim. "We've upset the balance of nature," Jo said. "Eliminated the top of the food chain. You have to play that role, otherwise you'll be overrun."

So, she'd set traps in the garage and, sure enough, caught as many mice as she had traps. It was disgusting, dealing with them, dumping the little bodies in the forest for scavengers. She had to do better than wait for law enforcement to do its job. She sat up, eased her legs over the side, and planted her feet on the floor. It was time to go hunting.

After breakfast, she casually mentioned she'd get back to work, that there was plenty she could do from home. Diana smiled in relief. In her office on the second floor, she dug out an old message from that reporter Bakewell at the *Syracuse Post* and sent a reply. She was ready to talk. Irene Bakewell had broken the story of Enceladus. Who better to take this on?

Bakewell wrote back, "Good to hear from you. Want to let you know you might not recognize me, though. The 'I' stands for Isaac now. I hope that's not a problem."

Problem? No. Confusing? Yes. The last thing she needed was someone claiming to be Bakewell but not really. It didn't take much searching to learn I. Bakewell was a respected reporter at the *Post*. Had been for years. His editor confirmed his history, including the transition. Isaac called by vid, his face familiar, if different. A resemblance in the lips, the smile. The eyes. Kind and wise, she'd always thought. Still she requested more proof.

"Here's something that was never published but that I know about you," he said. "Tara called you Pip."

Lyn leaned forward. "Yes. But why?"

Isaac smiled. "Short for pipsqueak, but also for the single pip on your collar, as a first-year at the Aerospace Academy. She had three when you two met. And Jill Faber said it was okay to reveal she'd been the anonymous source leaking Pulsar's plans for Enceladus. I don't take this lightly, even with source permission. It could jeopardize future investigations."

What a dolt she'd been, ignoring Bakewell as an obvious ally. And the risk Jill was taking by helping her and, unknowingly, the Johari, frankly stunned her. She nodded, reassured. "Hello, Isaac."

"How have you been? I'd be hurt you've ignored all my interview requests, but you haven't talked to anyone."

"Nothing personal." They chatted about her injuries and recovery then got down to business.

"I'm glad you called," he said. "I've been working on an article about the report of the investigation into the skim crash that killed Rachel Holness. Do you care to comment? Your name barely comes up in the NIB's report—"

"They've finished? It's only been a month. What's it say?"

"Inconclusive, but clearly intentional. A tracking drone fired from below. No specifics on who or why. No suspects, no indictments forthcoming."

Lyn sat back. She asked Isaac to keep her name out of his reporting.

"Deep background. You got it. If I can't separately corroborate anything you tell me, I'll let you know."

"Did the name Grus Moloth come up?" Lyn asked.

"No. Galaxy Cruises, right? What's the link?"

"Before we were hit, Rachel was telling me that Moloth bribed Earth Control to get the *Aphrodite* to space on the cheap. I've heard his family dealt arms in the war."

"Whoa," Isaac said. "You think he did this?"

"No idea. I let Jill Faber know, so Earth Control is looking into the bribes, but it seems possible. He likely hated Rachel. Never liked me much either."

"So not Pulsar?"

"Could be, but maybe not." Lyn gave him the names of the former executives, including Illumi Névé.

"Rachel's lawyer was former Pulsar? I did not know that. How high up?"

"Low level, legal department. But may well have kept up the interest over the years."

With the public line that Pulsar's intent was to militarize space and beat the Chinese, Lyn didn't want to go near the topic of aliens, so she left that out. Bakewell had revealed the group's role in the Enceladus disaster, and also proved the Chinese only wanted to get into space tourism. It added to the fiasco.

"Do you think Moloth was behind the explosion on the *Aphrodite*?" Isaac asked.

"I doubt he'd bomb his own ship."

"What about Illumi Névé?"

That hadn't occurred to her. But as former Pulsar, Névé would have an interest in closing space. Ne had disappeared until surfacing as Rachel's lawyer. "I suppose it's possible."

"What about Névé and Holness. Any reason ne'd want her dead? Or you?"

"Ne had a lot to gain from Rachel's lawsuit, so I don't see nem wanting her dead. Or me." She didn't say why, that the information in her head could only be retrieved if she were alive. But no harm in pulling nir name into this. Who knew what Isaac might uncover this time.

Isaac whistled. "Okay. That gives me something to work with."

Chapter 14

OMARA AND RO'S plans called for the Johari to gather in Las Vegas to board *Tenacity*, so it fell to Lyn to figure out what to do with them there. Enter M&S Enterprises. This level of favor required better than a vid call. By mid-October, she was well enough to travel. The burns had mostly healed, her arm and leg progressed to smaller immobilizers that let her walk and handle skim controls, but Diana refused to let her go alone, so she flew them down. They were greeted like VIPs, Miriam making a spectacular dinner and Sharyn putting them up in her best suite. They looked Lyn over carefully and muttered all the right things about how her recovery was progressing. After dinner, they settled in Sharyn's penthouse living room for drinks.

The room's walls were floor-to-ceiling windows on three sides, a far cry from her crew quarters on *Endurance*, with a small porthole. Wildfire smoke deepened the sunset to a spellbinding pomegranate. Two simple couches faced each other in front of a decorative fireplace, a glass coffee table between. A stone mantel held an antique clock and photo display. One photo of Sharyn's great-grandparents, former oyster farmers from the Chesapeake Bay, Lyn recognized from *Endurance*. Another showed her and Miriam smiling as they cut a ribbon in front of their first hotel/restaurant, beaming for the camera and surrounded by happy new tenants. Sharyn standing on the remaining section of China's Great Wall and another along Ireland's rugged coast.

"To what do we owe this royal visit?" Sharyn asked, handing Lyn a glass of whiskey. Lyn protested that she wanted to see them. Sharyn raised a hand. "Oh, I believe that, but I sense there's more. You've been more mysterious than usual these past few months."

Nerves set in. This wouldn't be easy, revealing this story. She sat next to Diana, took a gulp, and set her glass on the table. Miriam and Sharyn across from them shared a side-eye like they were bracing for bad news. If only this were as simple as a health update. "Trust me when I say that what I'm about to tell you sounded as crazy to me as it will to you."

Miriam shifted, more alert. Sharyn took a long sip.

She told them about the Johari. With each detail, she recoiled a little inside. It really did sound crazy. At the mention of extraterrestrial beings, Miriam let out a "No way!" When she said six hundred of them needed rooms in less than two months, Sharyn got up to refill their glasses.

"Just a few nights, but we can figure out something else if you can't or don't want to do this."

"That's a lot to take in," Miriam said. She looked at Diana. "Here I was expecting news you two were going back to space. I was prepared to refuse your plea to come along."

"Me too," Sharyn said. She stood by the window. Through the nonreflective glass, the sun had set, leaving dark to wall them in. No bright lights, just random twinkles, a few skims in the distance. A half-moon visible. "This feels dangerous. We can't risk our other guests."

"Plausible deniability," Lyn said. "We can frame it as a tour group coming through. There's no risk to you."

"But you got blown up!" Miriam said.

"Okay, maybe there is some risk. But that wasn't about the Johari."

Sharyn turned from the window. "Until the NIB gets wind or someone spills that we're harboring aliens. Does the government know about this?"

"Of course not. We could go to jail."

"Oh, great," Miriam said. "That makes me feel so much better. Thanks for putting us in the crosshairs."

Lyn didn't remember Miriam or Sharyn being the least bit obstinate on *Endurance*. No, their job was to follow orders. And she'd never ordered them to do anything like this. And she wasn't a captain anymore.

"Is this why you were nearly killed?" Miriam asked.

"I don't think so."

"You don't *think* so? You're not *sure*?"

Sharyn returned to sit next to Miriam. "What's this have to do with Rachel? What if we had let her come here and someone blew up a building to get to her?"

"This has nothing to do with Rachel. Well, maybe a little. Only in that she suspected aliens . . . never mind. The less you know, the better."

Miriam huffed out a breath. "That's rich. What have you gotten yourself into? That you're pulling us into?"

"We've had quite enough drama for one lifetime," Sharyn added. "Just because you're a danger junkie doesn't mean we are."

The room fell quiet. Lyn stared at her glass on the table, reached for it, then withdrew her shaking hand. They were right, of course. She had no business asking. Well, no harm in asking, but she couldn't expect them to do this. "I get it. I could have lied and made up a story about refugees needing help. You wouldn't have hesitated then, right?"

Their glances at each other spoke for them. The Lyn Randall they'd known for years had never lied to them.

"These aren't refugees," Miriam said quietly.

"And that's a cheap shot," Sharyn added softly.

They'd made their point. Lyn shut up, chastened. Miriam had been a refugee and knew about fleeing danger. She leaned in, elbows on knees. "I'm sorry."

Diana hadn't said anything. She didn't know these women like Lyn did. Now she rubbed Lyn's back. "Lyn didn't get herself or us into anything. If anyone did, it was me. The only way we could have avoided this was to have stayed in Rigil Kent." She looked at Sharyn pointedly. "And you wouldn't be alive. This isn't Lyn's fault. It's no one's fault. We came back, someone noticed the sheer impossibility of that, and guess what, aliens who've been here all along asked for a ride home. That's it. That's all there is to it."

Miriam swirled the amber liquid in her glass. "When you put it like that."

"I'm not a danger junkie," Lyn said softly.

"Hmm." Sharyn shrugged.

The story, the favor, sat between them, brittle and dangerous. Lyn's mind churned as she tried to figure out alternatives to this hare-brained scheme. She supposed the Johari could go right to the airstrip and board *Tenacity*. Then sit there for several days till everyone showed up.

"Well, I for one am not shocked," Miriam said, drawing Lyn's attention back. "After all we went through in Rigil Kent, I know anything is possible."

"But here, on Earth, studying us," Sharyn said, her tone less peeved, more curious. "I'm not surprised they want to leave."

They peppered Lyn and Diana with more questions, about Omara's role, the logistics of the ship. The mood evolved, the plan beginning to sound less deranged. She answered each question thoughtfully, carefully leaving them room to withdraw. They had to make this decision on their own, all facts on the table. They grudgingly admitted that Omara was taking on more risk, by pretending *Tenacity* would only take off for test flights. Their tenants would notice all the new arrivals, Sharyn pointed out. They weren't stupid. She ended up mostly in conversation with Miriam, who thought the idea of a tour group passing through might work. Sharyn dismissed that, noting it went against their mission and would be more noticeable than if they simply let the Johari slip in quietly.

"We're almost finished renovating the Grand Sunset," Miriam said with a questioning glance to Sharyn. "Think that'll do? If they're the only guests, it lessens the chance of a nosy leak."

"I think we can be ready in time," Sharyn said. Then she tsked at Lyn. "And I thought the only thing I had to worry about was you getting blown up."

"Poor Rachel," Miriam said. "I never met the woman, but if you were willing to help her, she had to have some good inside."

"No one deserved that," Lyn said to nods from everyone.

"Three hundred years," Miriam said in awe. "They must have no idea what they are going home to."

"I visited China last year," Sharyn said. "And Ireland the year before. It's funny the connection you feel. So visceral. Each place so different, but then I guess I'm different too. Yet my ancestors came here longer ago than the Johari did."

"At least China and Ireland were concepts you could understand, places to visit, movies to watch," Miriam said. "But a planet a hundred light years from here? That you had to pretend didn't exist?"

The tension eased out of Lyn as she listened to her friends talk. The plan was coming together, like the scaffolding around *Tenacity*. Would it be strong enough to hold them all up and keep them safe?

OCTOBER ENDED, THE Gaian signals likely commenced, and the last details fell into place. The Johari Fair in mid-November would mark the start of the Johari exodus to their planet. Ro would contact those leaving to be sure they were still willing and share instructions for meeting in Las Vegas. It also meant Diana faced saying goodbye to Antonia, her last link to Rose, her last chance to find peace in understanding how she could have loved a Johari, been loved by Rose, and never been told the truth. Lyn didn't know if they had used the traditional wedding vow—to love and support, in sickness and in health, till death do you part. But with that commitment came an understanding, a trust asked for and received. How much of a burden had it been for Rose to maintain that secret? For Antonia?

Lyn couldn't in any way grasp what Diana was going through. She could only imagine how she might react to either side of the question, Who are you? They'd once talked about theories that reality didn't exist at all. That everything was a mathematical illusion. Lyn didn't care to dwell on that. She accepted that what she saw through her eyes, heard through her ears, felt through her touch got processed in the brain, obeying certain rules she didn't have to be consciously aware of, to assemble "reality." She should be able to understand it, given the computing power in her brain. But some concepts stood outside perceivable reality. She wondered what it would feel like *not* to have a computer in her brain. She barely remembered life before it. With her brain threatening overload, it tripped a default to ignore all that and deal with the tasks before her: Expose Pulsar, avenge Rachel's death, get the Johari home, get this shit out of her head.

DIANA DID NOT return to work after Lyn's crash. She made the case to her principal that it would be better to take the year off and take care of her family. Thusly unburdened, Diana and Lyn set off for the Johari Fair in Mill Creek on a late Friday afternoon. Ani would be there too. She had said little about how things were going with Ruzena, but Lyn knew time was running out for them. In less than two weeks, they'd be heading to the rendezvous point and wait to meet the Gaians. Diana was tense too. This would be her last visit with Antonia at her house. They'd say goodbye forever on *Tenacity*.

Diana piloted since Lyn still tired easily. They chatted about agricultural fairs where farmers showed off their prize pumpkins and pigs, though Diana said the Johari focused more on sharing techniques. Lyn had been to carnivals and ag shows as a kid, but she wasn't prepared for this. It began as a glow on the horizon. Her first thought was a wildfire. The sun had set and the town was simply too small to throw out that much light. Diana didn't seem worried, though. In fact, Lyn detected a heightened sense of excitement as she sped up the Rambler and focused more on what was outside than their conversation.

As they neared the town, the glow resolved to a glittering spectacle, like a mini Vegas in its heyday. They had to land farther outside the town's no fly zone and join the line of cars, trucks, and skims inching along Main Street. The fair wouldn't open till morning and workers scurried about setting up booths and tents and stringing lights. Fields blossomed with a new crop—carnival rides. A Ferris wheel, rollercoaster, a line of booths, some contraption that rose into the air then plummeted to the ground. Lyn's worst nightmare. Other fields were set aside for visitor parking and camping.

They turned in at Antonia's house and pulled around to the back. She greeted them warmly. Gone was the snarky bluster of their last meeting. This would be goodbye and that was not lost on Lyn. Sure, she wanted to see how Ro was doing, but really, this was the point. Antonia plied them with food and drink, she and Diana carefully steering conversation away from said point, but the house was packed up. Photos off the walls, books off the shelves. No one was going to be able to take trunks of their belongings to Gaia, so everything had to be digitized or gotten rid of. How many other families in town were going through this? Instead, they talked about the fair, who would have the best ice cream, what concerts were worth lining up for. Diana and Antonia reminisced about past fairs with the missing family members.

The next morning, Antonia had breakfast ready when they came downstairs, and they ate quietly. As Lyn rose to clear the table and refill their coffees, Antonia offered Diana photos and mementos. "Take whatever you want. I can't take them with me."

The story Antonia was telling around town was that she was moving to another Johari community in Aotearoa. In reality, her things were being sent to an auction house, the truly personal items recycled.

Diana halfheartedly dug through a couple of boxes, glancing at items and setting them aside or barely touching the contents. In the end she took some photos of them all together. The rest, she said, she couldn't face. "I have her in my heart. That's enough."

The cats roamed among the boxes with a mix of curiosity and suspicion. Diana hauled the orange one out of a box. The cat clung to her shoulder and purred. "What happens to them?"

"Frank's taking them. He lives next door." Antonia took the cat from Diana. She grinned, but her sadness showed through. More losses. "I hate to think of them leaving this place, but Frank will let them roam."

The tabby squirmed, jumped down, and stalked off, tail raised as if to say, I've had enough of you weird beings.

The point of their coming may not have been the fair, but none of them would deny some fun, so they ventured out. In keeping with the Johari way, there were no high-tech AI-powered VR mystery escape rooms or anti-grav rides. Good old-fashioned, cheesy fun. A Ferris wheel, which Diana loved and Lyn hated; a Scrambler, which Lyn loved and Diana hated. Booths with every kind of locally made food or craft item from tools to clothing—no bio sensors in any of them. The main road-turned-concourse was lined with booths selling goods and food. Singing and music created a background soundtrack. Even the barkers sang out their lure to try a hand at ringing a bell or hitting a target. Diana bought an ax. For chopping wood. Lyn had pictured her more a low-tech optical telescope kind of girl. She bought a pair of goatskin boots.

In a bluehouse-turned-goat-barn, Lyn learned several farmers were selling their herds and assumed they were the ones who'd be leaving. Milk goats and meat goats and both kinds used for weed eating. She fake-begged Diana to let her have one, but she said they couldn't take care of Kat, let alone a goat.

"Kat doesn't need care," Lyn protested in her best teenage whine.

"My point, exactly," Diana said in her best teacher response.

The hardware store had been turned into a history exhibit. Here was the public face of the Johari. The only face for most of them. Plenty of outsiders came to the fair, it was a regional marvel, so exhibits displayed historical items and printed signs told the Johari origin story. Not the spaceship arriving from Gaia, full of curious researchers, but, Lyn read, a small group of like-minded individuals who decided that the Industrial Revolution wasn't for them and they'd keep to the old ways that got older and stranger as the decades passed. There was no specific founder, no one whom they revered or held as a queen or god. She'd never given the Johari much thought so was impressed by what she learned. They'd always been matriarchal. That also had set them apart. Women headed the families, controlled the finances, made the decisions. Wouldn't her dad love that, she snarked to Diana as they toured the exhibits. Among themselves, they didn't question it, but they'd taken a lot of flak from outside, which only made them pull inward more tightly.

That night they went to a community dinner followed by concerts and dancing. Dance floors had been put down in several of the bluehouses, with different bands—klezmer, countrypunk, classic country, synthetic opera. The Johari were known for their musical and singing talent, Diana said. "Rose had a beautiful voice."

Lyn's medbots kept her from getting drunk, but she enjoyed a happy buzz from the local fruit wines. Yet she sensed, or maybe imagined, an undercurrent of desperation in the crowds. Couples slow danced, clinging tightly. Some would go back to work after the fair, maybe a little hungover—no medbots for the Johari—never grasping the change under way. Others were leaving at the end of the week. Forever. Lyn wondered if she could tell from their body language which group was which.

Even Diana seemed distracted. Lyn pulled her up from her seat. "Let's dance."

Stiff and clumsy at first—it had been a year and a half since they'd danced at their wedding, and Lyn hadn't regained all her mobility. Still, it was Diana who stepped on Lyn's toes. She started to apologize but Lyn shushed her. Soon they melded together, moving in sync, a flow of turns and steps with neither directing the motion. Empathic gravity fusing them to the music. The next tune was peppy, and they remained in a slow sway, Diana's cheek pressed to Lyn's shoulder.

BEHIND THE SCENES, Lyn knew Ro was meeting with her senior leadership. Not the ones who ran the "unaware," as she called them, but those prepping to leave. While Lyn had a vested interest in making sure nothing went wrong, that no one leaked the truth of who these people were, she didn't need to be involved. Curiosity, that was all she had. Ro had the hard work.

There was no secret handshake or head tilt that would tell her who was among those leaving so they could chat in code about the weirdness of it all, so the next day she wandered the concourse with Diana and Antonia, stuffing themselves with lamb pies, veggie burgers, and fruits from the vendors. When her leg tired, they headed to the picnic area and bought still more food.

There, Lyn saw Ro sitting alone and looking a bit lost. Diana was still clinging to Antonia, so she excused herself and went to sit with her. They made small talk about the fair, the weather.

Suddenly Ro shoved away her half-eaten slice of cherry pie. "Have I done the right thing? For Gaia, certainly, but for us?"

Hell of a time to get cold feet.

"I envy the ones who don't know," Ro said. "We've built a really great community and, I'm now realizing, haven't kept as separate as we maybe should have. Knowing, I've always felt different, like I didn't belong. Going home to Johar—Gaia—felt like the only option, but now I wonder how much I've been changed by humans. For the better, I hope, but will the Gaians really accept us?"

Her eyes pleaded for confirmation. Technically, it wasn't too late to back down, but Lyn didn't need to say that. "I can't imagine what it's been like for your people all this time—both those here and those on Gaia." She told Ro about Sharyn's emotional connection to China and Ireland, countries she never lived in but where her ancestors had come from. "Whatever happens, they are your family and you'll adjust."

Ro scanned the crowd. "Our system is set up so that when we're told the truth, we're with others finding out as well. It helps to have friends to go through that with. But it's still a shock."

"Diana said learning about Rose felt like finding out late in life that you were adopted."

"But then we're left knowing we're different from the others. I look around here and I know who's leaving and who isn't. I don't know the others very well, and I feel bad about that. It's like we were a sect within a sect." She took a bite of pie, chewed thoughtfully, then set her fork down. "Do you think they have pie?"

That's what it came down to. The little things. Lyn had moved away from Montana, thinking she needed to flee. After the loss of Tara and her failed space career with Pulsar, she'd moved again. Touring with Omara and living in California hadn't helped. Was Montana the answer? At least she'd always had pie. "If not, you can show them."

"I never in a million years thought this would happen." Ro lowered her voice to a whisper. "Why'd you have to go and open a goddamn wormhole?" She didn't say it like an accusation. More like a longed for but still surprising revelation.

Lyn glanced at the crowd, the kids clutching toys and a parent's hand, teens chatting and laughing and flirting, the untested leader before her, who was actually asking the right questions because she cared, as a leader should. "I did what I had to do to save my people." She paused. "Just like you."

Chapter 15

LYN WAS A little surprised to see Ani at work on Monday and not spending the week with Ruzena. But then Ani told her Ruzena had made her decision—she was staying on Earth. Ani stood on the lower wing of the Ag-Cat, wiping the windshield with a cloth.

"How's her family taking it?"

"They hated it at first. Tried to talk her out of it. But they're coming around. She needs this week with them."

"You okay?"

Ani smiled weakly. "For now." She shoved the cloth in her pocket and jumped down.

This would be their last week before taking two weeks of "vacation." It was filled with work, and an eerie quiet. No calls from General Jacana, no visits to Jill Faber. A calm before the storm. Lyn hadn't heard anything from Isaac Bakewell, and it had been more than a month since they had talked. The wheels of justice turned slowly, she'd always been told. Tribal Court, however, moved faster, and Fúlli's "cousin" had agreed to work for Floret in exchange for clearing her name. Even Floret was satisfied after participating in the court proceedings.

By the weekend, the Johari began to arrive in Las Vegas, to a renovated hotel near the airfield. Most came by public transport, but for those arriving in their own skims, which they would no longer need, Sharyn quietly arranged vehicle transfers to other guests who could use them. For the most part the Johari stayed in their rooms, learning about Gaia from materials Beryl had sent during their last meeting and emotionally preparing to leave Earth. Ro had counselors ready for any who questioned their decision. Some did, but no one changed their mind. And, since none of them had ever been to space before, Omara briefed them on spaceflight safety procedures.

The mood, Omara told Lyn when she and Diana arrived, was of resigned inevitability as well as tense anticipation. "They spent years hoping this day would come, so while understandably nervous, there's also a marked excitement. Almost makes me want to visit my ancestral homeland. What's left of it."

On the last day, Sharyn recruited Ani, Ruzena, and a handful of Johari pilots to fly excursions around the region, over the Grand Canyon, viewing the restoration work in Lakes Mead and Powell after the dams were blown up in the war. But instead of returning to M&S Enterprises, the skims landed in a hangar at the airfield and the passengers boarded *Tenacity*. This was less conspicuous, Sharyn said, than six hundred Johari heading to the airfield all at once. The next day, they would take off.

Omara had been working with Jill on a series of test flights of an empty ship. EC wouldn't physically inspect the ship until Omara applied for an occupancy permit. This would be the fourth such "test." She was the only human crew listed, with support from Petra and Dr. Amos. In reality, for all the tests, Ani had been at helm, and Ruzena went along because she couldn't stand to be away from Ani, so Omara agreed. Plus, Omara told Lyn, she was a good pilot. "She reminds me of you in your younger days. Quiet competence."

Ani had reported to Lyn that on the second test flight, after the Gaians had begun sending their signal and based on what Beryl had told them to expect, they were able to confirm certain background noise was in fact Gaian. They just didn't respond.

The added benefit of Ruzena's continuing work on General Jacana's superluminal travel project meant she kept an eye on that progress. She was still on a test-pilot team, but so far, she said, they were only flying ships strengthened to withstand the stresses *Endurance* had undergone. "No sign of any machinery to open a wormhole."

As far as anyone knew, in particular Hellen Jacana and Jill Faber, Lyn Randall was busy at work, still recovering from her grave injuries. Diana Teegan was at home, writing a memoir since taking a sabbatical from teaching. Neither responded to press requests for comment on Omara Tours returning to space with a new ship. Omara herself declined to show off the new ship to curious media, which only ramped up anticipation for the eventual unveiling and the return of Omara Tours.

As for Lyn's family, they thought she was recovering at home and taking a couple weeks off, that Ani was in Puerto Rico visiting family. Fúlli would handle Lyn's projects as an expansion of nir responsibilities. She half-expected to become nir assistant when she got back. And she kind of liked that idea.

TENACITY'S BRIDGE WAS not as roomy as *Endurance*'s and on one level with big windows and plentiful view screens. No steep steps, no vertigo. Lyn took the captain's chair and, in a surprise move, Omara offered Ruzena the first officer's seat. Lyn had been under the impression Ruzena's role on the bridge would be to step in as "captain" only if they were discovered. Lyn couldn't be seen, and Tey was the only one licensed for a commercial ship.

"With the captain's permission," Omara said.

"Of course." Fact was, Ruzena knew the ship better than she did, and she respected Omara's opinion, both as owner and as someone who had worked with Ruzena.

Ani sat at helm an arm's length in front of the captain and first officer chairs and a short distance from the front wall of windows. Omara took the navigator's seat beside Ani, and Diana and Ro sat at the engineering station with instructions not to touch anything—Petra would handle engineering and navigation.

Down in the Medical Suite, a copy of Dr. Amos stood in his charging bay, ready to be of assistance to any Johari who needed it. He had opted not to change his gender, voice, or appearance. Lyn didn't know what internal conversation he had with himself to decide that, but she liked it. He was still, after all, Dr. Amos.

She watched Ruzena run through the checklist and admired her professionalism in the face of what must be an emotional wrenching. Ani responded with her usual, professional, "Aye, Commander." Lyn might not be a danger junkie, but she'd missed the adrenaline rush of takeoff, the excitement of leaving the bonds of Earth.

Diana and Ro had toured the decks, making sure the passengers were strapped into the couches in their cabins, suited and helmets in place. For most, this was their first time in space. Unlike the tourists on *Endurance*, these were not seasoned space travelers. Lyn could only hope nothing went wrong. Any panic could easily grow out of control and doom them all. While she had complete trust in the crew on board, there was no accounting for unknown forces out there, both human and Gaian.

I hope you aren't as nervous as I am, Omara said to Lyn through her mind link.

Why would I be nervous? I'm undocumented cargo, you're the owner.

Omara laughed out loud, causing a glance from Ruzena.

Tenacity was tractored out of the hangar and onto the launch pad. Ani was well versed in flying the ship by now, and Petra could do it on her own if she had to. Earth Control, however, was not ready for completely automated flights. Lyn hadn't gone on the test flights, so *Tenacity* was a new and pleasant experience. The ship lifted off smoothly, straight up from powerful thrusters, gaining an extra boost from the large anti-grav pad Omara installed in the ground. It had retractable wings, like *Endurance,* and they deployed smoothly for stability in atmosphere. When they reached altitude, Ani engaged the engines and they shot smoothly to orbit. For this "test," Omara planned to take the ship to the far side of the sun, cutting through Mercury's orbit, leaving Mars far enough behind them that a communications delay would buy them precious minutes if needed.

It took three days to reach the rendezvous point. Accommodations were cramped, with people piled into cabins and little extra room to relax or move about. This was not the luxury of an Omara Tours cruise. The Johari pitched in and formed their own kitchen crew, preparing the foods Omara squeezed on board as well as the space rations easily made with the Recyc-Alls. Lyn slipped back into her captain role and schmoozed her "guests." Now that they didn't have to hide their true selves, the Johari were open about their work and lives and what they hoped for on Gaia. She met doctors and writers and psychologists as well as farmers and mechanics and engineers. Families with young children and elders, like Antonia.

She compared these guests with those from past tours, which always included one or two complainers, for whom no amount of luxury or warnings about the constraints of a ship in space could please. But here she found no egos, no divas, no reluctance. That was remarkable, as Dr. Amos might say.

The Teys weren't the only ones leaving loved ones on Earth, yet everyone seemed to share a collective optimism that one day the two planets might keep in touch. "Not like we couldn't travel back and forth if we wanted to," Mr. Tey said with a wink at dinner the first night.

Lyn winced inwardly, realizing that if she did have the implant removed from her brain, with it would go the last remaining documentation for opening a Teegan wormhole. Only the Gaians would have the ability. But maybe soon, General Hellen Jacana would too. She decided to reserve a final decision on removing the implant until after she met the Gaians in person, had a sense of their technology, and could test her own gut feeling about them. Friend or foe weren't always clearly discernable by video calls.

TENSIONS WERE HIGH when Ani announced the ship was in position. Now they'd wait. The Gaians had been sending signals daily for almost two weeks. All they had to do was listen.

And there it was. The signal.

Lyn's stomach and heart signaled her excitement. This was it. Would this be Solstice morning, full of presents, or the worst movie plot where you scream at the character not to open that door? "Please respond, Ms. Parula."

Ro moved to the communications console and sent the coded response.

Dr. Amos joined them on the bridge and three grueling hours later, a comtunnel opened. Before them on the screen again sat Beryl, Pica, Salpin, and Quisca. Lyn was tempted to apologize if they woke them. Who knew what kind of schedule they'd maintained to be ready for this moment. After they traded greetings, they stared at Lyn.

"Captain, you've been injured," Quisca said.

She touched her face, the scars that melded her ear to her cheek and scalp. "They're healing. An unfortunate accident. I'm fine."

There was some time spent conversing and exchanging data in order for Lyn and her team to convince the Gaians that they were being honest and the ship wasn't filled with warriors. Ro assured them the passengers were all approved Johari, ready to return. Omara and Ro had arranged for a video feed to be piped throughout the ship. For the first time, the Johari were seeing their Gaian relatives. Likewise the Gaians could see waving Johari smiling and mugging for the cameras. Ro had selected a few to make statements, but the excitement washed through the decks.

Each step in the process had felt momentous, but all paled compared to sitting on the bridge of a ship filled with what were essentially refugees nervous and excited to finally arrive home.

For their part, Quisca and company seemed a bit stunned, faced with the enthusiastic Johari. Were Gaians just generally more reserved? Their eyes danced around their own viewscreen, from face to waving hand, to cheering Johari. Pica's light cheeks reddened noticeably. Beryl's eyes seemed wetter.

"Please—" Quisca began then seemed choked up. She started again. "Please convey our welcome."

"They can see and hear you," Lyn said.

Quisca inhaled a few deep breaths. Surely she'd prepared for this. Then she found her voice. "This is more overwhelming than I expected." The Johari quieted, listening. "I had words prepared, about how joyful it is to reunite with our family, but that hardly seems adequate. Human words, I confess, fail. May I greet you in our language?"

Ro stood. "That would be wonderful."

What came from Quisca weren't the unpronounceable tones they'd heard before when they'd introduced themselves, but a beautiful song. If there were words, they were indistinct, but a melody that rose and flowed, filling Lyn with peace and joy, like hearing a soaring symphony. You didn't need to know the words to a song to feel its emotion. The others joined in, making a gorgeous harmonic chorus. Even after they finished, the effect lingered and left everyone speechless.

Ro wiped her cheek. "Thank you. I think we understand."

Then a Johari woman began singing a beautiful piece Lyn remembered from her childhood, about missing and longing. One by one, other Johari joined in till there was a choral response to the Gaians' greeting. Another hush settled as they finished. Quisca thanked them. With a glance at her team, she announced the wormhole would open to allow *Tenacity* to pass through to Gaian space.

IT WAS STRANGE not needing TPCA or having to turn off gravity, but everyone strapped in with helmets in place. Who knew how a Gaian wormhole would be different from the Teegan version? That had been a rough ride, stressing the ship to the max.

Now, a distortion appeared in front of *Tenacity*. Petra called out the specs. A sphere formed, like the Teegan wormhole, and grew quickly, to Lyn's amazement. Through the opening, she could see stars, but also a ship.

"Captain, we're being pinged," Petra announced.

"By the Gaians?" Lyn said.

"No. By Earth Control."

Uh oh. Lyn muted the link to the Gaians and switched to mind link. They didn't need to hear this. *From where?*

It's an automated message in a relay, off a satellite in Venus's orbit. The time delay is seven minutes.

What's the message? Lyn asked.

It's a request for telemetry data. A bot's way of asking where we're going. Automated, unless someone suspects something and sent the command.

Lyn looked to Omara. This was not the time. *Let's ignore it*, Lyn said. *We'll pretend we never received it.*

Omara shook her head. *We can leave a lifepod behind. It can use* Tenacity*'s transponder codes and Petra can cover for us if needed. Until someone gets within viewing range, they'll think we're sitting here, quiet.*

Ro, not privy to this discussion, looked puzzled at the extended silence on the bridge.

Captain, I could go with the pod, Ruzena said.

That was an extraordinary offer. Giving up a chance to visit with her home people, miss saying goodbye to her family.

That won't be necessary, Lyn said, *Petra can handle the pod. But I appreciate your thinking of that. In another situation, it might be preferred.*

Ruzena gave a curt nod, looking slightly relieved.

Life pod ready to deploy, Petra said.

Launch lifepod, Petra, and respond to the ping. That should satisfy them.

Pod released, Petra said.

What did Earth Control want? Was it Faber or some know-nothing doing their job?

Lyn switched back to audio. "Ani, proceed through the portal."

Ani engaged the thrusters and they passed through smoothly. Alarmingly so. None of the shaking and turbulence of their trip back from Rigil Kent. That had been a dangerous, bumpy ride, and it had taken almost an hour to open the portal wide enough for the smaller *Endurance*. The Gaians had some sophisticated technology.

"Wow, that was . . . amazing," Ani said once the portal closed behind them.

Now Earth Control could look all they wanted but they wouldn't find *Tenacity*. Petra confirmed their location, a light year from the planet Gaia, HD 162827 d.

Ahead sat the Gaian ship. It looked nothing like an Earth ship. Hemispherical, it had a flat bottom and dome-shaped hull with a smooth surface. It seemed to shimmer in the starlight, like it was emitting its own glow. It reminded Lyn of sea jellies, an opaque translucence, but without the tentacles.

Only as they neared did she realize how big it was, maybe four times the size of *Tenacity*. She heard Omara's "mmm."

"A beauty, isn't it?" Lyn said.

"I'm immediately jealous."

The Gaians' vid stream blipped out as they closed the comtunnel and opened a vid channel through normal space, diverting Lyn's attention from the view of the ship. Quisca and Ro ran through logistics. Had Quisca's team been living out here on this ship since they started sending signals, or had they been able to get here in the few hours since *Tenacity* had responded? Either way, impressive.

There was no way to dock the two ships, so the Johari would have to be ferried over in lifepods. The Gaian ship's cargo bay was large enough that they could send all the pods at once. Petra could then fly the empty pods back to *Tenacity*. The Johari would remain in suits and helmets until they could be inoculated with Gaian microbes and until their own microbes could be purged. It would only take a few hours for the transition, Pica said.

"You are welcome to board and visit," Quisca said, "if you don't need to hurry back. I'd like to invite you to accept the inoculations that would enable you to remove your suits—and to visit our planet." She addressed Lyn. "I don't want to get your hopes up, but our medical experts believe, looking at your records, that the artificial implant can be removed. Not out here, however. It would have to be done on Gaia."

During the trip to the rendezvous point, Lyn and the others had discussed contingency plans should they be offered the chance to visit the planet, including undertaking precautions to protect their health. On Marao, it had taken several weeks for the illness caused by the planet's microbes to manifest, long after it was too late to prevent infection. Lyn's only concern was whether a week or a month later they could be harmed. Clearly the Gaians were familiar with how to do this, Ro had said, having done it successfully when the Johari arrived on Earth. Dr. Amos had reexamined the DNA Antonia had originally provided, searching for the marker Ro had mentioned on the previous trip. It was a simple fragment, he had found, easily detected and completely safe. He'd confirmed its presence in the Johari as they boarded *Tenacity*. This and the other data the Gains had given him eased any concerns he had about the compatibility of the human and Gaian microbiomes. He launched into a lecture on the details until Lyn asked him to skip to his conclusion.

"I would expect whatever protocol the Gaians will use to acclimate the Johari to their microbiome would also be safe for you. The Gaians' microbes are not like Marao's. Given the Gaians came to Earth and survived and I'm not seeing anything out of the ordinary—other than, of course, that these are alien—I feel confident you'll be safe."

Ruzena had been the most inclined to visit the planet. "Though it does trigger the Planetary Protection section of the Outer Space Treaty for when we return to Earth."

Lyn stared at her. Captain Tey had been the one to invoke that clause when *Endurance* returned and even tried to use it to prevent Omara from boarding. It meant they would need to remain in quarantine under Category 5, Restricted Earth Return until they could verify decontamination. "Really? You're bringing that up now? You of all people? Seems that horse left the barn about three hundred years ago."

"Apologies, Captain. I was only trying to—"

Lyn raised her hand. "I know. And you're right, but we've violated so many laws and treaties, why comply now?"

To be sure her crew hadn't changed their minds since that discussion, Lyn asked Quisca for a moment to confer. "Of course, take as long as you need." Lyn muted the call.

In the end, it would be up to her, as captain, to make the final decision. Jacana wouldn't stop till she got the tech from her brain. That didn't make her particularly objective, and going to the planet was an order of magnitude more dangerous. "I can't and won't ask you to go just so I can get this implant removed—"

They all spoke at once.

"I'm going with you, no matter what," Diana said.

"You're not going alone," Omara said.

"Are you kidding me? Miss this chance?" Ani said.

"I'd like to see it," Ruzena said quietly.

Dr. Amos waited for the others. "I expect to be able to monitor the procedures. I would intervene if I felt any of you were at risk."

Five sets of eyes were on her, waiting. They were all out of their fecking minds, Lyn thought, but with pride. A team working together was a beautiful thing. "Fine. And thank you."

She asked Petra her opinion of the Gaians' wormhole technology. "Could this have been faked?"

"I'm not detecting anything that would lead me to suspect this isn't all very real. When we went through the portal, I scanned the surroundings. While I'm unable to detect dark matter, the field dynamics clearly indicated a form of exotic matter holding the wormhole open. They are using the same concept, just with different material humans have yet to discover. Also, the exterior of their ship is a composite of materials not used on Earth—the basic elements are the same, just a different configuration. Without being able to board the ship, I can't know what purpose it serves or if it is used elsewhere. I'd love to get a look at their propulsion system."

It could be a trap. Get everyone off *Tenacity* so they could steal it or hold them hostage, but from what Lyn could see it was a tin can compared to the Gaian ship. Why would they bother? The ship didn't have a name that translated easily to English or any Earth language. The closest Petra could come up with was "potato sandwich," which made everyone giggle.

"Let's call it the *Spud*," Omara suggested to further laughter. It did resemble half a boiled potato.

Omara only worried that *Tenacity* shouldn't be "missing" any longer than necessary. She suggested, and Lyn reluctantly agreed, that Petra take *Tenacity* back through the wormhole and park until notified. There wasn't anything *Tenacity* could do for them here if the Gaians proved malicious. It was safer to send the ship back to Earth space and hope Petra could hold off any nosy Earth Control bots or suspicious generals. If the ship went missing, all hell would break loose. If its "crew" went missing, which was only Omara as far as anyone on Earth knew, that was, strangely, less worrisome.

"Pack a bag for a night or two," Lyn said, "and let's see what they've got." She reopened the link to Quisca. "We accept your invitation."

TENACITY HAD FIFTEEN lifepods, enough for the originally designed three hundred passengers and crew, and now they were one short. They sat inside the hull along the walls of the large muster area on the bridge deck. Omara had removed the seats, but to cram all six hundred in, they would be like crowded commuter transits. At least Omara had equipped them with artificial gravity.

Lyn didn't have Sharyn, or a large crew, to play traffic cop. She'd wanted her crew and Dr. Amos to stick together, but it made more sense for them to split up and take different pods. She reached for Diana's hand, their fingers interlacing briefly before they parted. Each stood by a pod door, and others Ro had drafted took the rest. They reminded everyone who boarded to move to the back, let others on, deploy helmets, and offered a reassuring pat on the arm and smile as needed.

Ro pushed among the crowd. "Families stay together, otherwise, take any pod. You'll be able to meet up with friends on the other ship." She reminded them to remain sealed until the Gaians had inoculated them. "Use the bathroom now, if you must. Who knows when you'll get to again, unless you want to pee in your suit."

Giggles and chatter echoed through the space. Parents bent over children, zipping helmets shut. Others helped elderly navigate with walkers and hoverchairs. A toddler screeched in terror when her mother tried to close her hood. Ruzena helped reassure her while the mother held her. Together, they got the helmet back on and the child settled, head on her mother's shoulder.

Finally, like a busy commuter platform, the crowd dwindled as they jammed into the pods.

"Let's get out of here," Lyn said through the com channel to her crew.

Ro stood frozen to a spot in front of an open pod door. Lyn ran over and gave her a reassuring pat on the shoulder. Don't fail me now, Aurora, she thought.

"I meant to make an inspiring speech," Ro said. "I meant to thank you."

"There'll be time for that on the other side." She patted her arm. "You did good."

Tears ran down Ro's cheeks. She automatically went to wipe them but bumped her faceplate, which knocked her glasses. She let out a weary laugh. Lyn gave her a playful shove to her pod and watched the door seal before entering her own.

One by one the pods popped out the sides of the ship and made their way like a line of ducklings to the *Spud*, Lyn taking the lead. The Gaian ship loomed, its smooth, pearly white hull glowing. Screens showed the line of pods behind her, so small in comparison. Only faint outlines marked what might be windows on the big ship, preventing a peek inside. A thrill of excitement and tension fought for control, curiosity winning out. The emotional calm of Quisca's song vibrated softly through her. Chatter through the com from the other pods made her feel less alone. The group in her pod were quiet, with only a muffled cry from a child in the far back. Windows along the sides gave them a view out.

The *Spud*'s cargo door slid open smoothly as they approached, like her garage door at home. At first the interior was dark, but as the door rose, she could see guide lights on the floor. The space was huge and clear, plenty of room for all of *Tenacity*'s pods. Racks of containers lined the sides, another rack held small ships, the *Spud*'s own shuttles no doubt. Lines and arrows pointed the way clearly, but someone in a spacesuit stood toward the back, arms held up, waving her in then pointing to the side. Where to park. She had to remind herself that this was an alien ship, otherwise she'd think she was setting down in any old commuter lot back on Earth. That both comforted and discomforted her. The mystery of how these people could be so human and so advanced deepened. Questions begging for answers filled her with a surge of confidence and commitment.

Once these fourteen pods landed and that massive door closed, there was no leaving without the Gaians' permission. Was this a horrible mistake? Through the opening to the main cabin behind her, everyone quieted, straining to peer through the windows, transfixed.

She shook her head to clear her mind. As she set down, she saw a line of people in suits and helmets, protected from the vacuum of space but masked and anonymous. Artificial gravity held them in place.

"How are you all doing?" she said through her local com to her passengers. She could hear them move and jostle against each other. Then chatter— "Okay." "Let's go." "I'm a bit space sick." Not surprising. Space took getting used to.

We landed on a ship from another solar system. Not a planet empty of technology like Marao. A threshold crossed that changed the world. World? Hell, her entire experience of reality. She mind linked to her crew on the other pods. *Any second thoughts?*

Not a good time for that, Diana responded, surprisingly calm and sure. Lyn might have expected her, of any of them to rethink this.

A loud *Hooah!* from Ani.

That's a little vague, Second Mate, Lyn responded with a laugh.

No second thoughts, Captain, Ani said, her voice pitched with adrenaline.

No second thoughts, Ruzena echoed with less enthusiasm.

Ditto, Omara said.

I'm not detecting any reason to abort, Petra said. Dr. Amos concurred.

Thank you, team, Lyn responded. She squirmed through the crowd to the side door and released the lock. She figuratively threw her heart across the threshold and flung open the hatch.

Chapter 16

STEPPING ONTO AN alien spaceship wasn't anything like she expected from movies and books. This could have been a busy transit station on Earth or even Clarke Terminal. The only clue was that the signs on the wall were incomprehensible. As the Johari filed off the pods, Gaians stepped forward to greet them. A sound system announced instructions: "You'll be led through a decontamination field. Please follow the instructions of your guides. Welcome to Gaian space."

Lyn gathered her team. Dr. Amos suggested he go first and report back what the field consisted of. *One would assume it's safe for humans, given the Johari will undergo this, but I'd feel better if you let me check it out.*

Not like they had any alternative, so Lyn agreed and he proceeded. The sound system described it as a nonthermal plasma process, which Dr. Amos confirmed. *Indeed, it is a UV-activated low-pressure plasma, much like that used on Earth. Perfectly safe.*

With that, she and the others joined the line. At the far end of the hallway, they entered a large lobby, like any grand hotel. High ceiling, potted plants, large windows, chairs and couches dotted the walls in conversation areas. If Lyn hadn't known she was on a spaceship, she'd never have guessed. Only the view, of stars, told her where she was. It chilled her to be reminded of the opulence of the *Aphrodite*.

More teams of Gaians, these dressed casually in jackets and pants and skirts and tunics that wouldn't look out of place on Earth, helped the Johari get back together with their families. The PA system let them know that the next phase would be a trip to Medical for inoculations. "When you are ready, just follow the escort."

Diana said it felt like the first day of college. Ro had disappeared into the crowd. With everyone in suits, Lyn couldn't tell one from another other than by size. Small children looked around in awe. Parents held little hands tight and for the most part everyone was pretty quiet. What were they feeling? Maybe like the refugees streaming through Montana on their way to Canada, or the boatloads of immigrants passing the Statue of Liberty in New York Harbor centuries ago. Have people always had this penchant to roam?

Ani and Ruzena clung to each other, searching for and corralling Ruzena's family—her parents, sister and brother, grandparents, and maybe aunts and uncles. Lyn was happy for Ani, but Ruzena had to be struggling. Where was home? Who was family? Would she ever see them again? She mind linked to Ani permission to stay with Ruzena and her family. *Whatever you and she need.*

Among the crowd, Lyn spotted Quisca's gray afro as she approached. "Greetings, Earthlings," Quisca said with what was clearly an amused smirk.

Lyn responded with a bow. "Take us to your leader."

Quisca laughed and held out her arms. Lyn wasn't sure what the appropriate greeting would be or what the Gaians' protocol was. Quisca must have sensed her unease. She reached for Lyn's hands and squeezed them warmly. "It's good to meet you."

"Likewise, but part of me can't believe this is happening."

"Neither can we." Quisca reached in turn for Omara, Diana, and even Dr. Amos, taking both hands in hers each time.

The crowded lobby was emptying out. Quisca led them to a couch and chairs by a window. "Unfortunately, you can't see Gaia from here. I can point out your solar system if you'd like."

"A dot somewhere out there, I presume," Diana said. "Do you have constellations? You know, patterns formed by the stars?"

"We do. The names wouldn't translate well, but the concepts are the same. We believe some might date back to the original settlers, reminded of the world they left. But we can't be sure. Most are named for various plants or animals on Gaia. What you call the Milky Way, we refer to as Snowdrift."

"There is so much I want to talk to you about," Omara said.

Quisca smiled. "I'd love that."

While they had been talking, Dr. Amos and Petra had been observing and analyzing the ship. Through her mind link, Lyn asked Petra what she thought.

Petra made the AI equivalent of a eureka, beeps and pings. *Interesting. My theory would be that the interior and exterior of the ship work together to absorb various stresses, everything from radiation to asteroid impacts and shear forces like you'd get from flying in atmosphere. There's even a temporal component I'm not able to understand. Bottom line, this is some seriously advanced technology. If this had been available during the war, the outcome would have been much swifter.*

Are you sensing weapons? Lyn asked.

No, although the potential to weaponize this technology must be considered. No doubt the Gaian defense capabilities would be superior to anything humans currently possess. But nothing offensive.

Omara joined in. *What's the difference? A defensive missile is that in name only.*

There is no missile technology on board the ship, Petra said. *I'm referring to shielding and deflecting. Humans could hit this ship with a nuclear weapon and it wouldn't so much as dent the hull.*

If what Petra said was true, the data in Lyn's head was rendered insignificant by what the Gaians were capable of. So much for eschewing technology. What an excellent cover for them on Earth.

She ordered Petra to send all the pods back to *Tenacity* except the one they'd need. Omara asked Quisca if it would be okay for *Tenacity* to head back to Earth space, explaining that an extended absence would be noticed. Quisca looked from one to the other as if questioning their trust but agreed. Through an apparent mind link, she sent the order and gestured to a window to watch the sphere form. On Lyn's command, *Tenacity* slipped away. She and Diana shared a look. Stranded. Again. Her stomach curdled only slightly. She was putting way more trust in these people than was perhaps warranted, but no one else seemed to share her misgivings. Omara looked like a child on Solstice morning, Dr. Amos stood quiet and impassive, no doubt scanning and analyzing everything he could through his wide-spectrum eyes.

"You do this so easily," Lyn said, struggling to think of an equivalent. "Like walking through a doorway, I guess."

Quisca twirled a hand in a circular motion but didn't offer an explanation. Not that Lyn could explain a Teegan wormhole, either.

"I'm so pleased you will come visit Gaia," Quisca said. "Shall we proceed to Medical?"

She led them through wide hallways while Omara peppered her with questions. Quisca said that yes, they did have a vibrant tourism industry and the ship was typical of the fleet. The ship's systems, Lyn noticed, were quiet and unobtrusive. No thrum through her feet or background noise in her head.

In the medical suite, they took off their helmets and received painless injections, much like the jetspray Dr. Amos used. They also were given translators. Tucked into an ear, it provided real-time translation in both directions. Dr. Amos stayed behind to talk to the Gaian medical team while the rest toured the ship.

People mingled on the various decks, the Johari circulating among presentations on what to expect on Gaia. Some perused shops on a marketplace concourse with restaurants that infused the air with intriguing aromas, making Lyn's mouth water. Hallway conversations buzzed with excitement, like a people finally returning home after a long vacation. A frisson of how lucky they were to have survived, even glad it was finally over, she noted with some regret. Was life on Earth that bad? What did the Gaians think of her crew, the humans? Probably primitive barbarians.

In the ship's engineering section, she asked about the technology they used to open wormholes.

The staff deferred to Quisca. She thought for a bit then said, "Do you mind if I speak in my language now that you have translators? I'm not as fluent in English as I'd like." She went on to describe in vague terms a technology much like the Teegan wormhole. Exotic matter used to hold open the throat. When she didn't get more specific, she said it was for their own sake. "It might be best if you don't know too much."

For their sake, Lyn mused to herself. Wouldn't General Jacana love to get her hands on this tech. She watched as another portal opened and they passed through to Gaia's solar system. No one had spoken, there were few controls, and the screens they could see were in a language they couldn't understand. The translator only worked audibly.

Diana watched the crew but shrugged. "I'm not getting a sense of how this works at all."

"We control the ship telepathically," Quisca said. "That would make observation more difficult."

The portal closed behind them, and ahead they saw Earth's twin. The *Spud* orbited Gaia at low altitude so the humans could see the planet as a whole. On the dark side away from their sun, cities sparkled, lights on dark velvet, like on Earth. It was one of Lyn's favorite views from orbit. The only difference here was that the cities were smaller and spaced farther apart. Not the huge swaths of light on Earth. Otherwise, the similarities were notable, and she reacted the same way as on first seeing Marao. That's *not* Earth? Clouds, oceans, land forms, mountains—with snow!—deserts. Polar ice caps! They passed a gray-rock moon with research stations and equipment. No one lived there full time. It was for research only, Quisca said. Nor was a retreat to another planet necessary.

During a meal in the dining center, the humans learned about Gaian foods and protocol. In general, Lyn observed, eating on Gaia was much like on Earth. Food on plate, hand to mouth. Instead of a variety of utensils, Quisca said, there was usually one, a spoon with short tines and sometimes a knife. The meal consisted of a stew and bread with fruit for a dessert. Very human, but Lyn tasted the first spoonful with trepidation. A bit salty but otherwise quite flavorful. Diana made a face. *It smells a bit foul*, she mind linked to Lyn. *Maybe fermented*, she decided.

Omara asked about the recipe, and Quisca admitted she'd requested the meal be more bland than usual, anticipating it would take getting used to. There were a variety of spices on the table, and Omara helped herself to several.

After, Quisca let Lyn visit the bridge to meet the captain and observe landing. It made little sense to her. The circular room was on the top deck, windows all around. Crew stood or sat, some even wandered around gesturing in seemingly empty air. There were no visible controls. All commands among the crew were telepathic, controls visible only to them, the captain explained. She kept a lively conversation with Lyn while commanding what on Earth would be a tense maneuver, seemingly paying no attention to her job, only the occasional pause when she relayed a command or received an update. Even when descending through the planet's atmosphere, no safety precautions were necessary. It was that gentle.

The *Spud* landed at a bustling transit station with smaller ships taking off and landing around them. Once they left the *Spud*, and their remaining pod, they'd lose contact with Petra. Quisca assured Lyn the pod, and Petra, would be well cared for at the terminal. *Have fun*, Petra said as they disembarked into a large, well-lit terminal. A domed ceiling let in bright light, scattered and shaded by hanging mobiles of colorful designs reminiscent of a solar system and its planets. The area was a combination of waiting room, check-in counters, and food court with restaurants dotting the walls. Signs, undecipherable to Lyn, and the translator couldn't help with that, seemed to mark various transit gates. A public address system spoke softly but clearly, announcing arrivals and departures. Lyn took out her translator to hear the language. For all its incomprehensibility, there was a lilting cadence to it, again like song.

She struggled to stem the overload of her first impressions of stepping onto another planet, one inhabited by very human-like beings. They were, in fact, humans. *Homo something-not-quite-sapiens*. Maybe more sapient than Earth humans.

The return of the Johari came with no media circus. No reporters, no cameras. Teams of counselors greeted the Johari and ushered them to waiting shuttles that would take them to a nearby campus for further orientation and acclimating. Much like refugees on Earth, the people were treated with care and patience. The counselors were the epitome of smiling reassurance. For those who were amenable, warm hugs greeted them.

Lyn and her crew stood to the side with Quisca, who would be their guide. Antonia came over, and Diana invited her to tour with them, but she declined. "I need to get on with my life. I say goodbye now or later. It's still goodbye." Her eyes were suddenly wet. She threw Lyn a sharp look and cleared her throat as if that could keep her from crying. "You take care of my only remaining daughter, you hear?"

"Yes, ma'am."

Diana and Antonia hugged for a long time then Antonia stepped away, turned, and joined a group of Johari. She didn't look back. Lyn put her arm around Diana.

"Friday's the anniversary, you know," Diana whispered.

"I know." Four years ago, three ships were swept away, and Rose Squires was killed.

Both the Gaians and Lyn had given Ani permission to spend the planet time with Ruzena and her family. Now, they clustered off to the side, Ani gripping Ruzena's hand. Soon, they disappeared through another gate and another shuttle.

Quisca led Lyn, Diana, Omara, and Dr. Amos through a doorway and outside into bright sunlight, a light breeze, and the scent of—what, Lyn had no idea, but it hit the back of her throat, like a spice. Not too sweet. Taking in a deep inhale, she realized how humid the air was. Not Syracuse humid, but refreshing. Puddles glinted sunlight. A shower had passed through. She spun to take it all in. There were trees and flowers and clouds in a blue sky and sounds she couldn't tell whether natural or part of the sound system of the station. For all she knew, here trees sang and animals only rustled. Dr. Amos turned in a slow circle, gazing upward. Lyn asked by mind link what he thought.

The air is of course breathable. CO_2 levels are under 300 parts per million, a third of Earth's, which would be analogous to preindustrial times. There are few of what we'd call pollutants. He hummed what Lyn took to be approval. "It's lovely here," he said out loud. "You might find the air a little rich. Be careful not to overexert."

Omara laughed. "Wouldn't that be refreshing."

Quisca motioned them toward a skim and took them to a hotel where they could freshen up and, when they were ready, she'd give them a tour of the city. Their rooms were much like any on Earth. While they couldn't read the brochure or signs on the walls, all they had to do was ask for a translation and the hotel's computer would answer. Any voice command was responded to.

"I suppose that means they're listening to everything we say," Diana said.

"You may request privacy at any time by saying so," the computer answered.

"Good to know," Lyn said. "Do you have a name?"

"A name? Computers don't have names. My dataset designation is—"

"Never mind," Lyn said. "Thank you."

Quisca led them on a walking tour, providing color commentary like they were old friends visiting. The city was the Gaian capital, holding the seat of government. It was clean and shopkeepers friendly and welcoming. It wasn't only a business thing either, Lyn noticed. People politely queued up for public ground transports, stepping aside for those getting off before boarding. Many smiled at and touched seeming strangers.

Tall glass towers rose over smaller, older buildings, but all looked to be in good repair. A mix, Quisca said, of businesses and residences. Trees lined even the busiest streets, and pocket parks dotted the neighborhoods with playgrounds, benches, or plant-filled oases. Children laughed and yelled to each other while kicking a ball around a playing field. Lizard-like creatures peered at them from boulders and stone walls. The shadow of a flying thing flicked by, a winged animal soaring skyward from a palm-like tree.

"Are those birds?" Omara asked. The sound was more like the buzz of insects.

"Not quite like yours. Ours are mammals. I'm afraid we don't have the pleasant birdsong you have on Earth."

OVER DINNER AT the hotel, Quisca continued her traveler's guide to Gaia. The dining room could have been any busy restaurant on Earth. Couples and groups sat around tables. Waiters—Gaians, not bots—carried trays of food and cleared away empty plates and bowls. The acoustics were such that Lyn could tell people were talking, even laughing, but she could only hear those at her own table. Windows faced a busy street with pedestrians and wheeled cycles as well as ground transports. The occasional skim flew overhead. A setting sun lit clouds pink. Dr. Amos joined them, receiving curious glances from the other patrons.

The planet's population was only three billion, Quisca said as they settled in, despite Gaia being roughly the same size as Earth.

"How did you manage not to overpopulate?" Omara asked. "It seems unrelated to any differences in behavior Aurora mentioned—humans being more competitive and Gaians more cooperative."

"That's not something we've had to think about." She supposed it wasn't an issue because they were matriarchal, and women had full choice and control over family planning—she headed the family. Men shared household and family chores. Family units were like humans'—mother, father, children. "And yes, we do have a spectrum of gender identities like you do though outside the male/female binary is relatively rare."

Women were the head of the household. They went off to work, they ran the government, they made important decisions. Fathers provided protection and food and cared for children.

"So, men don't have full equality?" Diana asked.

"Of course they do," Quisca said. "This is just the way we are."

Lyn and Diana shared a look. That's what they think. Quisca's fluency with English was excellent though her delivery was very neutral, Lyn realized. She couldn't tell from tone and inflection how serious Quisca was or whether she was trying to be funny or scolding. What even was a joke on Gaia? It reminded her of how challenging Fúlli was at first. Ne often meant one thing while saying another. Nothing important to worry about, but now, with an alien before her—or was she now the alien?—communicating intention mattered.

Quisca went on to describe the strong female friendships that men didn't have. Daughters left home to form new families and social groups. They dispersed, they became leaders. Sons stayed with the family, eventually caring for elderly parents. Mothers acted as matchmakers for their sons—daughters were on their own and the object of other mothers' matchmaking for their sons. Older women mentored young women.

"I think the Johari are going to be in for some adjustments," Omara said. She held up her glass. "This is delicious, by the way. Alcohol, I assume?"

"The same elements and molecules that make alcohol on your planet can do the same elsewhere in the universe, so yes. I'm glad you like it."

Diana took a bite of the steaming savory stew. "It actually tastes like chicken." She set down her utensil. "I'm trying to wrap my brain around how we could be so similar to start yet so different technology-wise now. I know a lot of years went by, hundreds of thousands, but does that really explain it?"

"Fortunately for us," Quisca said, "we knew upon arrival that resources could be exhausted and we had to come up with a better way. The reasons for us being here are unclear—we know we came from another planet, but lost in the fuzz of history is why. A lot changes in three hundred thousand years, but it's not hard to imagine we left because we had to. Space travel is extremely resource intensive."

"I'm curious that you aren't even more advanced," Lyn said, "given the head start. I expected molecular transportation, cyborg enhancements, that kind of thing. You've remained remarkably human."

Quisca smiled. "Thank you. I consider that a compliment. We did experiment with transporters. It proved too . . . well, the early efforts were so gruesome we shelved the idea. Something you might consider if you are doing your own experiments."

"We're not at that level, that I know of, but duly noted," Lyn said.

"As for enhancements, our medical knowledge has permitted us to heal most injuries without mechanical additions. We can regrow limbs, organs, everything but the brain itself. We never needed to create a super soldier, so it didn't occur to us to genetically enhance ourselves to monstrous proportions. We use our resources carefully. We don't extend life for the sake of extending life. No one wants to be a burden. We value quality of life."

Lyn was curious to follow up on that statement—did they control quantity of life? But Omara changed the subject. "You have no idea what other planet we all might have come from?"

Quisca shook her head. "Did we destroy it, much like you have Earth?"

That stung, but how did she intend that statement to land? Lyn pretended to adjust her translator, pulling it out enough to hear both the original speech and meaning. What Quisca said next, "Did we set out as explorers? Why you and us? Are there more on other planets? So many questions," felt neutral in her song-like language, until the last bit, "But for us to have found you Earthlings is truly gratifying," which comforted Lyn. She meant it.

"Yet we didn't know we came from another planet," Lyn said. "If that's what happened. Why?"

Quisca agreed it didn't seem possible they did not share a common ancestor, so somehow humans lost the knowledge of their origin. "We started out fundamentally understanding that cooperating was more productive than competing. Was it from lessons on our planet of origin?" She shook her head. "Alas, that's lost to history. Maybe it's simply because food is abundant here. And by cooperating from the outset, we've never devoted precious resources to weapons. We've been able to stay focused on inventions that benefit everyone. Though you certainly came up with some creative uses for former weapons, like missiles that become rockets and recycling armaments."

Lyn bristled at that last comment. Not the English words, which sounded complimentary, but the sensation the song gave her was ominous, like being insulted. Not unwarranted.

"Swords into plowshares," Omara said.

"We've been wondering how the wormhole that threw *Endurance* to Rigil Kent happened," Diana said. "Is it possible your people opened it? Even if by accident?"

"I don't see how," Quisca said. "I'm sure I'd know if an attempt to enter Earth space occurred."

"I've wondered if it was natural," Diana said. "We know there was an explosion on the *Aphrodite*. And there's a disk of dark matter in our solar system. Could some Teegan particles have been . . . I don't know. Charged. Released?"

Quisca stilled. "Intriguing." She didn't say anything for a long moment. Enough to make Lyn wonder if she was trying to concoct a story. "Forgive my pause. I'm not a physicist, so am not sure I understand enough to explain properly." She twirled her hand. "I don't know." Lyn interpreted the words as a resignation, giving up. The hand gesture a kind of shrug.

"I gather the particle you use to hold open a wormhole is different from what my parents found," Diana said.

"Correct."

"And . . . ?" Diana asked.

"That's all I'll say. If you don't mind."

"I do. But I won't press."

Quisca had a guarded look as she glanced from Lyn to Diana. While the Gaians had been more than generous to the humans and, especially, the Johari, Lyn detected tension, an almost palpable vulnerability in Quisca. It was like she was braced for a blow. Not surprising, given what she'd learned about humans was no doubt disturbing. If she was paranoid about Pulsar coming after her brain implant, imagine what Quisca thought of these barbarians before her.

"Tell me more about your healthcare," Dr. Amos said.

Quisca's shoulders dropped a fraction of a relaxing inch. "Obviously, we have illness and injuries, like you do. If someone is injured, say loses a limb, healthcare is freely accessible and they learn to adapt to loss or are provided the option of growing a replacement. Not all choose that route. All of our infrastructures are designed to accommodate everyone, whether elderly or—" She hesitated. "Well, you'd say disabled. But we believe everyone is able. Just . . . modified."

By the time they got back to their room, Lyn was exhausted, from the long day and her still healing body. They popped out the translators and rubbed their sore ears. Lyn told Diana how she listened to both Quisca's English and her own language.

Diana was intrigued. "Do you think she knew more about their technology than she let on?"

"No doubt, but overall, I didn't get a strong gut feeling that she was being deceptive."

"Gaia does feel a bit like Utopia," Diana said as they undressed and crawled into bed.

Lyn yawned and snuggled against her. "Makes me fear what humans would covet if they ever found out about this place. It's one thing to have advanced technology, which they clearly do, but I'm not sure they'd be prepared for the sheer rampaging greed humans are capable of."

THE NEXT DAY, Omara left with Beryl to meet government officials, Dr. Amos went with Pica to tour medical facilities, and Quisca took Lyn and Diana out of the city to visit the countryside and farms. They flew over lush green fields, lakes reflecting blue sky and white clouds, rivers full and wide. And forests. Vast, seemingly endless, stretching to the horizon. Also prairies and deserts. They passed through rain showers. It was hard to take in the beauty. Lyn hadn't seen anything like this on Earth other than in old movies and historical documentaries. It hurt her eyes and her heart.

Everywhere they visited, both urban and rural, they found art venues— theaters, museums, concert halls, even public squares filled with singing, dancing. There were no slums, no homeless, no exclusion zones of radioactive post-war landscapes. No mass graves. They weren't "handled." They could roam the streets as they wished with no Gaian escort. Through the translator, Lyn spoke with dozens of everyday citizens, shop keepers, transit drivers, office workers on break.

More than occasionally, they saw people embrace, kiss, even fondle each other. Neither Lyn nor Diana said anything at first, Lyn too embarrassed. Finally, Diana asked if everyone really did get along so well they could be so sexual in public. She blushed.

"It isn't necessarily a gesture of affection," Quisca said. "We diffuse tension differently from humans. Where you might put a fist through a wall, we touch each other gently. Sexual arousal in this case follows an explicit ritual."

Lyn detected no embarrassment on Quisca's part in her neutral description of what on Earth would cause giggles, blushing, and even disapproval. Here might be the main difference between Gaians and humans.

"That explains a lot," Diana said cryptically and changed the subject. Something for Lyn to ask about when they were alone.

"Could we visit a pole?" Diana asked. "And see snow?"

Quisca tipped her head. "Earth has snow, doesn't it?"

"Not anymore."

"Then you shall see snow."

They flew toward a pole, and the outside temperature dropped from summer in the city. Quisca pointed out the vegetation changing in response to shorter growing seasons and lower temperatures. Soon, they saw it, a white coating on the ground. Quisca flew until they were surrounded by mountain peaks draped in drifts like frosting, with craggy frozen rivers between peaks— glaciers. She set down on a glistening blue frozen surface. She hadn't thought to bring winter clothing, she said, so cautioned them to make the visit brief.

"Watch your step on the ice," she said too late as Lyn set one foot down and promptly fell flat on her ass. Diana laughed till she slid down a gentle slope away from the skim. She put her hands down then yelped from the icy burn. They ended up sitting and rolling in laughter, pointing to each other's fogged breaths, Quisca laughing with them like an amused parent.

Shivering, they slip-slid their way back to the ship. Quisca had a big grin as she flew them toward a snow-filled forest where dark clouds loomed. She set down in a small clearing of snow-draped spruce-like trees. It was snowing, flakes gently floating to the ground. Again Lyn and Diana flopped around when they left the ship, the snow knee deep. They gasped and laughed then quieted. Once Quisca shut down the skim's engine, silence drifted down with the flakes. Diana tipped her face back, snow melting down her cheeks. Lyn made a snowball. Their laughter echoed through the woods, snowballs flying back and forth till they collapsed, exhausted and sopping wet. Lyn lay down, astonished to feel so cold. And wet. Dr. Amos wouldn't know what to think of her biometric data right now. A shiver made her sit up. She helped Diana to her feet and they slogged their way back to the dry warmth of the skim.

"Thank you," she said through chattering teeth.

Quisca flew them back to the city, resuming her encyclopedic report of Gaia, Lyn's fingers aching as warm blood flowed, Diana's ears and cheeks bright red, their lungs scoured. As Ro had suggested, there were no large animals, Quisca said. Livestock consisted of a small goat-like creature. When Lyn asked about the prohibition against humans moving to Gaia, Quisca responded bluntly, no need for a gut reaction to her language. "I've come to think of the main difference between our worlds is that your motto is how can you help me, and ours is how can I help you? We consider Earth humans to be what you would call an invasive species. Aggressive, spreading, and an ultimate existential threat to us."

It wasn't like Lyn hadn't thought this herself on many occasions, but she stiffened at the candor. "That's not true of all humans," she said, compelled to defend her kind. "Many cultures have thrived on a collaborative concept, though perhaps not the dominant ones."

Quisca nodded in acknowledgment. "True. I stand corrected. It's one reason I hope we can remain in touch. Continue to learn about you."

Lyn was keenly aware that a culture of colonization thrived within those, like the G-Nerds, who had the greatest motivation and means to travel to a place like Gaia. It formed her overwhelming desire to protect it and other planets, like Marao. She couldn't blame Quisca for wanting to keep an eye out for a possible future invasion. "I understand. You are being more generous than I would."

THEY MET UP with Dr. Amos back in the capital. He was excited to report on what he'd seen at a medical center, the detailed research and vast amounts of data given to him to review at his leisure. They were equally curious, he said, to learn about human use of medbots. Their bots simply repaired damage and fought illness, not extended life, as human bots did. "They were quite surprised that life expectancy had not gone down from the war, and in fact had risen."

If the Gaians had any concerns about their information being revealed to the Earthlings, they didn't show it. The more Lyn learned about Gaia, the more she sagged into despair over what might have been for Earth.

Over dinner—Lyn was getting used to the flavors and enjoyed the meal—Quisca told her the medical team had sent word they were prepared to remove her implant, if she still wanted that. Dr. Amos described what he'd learned about the procedure, an advanced medbot that could travel through neurons and seek out and dissolve implants without harming live tissue. That the Gaians could perform surgery at that fine a level excited him no end.

"We have the technology to do this, just not the knowledge of how to go about it. It could be an exciting breakthrough." He might be an android—sorry, a doctor!—but he had a very human way of showing professional pride.

"This won't affect Omara's mind link, will it?" Lyn asked.

"No. That is superficial, working off brain waves and not embedded among your cells."

With his blessing, Lyn agreed to undergo the procedure.

The next morning, Quisca took her to a medical center, sleek and modern—a perhaps unusual term. Alien really, especially by Earth standards. Maybe it was because she was a VIP, but Lyn didn't have to sign in or wait. Compared to her room at that Worcester trauma center, this was light years ahead. Quiet, sunlit, no smelly disinfectants. Dr. Amos introduced her to Dr. Jura. She looked about Lyn's age but she had no idea what that meant on Gaia. She wore typical medical protective clothing, smock, cap over her dark hair. She snapped on gloves.

"Let's get you settled," Dr. Jura said, showing her to a recliner. They wouldn't be drilling into her skull, thankfully, and Diana was allowed to be with her throughout. Other doctors and nurses appeared and introduced themselves, but Lyn had no hope of remembering them all.

When the medical staff were busy gathering together tools and vials, Lyn pulled Diana in for a kiss. "Just in case. You know how much I love you, right?"

"Likewise. Remember, drooling zombie, I'm here for you."

They began with a series of noninvasive scans. Dr. Amos translated—from medical jargon to plain English—Dr. Jura's descriptions of the process and what she was seeing on the scans. Once she had a clear view of what was Lyn and what was the implant, she could design the treatment.

"I don't know if you were aware of this, Captain, but your implant shows signs of deterioration."

Lyn mentioned her hand tremor. "Do you think that's related?"

"We'll see, I suppose. I don't see anything dangerous at this point, but it might be good to remove this."

Jill and General Jacana had their own implants, and Rachel tried to alter hers herself. Lyn's last use of the implant was remembering why. Voices, Rachel had said. Weird obsessions. What if the implant itself was responsible for Pulsar's paranoia about aliens? How could she ask the doctor that without raising concerns about what humans back on Earth might be plotting? She let it go, relieved to be done with the thing. Maybe Dr. Amos could help Jill and anyone else who wanted it removed.

Technically, the Gaian nanobots could zero in on the specific information, the Teegan wormhole tech, and remove only that, but Lyn opted for a full deletion of all Pulsar technology.

"It's the best way to prove that I don't have the information squirreled away somewhere," she said. "I want every remnant of Pulsar out of me."

She was awake for the procedure, which consisted of an infusion through a patch placed on the side of her neck and connected to an IV bag. As the minutes ticked by, she felt only the sensation of knowledge leaking away. Not memories, though. Nothing changed there. Everything that had been erased by Pulsar and recovered by Dr. Amos remained intact.

"I can't believe this is enough to destroy all that data," she mused.

Dr. Jura corrected her. "We're not in the business of destroying things. Think of it as being recycled into healthy tissue or removed as a simple waste product."

Would she eventually pee out the specifications of a Teegan wormhole? Flush Pulsar's future plans for exploration and conquest down some Gaian toilet?

She was left with a mild headache and an eerie quiet in her head. "When I try to search for information, it's like I've lost the concept of how to access it. I used to think about something—say the orbital mechanics for launch, and I'd know the answer. I feel kind of dumb now."

"Welcome to our world," Diana said, giving her hand a squeeze.

QUISCA DROPPED LYN and Diana back at their hotel and casually mentioned there'd be a dinner that evening. That's nice, Lyn thought. Time to rest up and have a good meal before going home. She hadn't seen Omara all day. She'd been off in negotiations with Verius, head of the planet's government, and other leadership while Lyn was getting her implant removed.

"Verius wondered if you'd say a few words," Quisca said. "But it'll be a simple affair." Then she left.

They busied themselves packing. Lyn popped her translator out and rubbed her ear. "I think I might keep this."

Diana eyed her suspiciously. "For Dr. Amos to reverse engineer?"

Lyn laughed. "Hadn't thought of that, but we have our own, just not tuned to the Gaian language. I like listening to it. It's so melodic."

Diana shrugged and closed her bag. "No one on Earth speaks Gaian. What would you do with it?"

Lyn turned it in her hand. She flipped a tiny dial and put it back in her ear. "Let's see if it reverses. Say something."

"You are an idiot," Diana said.

Lyn heard an amusing tone. She laughed. "It works."

"And you're still an idiot."

While they rested, Lyn asked Diana what she'd meant about Quisca's explanation of sexual contact explaining a lot.

"Ah," Diana said. "I'd always noticed how affectionate Quin and Antonia were with each other. Such a contrast with my own folks. I took it to be more about what was abnormal in my life than what was abnormal among the Johari. And Rose was"—she paused—"very demonstrative too. I'll leave it at that."

Lyn rolled closer and touched Diana like she'd seen the Gaians. "Maybe don't leave it at that?" Diana smiled and kissed her.

DIANA SUDDENLY SAT up, waking Lyn. "This dinner is going to be big, you know. You don't host aliens from another planet, especially when it's not a secret, and don't end with a bang."

"Don't be silly. She said it would be casual."

"The president of the planet will be there. Trust me. This is big."

Lyn sat up. "You think they'll make an announcement? To do with Omara?"

"I'm more worried about what we'll wear." Diana scooted off the bed and rummaged through her bag.

They'd flown in their Omara Tours flight suits and had brought a change of civilian clothes, but that was it. Diana had bought a nice jacket from a shop in the city and Lyn bought one at a rural shop. Like a fine wool, and patterned with bright colors. The weaver had told her it came from an animal best described as a goat-like sheep. She'd seen herds in pastures. They were beautiful animals, their fleece naturally grew in bright greens, reds, and blues. It reminded her of the vibrant color of Pica's, Beryl's, and Salpin's hair. Those, she'd learned, were also natural. Hair color among the Gaians was a lot more diverse than among humans.

Diana held up the jackets. "Should we go shopping?"

"Where? And with what?" They were out of local currency, and Quisca would be back to pick them up in an hour.

Diana tossed Lyn's jacket at her. "At least take a shower. Do something with your hair."

"What's wrong with my hair?" She looked in a mirror. Okay, it was a little flattened and had a kink where she'd pulled it back into a ponytail.

After showers and a quick shine of Lyn's Johari boots, they raced down to the lobby where Quisca was waiting.

"Tell me we look okay for this," Lyn said with a hint of panic.

"Of course you do." For her part, Quisca looked the same as always in her simple gray tunic. She ushered them into her skim. "Humans find the strangest things to worry about."

They entered an impressively large building with columns and steps then Quisca steered them into a small anteroom where a dark-skinned woman waited. She wore a simple tunic and slacks, though with a bright pattern of blues and greens. Her erect posture combined with a bald head imbued the air with a regal presence. Sure enough, this was Verius, president of Gaia.

"How are you feeling?" Verius asked Lyn. "I was told the procedure went well."

"Yes," Lyn said. "I don't even have a headache. I'm very grateful for this."

"Selfishly, we are too." Her eyes flicked to Quisca. "While we are more than thrilled to meet you and are thankful for the return of our people, we can't help but be cautious. I hope you understand."

"I do. I look forward to learning how your talks with Omara went."

"I think you'll be pleased."

They chatted briefly about the sights Lyn and Diana had seen, their impressions of Gaia. She was so warm and casual, it was hard to remember she was their leader. Even shy Diana relaxed. Then Verius motioned them toward a doorway. They entered a crowded banquet hall, Johari and Gaians arriving and mingling and chatting in groups. The large room was not ostentatious. No gold ornamentation, no fancy chandeliers, but beautifully designed with a high ceiling and a large wall of windows overlooking a beautiful lake and sunset. Musicians played stringed instruments, flutes, horns, and percussion softly as background.

There was no particular attention paid to the arrival of the president or to Lyn and Diana. No shouted announcement, no musical fanfare. Omara and Dr. Amos were chatting with Ani, Ruzena, and her family by a table filled with appetizers.

Near as Lyn could tell, all the Johari were there. Ani and Ruzena looked happy for the most part. People mingled, many hugging and kissing in greetings. The Johari, like her own group, were more reserved. The president excused herself to confer with Omara, Diana went to get them drinks, so Lyn joined Ro by the window, momentarily alone. "How's it going?"

Ro smiled sheepishly. "It's a little overwhelming." She sipped her drink. "The booze is good, though."

"You okay with us leaving you here?"

She took a moment before answering. "Yes. I think so." She sighed. "They think we've been traumatized. They've offered counseling and medication."

"Medication? Sounds serious."

She gave a short wave of dismissal. "I have to admit, I feel very tense around them. Expecting some shoe to drop. At the same time, I feel an overwhelming sense of peace to have made it here. I have you to thank for that."

"Or to blame."

A smile and quick head shake. "Don't worry. We'll be fine." She looked around the room. "I'm glad there are a lot of us, though. We have each other."

"You're making me worry, Ro. I'm not dropping you off at summer camp. This is forever."

"I know. But didn't you find yourself adjusting to life in Rigil Kent? Thinking you'd never make it back?"

"I was terrified the entire time. But most of that was the responsibility of the hundred-plus souls on board, their lives depending on me and my crew. If we had been able to stay on Marao, maybe I'd have let go of Earth. A bit, over time. But there's something about home that pulls."

"Exactly. And for us, this is home. I didn't expect this to happen in my lifetime though I've been filled with a longing since I first learned the truth. So, we'll be fine. Please don't worry."

An announcement urged people to find their seats, that the meal would begin. Lyn's stress level rose despite the relaxing mood as she and her team were ushered to a table front and center, next to a low dais between them and the wall of windows looking out on a stunning sunset. Antonia sat beside Diana. They were joined by Verius, of course, as well as Quisca and her team. Ani sat with Ruzena and her family at the next table, and Ro at another with her family, her Johari leadership, and a few Gaians. The rest of the tables were a mix of Johari and Gaians. The musicians played off to the side.

What was proper etiquette? Did she risk embarrassing herself, and therefore all humans, in front of their president? Gaians seemed to prefer one-pot meals of stews and soups. But that was casual fare. She assumed this would be elaborate. Servers circulated with trays laden with bowls. At each table, one Gaian stood to help the server distribute the food. Beryl set a bowl of hot, aromatic stew before Lyn and worked her way around the table, serving the president last. Another server arrived with yet another laden tray. Beryl set bowls of salad and breads in the middle of the table and filled glasses with wine and mugs with water. Finally, she set a carafe of wine and jug of water on the table. It was all so familiar. Conversations had paused except for expressions of thanks, which Lyn repeated.

An urgent need for coffee hit her stomach and muscles. It'd been a long day, she was tired, but also hungry. Caffeine on top of nerves would not go well together. She sipped her water because she saw Salpin do that but didn't dare make a further move. Once they'd all been served, Verius mentioned where the food had come from, which farms, and thanked the kitchen staff by names. Miriam would appreciate this. Then they dug in. Lyn's nervousness melted with the first mouthful. A delightful mix of flavors and textures. Diana moaned beside her. Omara, on the other side of Verius, closed her eyes and savored the effect. Whether her taste buds were fully acclimated or these were better cooks, Lyn wasn't sure.

Verius smiled and raised her wine to her guests. "I'll leave the speeches for later, but welcome."

The dinner chat mingled with family-style passing of dishes and spreads—not quite butter, but herby and flavorful. Lyn carefully mimicked her hosts.

Beryl asked Diana about their tour of the planet. "Did you get to see Mount Joy?"

"We flew over it. Gorgeous doesn't even begin to describe your planet."

"I know of Earth only through reports and images. Tell me what it's like, now that you've seen here."

Diana shook her head. "That's a hard question. Earth used to be like this, but before I was born."

"Before the war?"

"Even longer ago."

Verius, listening in, asked Lyn her thoughts. "The same. It's bittersweet, being here."

"Bitter? Sweet? Two opposite tastes. How so?"

"It's an expression, to illustrate things can be joyful and painful at the same time."

Verius chewed thoughtfully then sipped her wine. "I like speaking with you instead of reading your languages. There are nuances that don't translate."

"Tell me about it." She remembered her translator and covered loosening it while scratching her ear.

Verius raised an eyebrow, if she had one, which Lyn noticed she did not. "Well, for instance, sometimes you say something but don't mean it the way it comes out."

Lyn covered a laugh. "Like what I just said. I didn't mean literally that you had to tell me what you don't understand. It's a phrase meant to be empathetic—that I understand."

"Yet you don't say that."

All she sensed from Verius was curiosity. "We have a lot to learn about each other." One thing that struck Lyn now, she said, was how low-tech Gaians were. "I haven't seen a holodisplay anywhere. And though you have robots and androids, people seem to do most of the work, even serving the food and drinks."

"An interesting observation." Verius swiped the gravy in her bowl with a piece of bread. "I do recall reports from Earth pointing out an increasing reliance on technology for simple entertainments and such. I suspect the difference is due to the resource cost involved." She licked her fingers.

Salpin, the engineer, said, "Simulations require vast amounts of energy. We've put that into superluminal travel and advanced materials and propulsion for our ships."

"Yet you don't use advanced AI," Omara said.

"By AI you mean artificial intelligence?" Salpin asked. Omara nodded. "We are certainly intrigued by your Doctor Amos." She gave him a warm look. "It's not that we don't make use of advanced computing. You've seen it yourself in how our ships are controlled. It's simply that we've focused more on enhancing our telepathic abilities in order to make the best use of our brains, which are more complex and yet somehow simpler than the enormous resources needed to provide external computing. We can, after all, simply give birth to new brains." She said that last with a chuckle, the truth of which made them all smile.

And in her tone Lyn sensed reassurance, nothing worrying. Surely, she was making too much of their language inflections.

"I agree that the efficiency of the human brain vastly surpasses my own ability," Dr. Amos said. "Perhaps a closer integration between what we call wetware and hardware isn't a goal we should be striving for."

"Your inclusion of yourself in that 'we' gives me great hope that you are on to something, as you humans put it," Verius said.

Lyn interpreted the light melody of her response as relief. She wondered if Verius was aware of the G-Nerds on Earth who longed to merge humans with computers. She mentioned she hadn't seen any open-pit mines or decimated forests, that on Earth you couldn't escape the scars of the past. Salpin said Gaia had three main continents, each more than large enough to support its population. But to be sure, they rotated their agriculture and forestry, always leaving most of the land untouched, and what they used was allowed to revert after a few years.

Quisca added, "We take only what we need, usually about a third, leaving a third for nature and another third for the next generation."

"Much like indigenous peoples on Earth," Omara said. "Treat the land to support seven generations. Not followed widely enough in the past, but governments are trying to be better stewards now."

"You say indigenous like it does not apply to you," Verius said. "Are you not all one people?"

Omara explained how humans moved around the planet throughout history, with distinct cultures, and often destroying existing populations. "It's not a happy history, but it's what we have."

Pica made a confirming murmur. "Yes, I recall reading about your . . . colonization patterns of genocide and ethnic cleansing, I believe it has been called. Most unfortunate."

Quisca shot her a look.

"My apologies," Pica said quickly, lowering her eyes, her cheeks blushing to match Salpin's hair. "I mean no insult. Shall we hug?"

Omara stiffened, her face flickered alarm. "I don't think that's necessary. No insult taken."

When the dessert was served, Verius turned to Omara. "I think now is a good time." They both went to the dais. The sun had set and lights were raised for them. Conversations quieted and everyone gave their attention.

"I'll be brief, that dessert looks delicious," Verius began. "We come together for a very special occasion. First, I'd like to welcome home our esteemed research team." She paused and raised her arms. Ro must have been prepped because all the Johari stood to a round of applause, which consisted of raised arms and waving hands. "It's impossible to convey my appreciation for all you've done over these past years and decades to bring knowledge of our cousins to us. At great risk to yourselves. I'd like to take a moment to hold in our hearts those who lived out their lives away from Gaia, those who made the ultimate sacrifice to protect us." She cupped her hands over her heart and the audience did likewise. "We have learned much about Earth over the centuries, but now to be able to meet our cousins brings a new dimension and meaning to the endeavor. I understand there's a saying on Earth: Be careful what you wish for. It might not be what you expected. Discovering Earth was a tremendous achievement. The first forays there were full of surprises. I won't elaborate on what we did not expect, but I am grateful for what we've learned, and I hope the future of our two peoples will be close and fulfilling."

In the Gaian language, Verius's speech had been a lilting melody, making Lyn's heart soar. From an official perspective, it seemed the Gaians weren't willing to keep that door shut. She supposed it could be diplomatic posturing and ultimately meaningless. Not like that had never happened on Earth.

Verius turned to Omara and put an arm around her shoulders. "I would like at this time to introduce you all to Omara. I am pleased to announce that we have taken the preliminary steps toward a continued relationship with her as a special envoy."

The room erupted in waves of applause. Ruzena, Lyn noticed, seemed particularly relieved. Ani beamed at her as she stood with the others in ovation.

"Someday we hope that will mean ongoing face-to-face interactions, but for now, we've given Omara a means to remain in touch," Verius said. "Nothing specific will be shared at this time, but the conduit of communication is open and available. As they say, the details are to be worked out."

"Oh, great," Lyn whispered to Diana. "Just as a target's removed from my back, one's placed on Omara's. I hope this isn't a brain implant."

"Just as no individual can survive alone without family and friends," Verius continued, "neither can a people without recognizing relations and allies. I extend my formal intention to be both a friend and ally to the humans of Earth as represented by Omara, Lyn, Diana, Ani, and the delightful Dr. Amos."

She opened her arms and bowed toward Lyn's table. More applause broke out. People stood and whistled or sang their approval. Verius raised her hand for quiet and gestured to Omara. Her turn to speak.

"I'm humbled to be in your presence." Omara opened her hands to the crowd. "This has been an experience humans have wondered about and even longed for, if usually with trepidation," she said with a disarming smile. "I look forward to getting to know you better and will take your example of hospitality and model of how to live a best life into my heart and"—she turned to Verius—"someday, I hope, to our own leadership so we can come together in harmony." She bowed. "Thank you."

When the audience waving slowed, Verius motioned Lyn to approach. "If you would, Captain."

This was no different from making a speech on tour, Lyn reminded herself, failing to force out the reality that while being in a different solar system wasn't a new thing for her, addressing a room full of extraterrestrial intelligent beings most certainly was. She concentrated on not tripping on the step up the dais. That successfully negotiated, she turned and faced the crowded room. Panic set in. She cleared her throat.

"Thank you for this kind, generous welcome. I had no idea when I set out on what was to be my last tour as captain what would follow." The sea of faces before her hit home with the impact of what had happened. "We simply never know what seemingly random events will propel us down a path with unexpected outcomes. The effort to save my ship, crew, and passengers turned into an alarm call for your people on Earth. Without the leap of faith Ruzena and Aurora gave me—which I admit I didn't make easy for them." She looked to Ro and Ruzena. "Learning about the Johari, the Gaians, and your way of life has been altogether eye opening, encouraging, and at times depressing. I'm not sure humans can rise to your level of sophistication. I for one am anxious to see where our now-joined paths lead. If we can resolve the mystery of our common origin, I can think of no higher purpose for the remainder of my life. I welcome any collaboration you offer."

That drew applause, and she had to wait to continue. She finished by introducing and thanking her crew. "We've learned that if you bring together the best minds, there are no problems too tough or emergencies too dire. I expect if the day ever comes that the rest of Earth can get to know Gaians, we'll find ourselves with truly profound mentors who can help guide us to a better place."

After more applause and singing, the three returned to their seats. Dessert proved equal to the main meal, and Lyn relaxed and enjoyed the conversation. Finally, as the event broke up, she gathered her team. It was time to go home. One last hug between Diana and Antonia, Ruzena and her family in a group hug with Ani. But it wasn't as sad a leaving as Lyn had anticipated. Hope hovered over them like the beautiful Gaian music.

Chapter 17

QUISCA HOSTED LYN and crew on a smaller ship to take their pod to orbit and open a wormhole to Earth space. Petra and the pod had indeed been kept safe, and Dr. Amos transferred all this observations to her. For security reasons, Quisca said, they'd first open a comtunnel to *Tenacity*. Petra, from *Tenacity*, responded to the hail with a curious answer, "When the cat's away, the mice will play."

That dumbfounded Lyn. Omara furrowed her brow, but not in confusion. "Nothing to worry about," she said for Quisca's benefit, but via mind link told the others, *It seems we will face a small problem on the other side*, and explained that she'd left Petra with a code to send if their trip had been compromised.

With T technology safely removed from her brain, Lyn didn't fear what anyone might do to her. *Not like we have any options. Let's see what the mice have been up to.*

To protect *Tenacity*, and whatever or whoever might be in the vicinity, Omara suggested the Gaians open their wormhole a half day's flight from *Tenacity*. Lyn said another goodbye to Quisca, and Ani piloted their pod through the wormhole and made their way to the ship. With hours ahead of them, Lyn advised naps. "Best to be rested before we face the fire."

RESUMING THE GUISE that Omara was the only crew, she hailed *Tenacity*. Jill Faber answered. "Welcome back. Have a nice trip?"

Lyn didn't know whether to be relieved or alarmed. A small ship registered to Earth Control was docked to *Tenacity*. They debated hiding on the pod and letting Omara handle Faber alone, but there really was no place to do that, plus Faber was on *Tenacity*. She knew it looked nothing like what Omara had specified to Earth Control.

"If the game is up," Lyn said, "let me take the heat."

"We are in this together," Omara said. "We'll take it together."

Faber greeted them in the muster area, hands clasped behind her back, her eyes widening in surprise. "Well, look what the cat dragged in." Her eyes roamed among them all, settling on Lyn. "Fit to fly, Captain? I didn't expect to see you here." Then she spotted Ruzena Tey, behind Ani. Her brow furrowed and she shot a look back to Lyn. "What's she doing here? You know she works for General Jacana, right?" Then she glared at Omara. "I thought we had an agreement."

"I can explain," Lyn said.

Jill rolled her eyes. "That's what they all say." Her anger radiated.

"We were testing the lifepod," Omara said casually.

"Really. The long-range sensors didn't detect you until about ten hours ago when you miraculously materialized. That seems to be your MO." She swept her gaze around the room. "Interesting layout here. Hundreds of tiny cabins, yet you don't strike me as the sort of operator who runs steerage tours. Luxury was always your thing. In fact, the specs you registered with Earth Control aren't anything like this ship. I think you all have some explaining to do."

"Over a meal. I'm hungry. You may as well join us." Omara swept by her.

Lyn mind linked to Petra. *What the hell happened?*

Petra responded, *She arrived yesterday, alone. I couldn't keep her off. I tried to argue that all was fine, but with Omara unable to respond, she invoked EC's emergency override.*

Lyn sighed. In case of emergency, Earth Control could unlock and board any ship to perform a rescue if the crew were disabled. A necessary but unfortunate loophole.

Omara linked to Lyn and the others, *Whatever you do, don't mention the Johari. Use the official designation HD 162827 d or Gaia. We may have to go with Plan B.*

Plan B? Lyn messaged back. *There's a Plan B?*

Just follow my lead, she replied.

Omara led the way toward the dining room. Dr. Amos lagged behind and messaged Lyn that perhaps it was best if he went to his office and recharged. Lyn agreed, considering the danger he presented to their little adventure. Jill could demand his logs, which at this moment were uploading to Petra who was transferring everything across space to Ruby Valley. While she could destroy Dr. Amos if she had to, it was no longer possible to erase Petra. As she walked and thought, Omara was dressing down Jill Faber.

"You realize you have illegally boarded a private vessel," Omara said, politely. "We hadn't sent an emergency message. I'm allowed to file a complaint, you know."

"We'll see about that," Jill said. "Falsifying documents won't help your case."

Omara stopped short when she entered the dining room. "Right," she muttered to herself. They had no chef or cooks. The Johari had done that. Omara continued through to the kitchen, waving for them to follow. Together they made dinner, Jill reluctantly going along.

"What did you think we were doing out here?" Omara asked as they settled around the captain's table. "Smuggling contraband?"

Jill locked eyes on Lyn. "Something far more interesting, I'm sure. You said you wouldn't use it again."

"I didn't."

Jill set her plate down with a loud clunk. "Let's cut the crap, okay? Save us all some time. I know for a fact that this ship disappeared for approximately six hours three days ago." She smiled condescendingly. "You think you fooled me with the lifepod transmitting your signal." She took a bite and moaned. "This is delicious." It didn't help her mood, however. "Unless you've invented cloaking technology, I need to know what you were doing." She pointed her fork at Diana. "Actually, especially if you've invented cloaking technology."

Omara ate a few bites. "Lyn tells me I can trust you."

Jill shot Lyn a look.

"What I'm about to tell you will not come as a surprise, I gather." Omara glanced at Lyn. "You may recall a message received from space, not Earth-based, back in 2115. Correct?"

Lyn did not have a good feeling about where this was headed.

Jill's hand stilled, fork suspended. "Mmm hmm."

"I don't expect you to believe me, but it turns out a group of aliens have been living on Earth for some time—anthropologists—who needed help getting home. I provided that help." Omara took a sip of wine while Jill silently watched her. "That message had been meant to reach these people, but was inadvertently intercepted."

A shiver ran up Lyn's spine. As if a cold wind had raced through the room sucking the air from everyone's lungs, they sat frozen, eyes darting. Diana visibly paled. Ruzena closed her eyes as if to block a blow.

Jill sniffed out a laugh. "Very funny. Try again."

Omara sighed. "It was quite a large group, hence the cabins. I'll refurbish when I get home. I think she's ready for tours, don't you?"

Lyn watched this spectacle, incredulous. What game was Omara playing?

"Where is this planet?" Jill asked.

"A hundred or so light years away. They can open wormholes. All we had to do was meet them at a rendezvous spot. Lovely people. Possibly cousins. Very human-like. Well, obviously since they'd blended in on Earth—"

Could they possibly get away with this from the sheer unbelievability of it? Could Jill be convinced Omara had gone insane?

Jill set her fork down with a soft clink. "You met with aliens."

"Yes."

There was a very long pause where Jill seemed to be deciding whether to believe this or not. No one moved.

"Very well," Jill said finally, quietly. She leveled her gaze on Lyn. "I'm invoking the Planetary Protection clause of the Outer Space Treaty."

Omara looked from one to the other, confused. "The what?"

Lyn closed her eyes. Omara knew what this meant. Was this Plan B? She matched Jill's serious, quiet tone. "That means you too now. Quarantine."

If Jill wanted to play the Space Treaty hand. Fine. Lyn would see her PP clause and raise her with one very annoying complication.

Jill folded. She pushed back her chair, like she could prevent infection by distance, and gave Ruzena a disapproving look. "Nice to see you again, Captain Tey. Isn't this ironic."

Ruzena froze, eyes wide and darting between Lyn, Omara, and Jill.

Jill continued to glare at her. "How'd you end up with this motley group?"

Omara stepped in. "I hired her. She's a very capable captain. Worked for Earth Control, so I assumed she was of the highest caliber. I'm hoping she'll consider a job with Omara Tours." She smiled at Ruzena, who managed a poker face. "When space closed, most captains went into other work." She tipped her chin toward Lyn. "Now that space is reopening, we're facing a labor shortage."

Jill put her hands in her lap and sat back. "You expect me to believe you met with aliens. I really don't have time for this. I flew out here myself because I didn't want anyone at Earth Control seeing the sensor data and raising an alarm. A ship goes missing—again—and we might never get space reopened. You are not helping the cause with this harebrained fairy tale. What. Is. Going. On."

Omara reached for her wine. "I suppose we can't really prove it, can we, Lyn?"

Lyn startled. "Um." All they needed to do was not mention the word Johari, and this could be handled. "She's probably right. Short of producing a little green person, I don't see how we can convince you. But yes, we visited another planet, talked to real, live aliens—who, I might add, have absolutely no interest in invading our planet. Heck, they've been there, seen what we're capable of, and scurried away. They weren't sure if they want to remain in contact, but I suppose we could call them and see if they'd talk to you."

Omara raised an eyebrow. Too much? Too late.

Lyn made a face. "Oh, but, drat, we have no way of doing that. They were the ones who opened the wormhole. And they removed my implant. That might convince you. You can check if you like, but it's gone. And, as I've said all along, so is the data we used to create the wormhole that brought us back from Rigil Kent."

Jill's eyes narrowed. "That's impossible."

Lyn smiled and nodded slowly. "I did have the data in my head. That's why I wouldn't let anyone near me. Sorry I had to lie to you, but I think you know the stakes." She went on to describe the aliens and their planet, an Earth twin light years away. "What they don't know—and we don't either—is how this happened. How'd two planets light years apart both produce humans? Sounds crazy, right?"

Crazy, and possibly treasonous to have withheld this information. Her vision tunneled down to Jill, the others blurring around the table. Draw the fire, Jill's ire, and let the others be. She babbled on about the theory of another planet with a common ancestor. "Think of it as the Africa of the galaxy."

"Why should I believe you?"

"No reason you should. No reason you need to. But I got the implant removed."

Jill stepped around the table to Lyn and leaned down to touch their foreheads. She pulled back abruptly. "How'd you do that?"

"I told you."

Jill returned to her seat. "Who are these aliens? What do they call themselves?"

"Their language doesn't translate very well," Omara said. "We decided on Gaia for the planet, so Gaians for them."

"You said they speak English."

"No, I never said that. The message in 2115 was English. But yes, the ones who were on Earth learned our languages, including English."

"There have been aliens on Earth, studying us." Jill shook her head. "I'm trying to fathom that." She looked at each of them in turn. "You're sure you weren't harmed? Probed? Examined?"

Ruzena released a nervous laugh. "Yeah, we're sure. Think about how it's been done right here. Scientists watch animals, even other humans, and try not to interfere, just observe. Why is it so hard to believe people from another planet might be curious about us, who look so much like them?"

"Lots of scientists dissect their research subjects. Early on they killed them first." Jill frowned at Lyn.

"Well, not in this case," Lyn said.

"Do you have pictures? Video perhaps? What's their planet like?"

"We weren't tourists," Omara said testily. "I didn't think to take snapshots."

"What about your AMOS system. Can I see its logs?"

This was dangerous territory. Dr. Amos recorded every interaction, every sound, including the many times they'd said Johari.

"I'll prepare a report for you," Omara said. "There's certain proprietary information we've agreed not to reveal."

Jill grunted. "Like the fake stuff."

"Believe or don't. I really don't care. We did what we say we did. We believe what we believe. You are a trespasser on my ship. I've said all I'm going to say." Omara flicked a hand at Jill, waving her off. "I think it's time you left."

Even the head of Earth Control didn't have the right to board the ship without Omara's knowledge or permission.

Jill folded her napkin. "Thank you for the delicious meal. Perhaps Lyn would escort me to my ship."

They made their way up to the docking deck, through hallways with small, empty cabins. Once they were alone, Jill said, "Skip the charade. The fact is, General Jacana tipped me off that *Tenacity* was acting strangely. She didn't want the military involved. Yet. She asked me to check it out. If you want me to help you, to protect you and Omara, you need to level with me."

So, the general was on to them. She needed Jill now more than ever. She sighed as if to signal she was giving in and pulled Jill into an empty cabin. They sat facing each other on opposite couches, their knees almost touching in the small space.

"Here's the truth. After *Endurance* returned, I was approached by a woman who told me she needed help getting her people home. That she figured I knew how. Because I did. So, I agreed. I asked Omara for a ship, and she kindly offered *Tenacity*. There were a lot of them, you see, so *Endurance* wasn't big enough. Yes, I used the technology to open a tiny communications tunnel and contact their people." Jill started to open her mouth, probably to yell, but Lyn pressed on. "And that's all. They took it from there. They have vastly superior technology and their wormhole was easy to pass through. We visited for a few days. It's a beautiful place. What Earth could have been. No wars, no pollution. They figured out how to live in harmony with nature and each other. Then we left."

"What about the implant."

"You saw yourself, it's gone."

"No side effects?"

"None so far—a tremor has disappeared, though, so that's good. They warned me it was deteriorating. Which means yours might be too. You need to leave Omara alone. This was my doing."

"And you trust these people? Why them suddenly and not anyone on Earth?"

"Because they haven't given me any reason not to," Lyn said. "Odd, isn't it? You get a sense of people. A gut feeling. My gut tells me we are more dangerous to them than they are to us. We talked about whether and how to let Earth governments know about this contact. It's historic, life changing, right? But their whole point was to learn about us undetected. Once we developed interstellar travel and *Endurance* returned, their study had to end, and they had to leave. As quietly as possible. They're afraid of us. That we'll do to their planet what we've done to Earth. You can see why they might want some secrecy. But I have to tell you, Jill, they have sophisticated technology. I don't think they realize how vulnerable we are, and it certainly hasn't occurred to them to invade us."

"So, you did do it. Open a wormhole. Not by yourself, I'm sure. I don't recall you being a whiz when it came to propulsion or engineering. Your strength is in your ability to work a team. I'm guessing you had a team on this."

"You're right. I'm no Vera Geller, that's for sure, even with the implant. But I know talent when I see it, and I'm good at solving problems. We had a very big problem in Rigil Kent. I really don't know what threw us there. And, no, it wasn't them. But I got us back. My team got us back, and I'll protect them to my last breath."

"Doesn't hurt to be married to a Teegan. Does she know how to do this?"

"Not entirely. So many worked on it that no one person had all the information needed. Except me." Lyn tapped her head.

"Not even Petra?"

"You read my report. She was reset to lose all knowledge of our trip."

"Pretty drastic. I never understood why you did that."

Jill didn't know. "Petra, and all AMOS systems, it turned out, had a prohibition against faster-than-light travel. Seems General Hellen Jacana, back in her Pulsar days, decided that would be a good idea."

Jill looked genuinely surprised. "I was not aware of that. And Jacana did it way back then? Why would it even be needed? Until you developed the tech, it wasn't in the realm of possibility."

"It was to Pulsar. If aliens were a threat, it had to be because they had the capability."

Jill's knee bounced as she chewed on this information. "Makes sense," she said, almost to herself. "They wanted it for themselves."

There was a time when Lyn revered Jill Faber. Trusted her with her life, trusted her to teach her not only how to fly in space but how to survive. And she had. Captain Faber had taken all the classroom lessons and personified effective leadership, motivation, and accomplishment. Unlike General Hellen Jacana, Lyn's opinion of Jill hadn't changed. Maybe mellowed. Now she felt more like Jill's equal.

Jill tried to cross her legs but banged the other couch. She crossed her arms and squirmed in the tight space. "This leaves me—us—with a problem. It's my job to notify President Woltman if and when extraterrestrial intelligence is contacted. I could go to prison if I hide this."

That was a complication Lyn hadn't expected. "Does Pulsar have the ability to open wormholes? Other than General Jacana."

"Not that I know of. Other than Jacana, I don't know that any Pulsar exist anymore."

"Jill, what's the harm in letting this go? End it right here and nothing more comes of it. We test drove a ship. That's all. You said all Jacana wants is the tech in my head. It's not there. If I can prove it to her without being killed first, that could end this."

"She'll want to know how you got the implant out."

Of course she would, and of course there was no way it could be done on Earth. "Oh, hell."

"Could Dr. Amos have developed this on his own?"

"Maybe." Lyn hedged here, not wanting to get Dr. Amos in trouble. She couldn't just say he did it, not without proof. If he could replicate the technique, pretending he'd come up with it himself, that would open a new can of worms, violating AI regulations set after the war, intended to prevent just this sort of rogue innovation. Weapons were one thing, this was another. Not deadly, but still against the rules. He could pass on information, but to invent something completely novel would cause intense scrutiny on him and Omara. She sagged against the wall, exhausted by lies and secrets. Stepping on that planet had changed the game, changed her, and she didn't know how to stop.

Jill slumped against the back of the couch and sighed in defeat. "We need this to go away the simplest way possible."

"Agreed. So why don't you just leave and we'll pretend nothing happened."

Jill narrowed her eyes and stared at Lyn's forehead. Right. The now-missing implant.

"We could go public," Jill said.

Lyn jerked upright in alarm. "Good god, why?"

"When you returned from Rigil Kent and Omara revealed you'd developed amazing new technology that should never be used again for the good of humankind, you became an instant celebrity. And untouchable. You got off lightly with a few interviews. If it'd been up to Rachel, she'd have strapped you down and dissected your brain to get that data."

"And now she's dead. I'm sure someone is still trying."

A grimace crossed Jill's face. "Pulsar's sole mission was to prepare Earth for battle with aliens. All based on that damn message. Jacana won't stop without a good reason. Maybe we can get away with informing the president and the general. I doubt either would be interested in publicizing this more widely."

Lyn couldn't really argue with that. Maybe facing the truth was the way to go. She didn't bring aliens to Earth, she didn't have to fix this problem.

Jill went on. "If Omara can give me proof." She held up a hand. "Curated to protect the identity of your alien friends but proves they exist. Removing your implant alone is significant evidence. We get Woltman and Jacana on board. What the president does then is up to her, but we get to step away."

"If Jacana can be convinced that message was purely innocent, related to these researchers and that they are not threatening, that would help."

"Hopefully. That's a big 'if.'"

"We'll need to talk to Omara, and you burned a bridge there."

Jill's tone softened. "You talk to her. I apologize. I was only trying to do my job and protect Earth. It's too late to help Rachel. You're right, she paid for a crime she didn't commit. Grus Moloth hated her for ruining his company." She leaned forward, elbows on knees. "I found the bribes she told you about. I've alerted the NIB."

"I've got Isaac Bakewell on this." She watched Jill's expression. "Did you know Irene was now Isaac?"

"Not till I called the *Post* for you." She sat back up. "What a quagmire. Someone wanted to shut Rachel up about the alien message. Moloth? Jacana? Who the feck knows."

"Or her lawyer. Ne's also former Pulsar."

Jill's eyebrows shot up. "They really are everywhere. We're supposed to be better than that. I'm with you on this. We want the same thing."

"Let's focus on Jacana. We get her on board and this is easier." Lyn needed to trust Jill. "What about the quarantine?"

Jill shook her head. "Nothing we can do about it. We're four days from Earth. Write your report to fit that timeframe. I never set foot on this ship. Got that? I can get us a meeting with the president."

THE MOMENT JILL'S ship disconnected from *Tenacity*, Petra told Lyn that Omara wanted to see her in her quarters, "Immediately." The urgency in her voice put Lyn on edge.

"What's going on?" she asked as she hoofed it down the corridor, only to remember that *Tenacity*'s muster area was not on the bridge deck. She reversed course and ran up the stairs two decks and to the owner's suite.

"She'll explain," Petra said.

Omara stood by the window, watching Jill's ship leave, hands clasped behind her back. "We have a small complication." She turned and motioned Lyn to the couch.

"Verius," Omara said.

Lyn was about to ask what about her when she materialized as a hologram right there in Omara's quarters. Omara appeared relaxed, but she was breathing deeply.

"Lyn, Omara," Verius said. "I understand the mission has been discovered."

"What?" Lyn said. She looked at Omara. "What's going on?"

Sheepish wasn't in Omara's vocabulary, but her expression veered that way. She rubbed her arms then faced Lyn. "I told Verius that Captain Faber learned about the contact. I only did it because we had an agreement"—she glanced over at Verius—"that we should be completely open with each other. It was a courtesy. I didn't intend—"

"Naturally, this is concerning," Verius said. "We knew there was a risk, so we have a contingency plan."

Lyn shook her head. "What plan?" She turned to Omara. "Is this Plan B? Because the only way Jill learned of the trip was because you told her." She shoved her hands in her pockets, finding the translator. Verius was speaking English. She fumbled for the switch that flipped the translation.

"I had no idea—" Omara faced Verius. "And Captain Faber has no details."

"What plan?" Lyn repeated, exasperated. She turned from Verius while pretending to adjust her hair behind her ear, popping in the translator.

"We cannot allow our existence to become known outside of our control— or your control," Verius said. "If Captain Faber is a threat to that, we can deal with her. We have options—"

Verius's voice, the music of her language, filled Lyn with deep dread and fear, not a benign let's try to convince her. More like when an orchestra gets to the climax and you know the hero in the opera is about to die. "What? No!"

"We have no choice," Verius said.

Verius hadn't said anything specific, but Lyn was sure this was bad. Very bad. "Captain Faber could be talking to her staff on the ground right now. And she's not the only one who knows about this. There are others on Earth who helped us, who know what we did, but nothing that would reveal Gaia. No one knows where we went. You can't be serious." To Omara by mind link, *How did this happen? What did you do?*

She responded to Lyn's panicked tone. *I don't think we need to be so dramatic.* Omara wasn't aware of the dire fate Verius had in mind for Jill.

"Please listen to me," Lyn said to Verius. "Jill, Captain Faber, is not a threat. I've known her for years. I just spoke with her and she offered to help, to keep this from getting out of control. She's on our side." Her mind raced, trying to imagine where this could lead. Now she could really use that damn implant. "Aurora spent an inordinate amount of time convincing me you were a peaceful people. She understands us. Talk to her. Please. Don't do this."

Verius didn't say anything for a long, excruciating minute. "We are peaceful. But we will protect ourselves. You must know that."

"Of course, and we're committed to protecting you. But don't you think continuing the dialogue we began is a better course? If that ship is destroyed, or disappears, there will be no end to the investigations." She saw Omara flinch. "I know for a fact they won't stop till they learn the truth. It's why I wanted that implant removed. I didn't want to be responsible for that information anymore."

Omara messaged Lyn, *Destroyed?* To Verius she said, "What exactly do you intend to do here?"

Whatever means the Gaians had to capture Jill or destroy her ship, clearly they could do it to *Tenacity* or any ship that posed a threat.

"If you kill her, I'll tell the authorities everything. I'll go to jail for it, but I won't let you do this." Lyn sent Petra a message to prepare to send an SOS and all the data to Earth Control if the Gaians appeared about to destroy Jill's ship or *Tenacity*. Her heart hammered as she messaged Omara, *What were you thinking?* The link couldn't convey how deep a betrayal this was.

I was thinking we had an accord. That the Gaians could be trusted. I'm as shocked as you are. I'm sorry, Lyn.

Verius held up a hand and made that circling motion. Lyn wished she knew what it meant—I agree? I give up? "I have requested Aurora join us."

The tension eased slightly. While they waited, Lyn relayed her conversation with Jill, ending with, "This doesn't have to end badly, for you or us. We can control how this is handled. Our tradition has been to depict alien encounters as dangerous because, frankly, that sells books, movies, and simulation games." She tried a smile. "Once our people learn how mundane first contact really is, they'll yawn and go on with life. If we do this right, build treaties and diplomatic relations, it would go a long way to protect you. And us."

Verius took this in, her face relaxing. She looked to the side and gestured someone to come forward. Ro appeared, looking confused.

Lyn filled her in, her eyes widening and mouth opening as the crisis crystalized.

Ro turned to Verius. "With respect, President—"

"Verius will do."

"From what I've learned in the short time I've been on Gaia, and from what I know of the humans on Earth, I understand your initial reaction. Dare I say, it's very human. Lash out when cornered."

Verius tipped her head, seeming to acknowledge the point.

"Lyn and Omara know the superior power of the Gaians," Ro continued, "even if it is intended to be peaceful. Humans would be crazy to try anything, but they have to know what they are dealing with to understand that. This is a tremendous opportunity, you said yourself, for us to join hands and learn our shared history."

Lyn waited. Omara shifted uncomfortably. Was Ro about to see three hundred years of research go up in flames?

"Who is this Captain Faber you confided in?" Verius asked. "How can she protect us?" The emotion in her voice was calmer, soothing.

Lyn explained her long relationship with Jill. "She has a family, children. She won't do anything that would harm them."

"It's been clear from the start, that you are far advanced from us," Omara said. "May I ask what weapons you have? With your research, you know more about humans' capabilities than we do yours."

"It's not a weapon, exactly," Verius said, now sounding calmer even in English. "As you know, a wormhole folds space. If the opening is inside a ship or a planet, even nearby, the spatial disruption can be devastating. At least for a traversable wormhole. Microscopic comtunnels are safe. Presumably you know this from your own use of the technology."

A tingle, like an electric charge, ran across Lyn's scalp. They could destroy the whole planet? Back in Rigil Kent, she'd asked Diana how well they could aim. What if they opened the wormhole in the sun. "We'd fry," Diana had said. She hadn't said the sun would be destroyed.

"The last thing we want is an arms race over wormhole technology," Lyn said. "This is beyond my ability to negotiate, so I defer to Omara, but it seems like setting up formal relations is vital now."

Ro agreed and said to Verius, "The Johari from Earth will need time to adjust. I can already tell it won't be easy. I don't regret the decision and haven't heard anyone say they'd rather go back, but we all need to understand that the worlds as we knew them must change. Not in big ways, but in good ways. I feel no shame in saying that I'm homesick already for Earth, because I'm also happy and at peace to be here, no longer having to hide who I am. We have to be in this together."

Verius took her time responding. "This Jill Faber. You trust her?"

"With my life," Lyn said.

"So be it, then." She looked at Omara. "Please let me know when you have reached out to your government and whether you will continue to have the authority to speak for Earth."

"Of course."

Verius and Ro disappeared, the call ended. Omara dropped onto her couch with a loud exhale. Lyn had never seen her so vulnerable.

"How did that even happen?" Lyn asked, trying for a conciliatory tone. "What 'means of communication' did they give you?"

Omara pointed to a cube-shaped box on her credenza, the lid raised. Inside sat a sphere, black, shiny, no buttons or controls. "This is a communicator. I touch it and Verius is notified. She then called me through a comtunnel. One that is holo-capable, apparently."

Lyn stared into the box, at the magic sphere. Yet another surprise from the sophisticated Gaians.

Omara closed the box with a thunk. "How did you know what Verius intended? She never said she would destroy Captain Faber's ship."

Lyn popped the translator out of her ear and described what the Gaian language sounded like, how it triggered her emotions like music. Omara blinked. "Yes, I recall the feelings the language evoked for me. Do you think she would have destroyed us too?"

"What would you have done?" This was an enormous sword dangling over their heads. "If General Jacana gets wind of this, she'll put me on a torture rack to get the data and build her own TPCA."

"I'm glad it's gone."

"Let's hope that's a good thing."

LATER, WHEN LYN had finished telling Diana the shocking turn of events, they lay in bed together, quiet and exhausted.

"I have to believe that deep down the Gaians are as good as we thought they were," Diana said. "Until Rose and I moved to Mars, we spent most holidays in Mill Creek with her folks. I always loved those times, but then would be so jarred when we had to return to Massachusetts or wherever we were at the time. The world outside Mill Creek felt wrong, like a desert surrounding an oasis. Unlivable. So, we moved to Mars. If you're going to live in an alien hellscape, we said, it might as well be actually alien. Living in biodomes, me teaching, her piloting. A completely unnatural existence."

"I wasn't sure Ro had it in her to lead her people," Lyn said, "but I saw in her some real spark of insight." In the end, Lyn decided, having first contact involve people already familiar with Earth and humans would be a good thing. "I think she'll be able to mediate this. I certainly hope so."

Had she done the right thing by helping the Johari get home and getting T out of her head? Funny to think Ro had also had second thoughts. Now the Gaians could destroy Earth and there was nothing she could do about that. Jill was right. The president needed to know and including General Jacana was critical. After that, she needed to step away, let go, and get on with her own life. Implant free. A sudden shot of grief hitched her breath. Oh, how she wished Rachel could be here for this. Her life ended with her feeling haunted, not understanding what was happening to her. She'd been let down all her life by people who were supposed to love and support her. Including Lyn.

Chapter 18

ONCE *TENACITY* NEARED Earth orbit, local messages started flowing in. They'd only been gone two weeks, but you'd think it had been another Rigil Kent tour.

"What's going on?" Lyn asked, listening to her personal com pod ping repeatedly, as much to herself as to Diana. They were the only ones being inundated, though. Scrolling through the messages, most were from her family and annoyingly vague. "Could they have found out we went to space?"

Diana also had several from her parents. *Are you okay? What happened? Please let us know you are okay!* She turned to the news. Nothing big had happened. Then the local Montana news. "Ah, a fire near Butte. They must be worried we were affected." She sent off a message that she and Lyn were fine, that they'd been visiting Omara in Nevada. "That should buy us some time to figure out what happened."

No longer needing any pretense, Omara had Ani fly *Tenacity* right to Ruby Valley. There, Lyn and Diana said their goodbyes and Lyn sent a message to let Miriam and Sharyn know the trip was a success.

For the last leg home, all was fine as they crossed the Idaho border into Montana, but once they flew over the mountains the scene turned apocalyptic. Blackened toothpick trees and charred ground stretched as far as they could see in each direction.

"Damn," Lyn muttered. Her heart sank seeing all the new growth obliterated.

Their cabin looked like a toasted marshmallow in the middle of a smoldering campfire. Ash swirled around them as the Rambler descended. Thankfully, the garage door opened. Diana rolled them inside, bringing along a cloud of ash. They sat for a moment. With the skim vents open the smell was strong and sharp.

"Let's see what's left," Diana said with resignation.

The house interior was fine. Kat greeted them with a purr and rub around their legs. "Last week, dry thunderstorms blew through," Kat said. "Lightning started the fire about ten miles from here. It's now burning north toward Missoula but expected to die out from lack of fuel after last year's burn up there."

Diana said the first thing she wanted to do was call Antonia. "Isn't that weird? She's gone. Not dead, but just as gone."

Lyn dropped onto the living room couch. "So much for a hideout."

Diana plopped down beside her. "We don't need that so much now that your brain has been fried." She nudged Lyn playfully.

"Tara and I planted trees. Now they've burned." If she were speaking Gaian, she'd sound like a dirge.

"Here?"

She shook her head. "No, farther south." She kicked the table. "What good is it to plant and repair and recover only to see it all go up in smoke again?" She wrinkled her nose. "I can't stand the smell. And we can't open windows."

Lyn got up and paced the room like an animal trapped in a cage. An endangered species with nowhere to go, no hope of a future. Diana sat still, watching warily. Not like she hadn't seen Lyn break down before. "Why does this keep happening?" Lyn said to no one in particular. "Damn you, Gaia!"

Wasn't it enough they were surrounded by archives of what Earth had once been like—documentaries, photos, lush descriptive memoirs of snowcapped mountains, amber waves of grain, cold waters filled with salmon, blue skies. You could convince yourself it had all been fiction, stories growing more mythical with each telling. But to see a functioning society that cared for the land, waters, and air. It reinforced how everything could have been so different.

She braced her hands on the windowsill, growling in frustration. Ash covered the outside sill, drifts in the corners of each pane. A gray version of the antique Christmas cards she'd seen with white snow on a frosted window. Frost didn't even exist anymore, never mind snow. Ash. The world was nothing but ash.

She dropped to her knees, arms crossed on the sill, head down. "Why am I doing this?"

"What are you doing?" Diana asked cautiously.

Lyn didn't answer. Tears silently dripped onto her knees. A heavy intake and sob brought Diana to her, holding her while she cried.

"WAKE UP." DIANA tossed a pod on the bed beside Lyn. "Check this out." There was an urgency to her voice that made Lyn roll over and groan. Morning light filtered through the ash-coated window. She flung back the covers and rubbed her eyes, swollen and sore. She grabbed the pod and squinted at the holoscreen, the news feed from the *Syracuse Post*. She let out a yip and sat up.

Two huge stories had broken while they had been away. Which was bigger? A special investigative piece alleged that Grus Moloth was under suspicion for the murder of Rachel Holness and attempted murder of Lyn Randall. A trove of documents showed the bribes he'd made to Earth Control and the link between him and his family's past as arms dealers. The tracking drone used in the attack on Lyn's skim had been purchased by an associate of Moloth's from his brother's company. As well, the former head of EC, Bernice Umbo, was being investigated for accepting the bribes.

Another story implicated Rachel's lawyer, Illumi Névé, in the bombing of the *Aphrodite*.

"A lawyer bombed the *Aphrodite*?" Diana asked, sitting beside Lyn.

They read on. No, the article said, ne had been part of a conspiracy to damage the ship and close space. President Woltman was going to appoint a special investigator to weed out any other former Pulsar staff or affiliates. The NIB had been alerted and considered Moloth a person of interest.

The articles were by Isaac Bakewell, revealing a host of accusations and evidence leading to the charges. They stared at the news feed. The article described Pulsar's plot to damage the *Aphrodite* and force a recall, closing space. All to give the group time alone to set up defensive and monitoring stations for an assumed war with China. No mention of aliens, Lyn read with relief. Névé had gone from its legal department to Earth Control's. A nobody, quiet, a desk jockey, but kept nir finger on the pulse of Pulsar's mission and befriended Rachel, and they stayed in touch after. Névé's job had been to make the company look legit legally, hiding the true nature behind the whiz-bang exploration outfit they presented publicly.

After breakfast Lyn checked her work messages. Several had come in from Isaac while she was away. She hadn't given him her personal address.

"I tried to contact you to get a quote for the articles, but you never responded," he said when she called.

She didn't bother to say she'd been out of range in another solar system. "I'm not surprised by Moloth, but Névé?"

"Someone squealed. A source knew someone who knew someone who contacted me. With deep, verifiable knowledge of what happened, who'd been haunted by the event all these years. The explosion was never meant to destroy the ship."

Isaac said Rachel had hired Névé at Earth Control when she took over for Bernice Umbo, another piece of work. She was the one who had taken the bribes from Grus Moloth and approved the *Aphrodite* on a fast track. As for Moloth, that link was more direct, Isaac said. "He's not very good at covering his tracks. Used a drone from his brother's company. Seems to be pure revenge."

Lyn sat on her couch, stunned. Suddenly everything sifted to neat piles. No more Pulsar after her tech, Rachel's murderer caught, the *Aphrodite* mystery solved. They still didn't know what caused the wormhole to open, but maybe Diana was right, and it was natural.

RETURNING TO WORK was like stepping onto an alien planet, and she knew exactly what that felt like. She just couldn't say so. Everyone was relieved to see her, thinking the only drama in her life was solving the bombing of her skim, Rachel's murder, and the fire at her cabin. Her dad asked about the fire.

"The cabin's fine," she said. But it wasn't. It was unlivable. She and Diana had talked about maybe it was time to move, someplace less vulnerable. But that would have to wait. She had one more task to deal with. No, two. Maybe three. First order of business hadn't even been on her radar until she walked through the door.

"Mom, we need to talk," she said, closing the door to her mother's office. Mom. Not Sarah, not boss. This was family, after all.

Her mother closed the document she was working on, and Lyn could tell in an instant that she was already bracing for bad news. She didn't meet Lyn's eyes and blinked long and slow. Lyn took the seat across the desk from her.

"I know I've been less than . . . conscientious about my work," Lyn began, "taking a lot of time off."

"You need time to heal, that's understandable," Sarah said with a wary caution. "Fúlli's gaining good experience."

"Thing is . . ."

Her mother closed her eyes. "Please don't tell me you're going back to space. With space reopening—"

"No. I'm not."

Her mother looked her in the eye.

"We need to figure out what to do with the cabin, find somewhere else to live. Diana might need to find a new job." This part was hard. "I'm not sure Montana is the best place for us. I won't have time to devote fully to the job."

Sarah straightened a photo and wiped invisible dust off her desk. "It's not out there, you know. You can wander the world, the stars, but everything you need is right here."

"You been reading *The Wizard of Oz* again?"

"I'm just saying."

This room had been Duncan's. Photos on the desk showed the whole family, including him, and one of her in her Vega, waving from the window. Her mother had taught her how to fly. The blanket tossed over the back of the couch had been Duncan's. This wasn't a shrine so much as a sanctuary. Here her mother could grieve in her own way, in private.

"Why me? Ethan and Theo have been living in California, not exactly a safe place with the floods and earthquakes. Kai's in Chicago and almost never comes home. Why do you need me here?"

"Not need. Want." She rested her chin in her hand, elbow on the desk, her cornflower blue eyes shining, lines radiating from the corners. "I never told you why we had so many kids. It made no sense, right? The planet doesn't need more humans."

Lyn shook her head, curious and confused. Her family was large, with six kids. None of her friends had more than one other sibling, or they were adopted.

Her mother took her time answering, her mouth quirking, eyes shifting as if trying to find a way to say something difficult. "We were fertile. Your dad and me."

Or awkward. Now Lyn knew why they'd never talked about it. What kid wants to know that? Her mother wiped a hand across her desk and scraped some speck with her fingernail. "That last regime—who shall remain nameless—" she said in disgust, "tested everyone. We were white and we were healthy, so in order to receive government benefits—food and fuel—we had to . . ." She didn't need to finish.

Lyn squirmed in her seat. Her parents had been born in 2100, before the war, and started having kids before it ended. She'd always wondered what kind of optimism that took and where could she get some. "They forced you?" The image was too grim to contemplate, yet her parents undeniably loved each other.

"Not forced, coerced. It was an arranged marriage, matched up by the Office of Population Control in Helena—what was called Helena at the time. Control going in both directions. Some were sterilized, some were . . . encouraged. You can guess which races got which track."

"I had no idea." She'd known about the eugenics programs at the turn of the century, the school curriculum covered it. But her own family?

"We didn't want you to know. Any of you. We love you. That's all that matters."

So much of her experience of her family had revolved around Duncan's death and the quiet void after. She hadn't had the vocabulary to express what she'd felt at the time, was much too young to understand. Over the years the stories had faded like worn cloth till she couldn't see the pattern anymore. Now she understood better how the Johari and even the Gaians had lost information. Not lost so much as altered over time, imperceptibly, unnoticed.

"I'm glad you told me. I'm not trying to hurt you and Dad. I'm just trying to get through each day."

Sarah smiled. "I know. And I love that about you." She straightened and said brightly, "Go. Do what you have to do." She transformed back to the solid ground Lyn grew up on. "We're here whenever you need us."

It didn't sound like a guilt trip but rather the unconditional love that was part and parcel of families as Lyn understood them. "I'm always here, you know. Even when I'm not."

THE NEXT TASK was harder. She left Diana to deal with fire investigators and real estate listings and headed to Ruby Valley. Jill had set up a meeting with President Woltman for the following Monday, so she and Omara had to get their story straight, and that meant a reckoning.

All the way down to Omara's, Lyn ran through her mind what had gone wrong that Omara blundered. Why had she trusted the Gaians so completely, and misjudged them so? She regretted that they hadn't spent their time on the planet with Omara. Who knew what she was being told and shown. There were cracks in the peaceful Gaian façade that only now registered as meaningful.

Quisca refusing to divulge technology, being so vague about how they doled out medical care. It had seemed reasonable at the time—conserving resources—and maybe it was. They simply didn't know the Gaians nearly as well as the Gaians knew humans, and that was a problem. All the more reason to continue a relationship. But what kind? Who should be the lead? Omara? That wouldn't be up to Lyn, but she now had her reservations.

Omara quietly ushered her into her living room. She motioned Lyn to sit, but she stood, arms by her side. "Let me have it," she said. "I need to know where we stand before we can go on."

All cards on the table then. "Jill could have been killed."

Omara winced.

"We all could have been killed for that matter."

Omara tilted her head in acknowledgement. "I didn't see that coming. I missed it." Her pain was evident in her face. Lyn wasn't used to seeing Omara in pain, feeling regret. She had no reference point for this. Whatever this was. A shift in the hierarchy? Was Omara no longer to be looked up to? She stood, paced the room, and stopped at the fireplace.

She faced Omara, arms crossed. "Are they listening in now? How do I know you haven't called Verius. What is that thing anyway?"

"I have not called her. They are not listening in. I was only told that my touch, and only my touch—my fingerprint or DNA, unique about me—would activate the Siq and alert Verius to open a comtunnel wherever I called from. It works by a form of quantum entanglement. It can't send information, it can't listen. Merely an alert."

"Siq? Is that what it's called?"

"That's my name for it. It means the shaft. For the channeled path leading to the ancient city of Petra."

"Why didn't the Johari have this?"

"It didn't exist then. That's all I know."

She told Omara what she learned on Gaia that now, through a different lens of understanding, seemed to stand out as more concerning. "Not that I think they were being duplicitous, but that we simply don't know them well enough."

"That was the focus of my conversation with Verius. A couple days touring their planet wasn't enough. They'd had three hundred years on Earth."

On that point, Lyn could agree.

"I also stressed that removing the data from your brain wouldn't end the research, and Verius admitted as much. She understood that letting us go and closing that door was a very bad idea."

"I wish she'd thought blowing Jill up was also a bad idea before she said it."

"You're sure that's what she meant?"

"She didn't deny it."

"No. She didn't," Omara said wearily. "None of us are as smart as we'd like to think we are." A statement she might otherwise had said with a quirk of a smile. Now it sounded sad, like a truth unearthed, a foundation of sand, not stone.

"That's certainly gotten humans in a lot of trouble over the centuries."

"Maybe the Gaians aren't so different."

Omara was a couple years older than Lyn's parents, and like them didn't talk much about the war, though she imagined their experiences were very different. Her folks were born and raised in Montana, except for brief migrations north into Canada then back when they were allowed. Omara had been rootless, wandering, not able to set down roots, so she'd ended up floating off into space. She was suited for it. Likely also for the job of being an ambassador to Gaia.

"I was really hoping they were," Lyn said.

"What we say and what they hear can be so different. The oldest, perhaps universal truth of humanity. Staying in touch with them is more important than ever now. Whether that's through President Woltman or someone else."

"Do you wish I still had the technology?"

Her face showed alarm. "No, of course not."

"You didn't keep a copy, did you?"

Her expression softened. "I thought about it, but no. I knew if I did that, you'd never trust me." She smiled ruefully. "I managed to lose that trust anyway."

"Not lost. Perhaps dented a little. To be repaired."

Omara nodded in acquiescence. "Shall we get to work then?"

Over the next several days, they pored through the information they had about the Johari—so they knew what to avoid mentioning—and the Gaians, so they could prove their existence and make clear the importance of continued contact.

By the time they were ready to head to Syracuse, Lyn was comfortable with their plan. If all went well, she'd hand off her responsibility to the Johari, to Gaia, and to any future of superluminal technology. Whatever role she'd played, whatever dominoes had fallen to bring her here, the fact was that first contact would have happened at some point. She simply happened to be in the path. Next steps were best left to others. Maybe, finally, she and Diana could come out from isolation and find out what normal life could be, together.

JILL FABER EXPECTED Omara's "curated" report proving the alien contact, so that's what Lyn and Omara presented to her. She greeted them in her office on the top floor of Earth Control, glass all around, a stunning view overlooking Onondaga Lake.

"No need for a privacy booth?" Lyn asked. "I was afraid we'd have to meet in a smelly barn."

Jill laughed, Omara squinted in confusion. "I'm not afraid of what we're discussing." Jill motioned them to her conference table. "You saw Isaac's reporting, I gather."

Movement on the cases of Rachel's murder and the bombing of the *Aphrodite*, coupled with the confirmed absence of the implant in Lyn's head, meant, Jill said, there was little left and what was would be revealed to President Woltman in a few hours.

Omara opened a com pod document and slid it over for Jill to review. She took her time, muttering and making slight adjustments. International agreements surrounding first contact were outdated, she noted, but had clearly been violated. She finished and closed the document with a shrug. Lyn waited for her verdict, like she was back under Faber's command.

"There's no detail about their planet," she said, "where it is, what it's like."

"You wanted proof of their existence," Omara said. "This provides that and protects them."

"It'll have to come out at some point."

"We can deal with that as needed," Lyn said.

"Bureaucratically, the main sticking point is that no response to an alien message or contact should be made without international consensus. I'm not sure a 'sorry about that' will suffice. I need to protect President Woltman if this gets out. Our saving grace is that all the original signers no longer exist. The upside of a global war."

"We can accept responsibility or blame for that," Omara said.

"That could be the least of our problems," Jill said.

That, and ensuring whatever happened next protected Jill, Earth, and the Gaians. With Jill's endorsement, they packed up their things and headed over to the president's office.

Chapter 19

THE SEAT OF the NAA government rested in an ancient building of red . . . brick? Lyn wondered. No, brownstone she decided. She shook her head. Used to be she'd only have to think about this building and all sorts of history, photos, and information would come to mind. Not without her implant.

The building perched at the top of a hill like a beacon, which maybe it was. On approach, she was struck by its gothic appearance complete with turrets and a tall bell tower. With a backdrop of dark gray clouds, she half expected bats to fly from the belfry. She remembered from high school history class that the almost three-hundred-year-old building had survived the war. Wounded, with blown out windows and shattered slate roof, it stuck up like a sore thumb. Or maybe a middle finger to fate. What better metaphor, the founders declared, to earn a place of honor in the new government.

She parked Diana's Rambler between Omara's and Jill's skims and turned to take in the view, the new nation's capital. Onondaga Lake shimmered in the distance, Earth Control's glass tower on the shore. A cool December wind tore at her, reminiscent of Montana. Syracuse was hilly and also windy. Together they entered through large wood doors into a wood-paneled lobby. Jill led them to the guard station beside a dramatic staircase that split at a landing and continued right and left. Lyn brushed her hand along a thick, carved newel post. "Is this real wood?"

"Most of it," Jill said. She pointed to a large window on the landing. "Originally it was stained glass, but was updated since its restoration."

The "window" glimmered and shifted, alternating views of the sky outside with photos of historic events and the restoration. Around them, people bustled about, the patter of feet on marble like the longed-for rain on a roof. Jill checked them in. She handed Omara and Lyn visitor chips. Lyn clipped hers to her jacket, the one she'd bought on Gaia. She also wore her Johari boots, for good luck. If these were fancy enough for Verius, they'd do for President Woltman.

"Third floor," the guard told Jill, who started up the staircase.

Lyn stared up the steps. Beautiful, but she wasn't sure her leg was up for it.

"Perhaps an elevator," Omara said. "My lungs will protest."

She was lying, of course. Lyn knew Omara liked to run through her desert property, up hills, in the heat. The president's office was not on the top floor.

That was reserved for ministry offices, where constituents could see their government at work and get a nice view.

At a reception desk, an aide showed them into the president's office. "Myrtle will be with you momentarily."

The curved far wall bore a vague resemblance to the old Oval Office of the U.S. White House, but this room was warm, with wood trim and a coffered ceiling. Three pairs of rectangular windows spread in a half circle. Above each a round, framed pane—Lyn struggled to recall the style. At one time she'd have known. Not clerestory. She shook off the frustration. That wasn't why they were here. Whatever they were, the light pouring in offset the dark wood. A thick carpet held sound. This would be a quiet oasis to work on issues of global importance.

A large desk was tucked off to the side, not the centerpiece, as though the president preferred to look out the windows and not have them at her back. Across from it a small conference table was laid with a pitcher of water and glasses. It was odd to be in this room.

"Should we stage a coup," Jill whispered. She was being chatty and friendly, with no idea how close she'd come to losing it all. Lyn groaned inwardly.

A quiet hum caught her ear and General Hellen Jacana appeared from the outer office.

"Good to see you looking better, Captain," Jacana said, holding out a hand.

"General," Lyn said, taking it.

She nodded to Jill and Lyn introduced Omara. They stood in an awkward group, waiting. General Jacana bounced on her toes, Jill stood at ease, hands clasped behind her back. Lyn glanced around the room like a tourist. Omara peered at the various statues, trophies, and books on shelves behind the table. Gifts and trinkets from various world leaders.

Myrtle Woltman had risen to lead the North American Alliance at the young age of sixty-five. She'd spent the war working with refugees, coordinating relief efforts, and serving late in the war as a communications specialist helping to spread news of the negotiations that ended the conflict and led to the new borders. No one was sad to see the United States vanquished, but its original ideals of democracy, rights, liberty, opportunity, and equality, though never fully realized, attracted a movement. Woltman was instrumental in implementing the goals of the Women's Revolution to see a new democracy founded in equality and codified in a constitution specifically protecting the rights of women, children, and nature. Without equity, she'd said during her campaign, we have nothing.

A side door opened and in strode the president. An imposing figure both physically and intellectually, she nevertheless carried herself with a casual, brisk manner, like any busy boss. She always insisted on first names, a contrast to General Jacana. Short, easy-to-care-for dark curls and her signature comfortable generic suit projected a no-nonsense attitude that had helped her win two elections handily, something no Black woman had been able to accomplish under the old U.S. system.

"Hello, hello," she said, extending her hand. Her smile made you want to smile back. "Have a seat." Once they were settled, she gestured to Jill. "Please, do tell me what this is about."

Jacana's gaze moved between Lyn and Omara, as though questioning why they were included in this meeting. Jill began, using her role as head of Earth Control to inform the president of a first contact with an intelligent alien civilization. As she spoke, Lyn watched General Jacana's face. It remained a blank mask. Too blank.

"What was the nature of the contact?" Woltman asked as she reached for the jug of water. She didn't seem terribly alarmed. So-called alien signals appeared pretty often, and were always innocent.

Jill put it as briefly as possible, that she'd been informed by Captain Randall that she had been approached by a group of people, emphasizing their humanity, with a need to return to their planet. "Seems they'd lost their own ship and, given Captain Randall's recent experience, thought she could help."

Myrtle froze, hand holding the jug. Clearly this wasn't the form of contact she'd expected. "People? Here? Not a signal from space or crazies who think they're aliens?" She set the jug down with a thunk.

"We've confirmed they were aliens," Jill said.

"Were? Where are they now?" General Jacana asked. She gazed at Lyn. "Did you help them?"

She was prepared for the question, yet she still squirmed in her seat. "Yes."

Jacana slapped her hand on the table and rocked back in her chair. "I knew it!"

Myrtle shot her a look to shut up. This was her meeting. She turned to Lyn. "I think you need to tell me what happened."

Here we go. She tried to tell the story briefly, only adding detail as questions were fired at her, mostly from General Jacana. She leaned forward, answering carefully, attentive, the way she'd focus on flying her Vega through turbulence, in control. When she mentioned the aliens had wormhole technology, General Jacana flinched. She emphasized the peaceful nature of the aliens, passive researchers, who ended their study once she and Diana had developed their own wormhole technology. That opened another round of questions by Jacana who was practically spitting at Lyn.

Finally, Myrtle raised her voice. "Enough." She placed her hands on the table. "Let's dial back the vitriol, please, General." She gestured to Lyn. "Please continue, and I'll ask the questions."

Myrtle asked for proof, and Omara opened the report from her com pod. "This is the DNA analysis."

Jacana glanced over the data. "Gobbledygook," she said, then clammed up when Myrtle glared at her.

Myrtle waved Omara to pass the pod to her. "Let me see that. I studied anthropology. I know a bit about DNA." Her eyes widened as she read the data. "How is this possible?"

"It's not," Jacana said quietly. "Some faked DNA."

Myrtle shot another warning look, and Jacana leaned back and crossed her arms. She rocked gently, impatiently.

"I don't understand. They're an advanced race, they have wormhole technology, yet they needed your help." Myrtle looked at Omara. "What's your role in all this?"

"They needed a ship," Omara said. "I provided that."

Myrtle turned to Jill. "And why am I only learning of this now?"

"I was not made aware of the contact until after they left."

Omara tried to take responsibility, but Lyn cut her off. "This was all me. They approached me. I became convinced of their harmless intent and asked Omara to help. Captain Faber had nothing to do with this. She detected our return and intervened. If she hadn't, I never would have said anything. This would be over and done with."

"On what authority?" Myrtle asked.

Lyn didn't say anything to defend herself. An artery in Jacana's neck pulsed. She flicked a glance at Myrtle then addressed Lyn. "You still haven't provided convincing proof."

Lyn wriggled out of her jacket. "Scan this. You'll see it contains fibers from no known Earth animal."

Jacana took out her com pod, set it to scan, and ran it over the fibers. She humphed the beginnings of acknowledgement. "Wait, how'd you get that jacket?"

Here's where things would get sticky. "I bought it from a weaver on their planet."

The room went quiet, like that proverbial moment when the cartoon character runs off the cliff and hangs there until the realization triggers the plumet.

"You went to their planet?" Myrtle and Jacana said together.

"How?" Myrtle asked.

"They provided the wormhole," Omara said. "We only opened a microscopic communications tunnel. They opened a wormhole from their side, and we transferred the people to their ship. They have tremendously advanced technology over us." She scrolled her report to the analysis of their ship, how the materials were not anything used on Earth.

"That we know of," Jill said, looking at Jacana.

Jacana pulled the holodoc toward her. Lyn expected her to dismiss this as faked, too, but her eyes narrowed as she scrolled through the data. She looked at Jill, Lyn, and Omara. "Why are you telling us now, after you've made contact." She shook her head with incredulity. "And *visited* their planet? Are you out of your minds?"

Myrtle ignored Jacana and leaned forward, seeming to drop her national leader role and allow curiosity to rule. "What's their planet like?"

Lyn, Jill, and Omara shared a look. Lyn raised a finger. She'd take this. She described the sibling stars and twin planets, how it was like Earth but before the devastation of climate change and war. Even if Jacana wanted to go in search of it, there were many siblings to choose from, never mind hundreds of candidate planets. She explained the theory of separated early humans—some to their planet and some to Earth. Millennia ago.

"No one had technology of any kind back then," Myrtle said. "How is this possible? Some other alien, or God, or . . . what?"

"We don't know, and they don't either," Lyn said. "But wouldn't that be something? If we could figure out where we came from and why we are here?"

General Jacana rose and stood behind her chair. "This is bullshit. Why are you wasting our time with this nonsense?"

"Because it happened," Lyn said. "Why would we make this up?"

"I have no idea. Fame?" Jacana waved a hand at the "evidence." "This could all be fake. You don't have a shred of actual proof. How convenient all the aliens have now gone home."

Omara turned to Myrtle. "Certainly, we can leave it at this. If General Jacana is not convinced, there's not much reason to continue."

"Well, I'm convinced. At least I'm going to assume this is real. First contact!" She leaned back and adjusted the sleeves of her jacket as though the aliens might walk through the door any minute.

It occurred to Lyn that General Jacana had every reason to end this discussion now, then go off and conduct her own covert investigation. She couldn't let this end here. "I have proof that should convince the general. They removed my Pulsar implant."

Jacana's eyebrows rose. "Really."

"You have your own. You've wanted access to my head ever since I returned. Well, take a look. All you want." Lyn went to her side. "Go on."

Jacana looked at the others. While she had been open about her Pulsar past, she'd never let on that she too had an implant. She sighed and touched foreheads with Lyn. She leaned back and looked at Jill. "What about you? Can you confirm this?"

Jill nodded.

"Implant? What is this implant? Pulsar?" Myrtle asked. "What's going on here?"

Lyn described the nanobot infusion that created a supercomputer in the human brain, where she'd stored the wormhole technology data. "After we returned from Rigil Kent, we were able to destroy everything except the plans and data that I'd had to upload to my implant because"—she glared at General Jacana—"we couldn't get home using the ship's computer. Since that data couldn't be removed, I refused to cooperate with authorities. It is now gone."

"You had the knowledge to open a wormhole all this time and lied?" Myrtle said in anger.

"It was for the best," Lyn said.

"And that was the last copy of the information?" Jacana asked.

"Yes," Lyn said.

Jacana scowled. "Too bad. It would have been nice to go back to the *Aphrodite* and collect some evidence. You heard about Illumi Névé, I presume."

Lyn's stomach heaved, Omara reddened beside her. "Yes," she said cautiously. She had vowed to bring justice to the *Aphrodite* victims. She'd brought back digitized records, everything she'd been able to collect from the wrecked ship. But the only evidence of an explosion they'd found was a vid recording of a flash. Was there any remnant of the explosive left, now floating for eternity? That could have been retrieved?

"Névé will no doubt claim a lack of proof of nir involvement. It'll be nir word against the technician who claims to have placed the bomb," Jacana said, her voice cold as the void of space.

Lyn sat grim-faced.

"I could have you charged," Myrtle said, back in the role of president. "Give me one good reason I shouldn't."

Jacana sat back down. She pulled the hologram of the Gaian ship's specs toward her then pushed it back again. She drummed her real fingers on the table. "During the war I was in an elite unit scanning the ocean floor for possible unexploded weapons to scavenge and reuse. We had to be resourceful to defeat a far superior enemy."

"What does this have to do—?" Myrtle said.

Jacana raised a gloved finger. "Deep in the Atlantic off the coast of southern Africa, we found what we thought was advanced weapons technology. A vessel of some kind. It wasn't crushed by the pressure. It looked like a space ship. Maybe an experimental craft that had crashed."

"Your point?" Omara asked.

"We couldn't retrieve the ship itself, but we recovered some pieces. When we analyzed them, we couldn't figure out how it had been made." She folded her arms and nodded toward Omara's holopresentation. "It was similar to that ship. Your alien friends' ship."

"Are you sure?" Lyn asked.

Jacana smiled, tapping her head. "It's all in here, thanks to Pulsar. I uploaded the scans after I received the implant."

Ro had said the Johari had been on Earth some three hundred years, that they'd landed in Utah, not crashed into the ocean. "Maybe it was their ship?" Lyn said cautiously.

"I don't think so," Jacana said. "When we dated the material, it came back as somewhere between two and three hundred *thousand* years old. We assumed it was an error, maybe caused by being in the ocean."

"Thousands of years old? I don't understand," Myrtle said. "Just what are we dealing with here?"

"I don't know," Jacana said, her eyes never leaving Lyn, "and we may never know, thanks to our friends here."

It seemed to take forever for Lyn's puny human brain to compute what General Jacana was saying. A ship hundreds of thousands of years old, not three hundred, not Gaian. Could the theory of a common ancestor be true? But how do you explain a spaceship that old, with clearly advanced technology that didn't exist when modern humans were barely leaving the savanna of Africa? Africa. Off the coast of which this ship was found. The Gaians had some memory, some documentation that they came from another planet. Earth humans didn't. Now she wished she'd asked more questions of Quisca and Verius. She slid her eyes toward Omara who sat perfectly still, no doubt formulating her next message to Verius. She pictured General Jacana going back for that ship in the ocean. She massaged a tense muscle at the back of her neck.

Myrtle turned to Jill. "What do you have to say for yourself? How'd this get past Earth Control?"

"It didn't get past her," Lyn said. "The only reason we're in this room is because she insisted on doing her job."

Myrtle groaned in frustration. "How did these aliens get to Earth, penetrate our monitoring systems, without being detected?"

"They arrived before Earth Control existed, before any SETI programs," Lyn said. She hadn't wanted to be so specific, but she didn't want Jill to suffer for something she had no control over. "They told us they'd been here since 1900. Before humans had even flown a plane."

Myrtle's mouth dropped open.

"1900?" Jacana said. "You're joking."

Lyn shook her head. "They were in contact with their planet, only becoming more careful as we developed aviation, radar, sensing technology, the space race. Then, when the message of 2115 was found, they went completely quiet, cut off from their own people for decades because they feared discovery."

"That was them?" Jacana asked.

Lyn admitted it was, that it had been a perfectly harmless communication that slipped through unencrypted. At Myrtle's confused expression, she explained the link between Pulsar, the 2115 message, and the aliens.

"Turned out Pulsar wasn't preparing to fight the Chinese. They thought the aliens who sent that message were going to invade Earth. But it was a misunderstanding. The message was intended for the Gaians on Earth."

"Pulsar is no longer a threat," Jacana said. "It has ended."

Both Lyn and Jill stared at her.

"You're sure?" Jill said.

"I am. I was the last of the executives to denounce the company and with the arrest of Illumi Névé, I don't know of anyone still active."

"Were you aware of nir involvement?" Lyn asked, a chill prickling the back of her neck. Could Jacana have had anything to do with Rachel's troubles?

"I was certainly aware that ne and Rachel Holness were former Pulsar and that they were working together. On what, other than the lawsuit, I have no information." Her expression softened. "I deeply regret what you went through, what happened to Rachel. But that was Grus Moloth and nothing to do with Pulsar, past or present."

"Please resolve your differences on your own time. I need to move on with this." Myrtle turned to Jacana. "You said the ship you found was hundreds of thousands of years old." She looked at Lyn. "But you say they've been here since 1900."

Even Lyn didn't know what this meant. She said all she knew was the research began in 1900, when the aliens found Earth. "I've no idea what General Jacana's talking about."

"And I have no idea what you're talking about," Jacana said.

Jill cleared her throat, like they'd forgotten she was there, the head of Earth Control. "Regardless of what's in the bottom of the ocean, for the time being I think we need to remain focused on next steps. How do you wish to proceed, Madame Pres—Myrtle? Our existing protocols for first contact don't assume we'll meet them face to face and speak the same language."

Myrtle rubbed her forehead. "I'm required by treaty to inform world leaders. This wouldn't be a good time to go back to the old ways." She chugged her water then turned her glass on the table, like it might divine an answer for her. "What if we went public with this?"

"Why would we do that?" Jacana asked.

Myrtle stilled Jacana with a penetrating glare. "Many reasons. Trust in government. Keeping an eye on how people react. So we can regulate any attempts to contact them."

"I can see the G-Nerds salivating over this. I think going public would be a mistake." Jacana's tone was measured, with a quick glance to Myrtle as if to make sure she was toeing her line, remembering who her commander in chief was. "The last thing we need is a space race to develop superluminal travel."

Lyn could practically see wheels in General Jacana's brain whirling. If this became public, it would be harder for her to work on it in secret. "I'd like assurance from the general that her research into superluminal travel will stop."

Myrtle shot a look to Lyn then back to Jacana. "Research? Are you working on this?"

Oops. Was the president the only one who didn't know? Lyn shrank in her seat.

Jacana appeared unfazed. "No doubt every government on Earth has been working on this since *Endurance* returned."

"Not this government. At least not that I've been aware." Myrtle let out a breath of disgust or disappointment.

Jacana tipped her head in subordination. "Apologies. I would have informed you if we had made any progress." Her eyes remained on Lyn.

Myrtle stood and stretched then went to the window, hands on hips. "Is second contact possible?"

"They are interested in diplomatic relations," Omara said.

"They are?" Myrtle said with surprise. "You might have mentioned that. Are there any of them still here?"

"No," Lyn lied, to protect Ruzena and any others who either didn't know they were aliens or were happy to remain a secret.

"And no humans were taken with them? We're not dealing with an abduction situation?"

"No," Lyn said. "They were adamant that no humans would be allowed on their planet."

Jacana watched her. "That sounds almost like a threat."

"It sounds like what it is," Omara said. "A guarantee that they'll defend their home world."

"You say they want diplomatic relations," Myrtle said. "Are there others out there they know about?"

"Not that we know of," Omara said. "They have a theory there's another planet where both groups originated from, but they don't know where that planet is." She was taking the diplomatic bull by the horns, answering before Lyn could. Regardless of Omara's flaws and missteps, in this case she was the best positioned to take on such a role.

"And who are they? What do you call them?"

"We call them Gaians and their planet Gaia," Omara said, "based on a pronunciation of what they call themselves."

"They are nonviolent, you say?" Myrtle asked.

"Yes," Lyn said. She described their matriarchal hierarchy and the lack of large game, that food was plentiful, so there was no reason to fight over resources. "Instead of competition, they use cooperation. They work together."

Myrtle sighed. "My goodness. Do you know how many wars have been triggered by arguments about why humans exist? Religious arguments. How did life get to Earth in the first place, let alone intelligent, modern humans? Evolution, sure. But there have always been theories that the building blocks traveled here from elsewhere. And a solar sibling makes sense. We know they are out there." She paused, thinking, then chuckled softly. "What if yet another alien planted us each on our respective worlds precisely to study us?"

She sat back down and rocked gently, her face contemplative. "First contact. This is *incredibly* exciting." She continued softly, more to herself than to the others. "I wish we hadn't lost so many records during the war. All those UFO sightings the military investigated. I wonder if any of them were real." Then she scowled at Omara and Lyn. "And you let them *go*."

The mood was turning in a direction Lyn hadn't expected. Jacana sat silent and still. Who knew what she was thinking. But President Woltman was a surprise.

Myrtle looked at Omara for a long time. "I'm trying to imagine the discussions you all had." A side glance to Lyn. "How do we contact them?"

Omara shifted uncomfortably. "I was given a means."

"A means," Jacana said. "How cryptic. Surely not cans on a string."

Omara's face hardened. "They gave me a device that will respond only to my touch and through quantum entanglement alerts Verius, their leader, to open a communications tunnel to me. So, no, not cans on a string."

Jacana returned a hard stare.

The sun had burned through the low clouds and brightened the room but not the tense mood.

"They may have won your trust," Myrtle said, "but I'll need to convince world leaders that Earth is safe from possible attack."

"How would you then like to proceed?" Jill asked.

Myrtle's chair creaked as she rocked. She stared off into space. "I wonder how many others are out there." She looked at each of them. "Don't you?" She gave a dismissive shake of her head as she rocked forward. "We need a plan. I suggest we inform senior advisors, the legislative leaders—all top secret for now. Then we can approach my colleagues around the world and formulate an announcement—" She turned to Jill and Omara. "If you two could stay, we need to talk about how to frame this. Clearly initiated by Earth Control, I'll need some plausible, yet vague answers to any questions." Then to Jacana and Lyn. "You are both welcome to stay if you wish."

"I don't need any more targets on my back," Lyn said. "Can you keep my name out of any public announcement?"

Myrtle agreed.

Jacana sniffed. "Like no one would suspect—" Myrtle cut her off with a glare. "I'll excuse myself. PR is not my strength, but I'm certainly available if you need me."

WITH THAT, IT was over. Lyn stood outside on the steps, blinking in the bright light. She should feel relieved, unburdened. She could go home. She and Diana had decisions to make. Pack up and move. Where? And to wait. For what? A warm thermal rose up the hill. So much for winter.

General Jacana pushed through the door and joined her. "May I walk with you?"

They crossed the parking lot together, Jacana rubbing her arm. "Bureaucracies make me itch."

"You're going after that ship, aren't you?" Lyn asked.

Jacana glanced at her with surprise, a feint, no doubt. "I don't see how I can. I'm a very busy woman. I wish I had the time to devote to it, but I don't, much as I'd like to." She tipped her face to the sun. "This isn't something you can pass off to a subordinate. I'm also more of a military strategist. Oh, sure, pulling a ship up from the ocean depths is easy, but then what? Any ideas?" She waved a hand. "Ah, but you have a life to get back to. No, I think this is finished."

They continued, side by side. The captain and the general. No longer adversaries but not quite allies.

Jacana pulled sunglasses from her pocket and twirled them. "You were right, you know, back there in rehab. My job *is* very boring. I'm not sure what I should do next, but leading an army that doesn't fight isn't very exciting."

"Just don't pick a fight with the Gaians. You don't have any limbs to spare."

Jacana stopped short and burst into laughter. "That's a good one!" The way her face lit up, clearly there was a time when life wasn't so serious for the vaunted general. "I don't want to fight," she said with a weary sigh. "But I do want some excitement. Who doesn't?"

"Me. I don't. I've had quite enough for one lifetime."

"Ah, but you had glorious adventures. I envy you that."

"Well, I wish you luck in whatever you choose. I can recommend Mount Everest. It's a challenge without the snow and ice and there are still plenty of bodies to recover."

"Been there. Stay in touch, will you?"

"I didn't think you needed my permission to track me."

"I'd prefer it," she said with a sincerity and kind smile that cut through Lyn's defensive reserve.

They had reached her skim. Diana's clunker. She missed her Sportster. And yes, she thought Jacana would have been impressed. A sigh. She could get in and fly away, but leaving Hellen Jacana on her own to do whatever she wanted with no supervision grated on her. What were the chances Omara could keep her from causing trouble? Impulsively, she whistled the Pulsar chant drilled into all recruits during hours of grueling training runs around the track. *We are Pulsar, Pulsar Proud!* Stupid, insipid, juvenile. But Jacana's head snapped around.

"Hellen, if you ever need a team of competent, discrete volunteers, I know some people." She couldn't believe she was saying this. Diana was going to kill her.

Jacana slipped on her sunglasses and gave a curt nod. "I'll keep that in mind. Take care, Lyn."

She waited till Hellen had launched her own skim, a newer, sportier Anaelan. The wind shifted. From the west now and carrying the smell of wood smoke. She climbed into Diana's Rambler and flew home.

Acknowledgements

Writing this book nailed for me the concept of tenacity, putting me through the wringer of research, a major rewrite, more revisions, filling of plot holes, refinement, and, ultimately, letting go. It's yours now. Phew!

I am thankful for many people, among them Sarah Cypher, at The Threepenny Editor, who once again made this a much better book. She remains the kind of cheerleader writers crave. The Bedazzled Ink crew are the best: My thanks go to Casey, Liz, and Claudia. To my Writing Group colleagues, your encouragement means the world!

And thank you, readers. I thought I'd left the crew of the *Endurance* in a good place, but your questions and my own imagining led me to an astonishing *What if?* that turned out to be lots of fun to write (when I wasn't crippled with anxiety and self-doubt).

Last, and first, to Beth, for the love that keeps me going.

I found inspiration in many places, but want to spotlight the female Yazidi fighters and Kurdish YPJ (Women's Protection Unit) that inspired my Women's Army and post-war New Era philosophy. I came across them when writing *Endurance*, and while they may not be a big part of the story, but they were key to the world building. Now, more than ever, I believe women can, and must, save the world. It's a lovely luxury to be able to skip over a devastating war and see what's possible on the other side. If we could only get there peacefully.

Research for this book took me around the world and beyond, virtually if not literally. That said, the ultimate responsibility lies with me, so all errors, intentional or not, are mine.

If you happen to gaze at the constellation Hercules, give a wave. You never know who might be out there.

Elaine Burnes is the award-winning author of the novels *Endurance* and *Wishbone* and short-story collection *A Perfect Life and Other Stories*. *Endurance* (Mindancer Press, 2022) won a 2023 Golden Crown Literary Society award for Science Fiction/Fantasy and was a finalist for the Ann Bannon Popular Choice Award. Her first novel, *Wishbone* (Bedazzled Ink, 2015), won a 2016 Golden Crown Literary Society award for Dramatic/ General Fiction and was a Rainbow Award Honorable Mention. *A Perfect Life and Other Stories* (GusGus Press, 2016), was a Rainbow Award winner. After years working in communications and editing for various publications, environmental nonprofits, and higher education, she now lives in and writes from bucolic western Massachusetts.

Visit https://elaineburnes.com to learn more about Elaine and her work.

Aim your phone's camera at the code.